MRS. ROBERTO

Van Reid is the author of *Cordelia Underwood* (*New York Times* Notable Book), *Mollie Peer*, *Daniel Plainway*, and *Peter Loon*. His family has lived in Maine since the eighteenth century and he now lives with his wife and children in Edgecomb.

MRS. ROBERTO

✺ OR ✺

The Widowy Worries

of the

Moosepath League

Van Reid

PENGUIN BOOKS

PENGUIN BOOKS

Published by the Penguin Group

Penguin Group (USA) Inc., 375 Hudson Street, New York, New York 10014, U.S.A.
Penguin Books Ltd, 80 Strand, London WC2R 0RL, England
Penguin Books Australia Ltd, 250 Camberwell Road, Camberwell,
 Victoria 3124, Australia
Penguin Books Canada Ltd, 10 Alcorn Avenue, Toronto, Ontario, Canada M4V 3B2
Penguin Books India (P) Ltd, 11 Community Centre,
 Panchsheel Park, New Delhi – 110 017, India
Penguin Books (N.Z.) Ltd, Cnr Rosedale and Airborne Roads,
 Albany, Auckland, New Zealand
Penguin Books (South Africa) (Pty) Ltd, 24 Sturdee Avenue,
 Rosebank, Johannesburg 2196, South Africa

Penguin Books Ltd, Registered Offices: 80 Strand, London WC2R 0RL, England

First published in the United States of America by Viking 2003
Published in Penguin Books 2004

10 9 8 7 6 5 4 3 2 1

Maps by James Sinclair

PUBLISHER'S NOTE
This is a work of fiction. Names, characters, places, and incidents either are the product of
the author's imagination or are used fictitiously, and any resemblance to actual persons,
living or dead, business establishments, events, or locales is entirely coincidental.

CIP data available

ISBN 0-670-03225-5 (hc.)
ISBN 0 14 20.0453 7(pbk.)

Printed in the United States of America

To my brother, Rick,
and
to my sisters, Terri and Cassie.

For everything that family does
for a person
—just by being,
and for everything else
they have done for me—
simply by being themselves.

✺ CONTENTS ✺

BOOK THREE
May 28, 1897 (Afternoon and Evening)

BOOK FOUR
May 29, 1897 (Morning)

BOOK FIVE
May 29, 1897 (Afternoon and Evening)

BOOK SIX
May 30, 1897 (Before Dawn)

BOOK SEVEN
May 30—June 2, 1897

EPILOGUE : THE WOMAN HERSELF
June 3, 1897

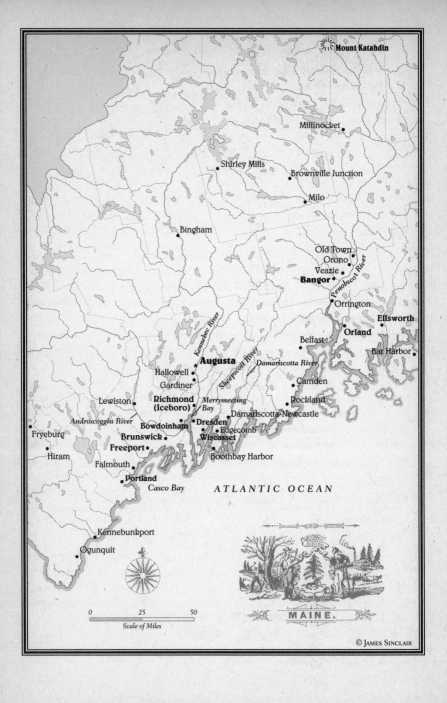

Mount Katahdin

Millinocket

Shirley Mills

Brownville Junction

Milo

Bingham

Old Town
Orono
Veazie
Bangor

Penobscot River

Orrington

Ellsworth

Belfast

Orland

Bar Harbor

Kennebec River

Augusta

Damariscotta River

Hallowell

Camden

Gardiner

Sheepscott River

Lewiston

Richmond (Iceboro)

Merrymeeting Bay

Rockland

Androscoggin River

Damariscotta-Newcastle

Bowdoinham

Dresden

Fryeburg

Brunswick

Edgecomb

Wiscasset

Hiram

Freeport

Falmouth

Boothbay Harbor

Portland

Casco Bay

ATLANTIC OCEAN

Kennebunkport

Ogunquit

MAINE.

0   25   50

Scale of Miles

© JAMES SINCLAIR

from *The Journal of H. St. Ronan*
Christmas Eve 1927

. . . *but couldn't manage it in a state of drink while standing on his head.*

Last night, the Charter Fellows were also up at the Dash-It-All, and quite intent on celebrating the holiday—the old duffers! We thought they would have a round or two and fall asleep in the corner somewhere, but Midlothian began to bluster about his prank the other day outside the police station, and old Durwood, Waverley, and Brink perked up like startled cats.

They promised us we didn't know what a good prank was, and regaled us with instruction on the art by way of reminiscence. Several stories we had heard before, particularly the one about the Egyptian sarcophagus that was displayed at the Public Library some years ago.

We were much surprised when the name of the Moosepath League came up, however, and amid the laughter we inquired what they could have in common with that respectable group of adventurers. It seems that one of the Moosepath League had been smitten by a woman parachutist, of all things—something about a boxing match and this woman landing atop the fellow and their getting tangled together. (Waverley proposed a toast to "The Provocative Tangle!" which we all liked very much.) Durwood then narrated how, some time after this historic event, he slipped a card with the woman's name on it into this fellow's coat pocket and presumably the man thought she had placed it there. As I am to understand—and Durwood was a little vague on this point—the upshot of the matter didn't come about till some months later.

The oddest—and perhaps the most pleasing—aspect of the story was that they seemed unconcerned with the sequel and believed that the prank in its purest form should be perpetrated and left alone. They were, in fact, quite sure that, "being cubs," we younger fellows were not up to the strict formulae of their code. Kenilworth gave them the raspberries.

There is more talk of repeal . . .

❧ PROLOGUE ❧
THE ASCENSIONIST

May 7, 1897

S kelly Wilson was fond of the rain, as he imagined it hid his footsteps, particularly amid the tangle of buildings above the York Street embankment in the western end of town. Here among the many levels of roofs and the crowded alleys between Brackett and Winter Streets the weather gave voice to a thousand surfaces, and a single drop of rain might splash twenty times before reaching the ground. The ancient materials, too, rattled more surely than did the stately brick and stone on the wealthier side of Portland.

Skelly was well nicknamed—he was pale and thin as a skeleton. There wasn't much to Skelly Wilson. His footsteps were like a cat's, rain or otherwise, but when one relies on silence and wit to earn their daily bread (or, as in his case, beer), one is thankful for whatever assistance nature provides, so Skelly was fond of the rain. People stayed indoors, if they had an indoors; creaks and groans in the back rooms were often lost behind the wind and weather, and stores and warehouses stood dark and empty. The rain itself, he imagined, hid his footsteps.

Skelly stood at the mouth of an unlit alley, his night-accustomed eyes articulating the dark wall of one building from the shadow of another. A single pocket of darkness was of especial interest to him tonight, as it had been for several days now; it had been only several days since he first took notice of the small window, covered on the inside with pasteboard. It was the pasteboard that drove him to distraction; he could hardly stand not to see what lay beyond and two or three days of careful study had been necessary for him to even guess where it led. On the pretense of visiting an acquaintance he had been through the building itself—a hodgepodge of rooms and cubbyholes and tiny annexes rented to people of meager income and as storage for out-of-port sailors; but when he *ciphered out* which door gained access to the same room as that window, he was confounded by an overabundance of bolts and locks. So Skelly turned his study back to that window and the jumble of roofs and gables about it.

The building went by its owner's name; "Down to *Bergen's*," people said.

Nicholai Bergen was a well-thought-of fellow, for such a place in such a section of town—an old warhorse who'd fought in the Wilderness Campaign. He was quiet and honest. His building was not much to look at, but folks living there did so in peace, more or less, and homecoming sailors could expect to find their belongings untouched. The block itself was not such a "den of iniquity" as others nearby. By day, it was next to respectable.

The window was small, but people couldn't imagine what Skelly might crawl through. He'd had a *business associate*, some years ago, who'd been amazed, in a stone-faced way, at Skelly's ability to squeeze through a narrow place. "A mouse will creep under a door," said the fellow.

It wasn't the size of the window that held Skelly back but the puddle beneath it. ("A small pond," he muttered to himself.) For a man who welcomed rain, Skelly wasn't so fond of water as a general thing, and he peered through the rainy darkness of the alley to consider the roofs and eaves nearby.

᠅S᠅

Blind, if not deaf, the room beyond the window sounded with the rain and dreamed in darkness till a scratching at the sash and a tapping at the pasteboard, like the work of a small animal, led to a single bar of gray among the black and the sough of a labored breath. The pasteboard came loose and dropped to reveal the silhouette of a shaggy head against the night beyond.

The increased sound of the rain was of more note than that of Skelly dropping to the floor of the room. He crouched below the level of the sash and listened. The rain without was enemy as well as friend now, for it hid other sounds than his—it masked warning as well as error. The grayness that entered with him—an ambiguous glimmer that was the end of the reflection of a reflection of light—barely gave news of the room's tiny dimensions. Skelly waited for his eyes to adjust to the dark, but they were not up to this depth of night and he fell to exploring with his nose and his hands.

There was a stir of odors—he could smell hide and wood and oil and other things beyond the dust. His nose brought him near the right-hand wall and a scent he could not identify. He brushed his hand past a series of objects on a shelf, some rough with fabric, others smooth with leather. He tugged at one of these and it levered into his hands before he realized that it and its neighbors were books.

"Gah!" he mouthed silently, but he opened the object in his hands and riffled its pages. Here was the unusual smell; he wrinkled his nose, smelling the paper and ink and must. Further along the wall there was the hint of perfume. His hands ran over garments—female garments (he chuckled to himself as he fingered these soft things); he managed not to kick over a row of boots and shoes—and again, a *woman's* boots and shoes; and then, along the opposite wall, he discovered several silky things that were folded neatly in heavy piles and seemed to have enough fabric in them to cover a house.

He ran his hands over these mysterious articles repeatedly. He ran his hand in between their cool, soft folds. He pressed his nose to them and thought he smelled summer. A strange and unaccustomed pang of sympathy (for *what*, he couldn't have said) touched something in him like a hand brushing a tightened line of gut. He laid his unshaven face against the material and drew in another breath. It *was* summer! But he had experienced summer for thirty-two years and had never known it to fill him like this; he suddenly knew a delicious sense of pain and longing and he fairly embraced the pile of soft fabric, closed his eyes against the near-blind darkness, and drew a shuddery breath through his bony nose.

Skelly's heart suddenly rose in his throat. The door behind him was ajar. He hardly dared to open his eyes, but, when he did, the soft light from a lamp in the hall clarified stripes of red, white, and blue upon the fabric beneath his cheek.

"I've been watching you, Skelly," came the steady voice of Nicholai Bergen, along with the creak of hinges. "Everyone knows you like to work on rainy nights."

Skelly sat up on his knees, startled as much by this intelligence as by Bergen's rugged form in the doorway.

"Just needed a place to sleep, Nick," said Skelly, realizing, even as he spoke, that his voice was too mewling and thin to elicit clemency from the old veteran.

"What are you doing there?" said the man in the doorway. "Get away from those things!" Anger rushed into Bergen's voice. He stepped forward, and, while Skelly let out a bloodcurdling cry, Bergen grabbed the narrow burglar and, in one movement, thrust Skelly through the tiny window as he might the plunger into the mouth of a cannon. He let go *this* plunger, however, and Skelly disappeared, conspicuous thereafter as only a splash and a series of offended shouts that rose up through the rain till Bergen slammed the window shut and replaced the chuck he had removed that evening.

Nicholai dusted his hands and wiped them on his jacket. He surveyed the tiny room in the glow of the hall light and made a mental inventory of the objects along the shelves—the books (he reached out and brushed the backs of some of these as if he might wipe away the trace of Skelly's presence), the garments and shoes (he righted a boot and set it properly next to its mate), the perfume bottles and the box of theatrical makeup, and finally the articles on which he had discovered the intruder resting his head. *What was he doing?* wondered Nicholai. He might have understood but never would guess the swarm of emotions Skelly had experienced as his sensitive nose detected the grasses and skies of summer. Nicholai touched one of the striped parachutes.

Some would have treated Skelly Wilson a little more gently, or wished they had after the first flush of anger, but not Nicholai. Skelly was part of Fuzz Hadley's gang, and everyone along the Portland waterfront knew that Fuzz was looking to take over Adam Tweed's place ever since that street boss was jailed the previous fall; but Fuzz Hadley, mean as he might be, held no terrors for a grizzled old vet like Nicholai Bergen.

The old man heaved a bit of a sigh, and his heart thrummed with a vibration not unlike that experienced by Skelly moments before.

Nicholai swung the door to so that he might look at the bill fastened to the wall behind it. The colorful printed image of a beautiful robust woman in a suit of tights and a theatrical skirt stood out from the surrounding print. She was not smiling, but she appeared regal and generous and kind. Something like a crown was in her raven-black hair. Her skirt wafted about her thighs and she consequently showed more of her well-rounded calves than was common to public experience. There was a blossom of red, white, and blue above her. She was descending toward a crowd of people, tiny with distance.

The legend read, NEWLY ARRIVED FROM EUROPE! EXCLUSIVE TO PORTLAND'S DEERING OAKS THIS SATURDAY! Three separate hours of a long past afternoon were noted alongside her hourglass midriff, and beneath her energetic figure was the astounding message that *Mrs. Roberto, of many European courts and audiences, will parachute in her patriotically designed parachute from an ascended balloon! 2,500 FEET! IN HER ATTRACTIVE SUIT OF TIGHTS!*

Nicholai had read it many times; he had a bill much like it in his own room, as well as several other attempts at representing the extraordinary Mrs. Roberto (in her attractive suit of tights). None could hope to do justice to the original. He scratched at his beard.

He was not a young man. He was not exactly a young man when he joined the Union Army, and *that* was thirty-six years ago; but Mrs. Roberto, in the flesh or on the page, spoke to him of youthful wonder and warm summer evenings and a breeze off the harbor on a bright summer's day. She was no spring maid herself, though less than half Nicholai's age (it seemed indelicate to conjecture any further on this point); but even a man of *his* years could consider Mrs. Roberto in her attractive suit of tights and feel like the youth who loves his schoolteacher or the young man who sits in heart-struck awe while the mature soprano commands the stage with her lovely voice and her operatic form.

Years ago, standing on Munjoy Hill with his grandfather, Nicholai Bergen had wondered aloud if the old man could still revel in a summer's day. Nicholai had been a pup then, and sassy to boot; but old Tor Bergen had given his grandson a droll glance and said, "An old man might *know* what a young man only *feels*," and turned his face to the sun.

"Summer comes again," said Nicholai to no one, or to himself, or to the room. He went out and closed the door behind him and inside the blind, if not deaf, room there was pitch dark and the sounds of locks and bolts being turned and thrust and then Nicholai's footsteps in the hall. There were the smells of books and perfume and bleached garments and silky fabric redolent with summer.

Outside Bergen's place, in the alley behind, Skelly Wilson stood and shivered. He had places he could go, a fire at the hearth of some saloon where he might warm himself and dry the muddy water from his clothes, and even a flophouse down by the waterfront where he could find a hammock. But he stood in the alley behind Bergen's place for an hour or more, shivering and feeling another unfamiliar sensation. One, of course, must first be informed of something to know its loss.

❧ BOOK ONE ❧

May 27, 1897

1. The Propitious Preservation
of Thaddeus Q. Spark

T he resemblance was remarkable, but beyond the immediate results of that first meeting too much should not be made of it. Perhaps the waning light of day—shadows cast eastward toward the waterfront—increased the potence of that initial glance by hiding the distinctions between them, distinctions that were, admittedly and according to those who knew both men, subtle. Beards, of course, like a forest, might hide a particular landscape, and we are, in this instance, dealing with two *exceptional* beards.

Thaddeus Q. Spark had worn a beard for many years, and few remembered him without it. He had been married in his beard. His wife Mable Spark (*née* Hicks) had never seen him without it, unless one counts the brownish tintype (which still survives) of a cherubic babe in his mother's arms. Thaddeus Q. Spark was of less than average stature and of more than average breadth of shoulder and depth of chest. His exceptional beard, as well as the thatch upon his head, was of a brown that showed the slightest hint of red when exposed to the summer sun; it protruded from his chin in a manner that some might have deemed pugnacious.

Resemblance ended when it came to their two voices, for Thaddeus Q. Spark spoke like the high end of a flute, and the man he was about to meet (while standing across the street from the Shipswood Restaurant, in Portland, Maine, some minutes after 7:30 of a Thursday evening in May 1897) gave forth with the tone of a double bass.

It was a pleasant evening, following a pleasant day, though a little breezy by the water. Characteristically dressed in the habiliments of the laboring class, Thaddeus looked more pugnacious than usual as he watched the traffic on Commercial Street; the fractious nature of his appearance was a little amplified by profound concern and a hint of annoyance. He was waiting for someone, and his wife and family would not have liked him to be standing there alone waiting for this particular someone, in the particular light of recent circumstance. He watched the street while patrons of the Shipswood Restaurant came and went and the day failed. Electric lights came on with the gloaming. Pigeons cooed from their perches along the waterfront roofs. Thaddeus had never been inside the Shipswood. He ran his own establishment some blocks to the west—the Faithful Mermaid (of which more anon).

For most of his life, the waterfront had been his close companion, and he hardly noticed the sights and smells and sounds—the scent of the water, the creak of the wharves and ships, the great prows looming from between shoreline buildings. With his hands behind his back, he paced a small portion of the sidewalk and nodded to folks as they walked by. One odd figure turned to walk backward as he passed—a wild-haired fellow whose clothes had not been laundered nor chin shaven very recently. He waved a hand as he receded with his reversed gait.

"Timothy wants to know what happened after Daniel Boone went up the Amazon," Thaddeus called after the man.

"He'll have to read it from someone else's pen," said the fellow.

"Oh, you must write it!" called Thaddeus a little louder to make up for the increasing distance between them.

"I've been fired! I must find other heroes to laud!" He almost tripped but continued to walk backward till he disappeared behind a group of men standing in front of a shop a few doors east on Commercial Street.

It was a shade after 7:30 when a cab pulled up to the curb, and even as the driver hopped from his seat, Thaddeus quite naturally stepped forward and opened the carriage door. A portly and bespectacled gentlemen of middle age began a happy "Thank you" as he stepped down, then stopped short at the sight of Thaddeus. The portly man had been in the process of lifting the hat from his balding head, but he lowered it again, said "Oh, Mr.—" and stopped short again.

"Evening," said Thaddeus, but his high-pitched voice only seemed to heighten the portly fellow's confusion.

"Good evening," said the man from the carriage. He held out his hand. "Tobias Walton."

Thaddeus shook the man's hand and said, "Thaddeus Spark."

"I am very pleased to meet you, Mr. Spark."

"Have a nice supper," said Thaddeus. "Come by the Faithful Mermaid some night for a bowl of chowder and a bit of something to wash it down."

"Perhaps I will do that," said Mister Walton. He glanced toward the head of the horse, where stood the driver and a young man of tall and lanky build. The young man was interested in Thaddeus as well, as was the handsome middle-aged woman who stepped down from the carriage on Mister Walton's hand. "Mr. Spark, Sundry Moss," said Mister Walton, indicating the young man. "And this is Miss Phileda McCannon."

"Thaddeus Q. Spark," said that man, his hat in hand.

"Mr. Spark," said the woman.

"Happened to be standing here," said the bearded fellow, still holding the carriage door.

"Thank you," said Mister Walton again. "Have a good evening, Mr. Spark," he added just as an unexpected gust of wind swept the street and his hat was lifted in the air.

The impish breeze did not reckon with the quickness of Miss Phileda McCannon, however. For one brief instant Thaddeus saw the fading light of day reflected upon Mister Walton's balding pate, but Miss McCannon's hand came up, swift as a cat, and gently fixed the homburg to its proper seat.

"Tobias Walton," she admonished with a smile that reached to her fine blue eyes. "You are not to lose your hat and instigate an adventure while my appetite is roused." She shook a finger as she said this.

Thaddeus chuckled, the familiarity between these two was so agreeable. The young man (had the portly fellow really said *Sundry Moss?*) joined the older couple and went with them into the restaurant. The driver climbed back to his seat and nickered softly to his horse. The cab rattled off and Thaddeus watched it rumble down the street; he turned his head and caught sight of his quarry coming toward him unsuspecting.

"Everett Darwell!" he called. "Where have you been this past week, and how do you expect a man to survive if he hasn't a pint of brew to sell?"

Everett Darwell came to a halt and looked in all directions, as if other folk might spring out of the shadows and demand answers. He was a small, wiry fellow, with a billed cap and no coat. "Blame it all, Thaddeus!" he shouted. "You know how it is!"

"No, I don't!" insisted Thaddeus Q. Spark. "Maybe you perhaps could tell me." He advanced on Everett.

"It's Fuzz Hadley, you know," said Everett warily. "He's taken a dislike to you since you and Jefford Paisley tossed his men out last month."

"Well, we didn't toss *you* out," said Thaddeus. He was almost within arm's reach of the man now, and Everett was looking for a place to bolt.

"No," admitted Everett. "But Fuzz takes exception to my selling to you, and I'm not of a mind to cross him."

Traffic on Commercial Street had slowed with the onset of evening, but those who did drive past or walk around them took note of the indignant man with the beard and the nervous fellow gesticulating as he talked.

"Well, if *no* one crosses him," Thaddeus was saying, "we'll just all knuckle under and he can do what he pleases."

"It's not for me to change things," said Everett quietly. "I'm just doing my best to make a living myself, Thaddeus." He looked up and caught sight of something that disturbed him greatly.

Thaddeus glanced over his own shoulder and saw Fuzz Hadley and several of his cronies coming up the cobbled sidewalk; he recognized Jimmy Fain and Peacock Hope, and there was little Skelly Wilson skulking in the rear. Thaddeus had anticipated this possibility, but that did not mean he liked it any better. He took a deep breath, and Everett might have heard something like a small oath come out from beneath that beard. "It's all right, Everett," said Thaddeus. "You go about your business. What business Fuzz allows you." He turned to face the approaching men, knowing that a moderately busy street would not put Fuzz off from making his point as he saw fit.

"I better stick and see what he wants," said Everett, but he was shaking.

"Mr. Spark," said Hadley; he'd been known along the waterfront as *Fuzz* for so long that people had forgotten why. Fuzz was not a tall man—in fact, only an inch or so taller than Thaddeus—but he was narrow and wiry, blessed with a natural muscularity that had only recently gone past its prime. He had retained a mean eye, however, and the loyalty of several fellows younger than himself. He wore no coat but sported a dark, striped vest with a gold fob dangling from the lower pocket; his round hat was pushed back like a kid's. Fuzz Hadley was not yet a waterfront boss, but he was acting the part.

"Fuzz," said Thaddeus. "Everett claims you object to his doing business with me."

"Everett?" said Fuzz. "He just thinks something might happen to him up that way, as you haven't put yourself under proper protection, Thaddeus. There are some chancy folk about. You might even say *dangerous*."

"You must be talking about Mrs. Kipply," said Thaddeus, speaking of one of the older laundrywomen that patronized his establishment.

Fuzz showed no signs of finding this humorous. His eyes went dead and all expression left his face. Thaddeus did not view this as a propitious signal. "Maybe you and the boys here," said Fuzz quietly, "ought to go down the wharfside and talk it over."

"Maybe they would like to come by the tavern some night and discuss matters," said Thaddeus, speaking with more calm than he felt; Fuzz and his men stood between him and his way home, but he thought he might get the jump on them and duck into the Shipswood before they nabbed him. Traffic was all but gone from the street, though he heard a carriage coming up behind.

"Never put off till tomorrow what you can do today," said Fuzz, which evidenced more humor and philosophy than Thaddeus would have credited.

"I was just telling him, Fuzz, how things were," said Everett Darwell.

Fuzz and his boys turned their collective gaze upon Everett, and Thaddeus knew his best chance had come. He was halfway across the street before anyone reacted, but he heard Fuzz grunt an order, and Thaddeus would need a proper lead to outrun Fuzz's young gang.

He hadn't precisely judged the distance of the oncoming carriage, however, and he had to pull up to avoid being run over. The driver had been ready to stop at the restaurant and with a shout he simply leaned back on the reins; the horse reared and let out a startled snort; the passengers inside made some noises and the streetside door to the carriage flew open. Turning back to his pursuers, Thaddeus caught sight of a man half stepping, half falling from the carriage, and this person took two or three stumbling strides before he bumped into Thaddeus's shoulder with a low "Ooof!"

The oncoming bullies stopped, and Thaddeus had the impression that they saw something that confused them.

"What?" shouted Fuzz Hadley. He had slowed his pace, but he walked a few steps more with his elbows levered out like the wings of an angry goose. "What?" he said again.

"I do very much beg your pardon," came a deep voice at Thaddeus's shoulder. Thaddeus could see, from the periphery of his vision (the only portion of his vision he dared consign in that direction) that the man beside him had lifted his hat. "Are you hurt, sir?" asked this fellow.

Fuzz and his boys had now come to such a complete halt in the middle of the street and they wore such expressions of confusion and, yes, alarm, that Thaddeus thought the chief of police had arrived. He dared a sidelong glance and saw something very like himself, dressed in the clothes of a wealthy gentleman with a newspaper under one arm.

"Good gorgeous George!" said Thaddeus.

The man with the newspaper returned his startled gaze, eyes widening above a prodigious beard. Two other men had climbed from the carriage and hurried to their companion's side. "Gentlemen," said one of these, a tall, blond, clean-shaven fellow, who himself had a newspaper in hand. "We saw it all," he pronounced.

Fuzz took a step backward.

"Very brave, trying to stop him," said the third man from the carriage, who tipped his own hat. He had dark hair, a handsome pair of mustaches, and also a newspaper in the crook of his elbow.

Fuzz narrowed his eyes as he sought to detect irony in this statement. He glanced from one bearded man to the other. Fuzz's gang, and the carriage driver, too, were studying the resemblance.

"Wouldn't want anyone hurt," said the blond fellow brightly.

This seemed an obvious sarcasm from Fuzz's point of view, but, more importantly, he was daunted by the very *un*daunted manner of these three fellows, not to say the obvious affinity between the first of them and Thaddeus Spark. "Gentlemen," said Fuzz. He tipped his hat cautiously and backed away. "Boys," he said to his men. They backed away as well. Peacock Hope tipped his hat. Jimmy Fain gaped, his jaw slack. Once across the street, Fuzz and the gang adopted a more usual form of locomotion and disappeared around the next corner.

Everett Darwell was long gone.

"Nice fellows," said the blond man. "And they have a distinctive way of crossing the street," he thought aloud. "They were abashed to hear praise, I think. Wouldn't you say, Thump?" He turned to Thaddeus when he said this, frowned, looked Thaddeus up and down, then caught sight of the man at Thaddeus's shoulder. "My word!" he said.

Thaddeus understood what the word was, and he took a second look at the short, broad-shouldered, bearded man beside him. The short, broad-shouldered, bearded man took a second look back. "Joseph Thump," said the man who looked so much like Thaddeus, and he put his hand out with a noticeable quiver. "Of the Exeter Thumps," he added.

"Thaddeus Q. Spark." Thaddeus shook the man's hand. "Of the Brackett Sparks."

"Christopher Eagleton," said the tall, blond man. "My goodness! The likeness is extraordinary! Isn't it extraordinary, Thump?"

"Hmmm," said Thump.

"Ephram?" said Eagleton, as he took Thaddeus's hand.

"My goodness' sakes!" said the third man, who had just taken note of the resemblance between the two men. "Matthew Ephram!" said this fellow. He referred to a pocket watch. "It's eighteen minutes before the hour of eight. Brackett. Is that in Massachusetts?"

Thaddeus hooked a thumb over his shoulder while he shook hands with Mr. Ephram. "It's a street over that way."

"Oh," said Ephram silently. "Nice evening," he said.

"Increasing clouds!" announced Eagleton suddenly. "Occasional showers expected, accompanied by warmer northeast winds!"

"High water at 8:48," said Thump.

"Gentlemen," said Thaddeus, "you can't know how fortunate was your arrival."

"Goodness!" said Eagleton. "It's fortunate we didn't run you over!"

Thaddeus thought that being run over might have been preferable to being caught in the clutches of Fuzz Hadley and his boys. Sweat stood out on his brow when he thought of it. Circumstances had grown precarious, particularly for a man with a family. "Thank you, gentlemen," he said, uncertain of what to do next; Fuzz would not be far away.

"Come inside with us," said Ephram. "You look a little peaked."

"You must have some refreshment," said Eagleton. Thump nodded.

Thaddeus didn't think the Shipswood served the sort of refreshment he was in need of. "Thank you, no," he said. "I really should be going home."

"You shall take the carriage, then," said Thump, and his fellows agreed. Someone put a bill in the driver's hand and instructed him to take Mr. Spark to whatever address he requested.

Thaddeus would have protested if the plan hadn't provided him with a means of outdistancing Fuzz. Once home, Thaddeus would have enough good company about to assure his immediate safety, and that of his family. "Thank you," he said. "Thank you very much. You must come to my establishment on Brackett Street, just off Danforth—the Faithful Mermaid." The three men seemed amazed and pleased with this sobriquet. "My wife is a first-rate cook," said Thaddeus, using the nautical turn of phrase, "and the doors will always be open to you."

They exchanged further pleasantries, and Thaddeus and Thump took another astonished look at one another before the tavern owner climbed into the carriage and was driven off.

"What a fine fellow!" said Eagleton. "Wouldn't you say, Ephram?"

"I would indeed," said Ephram.

"Thump?"

"Hmmm," said Thump.

"And what an unusual likeness," added Eagleton as they climbed the steps of the Shipswood Restaurant.

"Yes," said Thump.

"Those other gentlemen were rather shy," observed Ephram.

"Nice fellows, however," said Eagleton.

"Yes," agreed Ephram. He held the door. "I hope we meet them again someday."

⁂

"Look at that and tell me it wasn't planned! *Brave, trying to stop him*, they say! They paid the driver, too." As the cab drove off, Fuzz Hadley stepped back from the corner building on Union Wharf and watched it pass. He'd never imagined that Thaddeus had friends, not to say relations, in high places. It was a neat thing, their arriving the way they did; Fuzz almost had to admire it. "Jimmy," he said. "You stay here and follow those gents as best you can."

"Okay, Fuzz, but they seemed to know what they were doing."

Fuzz grunted. "So do I."

"They weren't a bit fearful," said Peacock.

They hadn't been, it was true, and if Fuzz Hadley was nervous about anything, it was of anyone who was not nervous about Fuzz Hadley—that and the cops.

"I thought I was cross-eyed when I saw the two of them standing there," said Jimmy.

Fuzz shot a look at Peacock Hope, who usually had something highfalutin to say. "Every *line in all the marked and singular lineaments of* the one were the *most absolute identity* of the other," said Peacock, which did not disappoint but, as usual, irritated Fuzz and confused him.

"You think they're meaning to take over?" wondered Tony Sutter, after he and the others had thought about Peacock's observation without much success.

"If they do, they've got a war on their hands," said Fuzz.

"What'll you do, Fuzz?"

Fuzz thought about it but could only come up with "I'll think of something."

They nodded at one another. Fuzz would think of something.

"Hankie, you'd better stay with Jimmy."

"Okay, Fuzz," sniffed a gangly fellow, who was drawing a handkerchief beneath his nose.

"Jimmy."

"Yes, Fuzz."

"Keep them close. If they take a cab, be sure to listen up where they're going." Fuzz nodded to the remainder of his retinue and ambled back onto the sidewalk. He headed west on Commercial Street but cast his eyes two or three times over his shoulder at the Shipswood Restaurant till it had dwindled from sight.

2. A Bill of Fare

The crowd at the Shipswood restaurant was bright with the spring weather, and the proprietor, Mr. Pliny, made the round of tables and played the gracious host while a violinist rendered sweet notes at the back of the main room. The restaurant was nearly filled to capacity, and everyone noticed when the first of the Moosepath League arrived to claim their usual table.

Laughter and cheer followed Mister Walton as he led the way through the dining room, and the humor he induced with a smile here and a happy jest there spread like a wake in good-natured ripples. The presence of Miss McCannon on his arm spread another, quieter ripple among the diners.

Phileda McCannon was five or six years younger than Mister Walton, who was soon to be forty-eight himself, and her straight and slender carriage made her seem younger still. Her dress inclined toward the plain, which only enhanced her natural grace and energy, and her features, which might have *seemed* plain in youth (particularly to herself), had in middle age aspired successfully to the attractive. In short, and as so often happens, the outer person had aligned itself to the inner till there was something so particular about her that men, whatever their age, found much to admire. She wore spectacles not unlike Mister Walton's, but they accomplished something very different upon her face.

The women diners at the Shipswood extended their hands as Miss McCannon was introduced, and the men stood and bowed. Mister Walton had rarely enjoyed anything so much as he enjoyed being seen with Phileda McCannon. Phileda, for her part, rather glowed.

Sundry Moss, Mister Walton's companion and self-termed *gentleman's gentleman*, brought up the rear of the trio. At twenty-three, Sundry was the youngest member of the Moosepath League; long and lanky, he held a readiness about him that had been proven time and again during the short history of the club—an *apparent* readiness that only added to the agreeable aspect of his features that otherwise may have been a shade less than handsome.

As was suggested by its name, and by its proximity to the waterfront, the Shipswood Restaurant began its existence with a patronage largely comprised of men who made their living on or by the sea; but the fame of the Shipswood's cook and the good taste and pleasant nature of its proprietor eventually gave rise to broader commerce, till this very night when it seemed that the customers within were very little concerned with matters nautical and about equally divided between male and female. The atmosphere of the dining room was less blue with the smoke of cigars and pipes than evenings past.

Once seated, Mister Walton and his companions chatted quietly, till they were conscious of some excitement outside their window. A cab had pulled up before the restaurant with a sudden jerk; the horse reared a bit. Sundry stood to see what was happening. Someone had nearly been run over, it seemed. "It's the fellow who looks so much like Mr. Thump," said Sundry.

"Mr. Spark?" said Mister Walton with concern. He craned his neck to see what was happening. "Is he hurt?"

"Only startled, I think. And there's Mr. Eagleton, and Mr. Ephram, and Mr. Thump himself."

"I would liked to have seen that meeting," said Phileda McCannon.

"It's happening right now," said Sundry. "But who are those fellows on the street, and why are they backing away?" Sundry had half a mind to go out and see what was happening but the fellows moving backward had already reached the opposite sidewalk.

When Ephram, Eagleton, and Thump entered the restaurant, they were in a high degree of excitement. "We have just met the most exceptional fellow," said Eagleton. "He bore a remarkable resemblance to our Thump, actually. We very nearly ran him down."

"Not for that reason, I take it," said Sundry, but Eagleton did not seem to hear this.

"We did meet Mr. Spark when we came in," said Mister Walton with a wry glance toward Sundry.

"Ever in the fore!" said Ephram. They quite admired Mister Walton's ability to stay one step ahead.

Mister Walton chuckled. "I believe it is my midsection that is in the fore these days," he said, patting this portion of himself.

Thump did not add much to this colloquy. He had been a little startled by the mirrorlike image of Mr. Spark.

"Who were those other fellows?" asked Sundry. "The ones walking backward."

"I believe," said Eagleton, "they had attempted to rescue Mr. Spark, who was running in front of our carriage."

"I might have guessed they had been chasing him," said Sundry.

Mister Walton cocked his head to one side, and Miss McCannon looked ready to ask Sundry to clarify this point, but Ephram said, "I think they were embarrassed when we praised them for their efforts," and it seemed worthwhile to go on to other subjects.

Mister Walton invoked the day's pleasant weather, and they rather expected a forecast from Eagleton but he seemed to be having trouble unfolding his menu. Ephram picked up the skein of thought, however, and impressed his friends by raising his water glass (the State of Maine had been under prohibition against alcohol for some forty-six years by this time) to offer the simple toast: "To Spring."

"To Spring!" concurred his companions, and several nearby tables joined them in the salute.

Ephram stood and raised his glass, saying "Moxie!" which, due to a previous misunderstanding, he and Eagleton and Thump thought to be a common toast. Mister Walton, Sundry, and Miss McCannon, all of whom understood this misunderstanding (yet did not have the heart to put it right), joined in heartily with a chorus of "Moxie!" Interestingly, this toast had acquired some fame at the Shipswood and certain tables echoed it just as heartily.

> "'In the spring,'" quoted Mister Walton,
> "'a livelier iris changes on the burnished dove;
> "'In the spring a young man's fancy lightly
> turns to thoughts of love.'"

"Oh, my!" said Eagleton. He blushed a bit, and when Mister Walton took stock of what he had said and met Miss McCannon's raised eyebrow, *he* reddened to the ears as well.

"I can testify to that sentiment myself," said Sundry, which admission surprised them all. He was a healthy-seeming fellow, suspected of harboring normal sensations, but he was generally closemouthed about personal matters.

"Oh, my!" said Eagleton again. (He might himself have testified in this vein, but would never have ventured to say so.)

"Well, I *can*," said the young man. "My father proposed to my mother in the spring, and I think it surprised him."

"Ah, well," said Phileda, "that *is* a sentimental tale," but Sundry had turned to his menu.

There was a decidedly British inclination to the bill of fare that night, and as Ephram had lately been reading *Wadleigh of Kent, or the Lady's Cousin* by Mrs. Henrietta Morstan-Stewbridge he led the table in championing the cock-a-leekie soup, roast beef and Yorkshire pudding, marinated cucumbers, and burnt cream.

"Hear, hear," said Eagleton, and Thump was heard to express his wordless agreement.

Phileda, who felt full just *reading* about roast beef and Yorkshire pudding, yet had faith in her appetite and ordered the chestnut chicken and chutney. "I am compelled to eat alliteratively tonight," she announced. Ephram, Eagleton, and Thump were impressed by this, and Eagleton jotted the thought into the notebook that he kept in his coat pocket.

When they had chosen their meals, and while they awaited the first course, Ephram raised his glass again and invoked his wishes for Miss McCannon's safe journey to Orland.

"Indeed," echoed a wistful Mister Walton, who had already expressed similar sentiments in the carriage. The others concurred.

Phileda accepted their good wishes with a smile and a nod. "I have put off dealing with my aunt's house all winter," she said, "so it *is* time, sad to say." She did look a little sad. Mister Walton did as well, and Phileda put a hand on his for the sake of mutual comfort. "But every instance that I leave you gentlemen," she added, "I fear I will be absent when you're off on one of your exploits." This was said with only a small bit of irony. "You do seem to save them for yourselves."

"Oh, we never intend, Miss McCannon," assured Eagleton. "They arise quite by surprise."

"If we feel one coming on," promised Mister Walton, "we will let you know."

"I must be satisfied with your word," said she, by which statement Ephram, Eagleton, and Thump suspected that Miss McCannon was being droll; no one could have had the smallest doubt of Mister Walton's word. "In any event," said she, "or should I say 'barring *unforeseen* events,' I shall return in time for Mrs. Morrell's June Ball." She gave Mister Walton's hand the hint of a squeeze before folding her hands before her.

Everyone was happier with this thought; Ephram, Eagleton, and Thump sighed in unison, they were that gratified by the image of Miss McCannon and Mister Walton attending the coming gala. After a moment's fond contemplation, however, they realized that Miss McCannon was sweeping them with something like an expectant gaze, and they were visibly startled when she suggested that *they* attend the ball as well.

"Ah, well!" said Ephram, who referred to Eagleton.

"My goodness!" said Eagleton, who referred to Thump.

"Hmmm?" said Thump.

"*And* Mr. Moss," she said, seemingly unsatisfied with the table's present level of alarm.

"The June Ball?" said Sundry as if she had suggested that he attend the next meeting of the Portland Ladies' Club.

"I think you would cut a lively swathe among the gentle flowers of Portland's elite," she added, looking as if she would like to see it.

"Good heavens!" said Mister Walton, as she had couched the sentiment in such dire terms.

Sundry crossed his arms before him and squinted an eye at Miss McCannon. He took in the faces of the charter members, pausing briefly at Mr. Joseph Thump, whose immense beard masked his expression but whose eyes were wide at the thought of *anyone* cutting swathes through gentle flowers.

"Ahem," said Thump.

"We must consider it," said Eagleton bravely.

"I believe you are right, Eagleton," said Ephram.

"Oh, well—!" said Eagleton, and with a wave of the hand he brushed off anything like praise.

"No, I certainly do," insisted Ephram. "What do you think, Thump?"

"Hmmm?" said Thump.

"It is decided, then," said Phileda puckishly.

This was news to the three gentlemen, and they wondered at what juncture the decision had been made and which one of them had decided. They thought it impolite to disagree with her, however, and simply nodded.

She had not done with them, however, and announced, "I shall expect each of your names on my dance card."

This brought renewed reserves of uncertainty into the faces of Ephram and Eagleton. Thump looked as if he had caught something in his throat. They had, the three of them, taken dance lessons at Mrs. De Riche's Academy of Ballroom Science more than two years ago, but only Thump had put to use what they had learned (famously, of course, with the extraordinary Mrs. Roberto).

"Eight minutes past eight," said Ephram.

"A turn in the weather is expected," said Eagleton. "Clouds gathering tonight, showers probable tomorrow."

Thump made a low noise.

"Very good, Thump," said Eagleton, though Thump had said nothing.

"Dramatic production, tomorrow night," said Ephram. "Tomorrow night, Portland Theater."

"I read something of it in the *Daily Advertiser*," said Eagleton, grasping at this welcome change of subject.

"*Portland Courier*," added Thump with a nod.

"'*Local patrons of the arts*'" read Ephram from the day's edition of the *Eastern Argus* which he had expertly opened to the correct page with a single movement. "Yes, '*Local patrons of the arts will be gathered Friday night to welcome Miss Ethel Tucker back to the stage of the Portland Theater, where she has known many a triumph and ovation.*'"

"Ah, yes," said Eagleton. They had seen her the previous fall while attending a play with Mister Walton, and they had been much impressed.

"Please, read on," said Mister Walton.

Thus encouraged, Ephram smoothed out the paper before him, lifted it again at a polite level before his face and started at the top of the article, which read as follows:

Local patrons of the arts will be gathered Friday night to welcome Miss Ethel Tucker back to the stage of the Portland Theater, where she has known many a triumph and ovation. When last she graced the "boards" of our fair city, she drew gales of laughter from her audience as the perplexed and marriageable "Kitty" in Hoyt's *Black Sheep*. In this production, she will, no doubt, elicit softer emotions in the dramatic role of a woman caught in desperate circumstances not entirely of her own making.

At 8 o'clock tomorrow evening, the curtain will rise on Elliot Hendrixon's *While She Waits in Silence*. Miss Tucker will assay the role of "Wanda McCintyre," a woman whose zealous nature leads her to throw over the man who loves her for the imagined honor of her family, the men of whom, unbeknownst to Wanda, are involved with dangerous and criminal activities. It is an innovation on the more common tale of the undeserving lover, and we are told that Frederick Mulbar makes the part of the jilted fiancé (who is also a secret emissary of the law) as noble and inspiring as he made his previous role (in the aforementioned *Black Sheep*) vain and absurd.

Those of nervous temperament might fairly be warned that from the moment Wanda comprehends the evil designs of her miscreant family, the tension grows tight as a drawn bow.

The evening will begin with a round of familiar melodies, sung by a double male quartet and led by Dick Jose. These will include "The Old Oaken Bucket," "In New Madrid," "The Bridge," and other old-fashioned songs.

But all the performers who trod the boards tomorrow night will understand, we hope, if we in the audience seem impatient for the entrance of Miss Ethel Tucker, whose lovely presence and dulcet voice will once again grace the Portland air.

"Dulcet voice," said Ephram; he was quite pleased with the phrase, as well as the honeyed tones it conjured in his mind.

"Very nice, Ephram," said Eagleton. "A very nice piece, but your reading of it, in particular, did great justice to Miss Tucker."

"Ah, well—"

"That *Black Sheep* was very funny," said Sundry.

"Yes," drawled Eagleton. Some of it had perplexed him, actually.

"*'The play's the thing'*," said Mister Walton.

"Is it?" said Eagleton, who was pleased to be informed.

"The play," said Ephram. Eagleton and Thump took this to be a new toast and they raised their glasses and echoed their friend.

"And Miss Tucker," said a suddenly bold Eagleton.

"Miss Tucker!" joined the others, particularly Ephram and Thump.

"To the ball," said Thump.

Ephram and Eagleton looked to one another with some hesitation; this salutation seemed to commit them, somehow. Ephram said "Hem," quietly and Eagleton said, "Yes?" Then they joined in with appropriate vigor.

"To the ball!"

"To the ball, Mr. Moss," said Phileda wryly.

"Barring unforeseen events," said Sundry as he raised his glass.

3. A Plan to Stave Off Melancholy

Outside the Shipswood, the assembled league paused to breathe the night air; the warmth of the day had roused the scents of salt and tar along the waterfront so that a hint of summer, when those smells are most potent, hovered somewhere in the darkness beyond the streetlamps.

"I saw seven robins in the front yard this morning," said Mister Walton.

Eagleton was much taken with this intelligence. "My mother used to sing a verse about robins," he said, and he had such a faraway look upon his face that his companions stilled their talk and considered the tall, handsome fellow till he spoke again, or, in this case, almost sang:

> "*The robin is a fairy creature,*
> *Sweet of voice, and fair of feature;*
> *One upon the grass so green,*
> *Is thought a visitor to mean;*
> *Two upon the tended lawn,*
> *Tells us soon the sun is gone;*
> *Three in any way or form,*
> *Conjures up a summer storm;*
> *Count four of this redbreasted bird,*
> *And true love's name will next be heard;*
> *Five means luck, and six means laughter,*
> *And happy tidings ever after;*
> *But seven robins hopping, dear,*
> *Will tell you some sweet child draws near.'*"

There was something in Eagleton's voice—in the song, and in the image of a mother singing it to her son—that caused Mister Walton to blink a little, and none of them were unmoved. Thump had something in his throat, and Ephram something in his eye. Sundry Moss, having taken his pause and a draught of air, nodded, as if in agreement with some newfound verity.

"That is lovely," said Phileda McCannon, and she reached out and squeezed Eagleton's hand. Eagleton reddened to the ears.

Sundry went ahead and spoke to a cabdriver, who waited with his horse and rig before the restaurant.

"Occasional showers tomorrow are probable," said Eagleton, by way of *good night* when the remainder of the party reached the sidewalk.

Thump shook Mister Walton's hand, and then Sundry's, saying, "High tide at 8:48," and Mister Walton beamed, as if this were the happiest of news.

Ephram bowed to Miss McCannon as he glimpsed at his watch. "It is 9:43," he informed them all.

"I think we will walk, thank you," said Eagleton when Mister Walton asked the three members if they would like to share the cab. Ephram, Eagleton, and Thump often chose to walk after these gustatory occasions. Their chairman was a famous walker and they felt it behooved them to exercise their ambulatory muscles, as chance offered, with the hope of someday nearing his energetic pace.

"The fog is coming in," said Sundry while he held the door of the carriage for Miss McCannon and Mister Walton. A sea mist had traveled the wharves and was now studying the nearest sidewalk with exploratory tendrils.

Ephram, Eagleton, and Thump continued to wave and forward their good wishes, particularly to Miss McCannon. They did not spare the driver their best, either, and touched their hats to the man as he chucked the reins and drove away. Mister Walton glanced out the carriage window as they turned up the hill, and caught sight of the three distinctive silhouettes beneath the streetlamp in front of the Shipswood Restaurant.

To begin with, it was a quiet ride to the City Hotel on Middle Street. Mister Walton said "You will write?" to Miss McCannon, and she replied sincerely "No doubt, as soon as I arrive."

Mister Walton made a small sound (a mild version of Mr. Thump's *Hmmm*) as an inward sort of expression captured his face. A certain question had been raised between himself and Miss McCannon, and Phileda, for reasons mysterious even to herself, had put off the simple answer.

Phileda McCannon had lived by herself for a good many years and perhaps realized, when Tobias Walton hinted at changing this state, that she had never appreciated the autonomy of her situation. She counted herself selfish and yet wondered if it were essential that she eke some conscious understanding of what her life had been thus far before moving into what it might be. She had never considered the satisfactions of being on one's own, having spent her adult life outstripping loneliness with purpose and swift motion. The worst of it was an inability to articulate her crowded emotions to her patient beau.

Mister Walton's response was puzzlement, just this side of hurt; his own lone state he considered unlikable and time away from Phileda to be wasted. It could be expected that his feelings would differ, as autonomy was something a man of his era (of most eras, to be sure) might take for granted.

Sundry knew that an offer on his part to go home by separate conveyance would be greeted by embarrassed *of course not*s and hasty *don't be silly*s, but they might otherwise have done him a favor, for he experienced the awkward silence between these two usually fluent people with a little impatience.

They stopped for traffic at a crossing and waited for the evening's last trolley to the Grand Trunk Depot to pass. "'*In spring,*'" said Mister Walton, almost beneath hearing, "'*a livelier iris changes—*'"

This reminded Phileda of earlier conversation, and as the carriage rolled forward again, she said to Sundry, "You spoke of your father's surprise when he asked your mother to marry him. Was your mother very astonished?"

"I'm not sure," said Sundry. "I think he had to mention it to her three or four times before he could get her to listen very closely."

Phileda made a silent *O* with her mouth. Mister Walton chuckled. They spoke then about Orland, where Phileda was going tomorrow, and Mister Walton's house, which he *had* thought he was coming to close up and sell when he returned to Portland the previous summer, and Moss Farm, where Sundry had been born and raised. Sundry had been home to Edgecomb over Christmas, but he was hankering to see it again. They spoke of the play that Ephram had read about.

All too quickly, they arrived at the hotel, and Mister Walton saw Phileda to the foyer, where he held both her hands in his and practiced a willful, if uncharacteristic, sigh.

"Toby," she said with more affection welling in her eyes than she might have cared to reveal in a public place.

"Shall I meet you in Hallowell when you come home?" he asked simply.

Feeling more selfish than ever, she nodded. She leaned forward and kissed him quickly and softly, then climbed the broad stairs of the hotel to her rooms. She had the image of the man standing in the foyer, looking lonely and perplexed, but when she went to the window the carriage was gone. She sat in the near dark, considering the still room and barely hearing the muted sounds of the hotel about her. *What was it about this loneliness,* she wondered, *that could attract her away from a man like Toby Walton? What perverse imp, or unarticulated fear held her in abeyance?* She had been a small bit annoyed at his indecisive courtship before he declared his love for her; she had kissed him passionately when he did declare it; yet as the winter wore on, she had grown fearful of what she had wanted and perhaps needed since meeting him.

She had been accused in the past of impulsiveness, but it often takes a good deal of preparation to appear unstudied and precipitate. Her mother (her dear mother) had been the only one to see Phileda as a *willful* eccentric. "It is well to be yourself, my sweet," her mother had told her once, "but you should not have to think about it so much."

There in the shadowed room, Phileda smiled through her tears to recall her mother's voice. Phileda was so practiced at something near carelessness with herself that she feared she might easily be careless with another. And perhaps she had. "It's not a problem, Phileda" was something her father used to say when she showed exasperation with a pent-up and cautious world. He could not have suspected (*she* could never have suspected) that his daughter was, in her own way, pent-up and cautious.

"It's not a problem," she said to herself there in the hotel room.

✴✿✖

Back in the carriage, Mister Walton's gloom was plain, and Sundry thought it polite to allow his friend and employer a minute or two to apprehend these honest feelings, but no more. The driver was turning the rig onto Congress Street when the young man said, "I thought those men must have been chasing Mr. Spark."

"What was that?" said Mister Walton, which proved how abstracted he was. "I beg your pardon," he amended.

"I think Mr. Spark was being chased."

Mister Walton took a moment to register this thought.

Sundry said, "It makes me wonder who or what he was waiting for when we met him."

Mister Walton continued to think rather than answer.

"They'll be planting at the farm," said Sundry.

The fog had not yet reached Spruce Street when they pulled up before Mister Walton's house, though the stars south and east of them were dim or altogether obscured. It had been a warm day for May, but it was good to get indoors as night reinforced its authority. A bit of the night had followed them in, Sundry thought, and it was a few minutes before he realized that it was not the hour but Mister Walton's distraction that shadowed them.

They hung their coats and hats in the hall and retired to the kitchen, where, as was usual, they discovered a sweet note, and something sweet to eat besides, from Mrs. Baffin, the elderly retainer who, with her husband, cooked and cared for 'young Toby' still.

"My word," said Mister Walton when he saw the small hill of lemon curd tarts on the kitchen table. "I ate so well at dinner, I'm not sure I can do these justice."

"She'll be disillusioned if we don't do something with them," said Sundry.

Mister Walton chuckled. "I'll get some milk from the icebox."

While Sundry brought the glasses down from the cupboard, Mister Walton made the discovery of an envelope beneath Mrs. Baffin's message. "A bit of mail for you," he said, and, lifting it to his bespectacled gaze, added, "from Edgecomb."

When the milk was poured, Sundry sat down and inspected the envelope, then his name and Mister Walton's address, the return address of *L. M., Moss Farm, Edgecomb, Maine*, and the three-cent stamp bearing the likeness of Washington. He helped himself to a tart before passing the plate to Mister Walton.

Seldom has there been so sturdy a relationship between a man and his employer that was yet so vaguely defined as that between Sundry Moss and Mister Walton and yet it troubled neither of them. Mister Walton had hired the young man very much on the edge of a whim, and Sundry had responded by proving invaluable as a companion and diligent as an extra hand. He might have been a butler, or even a valet, if Mister Walton had needed such attention, but he did bring in the wood and coal, and he was good at repairing things. He carried their bags when they traveled, which seemed to be often. He was, above all, an excellent companion.

No specific duties had been assigned, and no certain salary had been discussed, so the first time that Sundry discovered on his dresser an envelope with his name on it and money in it he had responded with embarrassment. It was as if his father had offered to pay him for milking the cows. It seemed absurd, however, that he would continue doing for Mister Walton for nothing, and Sundry dealt with the situation by claiming that he had been paid too much. Mister Walton informed him that the amount was perhaps too little. Both saw the wisdom of never raising the subject again.

So Sundry could help himself to a glass of milk and a tart while taking the trouble to serve what he was indulging in and see no contradiction in his behavior. Mister Walton, for his part, accepted Sundry's service like the generosity of a friend. Watching Sundry consider the letter before opening it, the bespectacled gentleman knew a vicarious pleasure that is only experienced through true friendship and regard.

Sundry finished one end of the tart, licked the tips of his fingers, and opened the envelope. A sheaf of paper came out, and he unfolded this to consider his mother's handwriting, which was the definition of fine and proper.

Dear Sundry,

It seems a long while since Christmas when everyone was here. I heard from Varius the other day, so I am thinking it high time I got another letter from you as well. He visited Uncle Cyrus last February and I have heard about their time together from both of them. Cyrus writes that everyone wintered well, folk and animal alike, though he says "Old Rheum" has taken up permanent lodging. A cup of Beth's birch-bark tea in the morning sets him up quite nicely, he says, and I will have to try this out on your father.

Varius drove on the ice straight down the Kennebec to Uncle Cyrus's, I am told, though I don't like to think of it.

Lillian Moss was writing about Sundry's twin brother, Varius. "My brother was up to visit my Uncle Cyrus last February," said Sundry. "Drove straight down the river."

"It is a picture," said Mister Walton. He and Sundry knew something about adventurous sleighing themselves.

Cyrus seems in a mood for reminiscence, and I wonder if he might benefit from more visitors. He tells of sitting on his porch now, with summer on its way, and thinking on meeting you at the station in past years. He did enjoy having young people around the place.

The young man could see his Great-uncle Cyrus as he read, and Sundry's face reported happy, if wistful, memories.

He speaks of Myrtle and Martin and how they wanted to be sure he would write hello to you. I always half suspected that Myrtle was sweet on you.

Had Mister Walton been privy to the details of the letter, and had he also been watching his friend close enough to detect a slight change in Sundry's expression he might have wondered if *Myrtle's* regard had not been entirely unrequited. He was, however, peering at his lemon tart, as if certain mysteries might be solved by the close observation of it. "Mrs. Baffin has put something interesting in this," he ventured.

Sundry broke away from his letter long enough to sample the pastry before him. For a long moment they ruminated over this enigma, and Sundry even wafted the tart beneath his nose. "There is something," he agreed.

I understand Cyrus's loneliness. The farm here is busy enough, but I have been missing small children about the place now that Bowdoin has turned ten and thinks he's too old to coddle. Things must be very quiet on Cyrus's farm of a spring day.

"My mother is suggesting," said Sundry, "and not too lightly, that I might visit Uncle Cyrus, up at Norridgewock."

"You used to stay with him in the summer, didn't you?"

"Five summers in a row."

"You always speak so fondly of him."

"He's a grand fellow," said Sundry, and he returned to his letter.

I wrote to him a few weeks back and told him about meeting Mister Walton when you both visited Edgecomb last September. Perhaps you can bring him up that way with you so that Cyrus can tell Mister Walton about all the mischief you used to get into.

"Mother would like you to meet him," said Sundry to Mister Walton, who had fallen briefly into a brown study. Sundry glanced at the next line in his mother's letter and said, "She sends her best greetings."

"And to her," said Mister Walton as if Sundry might communicate these sentiments then and there. Then seemingly from nowhere, he added, "Phileda will be taking the 7:15 east from Grand Trunk."

"We would have to get off at Brunswick," said Sundry.

"Which is some distance along the track to Orland and Phileda's destination."

"The Maine Coast Railroad runs from Brunswick to Waterville, a short jog on the Maine Central goes to Oakland, and from there the Springfield Terminal deposits a person very neatly at Norridgewock."

"I suggest," said Mister Walton, "that we allow whatever breeze or notion to nudge us."

"I *was* thinking," said Sundry in agreement.

"We will begin by visiting your Uncle Cyrus."

"Or Miss McCannon."

Mister Walton smiled. Then, as if to justify himself, he added, "I was going to see her off, but I will just see her off in Brunswick rather than Portland. And we will return in plenty of time to attend the June Ball."

"For *you* to attend," said Sundry.

"Phileda seemed quite struck by the idea of your going."

"Yes, she did," said Sundry.

"We will go to Norridgewock, and allow whatever breeze to nudge."

"I warn you, Miss McCannon may think you're on an adventure."

"If there is the smallest gleam in my eye, you must speak to me," said Mister Walton, his good humor restored. His heart was conscious of a reprieve. He would spend some extra hour or more, some few more miles with Phileda, and the thought of movement, of travel, stirred him from his doldrums.

Said Sundry, "If there is a gleam in your eye while Miss McCannon is near, I will let her draw her own conclusions."

4. Kitchen Implements and Animal Intuition

"The atmospherics tonight bode something further than spring," said Christopher Eagleton. Weather and its variability were his constant fascinations, and he read the prognostications every day in the Republican *Portland*

Daily Advertiser, which journal he carried, even now, beneath one arm. Though the oldest of the three charter members, his animated demeanor, his blond hair and clean-shaven face gave him the appearance of a younger man. He was the Methodist among them.

They considered the sky for a time, then at Ephram's bold suggestion they followed Commercial Street past the Sugar Refinery and almost to the Boston & Maine Railroad Depot, which was a portion of the waterfront they had rarely frequented. The lamps along this end of the avenue were bright, but fog had drifted off the harbor and the three friends were under the half-conscious perception that the buildings grew taller and more crowded, and the local surroundings dimmer and danker, as they walked. "I was very taken with your story concerning Miss Tucker at the Portland Theater, Ephram," said Eagleton when they had considered his atmospherics for a moment.

"You are very kind," replied Ephram—he of the fine mustaches. Ephram waved his copy of the city's Democratic journal, the *Eastern Argus*, by way of gesture. Matthew Ephram carried about him three or four watches, so that, in a quiet room, he might sound like a piece of clockwork himself. His home was vastly populated with clocks and chronometers and even the silent hourglass slipping the minutes between the gongs and cuckoos; and every Sunday he reconciled his pocket watches (and, from these, the clocks at home) with the timepiece in the vestry of Portland's Free Baptist Church. "Very kind," he said again.

"Not at all," insisted Eagleton. "It was marvelously read. Wasn't it marvelously read, Thump?"

"I believe it was." Thump appeared to be in deep thought, and this was often the case even if he wasn't. Perhaps it was his beard, or even his continued absorption with that deepest of subjects, the sea. Ships and the tide and all things nautical were Joseph Thump's hobbyhorse; he often read about sea matters and was even known to ask questions of sailors when he met them. He would check the tides each day in the *Portland Courier*, an organ that had once supported the Greenback Silver Standard Bearer Party, to which organ*ization* Thump considered himself allied, though it had been more or less defunct for the last ten years. He was an Episcopalian.

"It gratifies me that you think so," Ephram was saying in response to the praise of his reading. They paused and considered whether to retrace their footsteps or to ascend Park Street, which was a direct if *un*familiar route to more familiar environs.

"I have never walked Park Street," said Ephram, who was filled with new ideas tonight. Since Mister Walton had accepted the chairmanship of their society (in fact, since they first met him) Ephram, Eagleton, and Thump had become extremely bold; they had each purchased a telephone and a *number* in the local telephone exchange, Thump had read Stanley's account of the search for Livingstone (with his hair generally standing on end), and Eagleton had mentioned once that he would like to try riding a bicycle. With this spirit investing them, they resolved to take the street less traveled.

"I was rather struck by Miss Tucker in her previous performance," said Eagleton when they commenced the climb up Park Street.

"Yes," said Ephram thoughtfully. "I, too. I, too, was struck. What do you think, Thump?"

"Yes," said Thump. "She was very . . . striking."

The hill was not *very* steep, and yet they had already strolled some distance (this after a hearty meal) so their conversation was more deliberate while they put their energies into attaining the slope. The way was a little murky; the lower portion of Park Street was taken up with businesses and emporiums, closed at this hour and dark and quiet. Ahead of them, and a little to their left, there came the faint strains of music and voices. The temperature was dropping and the cloudless sky was salted with stars. The breeze from the harbor chased at their backs and fog billowed up behind.

Ephram, Eagleton, and Thump walked to distinctive beats—Eagleton occasionally pausing so that his friends could catch up with his long strides, Ephram's boots ringing the most regularly along the pavement, and the shorter, stouter Thump hurrying his pace to stay alongside his friends. It was natural that they would quickly apprehend a fourth, somewhat staccato rhythm that did not seem to belong to their efforts.

Ephram pulled up and said, "What's that?"

Thump looked behind them with a "Hmmm?"

Eagleton, who had been unaware of a strange tension growing within his own heart, shouted, "What?! What's that? What's what?"

This, in turn, startled Ephram, who said, "Good heavens!" and Thump, who turned back around and said, "Hmmm?"

"Was there something?" said Eagleton.

"I thought there was," said Ephram. "I thought I heard something."

They peered about and listened. They were in a section of the city they had never walked before and the street had grown darker still. Fog slunk up the cobbles. There was the sound of music and voices, a little louder now. A dog barked somewhere. Eagleton caught with his ear the rapid tapping that had engendered Ephram's first remark.

"There it is," said Ephram.

"It is up ahead, I think," said Eagleton, though a moment before he would have guessed it was behind them.

They considered the way they had come, but the fog looked thick and chilly in the halo of the infrequent streetlamps. There was a more inviting light ahead of them; to their left there was a well-lit block some distance down Danforth Street. When they reached this crossing, the music was clearer, as was the general roar that accompanies a crowd.

"Danforth Street," said Eagleton. "This is your territory, Ephram."

"Indeed," said Ephram, though he looked doubtful. He lived at the very western end of Danforth Street but had seldom frequented the more crowded lengths of that avenue. (To be accurate, he had only ridden through this section of his own thoroughfare and knew little or nothing about it.)

"Our friend Mr. Spark said that his establishment is just off Danforth Street," said Eagleton. "On Brackett Street."

"The Faithful Mermaid," said Thump. It sounded a pleasant enterprise.

"It's very busy down this way," said Ephram, peering at the distant movement and keening an ear to the voices and music.

"Hmmm," hmmmed Thump.

These nearby blocks appeared a little hectic, even (dare they say) wild. The long way around seemed good enough and they were about to cross Danforth Street, toward the center of town and away from this interesting commotion, when they perceived a person standing at the opposite corner. They stopped.

It was a woman somewhere beyond her middle years. Her dress was simple and she had no coat or hat. She wore an apron, which domestic accoutrement did nothing to dispel the sense of potential energy in her frame. There was in her hand a kitchen implement (a rather *large* kitchen implement) with which she tapped at her other hand, like a policeman with a truncheon. She was that type of female who strikes fear in otherwise valiant men, and who might have been termed "formidable." She glowered at the three friends. She was not physically imposing (not as tall as Eagleton, nor as broad as Thump), but she had an impressive sense of purpose about her, not to say tenacity, not to say displeasure—a sort of *raw* displeasure that the three men had not often encountered. Faced with the battlements of her folded arms, the kitchen implement in her hand (a rather *large* kitchen implement), and the brisk, intemperate manner with which she tapped her foot, the members of the club were more or less discouraged from further crossing the street.

Thump remembered reading once that kitchen implements were a principal cause of household accidents.

They considered her. She glowered at them. They stood in the middle of the crossroad. She tapped her foot. Ephram, Eagleton, and Thump decided (each to himself, and without actually consulting one another) that they did not know this woman and that the music and hubbub down Danforth Street was of great curiosity to them. Before they understood what they were about, they were striding down the eastern length of Danforth Street, where the sidewalks turned to wooden planks and the ditches were damp and muddy with recent rain.

"Perhaps we will find Mr. Spark," said Eagleton encouragingly.

"The Faithful Mermaid," said Thump again, and this was conducive to cheery thoughts.

The music down the street sounded merry, but there was a shout from ahead of them, and then a woman's scream that nearly lifted the hair beneath their top hats, and though the scream metamorphosed into high-pitched laughter they advanced with less certainty. Indeed, before the wild laughter had yet died on the air they were walking on their toes, looking as if someone had lifted them by their collars.

Soon they had walked almost a block; the voices and singing grew louder and more articulate but no more encouraging. The music was like a dear old tune played at several times the normal velocity and without benefit of common key among the musicians. Some doors up, a man stepped out of a well-lit and noisy building to amble the street in a circuitous manner. He sang as he walked—something about his beloved mother, his little gold ringlets, and his Sunday hat. Oddly the man was hatless and appeared to be bald.

"It's a very musical place," ventured Ephram hopefully. It was a very *bustling* place; the establishments ahead of them were glowing in the fog, and when the door to some house or tavern opened the sounds from within blared out as from a trumpet. A carriage trundled past and drew up before one of these places; a man and three women extricated themselves from this vehicle with some difficulty, and with further difficulty maintained their feet on the sidewalk. Eventually they clambered up a set of steps and disappeared inside.

The way ahead appeared less promising, and yet, when they turned back, the Moosepathians could still spy the figure of the woman at the corner. As they passed the circuitously ambling man, he stopped singing, stopped ambling (circuitously or otherwise), and let out a sudden and startling *"Whoop!"*

Thump had read somewhere (perhaps the same place where he had read about kitchen accidents) that certain animals (dogs, to be sure) were believed to have an ability to foretell earthquakes and other natural catastrophes, and he would wonder, later on, if this man had similar skills. Before the man shouted, the clamor from down the street persisted at the level of a dull and constant roar; one might have even considered getting used to it. But as soon as that single *"Whoop!"* was roared into the night, the undeviating ruckus fell into a momentary lull, which, as it proved, was the proverbial calm before the storm.

A cannon shot could not have seemed more deafening or more alarming than the sound that then spewed forth from a building just ahead of Ephram, Eagleton, and Thump on Danforth Street at twenty-four minutes past the hour of ten (Matthew Ephram's time).

5. No Way to Handle the Upright

The afternoon edition of the next day's *Portland Courier* carried a front-page item that commenced in this manner: *Some time before eleven o'clock last night, citizens at large on Danforth Street were witness to an extraordinary commotion, the origin of which was difficult at first to ascertain.*

All that Ephram, Eagleton, and Thump ascertained, when the front doors of the incongruently named Weary Sailor burst open, was that they had never seen such a mob of figures emerge from any place so swiftly and with so little regard for who or what stood in their way. The swarm of people fell out, or were hurled through the door as by some irresistible force, and the general cacophony they rendered into the night air was, indeed, like an explosion.

"Good heavens!" declared Eagleton.

"There seems to be a commotion!" agreed Ephram.

They thought it unconscionable to hie away if some disaster had occurred and so they crept up the sidewalk; no expressed consensus led them on, but only those unspoken attributes of obligation and curiosity, which historians of the Moosepath League understand to be a hallmark of that society.

They were not long in gaining the perimeter of the crowd, which formed a semicircle before the front door of a tavern. There was a distinctive aura about the mob that the members of the club had difficulty understanding. The gathering was wild-eyed and exhausted in appearance; some in the mob (men *and* women) swayed as they stood, and one or two propped themselves up by another's shoulder. One man was singing. Eagleton realized, with a start, that many of them had bottles or large drinking vessels in their hands.

The building they stood before was an odd old tavern with a short porch, double doors, and a balcony above. The babble of the crowd echoed off the side of the house, and as Ephram, Eagleton, and Thump approached it was difficult to understand the nature of the crisis; the din of many voices raised in ire and fear and even delighted excitement drowned away any single utterance that might define what had happened.

There was a resounding crash from within and the sign above the tavern door shook as if in a stiff wind.

"It is an interesting emblem on that placard," said Eagleton, though his friends did not hear him above the din. The sign depicted a man of the sea sleeping in a chair.

The Weary Sailor was not very conducive to repose just then, for through the crowd of voices there could be heard a powerful bellow from inside. There was another crash, and the mob greeted each of these thunderclaps with a collective shout. One voice in the crowd was heard to cry out "Put it on them, Gillie!" which provoked unexpected cheers and laughter.

People continued to gather before the tavern and the Moosepathians were pressed forward when they might have wished to step back. The noise fell away somewhat and an official-sounding proclamation rose up from the center of the mob as a single police officer plowed his way through. Thump could just see the man's hat and a blue-sleeved arm that rose up to indicate the need for order.

"Gory, people! Keep it down!" declared the policeman. He mounted the steps and considered the tavern doors, then turned to the crowd and addressed one man in particular. "What's to be had in *there*, Mickey?"

"It's Gillie Hicks, Calvin," said the fellow, amid several other similar, if unsolicited, answers.

Officer Calvin Drum looked the smallest bit daunted by this news; his face fell, but he took a deep breath that lifted his shoulders. "Gillie, eh?"

Another member of the city's constabulary, Officer Sam Skillings, was just then reaching the outskirts of the crowd, and as he made his way through he was informed of Gillie Hicks's presence within. A new clamor came from inside while the policemen conferred.

"What's he doing to it?" queried someone near Eagleton.

It sounded as if someone were dancing on the keys of a piano, which, as it happened, was not so very far from the truth.

Thump looked down to see a mist at his feet. Toward the harbor, fingers of vapor seeped from between the buildings, and there was an express chill in the air as the fog slipped over cobblestones and wrapped itself around people's legs.

"Gillie!" Officer Drum was shouting. "*What* are you doing?" There was no answer, and the policemen cautiously approached the tavern doors. These opened easily enough, but the portal beyond was blocked.

There was another jumble and clang of out-of-harmony notes, and then a third, and with each dissonant crash the crowd flinched in unison.

"Gillie!" shouted Officer Drum again.

There was a narrow bar of light between the lintel of the doorway and the object that hindered the officers' entry; part of a face appeared at this horizontal aperture. "Is that you, Officer Drum?" came a man's voice. Anything else that was said was momentarily lost beneath another unmusical crash.

"Who *is* that?" demanded the second policeman. A third officer, Malcolm Beam, was just then arriving, and he pushed between Eagleton and Thump on his way through the crowd.

"It's Safely Saturday," came the voice from within. The fellow thrust a hand out and waved at the policemen. "Gillie is taking the piano upstairs."

"What is he, drunk?" asked Officer Beam. The question was academic.

Officer Skillings climbed over the end railing of the porch and disappeared round the back.

Kachang! went the instrument in question.

"Upstairs?" said Officer Drum. "Safely, what is he doing that for?"

"I don't know, exactly. He and Duffy Wimple were kind of arguing, from what I could see."

Kachang!

"But upstairs?" said Officer Drum.

"Oh, yes. He's rolling it end for end."

"He must be thick into it," said the policeman, almost to himself.

"He's been drinking for nine days!" announced an expert witness in the crowd; the speaker's tone was scandalized but his thick tongue indicated that he himself might have been doing his best to keep up with Gillie.

"He's sober as a judge!" insisted someone else.

"He's just a little irked, is all," said another, and the crowd broke into raucous laughter.

Kachang!

Ephram, Eagleton, and Thump regarded the scene with open mouths and saucer eyes. They had never viewed, nor even suspected, such astonishing behavior, and it was a little difficult to believe.

"Yes, well," said Eagleton, his back stiff, his eyes wide. "Increasing clouds tonight. Showers possible tomorrow." A woman (and a rather wild-haired sort of woman at that) gave Eagleton a long glance. Eagleton, in turn, looked about for a means of retreat but he and his friends were hemmed in.

"High tide at 1:33," said Thump to the grinning fellow beside him.

"Twenty-six minutes before eleven," offered Ephram.

Kachang!

A tall and narrow man, well dressed and with a cultured accent, turned to Ephram and said, "I have always been interested that the piano is numbered among the *percussive* instruments."

Ephram had never thought very much on the place of pianos in the scheme of things. "My friend Eagleton," he said, "once met a gentleman who arranged piano stools around his dining-room table."

The well-dressed man's eyes widened.

"The backdoor is barred as well," said Officer Skillings as he reappeared at the edge of the crowd.

Kachang!

"He's almost up there," reported Safely Saturday from behind the barrier.

"Were they the adjustable sort of stools?" asked the cultured gentleman.

"I believe they were," said Ephram.

Officers Drum, Skillings, and Beam considered the barricade before them. Skillings took off his hat and scratched his head.

"That would be efficacious for people of unstandard height," said the man beside Ephram.

"We perceived that to be the gentleman's purpose," agreed Ephram. He could not help but admire *this* gentleman's acute comprehension.

Officer Skillings rapped on the barrier before him. "Safely," he inquired, "what is in the way here?"

"Gillie tore up part of the bar, and dropped it in front of the door."

"Can we push it aside?" wondered Calvin Drum to his fellow officers.

"He's got it wedged in here somehow," said the helpful Safely.

Kaching!! sounded the abused instrument.

The man beside Ephram looked saddened, and the Moosepathian would not have been surprised to see him doff his hat. "As they said of the aged soprano," intoned the fellow, "'I fear she is losing some of her notes.'"

Kachung!!!

Officer Drum gave the upended bar an experimental push, with no result; Officer Beam pitched in, and even when Officer Skillings, who was a tall, brawny fellow, lent a hand, the mass in front of the doorway hardly shifted.

Safely's face returned to the length of uncovered doorway. "He's reached the top floor."

"My word, Thump," said Eagleton. "This *is* out of common."

"It is extraordinary," agreed Thump. He wished that their chairman were here to lend his admirable philosophy to the scene.

"Are you standing on that thing, Safely?" wondered Officer Skillings.

"Let's try a window," said Calvin Drum.

Another face peered out beside Safely's. "Is that Officer Drum?"

"Yes, it is," came the calm reply.

"Officer Drum, Gillie Hicks is in an obstreperous frame of mind."

"Good heavens!" said Ephram.

Thump had wandered a little forward where the crowd had given a bit and Eagleton tried to follow him. Ephram took note of this migration, excused himself to the tall gentleman, and fell in behind.

Officer Skillings wrestled with one of the front windows.

The door to the balcony of the Weary Sailor gave way with a bang and all eyes rose as an upright piano came rolling into view. The instrument jarred against the railing, which let out an ominous crack, and the crowd gasped and retreated.

Skillings stepped down from the porch and craned his head back. "Gillie!" he called, as if he were speaking to a recalcitrant child. "*What* are you doing?"

A large face, the shape of a nicely rounded pumpkin (and with as little growing on it) peered over the length of the piano top. "Duffy won't play 'Heaven's Gracious Choir, Calling Sweetly Me to Join,'" declared this circular visage, "so he won't play *any*thing!"

"Gillie, what do you intend to do?"

"Just stand away, Officer Skillings—!"

"Where's Duffy?" called Officer Drum over his shoulder.

"I won't play it again!" declared a querulous-looking old man in the crowd. "No, I won't!"

"But Duffy—!" implored Drum.

"I won't!"

"It was my ma's favorite tune!" cried out Gillie Hicks in tears. He straightened to his full height now and the Moosepathians could see that he was a veritable mountain of a man. The fog had reached almost to the waists of the people in the crowd, and certain speculative threads of mist reached up along the posts that supported the balcony.

"Get down here, Gillie," ordered Officer Beam. "You're as cross-eyed as a flounder."

"I'm not drunk, if that's what you mean." Gillie looked uncertain about his footing, however.

"I'd hate to see him when he was," muttered Beam. "Duffy—!"

"I won't play it!" shouted Duffy Wimple. "I've played it every night for *seventeen* weeks and I won't play it again!"

"Duffy!" shouted Sam Skillings (everyone who spoke was shouting now). Sam pointed a finger at the old codger. "You had better get up there and—"

"I won't! I won't, I tell you! Gillie said I played it too fast, and if I *live* to take instruction from that dumb-as-a-pump chowderhead I'll eat my fingers!"

"Well, you won't play *this* again, either!" returned Gillie, and his head bent as he leaned into the instrument. The piano bumped the railing, and he drew it back a foot or so and tried again.

"Gillie!" shouted one of the officers.

Most of the crowd had scattered from the front of the tavern, the incoming fog billowing about them, and it was only because of this human ebb that Thump noticed that a decrepit-looking fellow beside him was lifting the wallet from his coat pocket. The thief had reckoned on the mob to mask his movements, what with bodies jostling bodies, but he had let himself focus too narrowly on his intended victim so that he was hardly aware of working, suddenly, in the open. He realized his danger in about the same instant that Thump realized he was being robbed, and Thump was so amazed that he almost didn't reach out in time to grab the man's sleeve.

"Gillie, you come down here!" Officer Skillings was shouting.

Officer Drum had joined Skillings on the wooden sidewalk to see what was happening when he noticed the smaller crisis between Thump and the thief. "Here, now—" began the constable as he stepped into the street.

As the pickpocket struggled to quit the scene with Thump's wallet and Thump struggled to stop him, a second man, who looked very much like one of the fellows who had been trying to *rescue* Mr. Spark earlier in the evening, stepped from the crowd and dropped to his hands and knees beside Thump. The Moosepathian almost toppled over this man's back, but there was one object in that wallet that was precious to Thump and these thieves could not have guessed at his resolve to keep it. Scrambling like a man on a cliff, and actually using his grip on the first thief's sleeve for a bit of leverage, he managed to raise one foot and stand on the back of the bent man.

Gillie Hicks, meanwhile, had paused in his efforts against the railing. He peered over the piano again. There was a general sigh of relief. Officer Drum glanced up at Gillie, imagined the moment of greater crisis to be over, and

took another step toward the thief, who dropped the wallet rather than suc-
cumb to either Thump's grip upon his sleeve or the long arm of the law.

The first thief bolted down the street. The second thief had fallen flat
upon his face and let out a terrific gust before Thump stepped off his back.
Officer Drum leaned into a cushion of fog to retrieve Thump's wallet from
the ground, saying, "Who belongs to this, then, eh?"

Above them, Gillie let out a grunt. A gasp rose up from the crowd.

There was a crash as the railing above gave way before the mass of piano.
Officers Skillings and Beam, Ephram and Eagleton, and several others in the
vicinity jumped aside or threw themselves back as the instrument pitched into
the air above the street.

The second thief leapt like a cat from his crouch and charged down the
street through the crowd. Thump stumbled, hands out, and collided with Officer Drum, throwing the policeman backward, and nearly falling on him as
he lurched another step. The piano's trajectory culminated in a thunderous
heap not three feet behind Thump but squarely on his pinched wallet.

The cymbal-like stroke of disharmonious chords overwhelmed every
shout and cry, and the dying notes of jangled piano wires and shivering slats
of splintered wood presided over a cloud of dust and a moment of heart-in-
the-throat astonishment. Only the dust and the fog shifted; the crowd and the
immediate participants in the scene stood, or lay, frozen. At the back of the
crowd, Fuzz Hadley and his gang were filled with amazement.

"Gory, Mister!" said Officer Drum to Joseph Thump when he had a moment to breathe. "I believe you just saved my life!"

Officers Skillings and Beam, as well as Ephram and Eagleton, were rushing to the side of their respective comrades.

"My word, Thump!" cried Ephram. "It was magnificent!"

"Ever in the fore!" declared Eagleton.

Thump had a finger in one ear; he was trying to determine if a near
sounding note was originating from within or without his head. Just behind
his right ear a goose egg was rising where he had been plunked by a flying
ivory key. After a moment's consideration, he decided that the note was indeed coming from inside his head. "High tide at 8:48," he articulated before
pitching backward with a docile expression on his bearded face.

A contrite-looking Gillie Hicks leaned his huge head over the broken
railing. "Everyone all right down there?" he queried.

❧ BOOK TWO ❧

May 28, 1897
(Morning)

from *The Portland Courier*
May 28, 1897
(Afternoon Edition)

NEAR TRAGEDY ON DANFORTH STREET

Piano Used as Instrument of Destruction!

Officer Calvin Drum Rescued by Local Club Man!

Some time before eleven o'clock last night, citizens at large on Danforth Street were witness to an extraordinary commotion, the origin of which was difficult at first to ascertain. Officer Calvin Drum of our city's constabulary came upon the scene soon after a mob of people were driven from a meeting place, which is celebrated by its patrons as the Weary Sailor. The building occupies the north block on Danforth between State and Winter. Officer Drum admits that he could imagine nothing short of a fire as being serious enough to send such a crowd into the spring night but understood that other forces were as compelling when he was informed of the inebriated presence of one Gillie Hicks inside the tavern walls.

Mr. Hicks is not unknown to the local police, nor to anyone who even occasionally peruses the court news, and as the suspect is of greater stature and girth than average men Calvin Drum is not loathe to admit that he was pleased to see Officer Samuel Skillings and Officer Malcom Beam arrive fast behind him.

A dialogue of sorts was initiated between Mr. Hicks and the officers, somewhat colored, we are told, by occasional reports from certain individuals who were temporarily trapped inside. Mr. Hicks, it seems, had uprooted the serving counters of the tavern room and blocked all entrances with the same. The crisis was understood to have begun by way of an argument between Mr. Hicks and a Mr. Wimple, who entertains the patrons of that establishment by his skill at the pianoforte, but who had refused to play a certain selection for the well-liquored Mr. Hicks.

To the astonishment of all, Mr. Hicks pushed the piano up to the second story of the building, rolled it out onto the balcony, and, following a brief discussion, pushed it through the railing and down to the street, where it might have killed Officer Drum, or caused him terrible injury, but for the quick action of Mr. Joseph Thump of India Street, who is a member of the recently formed club the Moosepath League (and a long-time subscriber to this journal, we are proud to say). Mr. Thump pushed Officer Drum from harm's way, much to his own risk, and was himself knocked insensate for several minutes, having been struck in the head by a flying piece of the shattered instrument. Those of our readers who have been following the extraordinary exploits of that society to which Mr. Thump claims allegiance will not be very surprised to read of this instance of courage and daring, for they have proved a remarkable company of adventurers.

The whole affair was over in a matter of minutes, but how close it came to altering the lives of Officer Drum and his family forever! None of us at this journal are aware of an instance like it, and while we applaud our constabulary and Mr. Thump we must take stock of what drink will do to a man, and how troublesome are the wild and immoderate occurrences, on a nightly basis, in that section of our otherwise law-abiding city.

6. The Family Spark

The establishment on Brackett Street had been known for a generation or so as the Faithless Mermaid till Mabel Spark had her way with the titular female. Sailors (and landsmen, to be sure) had always appreciated the inconstant qualities of the sea sprite as depicted on the sign above the tavern door. The mermaid was typical of her kind, with the upper portions of a beautiful woman and the lower portions of a fish. It was the upper portions that Mrs. Spark squinted at when she first came to the Faithless Mermaid. The mermaid was faithless, presumably, because she seemed most concerned with her reflection in the mirror, which she held at arm's length; her hair was cast behind her shoulders and her back was arched as if she were just waking. Mrs. Spark was sure the creature needed saving and a local sign painter (if not an artist) was hired to do the deed.

It was not enough for the mermaid to be covered by flowing tresses of golden hair; according to Mrs. Spark, she must "wear something," but in the process of painting the suitable apparel the painter proved a little clumsy and he was forced to do the job two or three times over. In doing so, the painter, who had also famously remade the signal heraldry for the Crooked Cat, a tavern two blocks to the west and one block closer to the water, augmented certain components of the mermaid's upper portions, and, somehow, in covering her up, made her a little less proper than she had been in her natural state. Mrs. Spark gasped when she saw the redeemed mermaid, but her husband put his foot down. She was dressed and he liked her as she was.

Nonetheless, the mirror was taken from the mermaid's grasp and replaced with a valentine heart; she became the Faithful Mermaid, and sailors (and landsmen, to be sure) evinced continued loyalty to her and admiration for the sign that bore her image.

Thaddeus Q. Spark had brought his wife and young family to Portland and the tavern in question in 1884, and as faithfulness overturned faith*less*ness so did the establishment's dark and dangerous reputation dwindle before that of a respectable enterprise. Thaddeus was himself more or less honest, if not entirely law-abiding, since his tavern served ale and beer and stout against the strict precepts of the State of Maine's prohibition. Mrs. Spark allowed nothing stronger (and not an ounce of rum), and the Faithful Mermaid gained the reputation as an illegal drinking establishment of upright character and with a rather attractive sign.

The greatest challenge on Brackett Street—and, indeed, along the length of the waterfront—was to raise a family; there were rough elements to be watched, bad influences upon a man's sons and unrefined sensibilities regarding his daughters. Thaddeus Q. and Mabel Spark's daughters were of a buxom quality, and all but their middle daughter, Annabelle, were gregarious by nature, neither attribute being much of an aid to a parent in his cautionary measures. Moreover, the boys were young rovers, if not absolutely wild; but they were good children on the whole. They were all good, and good-hearted, which in the end must stand for quite a lot.

The sign of the Faithful Mermaid swung in the slightest wind, and the sound of it creaking was both lullaby and *reveille* to eight-year-old Timothy Spark, who shared a small room with his older brother Bobby above the emblem of the tavern nymph.

Tim prided his young self as something of a Natty Bumpo—a Hawkeye of the city; he spent summer days on Brackett Street and in the surrounding alleys chasing and fighting enemy Indians with the warriors of his adoptive tribe, and stalking deer and bear and moose along the wharves with the flintlock his oldest brother, Davey, had carved from a piece of driftwood. Timothy knew the oaks and elms and maples of the city and Deering Park from their broad trunks to their tenderest limbs, and he traversed the roofs of the waterfront as he imagined the ancient tribes had walked the coastal hills; from the highest peaks, he and his friends (other boys less imagined than his Indian allies) watched the comings and goings of the harbor and numbered the pigeon chicks that called from their untidy nests among the eaves and gutters. The young pioneers hid from view of the busy streets like spies and sometimes came home with news and understanding that their parents could hardly credit.

Each night Tim drowsed to the sound of the creaking sign below his window and the comforting rumble of talk and laughter resonating up through the floorboards from the tavern room. Timothy slept well. He rose each morning to the squeak of the mermaid below his window and the clank of pots in the kitchen.

On the morning after the "Danforth Street Pianoforte Demolition" (as that event was dubbed by Portland's *Eastern Argus*) Tim woke in a single instant, as was his habit, and sat up in the next but was surprised to find his father seated in the chair opposite gnawing on a wooden match. Thaddeus Q. Spark had a way of occupying a chair, developed from years of waiting upon his customers' slightest whims, that indicated he would not be doing so very long; he always sat at the very edge of his seat, his hands on the arms of his perch (if it had any) or on his knees. His head erect, his attention forward, a sprinter could hardly want a better starting position.

This morning, Thaddeus's head was cocked to one side, just a tad, and his hands were folded in his lap; he sat well forward and looked like a good surprise would knock him out of his chair. "Good morning, Chief," he said.

"Good morning, Daddy." The boy scratched his nose, then his shock of blond hair. He rubbed his eyes and yawned. "What are you doing?"

"Waiting for you, I guess," said the father indulgently.

"You could have woke me."

"I could have."

"What is it?" asked Tim.

"How old are you now? Eight?"

Tim nodded. "Eight and a half."

The father nodded, his great beard wagging, and he chuckled, his high voice piping in short trills. "Chief Spark," he teased, but with a smile beneath that remarkable brush and enough regard in his expression that even a young lad like Timothy could not take umbrage. "Get dressed there, fellow."

"It's raining," said Tim. He peered from the window at the wet street.

"Well, it is," said Thaddeus.

"What is it, Daddy?"

"Want to come along with me this morning?"

Tim halted in the midst of pulling on his trousers. "Where are we going?"

"Your Uncle Gill got himself into a *fry* last night."

This interested the boy. "Is he all right?"

"He's in jail," said Thaddeus.

"Are we going to break him out?" wondered Tim.

Thaddeus let out a chirp of astonishment. "No, we're not going to break him out! Who do you think we are, the James Gang?" He laughed heartily. "Break him out! If your mother could hear it, she might help you try."

"Did they catch him at the wharf?"

"No, it wasn't that. He got himself in a fix, is all, but it would have been a tighter fix if not for the fellow we're going to visit this morning."

"Who is it?"

"You don't know him."

"Oh."

"Although, I dare say, you'll think you do when you see him." This observation occasioned something like a short laugh from Thaddeus.

Tim frowned again, but he liked a mystery. "Can Mailon come?"

"He can tag along," said Thaddeus. Mailon Ring was the next thing to an orphan. Mailon was a scrawny creature who waited outside the kitchen door for Timothy every morning. The day hardly seemed comprehensive to Thaddeus till he had seen that dirty face peering in from the alley. "He'll have to wait outside while we visit Mr. Thump."

"Mr. Thump?" said Tim. The name had an odd but oddly likable ring to it. When Tim was dressed and he had his rubber-soled *sneakers* on, they went to the rear of the house by a long corridor, then down the narrow back stairs to the kitchen. On the way, Tim could smell things cooking—bacon and biscuits and meat pies—and coffee boiling on the stove. The Faithful Mermaid's day was just beginning, and the older Spark children were busy with their mother bustling about the kitchen and tavern room.

"Tim and I are going to break Uncle Gill out of jail!" announced Thaddeus when he and his youngest son reached the bottom of the stairs.

"Father!" declared Mabel Spark (it being common along the coast of Maine in those days for wives and husbands to refer to one another as *Father* and *Mother*). "Talking like that before your son!"

A low whistle came from skinny little Mailon at the kitchen door. He stood close to the threshold so that the door's gable would protect him from the damp.

"What do you mean, *before* my son?" said Thaddeus. "It was his idea before it was mine. I thought maybe the two of you had discussed it."

Timothy's sisters Minerva and Betty thought this funny, but their humor was lost beneath their mother's protestations. "Good heavens, Thaddeus Spark!" she said. "I'll never guess what will come out of you next!" But she laughed herself, saying, "Break him out!" and she ruffled Tim's hair as she passed him, her hand covered with flour.

"Get some breakfast, Chief," said Thaddeus, taking his own turn at mussing his son's hair.

Tim sat down to a plate of bacon and eggs that his sister Minerva had served up.

"Have you eaten, Mailon?" asked Thaddeus.

The boy at the kitchen door nodded. Mrs. Spark wouldn't let the dirt-covered kid into her kitchen, but she always brought him a plate food if he was nearby at breakfast (and sometimes lunch and dinner). Mailon's mother was dead and his father nocturnal, and the lion's share of Mailon's sustenance came from the backdoor of the Faithful Mermaid.

"Timothy and I are going over to Mr. Thump's," said Thaddeus, leaning over the stove to consider a stew as it simmered.

"What are you going to do there?" asked Betty.

"Reciprocate," said the father.

Tim looked up from his breakfast and frowned. Betty turned about and rolled her eyes, which made Minerva laugh. Betty and Minerva were good girls, seventeen and twelve, respectively, but a good deal too pretty for Thaddeus's peace of mind. Their sister Annabelle, who was sixteen, was prettier still.

"You laugh, but my old ma used to tell me, 'Thaddeus, one must reciprocate!'"

"So does a pitman on a steam engine," suggested Davey, who was bringing dishes from the tavern room to be washed.

"Do you know what I'm talking about?" piped Thaddeus, one eye squinted in the direction of his oldest progeny.

"Not exactly," said Davey with a sheepish grin.

"I didn't think so. Wrecking a piano is a good deal less fractious than flattening a police officer, and we will reciprocate accordingly."

"I'd go myself and scrub his house top to bottom, I'm that grateful," said Mabel Spark, "but I can't help wondering what this Mr. Thump was doing over to the Weary Sailor, if he's the gentleman you say he is."

"He and his friends were lost, from what I hear tell," said Thaddeus. "I had invited them to come by and visit, and I guess they were on their way when they ran into your uncle's performance."

"You never told me where you met them," said Mabel Spark.

Thaddeus waved a hand in the air, as if he couldn't recall, or that it was too small a business to bother explaining. He hadn't told anyone about his short adventure in front of the Shipswood Restaurant.

Mabel Spark made a face but let Thaddeus go on this point. "I'd like to meet the man," she said, "and thank him myself."

"Oh, you'll think highly of him if you do," said Thaddeus, and there was the light of humor in his eyes that he did not trouble to explain. "He's a very *handsome* fellow."

"Oh, go on with you!" said Mrs. Spark.

"No, I wouldn't doubt, were anything to happen to me, but you'd up and marry him."

"My land, Thaddeus!" she said, and she swatted him with the cloth in her hand. "I can't guess what gets into you!"

Thaddeus laughed very happily, giggling like a child.

"He's probably homelier than a hedge fence," suggested Davey.

Something about this statement caused Thaddeus to scratch at his beard. "Believe me," said Thaddeus, "he is a very presentable fellow."

"Take an umbrella," said his wife.

7. Since Last Summer

"Sundry and I have had a change in plans," said Mister Walton when they met Phileda McCannon in the foyer of the City Hotel at quarter to seven.

"Have you?" she said, as if she had suspected this.

He laughed. "We are going to visit his uncle."

"How nice." She took the hat from his hands and brushed at the wet crown. "And he lives in—"

"Norridgewock."

"Which is—"

"Quite north of Portland, actually, but Sundry seems to think," Mister Walton confessed, looking into his eyebrows, "that traveling with you to Brunswick might do for the first leg of the trip."

"Does he?" Once she had groomed his hat to her satisfaction, she gave it back to him. Phileda was like her old self this morning, and had recovered enough from last night's misgivings to say "I knew I could count on you" in a manner that might have been admonishment or gratitude. She looked almost demure as she took his arm and they went out in the rain together, behind Sundry and a porter who were carrying her bags. Mister Walton held the umbrella. She smiled, looking down at the steps before them, like a child holding a cherished secret.

In the carriage she continued to hold his arm, which was not required, and she inclined her head a little so that Mister Walton thought, briefly, that she might rest it on his shoulder. Sundry considered the view out the window.

"Will the members be looking for you?" she asked quietly.

"They will forgive us, I think, if we leave town unannounced," said Mister Walton. "It seemed a little early to rouse them, but Mr. Baffin will ring them up later in the day and tell them."

The rain drummed on the roof of the cab. "If I were a gambler," she said, "I would wager money that there will be an adventure in this."

"Without the rest of the club?" said Sundry.

Miss McCannon laughed lightly.

Mister Walton patted her hand. "We will enter into no intrigues, nor court unusual company without you."

"Of course, there's my uncle," amended Sundry.

"Aside from Sundry's uncle."

The enclosed platform at Portland's Grand Trunk Depot was loud with the downpour, with the waiting train's impatient chuff of steam, the voices and movement of passengers and porters, hurrying footsteps, and finally with the call from the conductor of "All *aboard* for *Mar*tin's Point, *Fal*mouth Foreside, *Cumber*land Foreside, *Yar*mouth, *South* Freeport, *Free*port, *Bruns*wick, *and* points Ea-*aist!*" Clusters of electric incandescents gave off enough of a yellowish glow so that the rainy sky at either end of the high-roofed structure looked, in contrast, like twilight.

"I do love to ride in the rain," said Phileda.

Mister Walton nodded his agreement as he handed her up the steps. "Up ahead," he said pleasantly when they entered the nearest car and paused at the end of the aisle. There were, as yet, very few people seated, so it was a small surprise to his companions that it mattered to him what end of the conveyance they occupied.

But while they were standing at the platform, an abundance of red hair had caught Mister Walton's eye, the shade of which he recognized as surely as a familiar face. Once in the car, Sundry's gaze fell upon the red hair and the head of long, dark hair beside it, and he knew where they would sit.

Mister Walton and his companions approached the redhead and the brunette from behind, even as the countenance of a third woman, middle-aged and in winter colors, sitting opposite these two, came into view. This woman took note of Mister Walton with something like a start, but the expression on her face lightened slightly after her initial frown. Mister Walton paused at the shoulder of the redheaded woman and inquired, with undisguised delight, if the seats directly across the aisle were spoken for.

"Mister Walton!" cried the redhead, and if his delight was undisguised hers burst forth like a sudden beam of sunshine.

"Miss Underwood!" he replied with a happy chuckle, and his pleasure was not lessened as the beautiful young woman threw her arms about his neck.

"Oh! I can't tell you how wonderful it is to see you! Didn't I tell you, Priscilla, that we would meet someone?"

The dark-haired woman, perhaps a year or so younger than Miss Underwood, (which would put her just above twenty) looked as pleased, though in a quiet way, to see the bespectacled fellow. She gave the slightest nod to Phileda McCannon, and perhaps something slighter still to Sundry, who himself seemed unusually reticent in his greeting.

"Aunt Grace," Miss Underwood was saying, "I was just telling Priscilla we would meet someone today! I just knew it!"

"Mrs. Morningside," said Mister Walton with a bow to the older woman.

"Mister Walton," said Grace Morningside. She appeared uncomfortable with her niece's exuberance. "Cordelia," she said, "people will be wanting the aisle."

"My fault entirely," said Mister Walton, undaunted by the woman's reserve. "Miss Morningside," he said to the black-haired young woman.

Priscilla Morningside smiled sweetly. "It's so good to see you again, Mister Walton."

"You remember my good friend, Sundry Moss," he said to the three women.

"Of course we do!" said Cordelia, and she stuck her hand out in almost masculine fashion, which caused everyone but her aunt to smile, she was otherwise so feminine.

Sundry shook her hand and pronounced, "Miss Underwood."

"I have read such things about you both," declared Cordelia, "*and* the Moosepath League! Why, I thought *we* might have provided you with enough adventure! You remember Mr. Moss, Aunt Grace? Priscilla?"

Grace Morningside nodded curtly to Sundry; her daughter Priscilla barely met his eyes but said, "It is good to see you, Mr. Moss."

"It is my pleasure," he said quietly.

"And this," continued Mister Walton, "is my . . . very good . . . *friend* Miss Phileda McCannon. Phileda, Mrs. Grace Morningside, her daughter Priscilla, and her niece Cordelia Underwood."

Grace nodded in a stately manner, Priscilla smiled and said, "How very nice to meet you," but Cordelia, who brightened at Mister Walton's use of Phileda's Christian name, rather than the less familiar "Miss McCannon," gave the woman a wide-eyed smile and shook her hand.

"I have heard very definite things about you, Miss Underwood," said Phileda pleasantly.

"Oh, dear," said Cordelia, who looked as though she might laugh.

"If you don't mind," said Mister Walton, as he and Sundry and Phileda occupied the seats across the aisle. Another passenger begged their pardon and passed between. "Are you going to Ellsworth?" Mister Walton inquired; he knew Ellsworth to be the Morningside's home.

"Only to Freeport—well, to South Freeport," said Cordelia. "To visit Aunt Delia."

"You must remember me to her," said Mister Walton. "I recall with great pleasure the last Fourth of July with Mrs. Frost." Seventy-nine-year-old Delia Frost was Cordelia's *great*-aunt as well as her namesake, and Mister Walton had become very fond of the woman during his single outing with her and the Underwoods. "But I understand congratulations are long overdue," he said with sudden memory.

"Thank you," said Cordelia, for she was engaged to be married in June.

"And how is Mr. Scott?"

"Mr. Scott is very much 'Mr. Scott' these days," said Cordelia, as if this were an exasperating state of affairs though great happiness and mischief showed in her eyes.

"I am glad to hear it," said Mister Walton.

"Cordelia is glad to say it, you can be sure," said Priscilla, who had summoned enough courage to speak. She had marvelous long black hair but wore it in a manner that might have seemed more appropriate to a girl rather than a young woman. Her dress, too, was not as stylish or mature as Cordelia's. Mister Walton imagined that Priscilla's mother had some influence in these matters. Priscilla Morningside's features were a shade lengthy, which kept them from appearing quite as fine as her cousin's, but behind round spectacles her dark eyes were beautiful and expressive, and if her smile was not as immediately dazzling as Cordelia's it was easily drawn out by the present company. She appeared in a constant state of blush this morning.

"And may I guess at the maid of honor?" said Mister Walton.

Priscilla's smile deepened and Cordelia snatched up her cousin's hand; she still felt a little giddy, it was plain, when she thought about it all—the handsome and brawny hunting guide, Dresden Scott, their approaching nuptials, the wedding and reception. "Mr. Scott is building a house on my land outside of Millinocket," said Cordelia, and everything she said—the employment of the name '*Mr.* Scott' for the man she loved and the reference to '*my*' land where he was laboring on a house (their home-to-be!)—was filled with a happy wryness for which she had a particular genius. She who was born and bred upon a city street, within sound of the harbor buoys, was to make her life in the north and the interior where there were only outpost villages and scattered logging and hunting camps—but life was to be an adventure!

A family with five young children came clamoring down the aisle but sat some seats away. A man who didn't remove his hat sat in the seat behind Cordelia and Priscilla. Other folk wandered in and sat in small groups. Conversation about the weather could be heard. Someone was advancing their prediction about the local baseball team.

"All *aboard!*" came the last call of the conductor. He passed Priscilla's window, walking the length of the train and closing the doors to the passenger cars.

Mister Walton asked after Cordelia's parents and Priscilla's brother. Ethan Morningside, it was reported, had been clipping newspaper articles about the Moosepath League's exploits and keeping them in a scrapbook. "We have a future member, I am sure," said Mister Walton happily. Mrs. Morningside looked vaguely pained by this thought.

Cordelia said to Phileda, "Aunt Delia promises there is a dress shop in Freeport that is famous for its Boston fashions."

"Ah," said Miss McCannon, "the trousseau."

"Actually, Priscilla and I must have gowns for Mrs. Morrell's June Ball," said Cordelia with a conspiratorial air.

"Really?" said Phileda musically. "I plan to be back in Portland for the ball myself."

"Are you all going?" asked Cordelia. She was bright with her and Priscilla's errand, and brighter still with the unexpected company on the way. She could chatter without seeming nonsensical and be heard by people several rows away without seeming loud. "I warn you, Mister Walton," she said, "your name will be on my dance card."

"And happily," he said.

There was a noisy blast of steam from the engine and the train moved a speculative foot or so. The next hiss was less startling and the train shifted forward most of a yard and then another and then two yards and they could sense through the windows the gray light of the overcast day steadily approaching and then there was rain spattering on the glass and a view of the harbor on their right, with Munjoy Hill, the bowling hall, and the Portland Observatory above and to the left.

"Mister Walton was the life of the Freeport Ball last Fourth of July," Cordelia informed Phileda.

"Was he?" said Phileda with a sly sidelong glance at Mister Walton.

"And are you going, Mr. Moss?" asked Cordelia.

Sundry looked a little shy of the question. "I'm not sure that a country fellow would be of much use at a society ball, Miss Underwood."

"I don't know why not!" said she. "Wouldn't it be wonderful if Mr. Moss came to the ball, Priscilla?"

"Cordelia!" said Aunt Grace quietly.

Now it was Priscilla's turn to appear shy. "That would be very nice, I am sure," she said, hardly looking up.

"I may have to think about it," said Sundry, with a slight bow of his head. Cordelia and Phileda caught his gaze lingering on Priscilla Morningside as the young woman looked away.

"We will expect you," said Cordelia. Her smile broadened whenever she looked from Mister Walton to Phileda and each time that she caught sight of the fond expression on Mister Walton's face whenever *his* eyes fell upon Miss McCannon. She was aware, besides, of a potent sort of anxiety between Mr. Moss and her cousin. "We still remember your quick thinking and courage last summer, Mr. Moss," said Cordelia, referring to their shared adventure of the previous July. Then she added, "Don't we, Priscilla?"

"Oh, yes, certainly," said Priscilla, sounding anything but certain.

"I don't remember accomplishing very much," said Sundry.

"Sundry will hear no praise of himself, I'm afraid," said Mister Walton, quick to rescue his friend.

"We will trouble him with it anyway," said Cordelia. "Won't we, Priscilla—Ow!" Priscilla may have accidently kicked her cousin's ankle as she shifted her own feet.

Mrs. Morningside said little, to begin with, though Mister Walton politely referred to her in each matter. Grace Morningside had the demeanor of someone who was born old. Grace had lost her husband several years before and had yet to completely shed her widow's clothes. She was a thin, not unhandsome woman who gave the outward appearance of a wisp until things became difficult (or she deemed them difficult), whereupon she might surprise everyone with the weight of her opinions and abilities. For the most part, however, she *sometimes* suffered from headaches and fainting spells.

But when asked, Grace explained that they were staying with the Underwoods until the wedding and managed to offer further details about that event. Phileda and Cordelia carried the lion's share of talk. There were several stops before Freeport, and other travelers came and went, but the rainy miles clicked by all too quickly. Soon the station was announced and the one party prepared to get off. Mister Walton would have gone out with them if Aunt Delia had been there to meet them, but he said his good-byes instead in the aisle of the car. Good wishes were passed full circle, and at the last moment Sundry gave a curt nod and said he would see the women out. Mister Walton watched his young friend stride ahead of the trio, a little surprised at this level of gallantry.

"So this is the Cordelia, for whom you left my side last summer," said Phileda recalling how Toby had gone to Millinocket to volunteer in the search for the kidnapped young woman.

"Well, yes," he said with the slightest hint of apology.

"I think her well worth it," said Phileda. "But how often has Sundry seen Miss Morningside?"

"Only the once, I think, when we visited the Underwoods last July."

"She is a lovely young woman," said Phileda. "Very sweet." She shifted to the other side of the aisle so that they could look out on the platform.

"Yes," agreed Mister Walton, still a little surprised. "It only takes one look." And he gave Phileda a particular look when he said this. "He has mentioned her a time or two, now that I think of it, but he's kept any feelings a secret . . . till now."

"Well, he would, wouldn't he?" She took Mister Walton's arm. "He must go to the ball, and that is the final word."

Mister Walton chuckled. "He doesn't seem very keen on the idea."

"He told Miss Morningside he would think about it."

✳ᏕᏒ✳

Stepping onto the rainy platform of Freeport Station, Sundry gave the conductor a meaningful nod and the fellow retreated a pace or two. The young man stood with his hat off and his head getting wet. Grace looked a little suspicious, but once she had unfurled her umbrella she took Sundry's offered hand and nodded her thanks.

Cordelia managed to get herself in front of her cousin and brightly thanked Sundry when she came down. "Good heavens, Aunt Grace!" she said, scooting beneath the woman's umbrella. "That man looks *just* like the Prince of Wales!" Aunt Grace had met the prince on his visit to Portland when she was a very little girl and counted it a prominent moment in her life. The reference was surprising, and a little confusing, to her. She turned away from the young man who was about to hand her daughter down and looked through the rain in the direction that her niece was pointing. "Right there, Aunt Grace! Why, he has a striped waistcoat!"

Sundry heard none of this. Priscilla Morningside hesitated only briefly at the top of the steps before putting her hand out.

"Thank you, Mr. Moss," she said, somehow looking down with her head and up with her eyes. It was not a calculated expression, but it had every effect of the most practiced coquetry. She stood where she set her feet, unmindful of the weather, then stepped a little closer to him so that another passenger could reach the steps. The family with the young children had climbed down and were noisily hurrying toward the station house.

Sundry thought for a moment that his voice might not function properly but then he managed to say "It's good to see you again, Miss Morningside" without causing himself too much embarrassment. "You should get under cover."

"Yes," she answered in a breath, a very small smile on her lips and a very large one in her eyes.

"Priscilla!" declared Grace. "Get under cover! What are you about?"

"Mr. Moss," said Cordelia, "you must come visit us someday soon, in Portland, before the wedding." She stepped back into the rain to shake Sundry's hand again, managing at the same time to delay Priscilla's departure.

"Yes, thank you," said Sundry quietly.

Priscilla had hardly moved since he let go her hand; her nearness to him, and Cordelia's example, gave her every excuse to offer it to him again. Her shoulders were unnaturally lifted against the rain, or her mother's disapproval, or her own reticent nature.

"Cordelia, I don't know what you were talking about," said Grace. "He didn't look a bit like the prince. The prince has such a noble bearing and a grand beard. You would recognize him in an instant. Priscilla, come. We must find a porter and a carriage."

"Bye," said Priscilla simply before letting go of Sundry's hand.

He nodded and gestured with his hat.

The conductor must have been a man of sympathetic nature, for he crossed before Sundry and stood in such a way that the young man might appear to be speaking with him while he watched Priscilla hurrying through the rain with her cousin and mother. "A very pretty young woman," said the man.

Sundry didn't remember to put his hat back on.

When the women had gone round the station with a porter, the conductor walked back toward the station house calling, "All *aboard* for *Free*port, *Brüns*wick, *Cooks* Corners, *Har*ding, *New* Meadows, *Ba*-ath, *Wis*casset, *and* points Ea-*aist!*"

"They are lovely young women," said Phileda when Sundry returned.

"Do you think?" he replied.

"They are going to the ball."

Mister Walton was looking out the window.

"I hope they find something nice to wear," said Sundry.

8. The Attempted Reciprocation of Thaddeus Q. Spark

Mr. Joseph Thump peered from his parlor window and thought that there was a good deal of foot traffic along India Street for such a rainy morning. The oak before the house where he kept rooms drooped with newly budded leaves and dripped with an accumulated mist that also gathered on the window and warped his view. The macadam pavement of India Street glowed darkly. Several people beyond the gate and along the sidewalk appeared to take an interest in the house this morning. Perhaps a branch had come down. He leaned, first to one side, then another, bending his eyes toward the lawn.

"Hmmm," he said himself. He slipped from his jacket pocket an almanac of tides (complete with adjustments for several localities along the immediate coast) and opened this to the appropriate page to consider the hours and minutes of high water that day. Every day, Thump compared the predictions of his almanac with those in the newspaper, and occasionally the *Portland Courier* and *Captain Farthing's Almanac of Time and Tide* would disagree as to the exact moment of high water by as much as two or three minutes. He never felt quite right on such days.

As it happened, he felt a little out of kilter today, though for other reasons. Near at hand, upon the table by his favorite chair, was his crushed wallet. In his vest pocket was the item he so forcefully rescued the night before; he took this article from the pocket now, as he had done a dozen times since rising this morning, and considered it with a deep sigh.

There was a light rap at the hall door and he knew this would be his landlady, Mrs. Wilbur, with breakfast. Mrs. Wilbur and Millicent, the maid, set his place and arranged the several trays and plates and the day's edition of the *Portland Courier* in the little dining room across from the parlor, but he waited till they were nearly done before he came in and thanked them. Mrs. Wilbur saw immediately the welt on his forehead.

"All that's good, Mr. Thump!" she said. "What has happened to you?"

"I was struck by a piano key, Mrs. Wilbur," he reported. "Thank you for asking." His head was still ringing a little, now he thought of it.

"My stars, Mr. Thump! That's a nasty swipe. Did you fall?"

"No, Mrs. Wilbur. The piano did." Thump was lost in recollection and did not consider the image this news, coupled with his bruised head, might engender in a person's mind.

"Well, I don't wonder your head should ache," said the astonished woman. "Take some tea and eat hearty, sir." She scooted the maid out before her. Millicent was a plump young woman who was not easily roused from a generally bland expression, but she had taken great interest in the idea of a piano falling on Mr. Thump's forehead. "Out, out," Mrs. Wilbur said as she hied Millicent from the hall.

Something occurred to Thump as he regarded his breakfast and he returned to the parlor to look from the window again. What he saw roused a deep "Hmmm" of curiosity from him.

He was sorry not to do justice to his breakfast this morning, only managing a serving or two of sausage and eggs and toast and jam and smoked trout and potatoes and tea. He tried a sweet roll after this and felt quite done in, which was not like him. He had poured himself another cup of tea and wondered if it would be proper to go back to the parlor with it. He often referred to Mister Walton (or the Mister Walton in his mind) when he was faced with such quandaries and could not imagine the good man objecting to a body sipping tea on his feet. Consequently, Thump found himself standing at the parlor window considering the crowd on the rainy sidewalk and completely forgetting the cup and saucer in his hands.

Several of the people standing beyond the gate were some of the same several people who were standing there when he last looked, *and* when he had looked the time before that.

There was a small familiar rap at his door and Mrs. Wilbur leaned in from the hall. "Mr. Thump?" she queried in a strange little voice.

"Hmmm?" he said.

"Mr. Thump, there's a Mr. Spark to see you." She looked very searchingly at her boarder, as if she had not seen him properly before.

Thump felt strange, standing in the parlor with his cup of tea and saucer, and stranger still standing at the door with them. Mrs. Wilbur took no note but only looked at him some more, and said again, "A Mr. Spark to see you, Mr. Thump. I told him you were injured and he seemed to know it."

Thump frowned thoughtfully, an expression that remained hidden behind his beard. Mrs. Wilbur was waiting. "Mr. Spark?" said Thump.

"And a boy," said she.

"And a boy," he echoed. He was reminded of Eagleton's poem of the night before, but he had not seen seven robins; that had been Mister Walton. Thump *had* seen some robins the day before, but he had not counted them.

"They seem a little—" began Mrs. Wilbur in a confidential tone. "Well, a little rough around the edges, if I might say it, though if they're friends of yours I'm sure they're nice enough."

Mr. Spark, thought Thump. He only knew the one Mr. Spark, and that was the man who was nearly run over by their carriage yesterday evening. He hadn't considered that fellow to be *rough* and thought it untoward of Mrs. Wilbur to suggest such a thing. He didn't know many boys either, though he had spent some time in the company of a little fellow of four or five last fall and thought him pleasant. He was further disconcerted to notice that Millicent was staring at him over Mrs. Wilbur's shoulder. It did not occur to him that they were startled by the resemblance between himself and Mr. Spark.

"Shall I tell them you're indisposed, sir?" said Mrs. Wilbur.

Again, he thought of Mister Walton and could not imagine the chairman of the Moosepath League agreeing to any such subterfuge; the chairman would be glad of company and perhaps Thump had invited Mr. Spark to drop by, though he didn't recall. "I will put my cup and saucer down," he said decisively. "You may show them in, Mrs. Wilbur, and thank you."

⁂

This was the prosperous side of town and Timothy Spark had not spent much time here. He thought the house on India Street was splendid, with its granite steps and wrought-iron fence; everything was outsized and marvelous— the great front door, the spacious hallway, the broad, dark stairs. While the landlady let them in, Tim waved to Mailon, who waited on the sidewalk in the rain. Tim's father shook his umbrella closed and gripped it in one large paw.

Thaddeus gave his son certain last-minute instructions as the landlady led them up to the rooms of the mysterious Mr. Thump. The maid stood at the railing above and watched with undisguised interest while Tim and his dad mounted the stairs. Both women stared at Thaddeus Spark till the boy looked to see if his dad had food in his beard.

The landlady stopped them at the head of the stairs. Tim sensed an unfamiliar stillness beyond the door that led to Mr. Thump's apartments—not simply a lack of many voices and lives jostling elbow to elbow but a palpable *near silence*, as if thought itself (but only thought) had thickened into something real. It was an alien sensation that perplexed the boy.

The landlady knocked lightly, and when the door was opened and she had announced them Tim saw past her elbow the man called Mr. Thump.

"Yes," came a deep voice.

"Mr. Spark to see you, Mr. Thump," said the woman. "And the boy."

Tim's mouth opened and hung there. There were three elements about Mr. Thump that did *not* resemble Tim's father: the first was Mr. Thump's expression, which appeared uncertain, while Thaddeus typically exhibited more confidence than a card shark at country house poker; the second and third were Mr. Thump's expensive trappings and the deep rumble of Mr. Thump's voice. It was most extraordinary to see his father's likeness dressed in such prosperous clothes, and speaking in oboelike tones.

"Mr. Thump," said Tim's father.

"Mr. Spark," said Mr. Thump as he let them in; his expression indicated that the resemblance between himself and Thaddeus continued to surprise him as well. The visitors held their caps before them, their raincoats damp; Tim was fascinated as he scanned the hall furnishings and the glimpses of parlor and dining room that could be seen from the door. His father smelled strongly (and pleasantly, Tim thought) of lye soap.

"I do hope we waited long enough for you to rise and have some breakfast," said Thaddeus. "I have come with double gratitude this morning, to thank you again for your presence on Commercial Street, but mostly to thank you for your Christian behavior of last night, *and* to offer whatever services my family might humbly provide you for saving my wife's uncle."

Tim's father had not taken into consideration Mr. Thump's knowledge (or lack thereof) concerning Mrs. Spark's family. Thump did, in fact, attempt to reconcile this man's wife's uncle with the young police officer Calvin Drum. "It was more in the way of an accident, sir," he said quietly.

"You are kind to say so, Mr. Thump," said Thaddeus, misunderstanding the man's meaning. "But Gillie is *liable* to accidents, and the worst kind, for sure. It takes quite a lot of accident to get a piano up a flight of steps and over a balcony railing, and I told my wife as much this morning after we visited him."

"Your wife's uncle, Mr. Spark?"

Mr. Spark answered in the affirmative with that abrupt Yankee inhalation that has busied linguists and baffled imitation. It was, in fact, the famous *'ayuh'* that sounds differently on every peninsula in the State of Maine, and never anything like the letters that have been assembled to represent it.

Mr. Thump ventured forth again with, "Your wife's uncle is—?"

"Gillie Hicks," confirmed Tim's father with a nod. "And had you not pulled Calvin Drum to safety, Mr. Thump, Gillie would be looking at the rest of his life behind bars. He's an old *rounder* from way back, but it would have broke Mabel's heart to see him plunked for murder."

"Certainly, I am glad for her," said the gallant rescuer, though he looked far from *certain* about anything.

"I knew you would be." Tim's father stood straighter, now that he had gotten this out of the way. "Now, 'one good turn deserves something else,' as the saying goes, Mr. Thump." Thaddeus accepted the dearth of response as an invitation to continue. "'Reciprocate,' my old ma used to say, and it was not many years ago I asked someone what she meant. I heard something like it last winter at church. We go sometimes, Mrs. Spark and myself. And she says to me this morning, Mrs. Spark did, 'Thaddeus, you find where Mr. Thump hangs his hat, and you go down there and offer up some service for his saving Uncle Gill.' I was of the same mind myself."

"I assure you, Mr. Spark," rumbled Mr. Thump, "the necessity of any such . . . service is . . . unnecessary."

Thaddeus didn't seem to hear this. "You would do us a great favor, Mr. Thump," he said, "by allowing us to do you a favor." Recalling the presence of his youngest son, he put an arm over Tim's shoulders and drew him forward. "I beg your pardon," said Thaddeus. "This is Timothy K. Spark, my youngest boy. He's a little thin but he's wiry. Perhaps you might find him useful, running errands or the like. He can spit-shine a boot so's you can see your face in it. I put him at your full disposal."

Tim's father gave Tim a gentle whack on the back and the boy stepped forward. "Pleased to meet you, Mr. Thump," said Tim, which greeting had been carefully rehearsed.

"Yes," said Mr. Thump. He shook the boy's hand carefully. The elder and younger Sparks could not know that it took all of Joseph Thump's *Waltonian* observation and knowledge to respond to such a crisis. "I couldn't accept your generous offer, Mr. Spark," he said, "for something that so little put me out of my way."

Tim's father was a sympathetic man; he told the family later that they would only abash Mr. Thump by pressing their desire to *reciprocate*. "Ah, well, Mr. Thump," said Thaddeus, "we'll bide a while for another opportunity. Gillie's in the lockup, by the way, and sends his best."

Mr. Thump had the look of a man who had never been sent anyone's best from jail, but he managed to mumble something encouraging in return.

The landlady, still at the door, swung it wide now to encourage Tim and his father to exit. She continued to glance from the taverner to Mr. Thump with wide eyes. "Saved a man's life, you say?" she queried Tim's father when the door was shut and they descended the broad stairs.

"What did he say?" asked Thaddeus's cousin Ira when the father and son reached the sidewalk. "Does he live alone?" wondered Ira's wife, Minnie, and half a dozen other queries were registered from the relatives and acquaintances in the crowd gathered outside Mr. Thump's house.

"He's a very private man, our Mr. Thump," said Thaddeus as he and Tim came through the gate, "and we will *reciprocate* in a likewise manner."

"You should see the place!" said Tim to Mailon, who had been standing in the rain and looked a little better laundered than sometimes. "He does look just like you, Daddy," said Tim. "What does *reciprocate* mean?"

"It means 'Do unto others as they have done unto you,' which is a very Biblical phrase and much sought after among Christian people. Good morning, Calvin," said Thaddeus. Officer Drum was striding up the sidewalk.

"Thaddeus," said the policeman. "What brings you here?"

"We came to pay our respects for Mr. Thump's quick action."

Calvin Drum was on more or less friendly terms with the Sparks, but he never imagined they valued him so. He knew immediately why they would be thankful to Joseph Thump. "Right you should," he said with a nod. "Gillie would be up to his neck in it if Mr. Thump hadn't acted as he did."

"We are quite aware, Calvin, and also pleased that you were unscathed."

There was something a little backhanded about this, but Calvin Drum had a sense of humor and he grinned with one side of his mouth as he turned into the gate. "I am much obliged," he said quietly. "Half thought you and Mr. Thump were brothers, for a bit." He paused then, on the sidewalk, his face screwed up into sudden thought. "You're not related, are you?"

"We both descend from Adam, I suppose."

Officer Drum nodded. He marched up to the front door of the house on India Street, put his hat in the crook of his elbow, and swung the knocker.

"Do we?" asked Tim.

Thaddeus patted his son's shoulder with a high chuckle, saying, "You keep about, Tim. Stop by here now and again and you'll have reason to reciprocate before you know it."

"What should I do?"

"You might just hail him a cab or . . . well, I don't know. Something will occur. Trust that it will."

"Can Mailon help?"

"Yes, if needs be. Pay for some of his meals, I dare say."

"Should we follow him?"

"Mr. Thump? You might. But remember, he's a private fellow. The less he knows you're about, the happier he'll be."

The front door to the house opened and Mrs. Wilbur stuck her white head out to inquire who was knocking. Calvin Drum greeted the woman. Thaddeus looked up at the house and thought he could see Mr. Thump standing at a window. There were some interested comments along the sidewalk, and they all waved. After a moment the figure in the window waved back with a small gesture.

Across the street, standing almost behind the trunk of a giant elm, Fuzz Hadley's boy Jimmy Fain forgot that he was supposed to remain unseen and waved to Mr. Thump, too. He thought for a moment that it was Thaddeus up there, which was confusing since the taverner had come out of the house and gone down the street.

Thump saw Jimmy across the street and included him in his wave. Turning away from the window, he felt peculiar. In hand was the cherished object from his wallet—a small white card upon which a particular signature had been affixed. He considered it now, as he had a thousand times since he first discovered it so mysteriously. In January, he had thought there was the faint aroma of rosewater about it, and though he knew there was no scent left now (if there ever had been any), he held the card beneath his nose, almost in the attitude that a courtier might have taken to kiss a lady's hand.

9. Letters from the Wide World

Ezra Porch peered narrowly through the upstairs railing to the hall below and blinked. His sharp ears caught the sound of rain at the door. The tall clock ticked just beneath him, but out of sight from where he crouched. Mother Pilican was in the parlor, puttering at something in near silence; Ezra caught only a faint glimmer of sound, a mere suggestion of movement. She might have set an overstuffed pillow onto the sofa, but such was his complete understanding of the house about him that he knew it, even in a lazy drowse.

His eyes widened suddenly and his heart took an irrational leap. The front door opened with a *woosh!* and he knew it was Dee, who often entered like a gust of wind. Weather puffed in with her, and it was something more than that gentle spring rain poets speak of, yet Dee had only a short wool jacket and a scarf over her head. She shut the door with a thump, pulled off the scarf, brushed some stray drops from her hair, and shook the jacket when she had got it off. She was damp all over but unperturbed.

A bit of dark brown hair had fallen from the bun behind her head and she brushed this behind an ear. "Ezra Porch," she said, for she had caught sight of him now. He knew his purr could probably be heard in the next room and was not ashamed of himself. He flexed his yellow paws beneath him and almost closed his eyes. "Ezra Porch," she said, "you got into my wastebasket this morning and strewed paper all over the floor."

He did close his eyes then. There was nothing that gave him more pleasure than to have Dee scold him.

Mother Pilican could be heard "tut-tutting" in the parlor. "Mr. Porch, what have you been up to?" she said.

"He's been a naughty boy," called Dee to her mother. "Where's Uncle Fale, Mom?"

"He's out in the barn, dear."

"There's a letter here for him." Dee realized her boots were wet and she made a face. Ezra Porch purred. Dee considered her feet for a moment, then decided to chance her mother's eyesight.

With her wheelchair pulled up by the parlor fire, Mrs. Pilican was sewing a patch on a pair of Uncle Fale's trousers. She looked up over her glasses when Dee came in and said, "You've let your feet get wet."

"Yes, Mom," said Dee. It might be presumed that a thirty-four-year-old woman would know this, but Dee had expected her mother to mention it.

The older woman's eyesight was not keen, but she had put two and two together, so to speak. Dee had never been one to hurry in from the rain.

Dee looked handsome, if not beautiful, in her white blouse and tartan skirt of blue and green. She had a large cast to her features that had not drawn suitors, though there was a *presence* to her otherwise, in the physical sense, that other women might have envied. She was perhaps as comely as she had ever been as she neared middle age, and Mrs. Pilican knew that even the young minister at the Methodist church was pleased (in a not entirely ministerial way) to shake Dee's hand after services of a Sunday.

"It's taken the men here these thirty-odd years to see her," Dee's Uncle Fale had said to his sister only a few days before.

"They're all head down at their labor," Mrs. Pilican had replied.

"I was much the same," he admitted. "If she had been in the wide world she'd have married a count or a duke or something." Fale Field himself had not been in the *wide world* for many years, but he gleaned what he could from the newspapers and magazines.

Mrs. Pilican had smiled down at her own work. "I don't suppose Portland counts for the wide world these days," she said. The old woman had come from Portland, many years ago, but hardly remembered it now, past the greater events of her life. The thought had made her sigh, though, for in another month or so Dee would be summering, as she always did, in the city.

"Something from Mr. Siegfried," said Dee. She had been to the post office and carried two or three envelopes and a magazine.

"Oh?" Mrs. Pilican was pleased. There would be a royalty check against her latest work, but what she most looked forward to was Mr. Siegfried's accompanying letter, which was always courtly and old-fashioned. She took the envelope from her daughter and considered the elegant handwriting.

Dee settled into the captain's chair on the other side of the room. An issue of *St. Nicholas* magazine dropped from her lap and fell open, and when she picked it up, something on the contents page caught her eye; she wasn't even sure what it was until she opened the periodical again and found the title *The Mystery Behind the Myth of Persephone*. It was a children's journal, despite this profound article; the Pilicans still subscribed, though Dee and her siblings were long grown and, save for Dee, scattered by work and fate, and though Mrs. Deborah Pilican seldom wrote for the magazine anymore.

"My, it's a day for letters," said Dee. "Teddy and Bill," she said, holding up the envelope.

"They'll be here next month," said Mother Pilican. Life was a mixed blessing: Teddy and Bill (her niece and nephew Theodora and William Field) would arrive for the summer and Dee would leave a week or so later.

The sound of hooves on the main street of Dresden Mills gave Dee reason to look up from the letter in her hand and peer out the window across the room. A horse and carriage clopped by in the mud and rain. She always liked to imagine where people were going. "Dr. O'Hanrahan," she said.

"Mrs. Beal is due," said her mother.

A door at the back of the little Cape shut and Uncle Fale strode in.

"The Grand Army of the Republic calls again, Uncle Fale," said Dee. She handed him the third envelope.

"Thirty-two years this month," he said. He thanked his niece, retrieved a pipe from the mantle, and sat down with the news from the G.A.R. that was sent out to veterans four times a year.

Mrs. Pilican opened her letter from Mr. Siegfried. He asked after her and those close to her with all best wishes and compliments. She remembered meeting him and all the fuss they'd made and how gracious he had been. It had only been that once, but she imagined she knew him well. Only after she had read the short letter two or three times over did she think to look at the check that accompanied it. "Oh, my!" she said aloud. "*Mrs. Babbington* is doing quite well."

"And you thought she was overwrought," said Dee.

Mrs. Pilican laughed. "I gave her reason, I suppose. I am trying to be nicer to Melanie Bright. I may use my own name for this one." Deborah Pilican liked to alternate her pen names, since she was a swift writer. She had grown fond of these alter egos, and the author of *The Misery of Millicent Babbington*, known to the world as Mrs. Rudolpha Limington Harold, was an especial favorite since she was the smallest bit scandalous.

Dee shivered suddenly. She brushed at the damp on her sleeve.

"Out without your rain gear again," said Uncle Fale, nodding toward her wet hair.

"It wasn't raining very much when I left," she said, which was a reply that had been heard before today.

"There's not much to a snowstorm when the first flake falls," he countered, and this had been heard before as well.

"I will get the slicks out next time," she said. It might have been a conversation two weeks ago—or twenty years.

Uncle Fale chuckled. The idea of Dee in anything so *cautionary* as a slicker amused him. "Maybe in a hurricane," he thought aloud.

The rain chose this moment to rattle the window behind him.

"It's not too early for tea, is it?" wondered Dee's mother.

"I'll get it," said Dee.

"No, you come over by the fire and rehearse Teddy and Bill's letter. I'll get the tea, and then you read their news to me. Toast and jam?"

Dee and Uncle Fale agreed to this plan, and Mrs. Pilican wheeled herself into the kitchen. Dee stood before the hearth and read the letter.

There was the sound of *padding* down the carpeted stairs and Ezra Porch appeared from the hall. He almost fell over, nuzzling the doorpost, then he let out a birdlike *chirrup* and went over to Dee. She let him rub against her skirts for a moment before she sat and pulled him onto her lap.

She shivered again and thought of Persephone, rising every spring and returning every fall. How very unlike the Underworld was Dresden, Maine, which Dee loved and lived in for nine months of the year; but how very much like Persephone she felt when July drew close and she left for Portland. How very much she loved her mother and her uncle, how very satisfied to be a doting daughter and niece for three-quarters of her life, and how very much she looked forward to becoming someone else when she spent her summers away.

Last night she dreamt that she was flying, and even now she could close her eyes and recall the effortless sensation, the darkness of town, the night forest rushing beneath. She stroked Ezra Porch, and the yellow cat rumbled in her lap. Like all animals, he was mad for Dee, though her attentions were often delivered without conscious motive. She was drawn to stroke his back even as the wind was to ruffle the oak tree before the house.

Uncle Fale watched her. He had seen Dee "disappear" like this a thousand times. She had only to stroke a cat's fur, or a horse's muzzle, and an odd expression came over her—something between happiness and loss. "Errol Husting died," said Uncle Fale.

"Oh?" Dee came out of her trance.

"Last Christmas Day."

"Oh, dear," said Dee. "I am sorry. Did you know him well?"

"Not at all, dear," he said. "But we fought against him and his Georgians back in '63. He was a canny soldier and a grand gentleman." Uncle Fale looked up from his letter, but he was lost in the past.

Dee stroked the cat's silky back. In *her* silence, she slipped forward again, toward summer, so imbued now with her dream of flight.

10. Not Quite Good-bye

As the train pulled into Brunswick, Mister Walton gazed from the window with the sort of interest that can only be aroused by prior experience. The town of Brunswick has come in for its share of significance in the history of the Moosepath League, and by the spring of 1897 it had already provided the backdrop for an auspicious meeting that led to a gun battle upon the Sheepscott River and the rescue of a child, and also for the first (but not the last) Moosepathian attendance at the elusive Merrymeeting Tavern.

Pulling into Brunswick Station, it was natural that Mister Walton would see in the broad main street and the handsome white homes leading toward Bowdoin College a *possibility* of adventure (with rain to add a sense of mystery), and that the impish glint he and Sundry had spoken of the previous night would be evident in his bespectacled eyes. The expression made Phileda smile, though she would be quitting Toby's company for several days now. He let out a sigh that belied his fascination.

As for Sundry, he was of a thoughtful mein these last miles.

The interior of the train darkened as it chuffed to a halt beside the station house. The rain at the windows increased. Steam and mist mingled on the platform, and the conductor waited beneath an umbrella while people got off. Phileda came out with Mister Walton despite his protests.

"I won't melt," she insisted. They watched two or three men board the train while Sundry claimed the baggage. Phileda touched Mister Walton's cheek with her gloved hand. "I am quite jealous of Sundry's uncle just now, meeting you for the first time."

"He hasn't had to put up with me these past few months," he said with a smile on his face.

She smiled wryly and narrowed one eye at him. "That's not what I meant," she said. He must know this, of course, but she was learning that sometimes it profits one to be sure.

"I know," he said simply.

Then she undid one of his coat buttons, simply so that she could button it again. When she was done she brushed at her work. Something filled her when she looked back at him. "We must talk when I get back," she said, and the look upon her face needed no further explanation or assurance.

Toby nodded. Something had filled him as well, and he sighed.

"The June Ball, then?" she said.

"Yes," he replied, which syllable used about all the air left in him.

Then she kissed him softly and gave him one more glance that would have done a flirtatious schoolgirl proud. She exchanged a wave with Sundry, who was hurrying the bags inside. When she was in her seat again, she pulled down her window and said to Mister Walton, who was standing below, "You're being rained on."

He was indeed, with his homburg in hand, his overcoat damp, and his bald pate shiny. "I am impervious," he said contentedly.

"You'll catch a cold," she replied with mock severity.

"All *aboard!*" called out the conductor as he strode the length of the platform. The litany of stops tumbled out of him like a chant. He glanced from Mister Walton's hat to the pleasant face of Phileda McCannon at the window. "I met *my* wife on the train," said the conductor.

"Did you?" Mister Walton had not taken his eyes from Phileda.

"She was the engineer's daughter. There was a carload of us coming home just after Appomattox, and she was with some girls who sang patriotic songs for us on the stretch from Belfast to Bangor. I struck up some talk with her when they were done, thinking I might impress her in my uniform, but she hardly noticed me till I fell into a rhododendron outside Bangor station."

"It is an unusual form of courtship," said Mister Walton mildly.

"Her father liked it, too," said the conductor, then he shouted, "All *aboard!*" He climbed the nearest steps, held the rail, and leaned out to see if any straggling passengers were hurrying to make his train.

"What was he saying?" asked Phileda, who did not fear the appearance of curiosity.

"He met his wife on the train," called Mister Walton.

She mouthed an *O*, then said, "Was he the conductor, then?"

"No, but he fell into a rhododendron." Mister Walton smiled up at her, and added, "It made *her* laugh, too, evidently."

Phileda sat back in her seat, face forward, almost as if something shy had come over her. Mister Walton was thankful for this brief moment to watch her with impunity.

"All *aboard!*" shouted the conductor one last time from the steps of a car further up the train.

"Take care," they said to one another. Phileda's expression grew mischievous and she blew him a kiss just as the train began to move. He was a little startled, as if something physical had actually been thrown his way. It was a moment before he thought to return the gesture. A gout of steam obscured his view and then her car was foreshortened by distance and her window was invisible to him.

"She wants to talk to me when she gets back," said Mister Walton. He could sense rather than see Sundry Moss at his side.

"Does she?"

"That's what she said." Mister Walton had his hat on now and he took his spectacles off to rub them with a handkerchief. "For the first time since she and I met, I don't feel *down*, now that we're parted. I miss her already but I don't feel sad, somehow. It's not the same thing."

"Maybe 'when she gets back,'" suggested Sundry, "is a little like saying 'when she gets home.'"

There *had* been something of that in her expression, thought Mister Walton, though he hadn't considered it in so many words. Sundry's construction pleased him. "Well," said Mister Walton, "on to Uncle Cyrus."

Sundry nodded once. "Barring unforeseen events."

✳✺✦

It took a mile or so for Mister Walton and Sundry to accustom themselves to the *clickety-clickety* of the Main Coast rails after the *clickety-clack-clickety-clack* of the Maine Central's. It took *more* than a few minutes to accustom themselves to the lack of female company. The day had started well, with Cordelia and Priscilla and Mrs. Morningside, as well as Phileda McCannon; now they were two bachelors, and the rainy day seemed a little deficient.

Their car was largely populated by newspaper-wielding men in bowlers and stripe-vested drummers with sample cases at their feet, with only the occasional feathered hat to break up the monotony. Mister Walton and Sundry considered the passing scenery and the weather. Mister Walton quite liked the rain, but he was glad not to be looking out at it from his parlor window. Sundry was of farm stock, and rain was like answered thirst, but it matched a pensive mood all too well.

Some folk need the rain for the sake of the soul, and perhaps one of these people can recognize another or simply search for the face that is *not* glowering out at the storm. There were a lot of sour looks reflected in the train windows, ghostly frowns filled with the passing landscape, but one man, sitting across from Mister Walton and Sundry, appeared content, with a pleasant smile in a close-cropped salt-and-pepper beard. Mister Walton took note of him and nodded to the fellow when their glances met.

"Good morning," said the man with the pleasant smile.

"Good morning," said Mister Walton.

"Yes, it is good."

"I believe you," said Mister Walton. "I like the rain myself."

"My wife liked a rainy day," said the old fellow.

As this last sentence was couched in the past tense, Mister Walton gleaned from it as much sorrow as serenity. He smiled softly and nodded.

"I was thinking of her," said the pleasant man. He looked ahead again and seemed to forget Mister Walton across the aisle.

Mister Walton was a little stunned, and a little saddened. He directed a rueful smile toward Sundry and said, "Hmmm." The young man, too, had been pulled from his own reverie and looked at a loss for words. "Hmmm," said Mister Walton again, quietly so that he hardly heard himself, and looking out at the gray day he thought the rain looked colder.

The whistle rang out, announcing their approach to Bowdoinham, and Mister Walton unexpectedly found himself waking from a strange sleep. Sundry sat straight in his seat, looking ahead like a sentry. Mister Walton blinked and apologized to his friend for nodding off, but Sundry only answered with a short laugh. The man with the pleasant face was gone.

The outskirts of Bowdoinham village appeared. The fields closed in and folded round them. The whistle shrieked again and a trestle growled beneath the train as they crossed a branch of the Cathance River. Merrymeeting Bay hove into view. Steam billowed past the windows and the rain increased as the train chuffed to a halt. Mister Walton, who had traveled in many a railroad car, thought the arrival at Bowdoinham Station felt a little rougher and more precipitate than might be expected.

The conductor appeared at the end of the car and cleared his throat prefatory to an announcement. "We are having some difficulties that will delay us half an hour or so," he told them, occasioning some groans and protests. "If anyone would care to stretch a leg," he added, "we will voice the train ten minutes before departure. One of the boys has gone up to Fink's Store to ask them to put a kettle on."

Some of the passengers looked indecisive, but others rose. Mister Walton yawned. "I could benefit from a cup of something hot," he said.

"I've never been to Bowdoinham," said Sundry, which state of affairs seemed reason enough to step out and look around.

"Well, then," said Mister Walton, "let's find Mr. Fink's store and see if the kettle is boiling?"

11. Oak and Elm

The oak in Mr. Thump's yard was a perfect place to perch, the tree having recently leafed out to provide the sort of screen that a crafty Indian most preferred. When the street was clear and Mr. Thump had left the window, Tim and Mailon vaulted over the wrought-iron fence and scaled that tree like squirrels, scrambling into the highest, rain-soaked limbs.

"Are there Indians on India Street?" wondered Mailon.

"You don't have Indians in India," said Tim, a little exasperated. He threw the hood of his mackintosh over his head and squinted against the drops.

"No?"

"You have *Hindoos*."

"Why do they call it India?" wondered Mailon. He wore one of Tim's old jackets and he hunkered his head beneath the collar.

"I think they thought they were Indians when they got there," replied Tim, not entirely sure who *they* were and hoping that Mailon wouldn't ask.

He didn't. Mailon was studying this lesson in geography. Tim hissed and pointed back toward the street. Mailon scanned the neighborhood but could discern no war parties or even a herd of deer.

"The elm across the street," whispered Tim.

Mailon applied his hawklike gaze to the tree in question and glimpsed the figure hiding behind it. The kids lay upon their respective branches, their breathing all but stilled, their limbs frozen. It was almost too happy to believe: To spy a spy! But had *they* been seen in turn? Tim leveled his gaze along the stick he had carried into the tree till the man behind the tree leaned into view once more. *Got him!* thought Tim. He thought he knew the fellow, who was looking up at the elm, as if the tree, instead of the sky, were raining on him.

Wait out a storm beneath a tree and get wet twice, thought Tim. He had read this in a true account of Daniel Boone's adventures in Africa. Tim wasn't exactly dry himself.

"It's Jimmy Fain," whispered Mailon.

Tim wondered why Jimmy Fain would be spying on Mr. Thump. Jimmy Fain was one of Fuzz Hadley's gang.

"What's he doing there?" wondered Mailon.

Tim waved him to silence. *Did the man see them in the tree?* seemed the important question. But the Indian scout must first know patience. The quarry will reveal itself if only the scout waits, noiseless and still. Tim scanned the street, hoping to find other secretive figures peering from behind trees and bushes.

The voice of someone calling "Sir!" pulled Tim's attention back to the elm across the way and the door of the house that it fronted. "Sir! You, there, sir!" A man of middle years—a butler or a servant—stood on the stoop. Tim and Mailon knew the man was speaking to Jimmy Fain before Jimmy did. The servant considered the rain as he might an obnoxious odor, then stepped down onto the brick walk and approached Jimmy at an oblique angle. "Sir!" he said again. "What are you doing there? You, there!"

Jimmy stepped from behind the tree and pointed to himself.

"You, there!" said the servant.

"What's he doing?" called an elderly woman at the door.

"I don't know, ma'am," replied the servant. "As to motive, he seems vague." The servant then turned back to Jimmy, saying, "What are you doing? That is a private elm, you know," but Jimmy had reached the sidewalk by this time and was walking hurriedly up the street.

The boys in the tree stiffened like cats, ready to pounce, and Mailon said, "Do we follow him?"

Tim wasn't sure what to do, but following a spy seemed much more important (not to mention, more interesting) than waiting in front of Mr. Thump's house on a rainy day.

The servant was returning to the front door of the house across the street, and the elderly lady was leaning out into the weather to watch Jimmy Fain disappear up India Street. The two boys came down the oak like jungle creatures and lit upon Mr. Thump's lawn with less noise than the rain. They scurried across the lawn, over the fence, and up the street in the wake of Jimmy Fain (or the "spy," or "that curious man standing by the elm," according to a person's point of view).

"Gracious!" declared the elderly woman. "What is the street coming to?"

12. Rain and Roof

Jimmy Fain charted a rainy, meandering course on his way to Danforth Street, and Tim and Mailon followed him every step of the way. It was a little strenuous keeping out of sight while trailing their quarry around the city. Jimmy wasn't really dressed for a stormy day, but he did not hurry from shelter to shelter; he darted from one side of the street to other, as curious as a stray dog, peering into backyards and stopping to watch more industrious individuals at their labor. Tim wondered if Jimmy was deliberately attempting to throw them off his trail, but that was surely ascribing too much conscious motive to his wanderings.

"What's he talking to *him* for?" wondered Mailon when Jimmy stopped to chat with a cabby on Middle Street. The boys peered through the rain, between the palings of a picket fence.

"What's in there?" asked Mailon when their quarry strolled into a narrow alley off Plum Street. Tim and Mailon crouched behind a fish cart.

"Look!" Mailon almost shouted. Jimmy Fain appeared from between two buildings some distance up the street and they bounded after him.

On the corner of Danforth and Winter Streets, Tim tugged at Mailon's sleeve and scrambled over a fence and up a shed roof. The rain had lessened, but the slates of the adjoining roof were still slick and Tim had to help Mailon along. They caught glimpses of Jimmy as they traveled the peaks and eaves, then they came to the widow's walk overlooking Doten's molding mill. Here they perched in the drizzle and watched for Jimmy on the street below.

A gull soared almost within reach. There were days, up here, near the sky, when Tim feared he might just try to touch one of those birds without thinking—just reach out and pitch himself over the rooftops. He looked away when this thought pinched his heart, and now he looked down at his feet.

Mailon's stomach growled.

"I'm hungry," said Tim.

Mailon glanced at Tim and gave a sigh. Mailon would never say that he was hungry, but he was always glad to join Tim for a meal. Tim always said he was hungry for both of them, sometimes when he wasn't hungry himself.

The rain left off for a time and a streak of sun pierced the clouds, so that pigeons and terns and seagulls wheeled up from the eaves and rooftops as if they were starving for light. A steam whistle sounded from the docks. A schooner was coming in as the rain stood out to the harbor. From the roof, the boy's sharp eyes could make out the very instant that the schooner passed out of the line of storm.

Without warning, the trapdoor in the middle of the widow's walk came up and Mr. Ealing, who owned the widow's walk and the surrounding rooftop as a consequence of owning the entire building and business beneath, tromped up the narrow stairs to view the water. He turned as he dropped the trap and looked at the boys.

He was not surprised to see Tim and Mailon. "I thought I heard prowlers up here," he said. He had a large pipe, a raincoat with the hood thrown back, and a captain's hat on his gray head; he was a man of business and not the sea, though the sea was his business. "Kind of greasy on those slates today, isn't it?" Mr. Ealing had heavy features and bushy gray eyebrows.

An enormous bird lit upon the roof just below them, a Goliath of a black-backed gull, and Mr. Ealing did indeed call this creature *Goliath*. As was usual, the shipping magnate had a bag of peanuts in his coat pocket and he tossed one of these delights, still in its shell, to the bird. The gull hardly put itself out reaching for the gift, and Tim didn't even see the bird swallow. Mr. Ealing held out the bag and Tim and Mailon each took handfuls for themselves. The peanuts were warm. Mailon even threw one to the gull.

The wind blew a little and the rain rose again to a slight drizzle.

Mr. Ealing squinted against the wet. "What brings you up here on a day like this?" he wondered.

"We were spying on Jimmy Fain," said Tim. He seldom held anything back from Mr. Ealing.

"Were you?" said the man. He tossed another peanut. A smaller gull banked nearby but knew better than to attempt a catch or settle upon Goliath's rooftop.

"He was spying on a friend of my father's," said Tim.

"Was he?"

"He looks just like my father," said Tim.

"Jimmy Fain?"

"No, my father's friend. Mr. Thump."

"Thump, eh? Do you mean the Thump's over that way?" Mr. Ealing pointed east. "The Thump and Chaine Atlantic Corridor Shipping Firm," he quoted as if he could read the sign from where he stood.

Tim didn't know.

"So, where's this Jimmy Fain now?" asked Mr. Ealing.

Tim shrugged. He had lost interest in the man. He couldn't imagine that Jimmy had any important errand, wandering the city the way he did, but he'd been fun to follow.

"There he is now!" said Mailon. He was leaning against the rail of the widow's walk and pointing down at Danforth Street.

"Who's he talking with?" wondered Tim.

"A short fellow with a bad temper, by the looks," said Mr. Ealing, who had his old spyglass trained upon the scene below. "Take a look."

Tim loved the old brass instrument since that day when Mr. Ealing first caught him up here and finished reprimanding him by feeding him peanuts and letting him share in the long view of the harbor and environs. Tim placed the glass to his eye and swept the street below till he caught sight of Jimmy Fain cowering before a shorter, wildly gesticulating fellow. "It's Fuzz Hadley," said Tim. There were several men hanging about with Jimmy and Fuzz.

"Jimmy's one of Fuzz's boys," explained Mailon.

"Fuzz is awfully mad about something," said Tim.

"Only dogs get mad," said Mr. Ealing.

"What's that?" said Mailon.

Mr. Ealing changed the subject without announcement. "If you have answered all the requisite questions, perhaps I may inspect the observatory and see who is coming in."

Tim handed back the glass, and they waited on the widow's walk while Mr. Ealing took in the flags on Portland's beloved observatory tower. Built on Munjoy Hill in 1807, the lofty structure was used to sight incoming vessels and thereby report to the rest of the city, by way of flags and signals, the identity of the ships and the firms to which they belonged.

"She's Burnham's *Revere Belle*," reported Mr. Ealing, "in from Hawaii."

Tim turned back to Danforth Street. Jimmy Fain and Fuzz Hadley and the others were gone. He wondered what Fuzz had been angry about. Maybe he was giving Jimmy the devil for being caught by the old lady and her butler, or maybe Jimmy told him that he'd been followed.

Then Tim wondered what Jimmy was doing spying on Mr. Thump in the first place. Could Fuzz be thinking of robbing Mr. Thump's house?

"Maybe we better go back to Mr. Thump's," said Tim. "Dad said I should watch out for him." Tim said to Mr. Ealing, "Mr. Thump saved my Uncle Gill from killing a policeman with a piano."

"Tried to kill an officer of the law with a piano," said Mr. Ealing thoughtfully. "I lived next to a little boy once who *almost* killed me trying to learn the violin."

Tim appeared awed by this, but then a smile crept over his face. "We better get back to Mr. Thump's," he said again, then he remembered how Mailon's stomach had rumbled and added, "after we drop by home for dinner."

They were going to climb back over the railings and descend the roofs, but Mr. Ealing insisted they take the official route through the trapdoor and down the several flights of stairs to the street. (It was not the first time; Mr. Ealing's employees could never figure where the kids came from and he liked very much not telling them.) In a few minutes, the man was standing on the front steps, eating the last of his peanuts and watching the Indian scout and his *brave* ally scamper in the direction of Brackett Street and the Faithful Mermaid.

13. *Sus Scrofa in Melancholia*

Mister Walton's nose detected the recent use of the coffee grinder when he and Sundry entered Jonas Fink's General Store and Post Office. Other smells lurked behind this welcoming aroma in the lamplit interior, perhaps betokening some fresh purchase—a bag of penny peppermints for the old man who sat beside the stove, his white beard waggling as he spoke or jawed one of the sweets in his near-toothless mouth; the scented oil in the dark hair of the young bachelor blacksmith, a tall, wiry fellow in his leather apron standing by the candy counter with a bottle of sarsaparilla; or the sharper presence of a pickle in the clutch of a red-shirted fellow, who made noisy work of his fat, green prize as he listened to local gossip from the proprietor himself.

The rain had brought several villagers, if not a lot of actual patronage, into the store, so that the addition of a dozen people from the train gave the long, low room the atmosphere of an unexpected celebration. Someone recognized an old acquaintance and launched into reminiscence and news, and a drummer cornered a suspicious farmer by the dry-goods shelf. Three women off the train joined a local wife to look over the yards of fabric and colored yarn at the back of the store. Mister Walton and Sundry came in from the rain and returned several friendly greetings.

"Some sort of broken pipe, says Duddley," informed a gentleman by the door. Duddley, Sundry guessed, might be the engineer, quizzed on his way to the telegraph office two or three doors down the street. "A drive pipe, he says," added the gentleman. "They have pipes on those trains, I guess. It's why they smoke, I bet." He was a moderate-shaped fellow with a thin, serious face that had been shaved a week or so ago. He had a sleepy eye that drew attention to itself. "I told Duddley they might carry a spare or two, and he allowed how they might."

Sundry nodded at this sage discourse.

"I told Duddley how I had a pipe or two I might lend out, and he allowed how he'd see what was needed and come by if I could help."

Sundry continued to nod. He was attempting to ascertain the degree of humor in the man. Mister Walton, in the meantime, was pondering the many wares in Jonas Fink's General Store and Post Office—canned goods and patent medicines, bins of penny candy and brightly wrapped saltwater taffy, bags of flour and salt and sugar, and small household contraptions. By the near corner he maneuvered around two old fellows, who were comfortably established in a pair of ladder-backed chairs and contentedly squabbling about one of a series of contentious subjects.

Beamus Caterwood and Ernst Feldspar had been enjoying their later years (on the porch of Fink's General Store and Post Office when the weather was clement, and by the stove when it wasn't) for as many years as most people in Bowdoinham could, or cared, to remember, and nothing gave either Beamus or Ernst very much more enjoyment than the other's irritation, for other than their place of rendezvous they agreed about nothing in life or philosophy.

Ernst had regulated the course of their present dialogue by declaiming his lack of use for the "forty-odd or however many other states there were in the country," as he hadn't ever visited any of them, and wasn't entirely sure, in any case, that he had ever benefited by their existence. Beamus got off a salvo by suggesting that the "forty-odd or however many other states in the country" had themselves benefited by Ernst having stayed put.

"Now, what do they do in Colorado that I should be thankful for?" wondered Ernst after his initial burst of outrage.

Beamus wasn't sure but felt justified in praising the people of Colorado for keeping their distance from Ernst. "They've put the Mississippi and half the country between you and themselves, and I admire them for it! Besides, they have more gold in their mountains than anybody!"

Debate continued along these lines—a ramble through American geography that was neither alphabetical nor maplike in its progress—and when Mister Walton approached the two dusty combatants, he was summarily snatched into the clutches of their disputation. As it happened, he was attempting to explain the rationale behind the State of Iowa when Jonas Fink came up to see if he might help the portly fellow by rescuing him from Beamus's and Ernst's truculent eddy.

"I've never heard of such a thing!" Ernst was declaring.

"I was just saying," said Mister Walton to Jonas as the proprietor approached, "that Iowa's an important pig producer."

Unaware of the present topic of debate (and perhaps due in part to a contracted verb in the bespectacled man's sentence) Jonas was under the misconception that Mister Walton had said "I was just saying that I *was* an important pig producer."

"You don't say!" said Jonas, his interest up. The subject of pigs, as it would soon be revealed, was something of a preoccupation for the local community. "Where is that?" asked Jonas, wanting to know where Mister Walton had produced all these swine.

Mister Walton was unaware of the misunderstanding, and his knowledge of Iowa's agriculture was not specific. "All over the state, I guess," he replied.

This seemed tentative to Jonas but he pressed on. "What sort of pigs?" he wondered aloud.

Mister Walton had to think about this. His brow knit while he considered the various breeds of pigs that farmers in Iowa might deem worthy of their industry. An amiable expression crossed his face, but to Jonas it indicated a surprising lack of certainty. "I don't know," said Mister Walton, throwing his hands out to signify monstrous creatures. "Great big ones!"

So far, for a man who had produced pigs in important numbers, this affable gentleman had shown to Jonas a wonderful lack of cognizance regarding the *where* and the *what sort*.

"*I* never ate one of them!" insisted Ernst.

"You don't know as much as a goose knows about God!" said Beamus.

Mister Walton had his hat in hand, but he raised it in salute and excused himself from the immediate vicinity before Ernst began to explain just what he *did* know about the Almighty.

"I have coffee boiling on the stove out back," said Jonas Fink. "Let me get you a cup."

"That would serve nicely on a rainy day," said Mister Walton.

Jonas ambled back behind the counter, stopped beside the man in the red shirt with whom he had been conversing, and spoke a word or two before disappearing into the back room. The red-shirted fellow turned his gaze to Mister Walton and considered the portly man, then he gave a nod to the farmer's wife and spoke to her, whereupon one of the other locals hovered beside them and these three discoursed for some moments.

Mister Walton wandered about the store, greeting the locals and his fellow stranded passengers, till Jonas and his wife came out with a tall pot of coffee and a dozen cups, along with a pitcher of cream and a bowl of sugar. People gathered at the counter, and Sundry and Mister Walton found themselves the center of pleasant conversation. Sundry bought some cinnamon buttons.

"You should meet Vergil Fern, sir," said the man with the red shirt.

"Oh, yes," said the farmer's wife. "If you have a moment, you should ride over to Vergil's and say hello."

"Should I?" said Mister Walton, his eyes wide behind his spectacles. The young blacksmith appeared to take as much interest in this suggestion as Sundry did, and they both moved closer to the conversation.

"He's all in about that pig of his," said a second fellow.

"All in?"

"He's morose, sir."

"I am certainly sorry to hear it," said Mister Walton with great feeling. "What is wrong with the poor pig?"

"It's the pig that's morose," explained the man with the red shirt.

"I beg your pardon?" said Mister Walton.

"You've never seen a pig so blue in all your life, sir," said the second man. "I was over to Vergil's the other day, and it quite cut me up."

"My goodness," said Mister Walton. He turned to Sundry.

"I never could endure a sad pig," said Sundry.

"You should go up and take look," said the second fellow.

"That's a prize animal," said Jonas Fink.

"Oh, yes," said the farmer's wife.

Mister Walton might have inquired why they thought that he in particular should view this specimen, but large matters often turn upon small and the small matter at that moment arrived in the aspect of the train conductor, who announced that a new drive pipe was not to be had at short notice and that they were waiting for the next train to come up the line and take them with it. Another forty or fifty minutes wait was in the offing.

Sundry was interested that these people were so keen on Mister Walton seeing this pitiable pig, and he saw that others also wondered. A quick whisper in the ear of the curious from one of those in the know occasioned an assenting nod; Sundry watched this form of communication make the rounds of the store. "Where does Mr. Fern live?" he asked when the conductor was gone.

"A mile or so out of town," said Jonas Fink.

Mister Walton was about to say "Perhaps another day—" when Sundry suggested that they find a rig and drive out to view this melancholy creature.

"Do you think?" said Mister Walton. "I wouldn't want to miss our connections."

"There'll be trains all day," said Sundry. He wanted to see this celebrated pig. "I'll go over and have our bags held at the station in case we miss the next one."

Several sensations visited Mister Walton. He was a man of great empathy, to begin with, and the thought of a sad pig was enough to arouse his kinder inclinations; he was, to be sure, quite taken with the eccentric notion that a chance visitor must inspect such a creature; lastly, he had the peculiar feeling that he had experienced something like this before. "Will Mr. Fern mind our coming by unannounced?"

"Goodness, no!" declared several people, and, "Nothing he'd want more!" and, "You'd do us all a favor."

"Then by all means," said Mister Walton, greatly amused, "let us see this disconsolate creature. Perhaps the company will do him good."

"I'll drive you there," said the blacksmith.

"Johnny would just as soon get a look at Vergil's pretty daughter," said the man in the red shirt.

The blacksmith ignored this but there was a laugh or two as he led Mister Walton and Sundry out into the rain. "Come over the shop with me and I'll get the rig up."

"What's this pig's name?" asked Sundry.

"Hercules," said Johnny the blacksmith.

"I think the rain might be letting up," said Sundry, who may have been more intrigued by the notion of visiting Fern Farm for the mention of a pretty daughter. When he said this, however, something rumbled out of the west.

14. The Family Fern

Vergilius Fern was the embodiment of several contradictions, it seemed, and the more Mister Walton and Sundry heard about him from Johnny Poulter the blacksmith, the more eager they were to meet the man. Mr. Fern was the local schoolteacher who had (some years before, and unexpectedly) come into a moderate inheritance, which fortune seemed out of keeping with the common perception of his livelihood, but he used a good portion of his newfound estate to improve the local school and continued to teach there. He had become interested in husbandry in recent years, and, then, so interested in the animals he husbanded that he lost *all* interest in marketing them, or using more than the milk from his cows, the eggs from his chickens, or the natural consequence of feeding them for the embellishment of his fields and gardens. At first the agricultural circles at Bowdoinham were disdainful of his *pet* cows and hens and sheep, but soon the neighborhood became familiar with these long-lived creatures and proportionately concerned with their well-being.

Johnny Poulter explained all this while Sundry helped him harness the little mare that would take them out of town. The blacksmith's rig had a short canopy, but they were glad that the rain had slowed; Mister Walton and Sundry got damp, nonetheless, and Johnny was altogether wet, though the young man's spirits grew brighter as they went. "Mr. Fern will be home for lunch with his own children soon enough," he said, "but Ruth will be glad to entertain you in the meanwhile."

"I hope we won't be imposing," said Mister Walton.

"Not if you've come to see his pig," assured the blacksmith.

"This must be an uncommon creature."

"You'd let him in the house, if he could fit through the door." The blacksmith drove the rig up on a bank, above a place in the road where the recent rain had formed a muddy pool. They could see where another wagon or carriage had been stuck. "He's a rare teetotaler," said the blacksmith. "Mr. Fern," he amended, to be sure they understood that he wasn't speaking of the pig.

"Are teetotalers so rare in these parts?" wondered Mister Walton.

"Not at all," said Johnny. "It's simply a matter of degree."

Mister Walton was amused. "I didn't realize the philosophy came in increments," he said.

"There are all *sorts* of teetotalers."

"I am amazed."

Johnny Poulter smiled. "Let's see—there's the teetotaler who won't drink on Sundays, and the one who won't drink before the preacher—"

"And, of course, the one who won't drink before the preacher does," suggested Sundry.

"Good heavens!" chortled Mister Walton.

Johnny was easing the horse and rig back down to the road. "There's the one who won't drink before a woman."

The two young men were able to name an extraordinary range of teetotalers, but it was more in the way of a game than anything like cynicism. Mr. Fern, according to Johnny Poulter, was a great temperance man and a despiser of anything spirituous beyond the soul itself.

They passed through a small grove of birch and oak and mounted a short hill, from which lookout they had their first view of Vergilius Fern's farm.

This collection of buildings appeared at variance with itself. Tucked against the southern side of a green knoll and beside an ancient stand of lilacs, the original house—little more than a hut—had been appended to in grand, if haphazard, fashion, so that the whole enterprise had the look of an immense body with a tiny head. The spacious barn, too (an oddly proportioned construct), lived in something less than visual harmony with its predecessor—a humble shed, that held a conspicuous position upon the property.

The small buildings beside the large gave rise to some peculiar yards and corners, and everything was surrounded by handsome wooden fences, which, in turn, were occupied by diverse species of contented farm creatures. As the carriage descended the hill, Mister Walton could believe that these animals lived in complete confidence of their continued well-being; everything appeared to hang from placid moment to placid moment, and he imagined that even the rain should not distress a soul (human or otherwise) at Fern Farm.

"Hercules will be over there, I believe," said Johnny. He pointed to the tiny shed.

"In the little building?" asked Mister Walton.

"No, behind it," came the reply. "Or thereabouts."

"But there's no fence around it."

"Hercules has the run of the place. He was something of a watchdog before he fell into this gloom of his." Johnny was pulling them into the farmyard, and the door to the little portion of the house opened to reveal a young woman (the pretty daughter, as it happened) who waved and smiled.

"Good morning, Johnny," she called sweetly. She had auburn hair and freckles across an upturned nose, and all three of the visitors were better off for her smile.

The blacksmith gave a surprisingly tentative wave in return before jumping down. Cheerful and talkative on the journey out, he now appeared diffident. Mister Walton felt a little stiff riding in the damp and he groaned and laughed ruefully as he climbed out after Sundry. They didn't hear the first of Johnny's conversation with Miss Fern, but, as they approached the door they saw that an older woman—short and round and pleasant—stood behind the daughter, and the blacksmith said, "Mrs. Fern, Madeline, this is Mister Walton and Mr. Moss. Mister Walton, Mr. Moss, may I introduce Mrs. Ruth Fern and her daughter Madeline."

Mrs. Fern was a bright cherub of a woman, with shining button blue eyes and hair a little redder than her daughter's. Her cheeks were red, her nose was tiny, and she had, besides, every appearance of vigor and health. "How nice of you to come look at Hercules, Mister Walton," she said.

"Father and the children are so worried," said Madeline.

Mister Walton blushed, the more so since he could not for the life of him understand how his looking at Hercules could be such a boon. The blush endeared him to his hosts, and Mrs. Fern insisted that their guests first come in from the rain.

Mister Walton and Sundry stood in a little hall while Johnny hung back. "Come in, come in," Mrs. Fern insisted several times over. "Get out of the damp, Johnny. Vergil will be home presently for his lunch—and the children with him."

"Mr. Fern teaches school?" said Mister Walton.

"Yes, up the road. He can't bear to let it go, and I dare say the children can't bear to let him."

"Come in, come in," she said again. This phrase had got them into the hall and taken their coats off, and now it drew them through the narrow precincts of the original house, where they found a kitchen and pantry, into the newer wards and a handsome, spacious parlor.

The furnishings were a pleasing miscellany of the rustic and the elegant—a rough old rocking chair that might have predated the original house sat beside the chintz-covered love seat, and a hand-carved bootjack peeked out from beneath the overstuffed hassock. But Mister Walton was straightaway taken by a large portrait of a very large white pig and an old-fashioned country squire that hung above the fireplace.

The long-faced man in the painting (thin as the pig was wide) was dressed in such outmoded clothing that Mister Walton might have thought the picture a hundred years old if a banner across the pig's middle hadn't declared the creature to be "Hercules." Man and pig alike looked as placid and amiable as two such specimens could be; the man stood, hat in hand, and looked ready to fall asleep and the pig grinned like a dog. Mister Walton admired them both and didn't like to think of either of them as troubled.

"Make yourselves at home," said the farm wife, her eyes disappearing behind plump red cheeks when she smiled. Mister Walton and Sundry gladly acquiesced, but Johnny Poulter stood by an overstuffed chair and looked uncertain. The women scurried back to the kitchen for refreshments against the weather, and they had not returned with these remedies before a good deal of noise and discussion was heard from the front of the house and the guests surmised that "Mr. Fern, and the children with him," had arrived for lunch.

Two little boys charged into the parlor, then two young girls, and the guests rose as a tall and narrow man with a tall, narrow face strode in behind. He was dressed in fairly fashionable, if well-worn, clothes, but they hung on him as on a drying rack. "Good day, good day," said he who was so obviously the squire in the portrait above the mantle. He did not look as placid, today, but he took his each guest by the hand and said, "How extremely kind of you to come by," and, "Johnny, how are you?" His eyes were great, sad things and his nose occupied an extraordinary amount of his face.

Johnny was, at that moment, besieged by the children, who must have thought he was best greeted as a sort of conveyance, for they had climbed atop of him and one was shouting "Giddyap!"

To add to all this sociable chaos, an elderly woman in dark clothes, high-buttoned boots, and a house bonnet arrived from the back of the house to be introduced as Mr. Fern's Aunt Beatrice. When the elderly woman had been appropriately charmed by Mister Walton, they all watched Johnny and the little Ferns frolic on the floor. The children—introduced, when they could be singled out of the heap, as Bonny and Susan and James and Homer—continued to use the blacksmith like a horse, and he seemed content to perform this service and even laughed as he rode them around the room; he had not behaved half as confidently when Madeline was near.

Mr. Fern smiled, but sadly, at the scene. "Children feel everything so keenly, Mister Walton," he said. "And they feel every *thing*, so that their little hearts are tugged this moment by trouble, then that way by laughter. Only moments ago they were fretting like one mind over poor Hercules."

"I am sorry to hear that your pig is unwell," said Mister Walton.

Mr. Fern accepted this sympathy with a gracious nod. His brow formed a careworn arch over his face. "Shall we go see the poor fellow," he said.

Mister Walton was agreeing to this proposition when Mrs. Fern and Madeline bustled into the room carrying trays and cups and a great pot of tea, and Mrs. Fern remonstrated her husband for forgetting his manners. "They have only just arrived, Vergilius," she insisted. "Let them dry off from getting here before you damp them down again with trekking about the yard."

"Yes, of course, of course," said the man. He indicated that his guests should be seated, and then he plunked himself onto the love seat with a lugubrious sigh. "I beg your pardon," he said, "but Hercules hasn't been himself for a month or more and we're very anxious for him." Johnny Poulter collapsed beneath the weight of children and one of the little boys broke away from the blacksmith's back to leap into his father's lap.

"What's happened to him?" asked Sundry. He accepted a cup of tea and a piece of cake from Madeline with a smile and a "Thank you."

Johnny did not miss Sundry's appreciation of the eldest Fern daughter and decided it was worth his while to pay attention. He righted himself on the floor and, with only two or three of the children hanging from him, found a chair to sit in. Sundry did not miss Madeline's quickness to wait on Johnny, nor Johnny's continued awkwardness; the blacksmith dropped his spoon and very nearly dropped his cup, and he excused himself several times over.

"That is the enigma, Mr. Moss," Mr. Fern was saying. "Hercules hasn't failed in any manner but his happy temperament." He turned to Mister Walton, who he seemed to think was the expert among his guests. "He was an extraordinarily satisfied pig, was our Hercules, Mister Walton."

"I can believe it, if the portrait above the mantle is any evidence," said the bespectacled fellow. "How does his discontent manifest itself, Mr. Fern?" Mister Walton had grown quite alarmed for the creature.

"Hercules is very sick," said one of the children. The young ones lost a measure of their careless delight every time the pig's name was invoked.

"It is complex, sir," said Mr. Fern, "to demonstrate by rudimentary explanation, but if ever there was a glum pig, he is the individual."

If ever there was a glum man! thought a solicitous Mister Walton.

"He doesn't occupy himself," continued Mr. Fern. "He doesn't greet *company* anymore, and I never hear him patrolling the yard of a night, as used to be his habit. But the true affliction is something separate from—or, rather, in addition to—those fluctuations."

"He's very contemplative," said Mrs. Fern.

"Pensive, even," said Mr. Fern.

"Oh, it's deeper than that," said Madeline. "Mister Walton, you have never seen such a melancholy pig."

"Perhaps he has gotten lazy," said the elderly aunt, but she looked uncertain of the hypothesis when the attention of the room fell upon her. Mister Walton thought she evinced discomfort with the subject in general; perhaps she thought pigs an unsuitable topic for parlor conversation.

The remainder of the family did not share her opinion, and Mister Walton grew misty-eyed simply viewing their distress. "I wish I knew what to say," he admitted.

"Has he lost weight?" asked Sundry, who knew something of farm matters.

"He has not," informed Mr. Fern.

"Has he had the society of other pigs?"

"We conveyed a sow from an adjacent farm two weeks ago, but he displayed not the slightest interest," answered the man.

"He was always such a chivalrous pig," said Madeline wistfully.

"The sow stayed two days, then walked home," said Mr. Fern.

Mister Walton was lifting his cup at this juncture and only hesitated briefly before taking a tentative sip. He glanced to Sundry, but his friend seemed as concerned as the family and as mystified as Mister Walton himself.

There was a strange color to the atmosphere when they stepped out—more like dusk than so close to noon on a day in late spring. The rain had dwindled to an occasional spit, and the wind had shifted into the northeast, bringing with it a small chill even as the sun made brief appearances among the clouds.

"Hercules!" called Mr. Fern, when they paused before the front door, and "Hercules!" called the younger children. Mister Walton heard quacking, and then a low grunt, as might be expected from an old curmudgeon who doesn't want to be disturbed.

"He's over by the barn," said Vergilius Fern. Looking quite blue, he led the way with his long strides, pausing by a tethered goat whose crown he scratched as he passed; around the side of the little shed before the barn they found a colossus of a white pig stretched out on his side amidst a flock of softly quacking ducks.

Sundry had seen some prize pigs in his time, but he didn't know when he had seen such an enormous one as this. Hercules was long as well as massive, so that he looked like a small cow lying there as his white side gently rose and fell. The creature hardly acknowledged his visitors, even when Mr. Fern informed the pig that Mister Walton and Sundry had come expressly to see him.

Mister Walton half thought it was some beast of legend lying there before them, and when asked if he would like to make a closer examination the portly fellow lifted his hat, scratched his head, and shifted from one foot to the other before stepping forward. The family and Johnny Poulter waited, as they might while a doctor considered his patient. The ducks quacked sociably and parted ranks as Mister Walton and Sundry approached the giant animal. When the two men were within a yard or so of the pig, they paused and leaned forward. In a low tone Mister Walton said to Sundry, "This is very curious, don't you think?"

"Well," said Sundry. "It is." Mister Walton wasn't sure whether they were speaking of the Fern family's odd interest in his seeing Hercules or of Hercules's inexplicit ailment itself. A duck came up to the portly man and gazed at him.

Hercules swung his great head around and Mister Walton had never seen such a look of gloom upon the face of an animal. The ears drooped in a most downcast manner, the chops formed an almost human frown, and those pig eyes were red and bleary, so that the guests could believe the beast spent its days and nights weeping.

Mister Walton glanced back at the family again. To Sundry, he said in the same quiet tone, "They seem, almost, to think that I have some expertise in the sphere of pigs."

"The subject first came up at the store," said Sundry. "Did you display some genius there?"

Mister Walton chuckled quietly. "I believe that I was singularly *un*geniuslike." After a moment he said, "Do you know, it reminds me of the time those people at Wiscasset thought I was a big game hunter."

"You rescued *that* animal," said Sundry, clearly with every faith in Mister Walton's restorative powers. "You didn't say anything about pigs at the store?"

"I did mention," admitted Mister Walton, "to the two older gentlemen in the corner that there are a good many pigs in Iowa."

"*That* doesn't seem to put you in the running, somehow," said Sundry. He glanced back at the Ferns, who hung back as if he and Mister Walton were in the most serious consultation. "Does he mind being touched?" Sundry asked.

"Not at all," assured Mr. Fern. "Dismal as he is, he yet appreciates a tender scratch upon the belly."

Sundry *scooched* beside the creature and cautiously rubbed the massive stomach. Hercules let out a long sound that was half groan and half sigh, and gazed blearily into the middle distance. The ducks replied in a soft chorus and wandered about the pig in a companionable manner.

"He seems almost human," said Mister Walton. It made him sad to look at the pig. Sundry let out a sound that might have come from their friend Mr. Thump. "What is it?" said Mister Walton.

"Do you know what sort of human he reminds me of?" said the young man quietly. "Do you remember the *Dash-It-All Boys*?"

"How could I forget them?"

"Do you remember last December when we found them at the station?"

"They were suffering from a night of excess, I believe," said Mister Walton in a near whisper.

Sundry made that Thumplike sound again. "That groan Hercules gave out just now reminded me very much of one I heard from Mr. Waverley."

Mister Walton thought on this. "Are you suggesting," whispered Mister Walton, "that this pig has been drinking?"

"Perhaps his slop has fermented."

"I can't imagine he gives it the opportunity."

"What does he eat?" wondered Sundry of Mr. Fern.

"Whatever we eat," said the man, looking from Mister Walton to Sundry as if he wondered who the expert really was.

"Perhaps it was only Mr. Poulter's discussion of teetotalers that put me in mind," said Sundry.

The pig gave out another humanlike groan, blew a sigh, and barely shifted himself. Sundry's eccentric notion had taken root, however, for Mister Walton suddenly imagined that the animal looked regretful.

"What do you think ails him?" wondered Mr. Fern anxiously.

Mister Walton shot a startled look at Sundry, but his young friend only gave a quick wink and looked away. Mister Walton could not imagine why the people at the store and now the Ferns, thought he would know *any*thing about pigs, but it seemed the moment to disabuse them on this issue. "I must be truthful, Mr. Fern—" began Mister Walton.

"Mister Walton would have to know more to form an opinion," said Sundry.

Mister Walton almost laughed, for no statement could be more accurate.

"Of course," said Mr. Fern. "You must stay to dinner, if you are not pressed to be elsewhere, and then we can answer your questions to the best of our abilities."

Mister Walton looked ready to speak again—that is, he looked ready to express some opinion or offer an important smattering of news. He took a breath and the whole family waited upon his word. Sundry nodded by way of accepting the invitation, and Mister Walton said, "Thank you, Mr. Fern. That would be very nice." When the Ferns had gotten a few paces ahead of them, Mister Walton turned to Sundry and said quietly, "Do you know anything about pigs?"

"We do raise them at Moss Farm," said the young man, his hands behind his back as he strolled. He seemed unperturbed.

Mister Walton glanced back at the stricken creature. Hercules let out something like a snore, and the portly man wondered, briefly, if pigs dreamed.

BOOK THREE

May 28, 1897
(Afternoon and Evening)

15. What He Once Had Been

"They do, of course, . . . pigs . . . dream," Vergilius Fern said when the subject of porcine sleep was raised and Mister Walton posed the question. "Everyone has seen a dog chase rabbits in his sleep," explained the farmer, "and pigs have at least the mental faculties of an old bloodhound."

Mister Walton would not have contradicted the man, even had he any experience of pigs by which to do so—Mr. Fern was that fond of the enormous creature in the yard; no one would have willingly offended him. As it happens, pigs do dream—or, at least, Hercules did that afternoon, drifting from his deep gloom to the solace that sleep can harbor. He dreamt of what he once had been, what (in his large porcine heart) he had aspired to, and what he once imagined himself to be.

Watch a dog imagine himself to be heroic and noble and without any dire circumstance to test him he will yet embody those salutary traits; it is the thought that counts. See a cat stare into the underbrush, where only the wind stirs (perhaps); she is imagining herself as stealth and danger incarnate. (Even a kitten has this capacity.) The cat may pounce wide of her prey, but she will walk away with that certainty of stealth and danger unhindered.

Hercules had once been the very soul of Fern Farm because he had thus imagined himself, applying his vision with goodwill and an admirable work ethic. Not all strong men will bend themselves to difficult tasks, and many a man who lacks in physical strength will *think* himself through a heavy burden. Hercules once rescued young Homer from a feral dog, and many were the times he stood between a night predator and the frightened ducks, not simply because the pig was large or capable of anger but also because he imagined himself as watch and protector of his family and estate.

"We do not mourn because we are old," said some philosopher, *"we mourn because we are no longer young."* Dreams were sweet and bitter to Hercules in those days. Sometimes they were formed of beautiful images that hurt with

the melancholy of loss. One recurring muse took him to the very nurturing belly of his mother, among the warm, restive bodies of a dozen siblings; it was perhaps more a *dream of species* than a personal memory, but when it came he whimpered in his sleep like a lonely child.

Another vision took him through flower-strewn fields with Farmer Fern, fast as the wind, light as duck's down; sunlight obtruded the shadows of the farmer and his family, but Hercules knew their presence as he bounded over the bright hills.

Or he would simply know himself as the farm and that the farm was him, one existing in the other, like the egg in the chicken and the chicken in the egg. He had flashes of real things—luminous memories of visitors, friendly pats and scratches between his ears, the darker recollections of self-imposed night watches when the weasel or the fox prowled the inner wards. Hercules had been endlessly hungry for his exertions and had eaten all he needed as reward. He was a great white whale of a pig with a heart to match; but his appetite had betrayed him.

He might even have sensed something perilous about the slops fed to him ever since a certain figure first crept onto the property weeks ago with the promise of a midnight snack. He might have told himself "Never again!" as he groaned and gloomed through another day, but the midnight slops would come again and the remainder of the night would be lost in a strange haze, till the sadness and despondency of another all-too-brilliant morning barely roused him from his unaccustomed lethargy. He did not mourn simply because he felt ill and dejected, he mourned because he was not what he once was, or what he had imagined himself to be.

Everyone suffers his frailty. Hercules dreamed his melancholy dreams and his friends the ducks quacked softly, solicitously about him.

But why would he always return to that beckoning swill of hazardous spirits? "Well," said Sundry, when all was said and done, and with his customary inverted logic, "that's why they call them pigs."

⚜

If the Ferns and their farm seemed self-contradictory, Mr. and Mrs. Fern were nothing but complementary to one another in the procreative sense; the long aspect of the father had merged with the round countenance of the mother to form a bevy of handsome children. Madeline was not alone in catching the eye, for every one of her siblings bore up to close scrutiny and seemed, in the opinions of Mister Walton and Sundry, to match a comely appearance with attractive manners and a ready smile, even if the best of manners must give way to curiosity sometimes.

"Mister Walton doesn't talk much about pigs," said Susan to Sundry at the dinner table.

"Doesn't he?" said Sundry. "Ah, well, Sherlock Holmes never talked about a case while he was pondering it."

Hearing this, the young woman considered the portly gentleman at the other end of the table with renewed awe.

Mister Walton was adept at happy conversation, and, like many intelligent and curious people, could appear, unintentionally, to have command of many a subject at hand simply by asking questions; however consciously, it was also a method by which to direct the topic of discourse, and Mister Walton inquired about the farm, about Mr. Fern's school and his pupils, and about the Fern children and their pursuits, but never raised the subject of pigs.

As it happened, the guests were not yet sat down to dinner before they were invited to stay for supper, and they would not sit to supper before they were invited to stay the night. Mister Walton might have graciously declined both invitations on the grounds that they were on their way to see Sundry's Uncle Cedric if Sundry had not (in each instance) spoken for them first and accepted. "I don't wish to keep you from Norridgewock," said Mister Walton when he and Sundry had a moment by themselves.

"*'Whatever breeze or notion,'*" quoted Sundry. Johnny Poulter eventually had to return to work, and he offered to take Sundry back to town to retrieve the bags and hire a carriage. The Ferns insisted that Johnny stay for dinner first and the family and their guests gathered about a well-laden table. Mister Walton was delighted by the company of young people at dinner, and he thought that Madeline Fern in particular might represent a very *pleasant* notion to his friend.

Following dinner, Mr. Fern sent one of his sons back to the schoolhouse to tell the other children that afternoon class was dismissed. Seldom does a herald so enjoy his task. "They didn't riot, did they?" asked the teacher when the boy returned. It was pleasing for Mister Walton to see that Mr. Fern had retained his sense of humor through the family's pig crisis.

"They gave you three cheers," said the boy.

"They are good students on the whole," said Mr. Fern to his guests, "but an unexpected holiday is never despised."

"I should be concerned if it was," said Mister Walton.

The ragged end of the storm blew overhead as Sundry and Johnny set out; small, dark clouds chased hard upon a field of gray. The Ferns and Mister Walton stood in the yard to wave the young men off, so that Sundry might have thought he wasn't coming back. He glanced over his shoulder once they were under way and smiled to see Mister Walton standing with his hands folded behind him and his head back to look at the weathercock atop the barn.

"Mister Walton doesn't seem like a pig farmer," said Johnny Poulter when they had gone over the hill.

Sundry was interested to hear it but betrayed no surprise. "Doesn't he?" he replied.

"Like almost anything else, I guess."

Sundry considered Johnny carefully and could see no guile or wryness in the man. "Appearances can be deceiving," he said, wondering why Mister Walton *should* have looked like a pig farmer.

"It's true," Johnny agreed. "Mr. Fern doesn't seem much like a farmer."

"Madeline is very pleasant," offered Sundry.

It was Johnny's turn to consider Sundry. "I *had* noticed," he said.

"I thought she was glad to see you," said Sundry.

"Did you?" said Johnny, and that amiable caution with which he regarded his passenger melted in a heartbeat. Sundry was working more on intuition than hard evidence, but he had guessed at a mutual admiration between Madeline Fern and Johnny Poulter. "Ach!" said Johnny, as if thoughts on this course were pointless. He was an even-featured, dark-haired fellow, with a bit of dirt beneath his fingernails and a smudge of something on the back of his neck, but he was smart and had proven to have a sense of humor (the surest sign of intelligence, according to certain intelligent men). "I can hardly speak to her," said Johnny, and he smiled ironically.

Sundry waved a hand to indicate how inconsequential this was. "Mister Walton says that listening is the first signal of good conversation."

They both looked ahead then and said nothing till Sundry laughed and Johnny laughed with him. The blacksmith then began to explain to Sundry what Sundry had already supposed.

There is an aesthetic sort of pleasure that men derive from praising the women they admire, and one might think that a young fellow like Johnny was holding the apple of his eye in the palm of his hand when he described, in decorous fashion, the many accomplishments and fascinations of Madeline Fern. Simply hearing them, Sundry half fell in love with her himself.

Jonas Fink was standing on the steps of his store as they went by and he called out to Sundry, "Anything you need?"

"I don't believe so," said Sundry. He wondered again how the notion that Mister Walton would know something about pigs had first taken flight.

"I thought maybe your friend had sent you back for a cure," said the store owner.

"He's still studying on it," said Sundry.

Johnny Poulter dropped Sundry off at the station. The mechanics were still working on the first engine, which was pulled up on a siding, but another engine had been brought up the line and the train was long gone. Sundry and Johnny parted on good terms, though the blacksmith might have felt some jealousy toward anyone going back to spend time at the Ferns'.

"Fix that creature up, yet?" wondered a man at the railroad station. Several other heads came up and Sundry knew that the whole town was talking about Hercules and the two strangers who'd gone out to see him.

"It's no simple thing to gladden a pig," averred Sundry, and the railroad man nodded at this wisdom. While he was at the station, Sundry wired the Baffins at home as to his and Mister Walton's whereabouts. On the way to the livery, he passed Fink's General Store and Post Office, where certain locals were still gathered. It did not take them long to detect his presence, and he was met with a barrage of questions. "How's the pig?" asked one fellow.

"Not inspired," said Sundry.

Another farmer was leaving town when Sundry reached the livery stable with his and Mister Walton's bags. "How's old Hercules?" asked this fellow, after he'd offered to take Sundry back to Fern Farm.

"No better," said Sundry.

"There's some would be glad to do *that* well," said the man.

Sundry offered nothing more, though the fellow must have been curious. The farmer refrained from further questions. "What's it going to do tomorrow?" wondered Sundry, looking into the sky.

"We'll know more about it tomorrow night," said the farmer, who could be as helpful as Sundry when need arose.

✻❦✻

"Like water off a duck's back," might be an appropriate phrase to characterize how life generally affected the outward poise of Sundry Moss. In most circumstances, Sundry's inner self remained as calm, but it was spring and he had recently spoken with a young woman who had, at their first and only other meeting (and unknowingly), startled his heart like an unexpected gunshot. As a rule, it was not difficult for Sundry to keep his head, even when all about him might have lost their composure; indeed, it *was* difficult for him to acknowledge those rare moments when his nerves were genuinely struck, during which instances his *practiced* calm served him well.

Suffering quietly from his too-brief experience of Priscilla Morningside, it did not hurt his condition that he suffered it in the general purview of a lovely young woman like Madeline Fern. Madeline could not make him forget Priscilla, nor in any way replace her in his estimation, but Miss Fern's beautiful smile and sweet demeanor did hoist his spirits.

The Fern plantation, too, was natural balm to Sundry, so, upon his return, when the family dispersed to their afternoon chores, he quite gladly joined them. He took visible pleasure in tending the animals, relished the familiar scents and sounds of the vast barn, and even took a turn in the rope swing that hung from the rafters. Eventually he wandered outside and explored the grounds, strolling fence and field as a tourist might walk the ruins of a Greek amphitheater. A rural upbringing provided Sundry's eyes and ears with the means to interpret signs that must have escaped Mister Walton; the repair and order of things, the health of the livestock, and recent events were made plain to him by small and (to the unseasoned eye) insignificant details.

When Mister Walton and their hosts came out of the barn, they found

Sundry considering a single rut that ran like the track of a wheelbarrow along the lawn from one corner of the house to the side of the barn, where a ladder lay on its side. "Working on the roof?" Sundry asked Mr. Fern, his hands behind his back as he looked up.

Vergilius Fern also tipped his head back to consider the top of the house. "No," he said with a puzzled expression. "Should I be?"

Sundry only shook his head.

"I'm not very fond of heights, to be honest with you," added the farmer.

"I like my feet on the ground," admitted Sundry.

"You don't think Hercules has been up on the roof, do you?" said Mr. Fern, exhibiting more wryness than his guests would have credited.

"Have you tried keeping him in?" wondered Sundry.

"We kept him penned for three days, though it broke my heart to do it, and I saw not a whisker of difference, Mr. Moss."

Sundry turned his back to the house and approached the corner of the property inhabited by the unfortunate pig.

"It's very nice of you to be here, Mister Walton," said Mr. Fern.

"It's very nice of you to have us, Mr. Fern," replied the portly fellow. He had taken off his spectacles and was rubbing them with his handkerchief.

"I trust you have been thinking about our Hercules."

Mister Walton reestablished his spectacles upon his nose and peered after Sundry. "Yes, we have," he said a little absently.

"Mr. Moss is a bit of your right hand, I surmise."

"A bit of my right arm, Mr. Fern."

Mister Walton marveled at the many stories the Ferns began to tell about the creature. The pig could pull a cart and play hide-and-seek, if the children were to be believed, and Mr. Fern related how Hercules had earned his name (when he was merely large, and not enormous) by driving off a stray dog that had threatened little Homer.

In better days, Hercules had acted as footman by greeting visitors at the hitching post and as night watchman by patrolling the grounds of the farm at odd hours after sunset. The pig seemed impervious to the heat of August and the chill of January, and on pleasant evenings he sat on the veranda, grunting to Mr. Fern's orations of Longfellow and Poe. All this Mr. Fern expressed in regretful tones, as if his porcine companion had already gone to his reward, and the more Mister Walton heard about the remarkable pig, the more he wished he knew how to help the beast.

Hercules let out a long forlorn sigh, and Mr. Fern echoed this with one of his own. "He's a good pig, Mister Walton," said Mr. Fern.

"I've never known one better," said the bespectacled guest.

Mr. Fern produced a handkerchief from a vest pocket to dab at his eyes. "That's very kind of you, sir," said Mr. Fern.

They were still communing with the depressed pig when someone rang the dinner bell and Mister Walton followed his host back to the house. Sundry lingered by the flower beds but then caught up with them, and Mister Walton noticed that his trusted friend and companion seemed almost cheerful.

from *The Dresden Herald*
for the week of May 28, 1897

NEWS IN TOWN

Come lads and lasses to the fields,
(For Summer is a comin' today)
Where Winter's heavy mantle yields,
To the merry morning of May.

The flowers bloom in splendid hue,
(For Summer is a comin' today)
The trees leaf out for all to view,
In the merry morning of May.

Oh, who draws nigh in gold and green,
(For Summer is a comin' today)
The Lass of Spring, fair to be seen,
On this merry morning of May.

So sings the ancient ballad, but it is a ballad from across the water where Spring spreads light and warmth over the English Counties, or it is a song for these shores, but in southern climes. Here in Dresden, Spring is the more welcome for heralding the summer that June all but ensures. April will have her crocuses, and May sports the tulip and the jonquil, but June is the lady whose promise breathes life into the fields of Maine and coaxes the leaves of the trees and the wildflower to peer from their buds.

Poets by Winter's hearth speak of blue-eyed, green-gowned May and seem forgetful of swarming blackflies and muddy byways. Elias Judkins didn't forget, and he tells us he purchased a spyglass with which to keep an eye on his back field. The blackflies were so thick there, last Tuesday, that he could see them like a shadow from his parlor window, and he gave up repairing a wall when he spied them, saving himself a trip over field and brook. He came into town then and spent part of the day at Labarge's General Store trading memories with some of the village patriarchs.

Sally Innsey came in for a sack of flour and baking powder for Mr.

Innsey's biscuits and said a warren of rabbits had appeared over on the south side of Calls Hill. Some who sat about the store remembered how Jack Crosby and Barne Baker raced their horses from Cork Cove to the Great Bog and Jack's mount shied as a swarm of rabbits scurried from a hole down by Nequasset Brook. Jack fell off his horse and right through the ground into the warren, and Barne graciously called the race against interference.

Mrs. Henrietta Lincoln has not been feeling well of late and several neighbors have been by to offer her company. We all wish her a speedy recovery.

Mrs. Anne Babcock is back from visiting her sister's family in Thorndike, and Mr. Babcock must be pleased to have her, as he is by his own admission, "no better cook than an old sinner deserves."

Mrs. Gemma Cooley's cat ruined part of a skein of yarn she was using to make her son James a sweater, and if anyone has some gray yarn she would gladly trade with them so she might finish it.

On Monday, Burthold Handy received a letter from his brother Beale in Hawaii and he shared it with folks at Grange on Wednesday night. Everyone was greatly interested in the descriptions of the island flora, the volcanic heights, and the strange customs of the people. Beale is foreman of a pineapple plantation on the island of Oahu.

Oliver Worthen reports that his dog Petunia littered a dozen pups this week. That was litter indeed!

16. The *Afternoon* of May

Ezra Porch was up in the lilacs when Dee came out that afternoon. He liked this place and often peered out at the life of the village from the screen of branch and leaf. If he were still enough, birds sometimes roosted here; he might dare grab one if Dee wasn't in sight. He thought himself very wicked and was content.

A breeze fell off Orchard Hill and swept with it the scents of the Kennebec River as it passed. Even a human might smell the water and the intervening earth on a day when the sun roused these scents into the air.

Dee opened the gate and stepped into the street. There were still some muddy places from the morning's rain and she described a crooked path on her way to the post office. She had not gone far, however, before she slowed her pace and then stood for a time looking up at the sky, where bright, scratchy clouds lingered in a pale blue. There was enough of a breeze to keep the bugs away, she thought. She had a small hat and only a shawl about her shoulders for a wrap, but the sun was strong, and she set out past the school, up the field in the direction of the river. The grass was barely damp, but the ground gave like a cushion, still soft with the morning's rain.

She climbed over a fence rather than walk to the stile. A bramble caught her sleeve and she pierced a finger releasing herself. "A toll on every road," her Uncle Fale often said. Dee had a small taste of blood when she put the finger to her lips. Then she shook the sting from her hand and scaled the little rise beyond. There were sheep on the other side of the hill, and she could see before her, just east of where she stood, the broad Kennebec; when she glanced to the west, over her shoulder, past her home and a grove of trees, there was the smaller Eastern River. Near an inlet of the Eastern were two small islands, bristling with alder and willow. She remembered that there was a table of rock somewhere near, and she cast about the hillside till she found it.

Pulling her shawl tightly around her, she sat upon the gray surface of ledge and watched for ducks on the river. She looked to the clouds again and thought about the wind—how fast it blew, where it had come from, and where it went. A swarm of blackflies milled below her on the hill, but the breeze never let them rise very far above the turf.

Looking back toward the Kennebec, she saw someone walking the meadow—a man taking long, purposeful strides in her direction. Dee looked about her and could find no other goal but herself. She thought of walking back to the village before the man got near, but it was too obvious that she had seen him, and her curiosity was up besides.

It was not long before she shaded her eyes to get a better look, and not much longer before she was able to descry Olin Bell making the steeper southwest slope of the hill. He kept his head up, though it was natural to look down as he climbed. At a certain distance she smiled at him, and Olin stopped and called to her. "Good morning, Dee."

"Good morning, Olin," she replied. He might have skirted the hill then, if he were going somewhere else, but her friendly tone was like permission for him to approach. She stayed seated as he came.

Olin Bell was about two or three years younger than Dee. She remembered him from school and thought that he hadn't changed very much since those days. He still had the same pale hair, pale blue eyes, and pale freckles across his face. He was a tall man, strong and broad shouldered. He had recently inherited his family's farm when his uncle died. Dee could see the place from where she sat, neatly placed among a line of maples and along the banks of the larger river.

"I thought it was you," he said as he drew up a few feet away.

"Wiser people would wear more than a shawl today," she said, as if she had been identified by this shortcoming.

"The sun's warm enough," he said.

"Or wiser people have more to do with themselves," she posited, seemingly bent on self-deprecation.

He did not answer this but looked about them, and she watched him and watched the places he set his gaze. "There are a lot of people who don't look at things," he said after some thought. He had not been searching for an answer, Dee thought, only a way to frame it. "Uncle Tim said your mother would walk the fields," he added, as if this were reason enough. "Just as you do. Back when she *did* walk."

"It is a necessity," she replied.

He nodded. He leaned down and snatched a blade of grass from the turf, then wound this about a finger. He had boots on; their uppers were muddy but the grass had swept the vamps clean. He took a large breath and looked past her out over the Eastern River.

Oddly, Dee was suddenly a little fearful of what Olin might say. *But Olin Bell?* she wondered to herself. She chanced a look in his direction and observed a handsome profile against the sky.

He said, "Jimmy Baker and I made a raft from some boards we got out of an abandoned barn down by the Stafford place and used it to explore those islands. We thought we were pirates."

Dee liked the image. "You would never have invited a girl, I suppose."

"Didn't know enough to," he said with a laugh. "How *is* your mother?"

"She has her bad days, but winter's past and the sun will do her good."

He nodded again, looked out at the meadow, then turned back and smiled. "Can I tell you a secret?" he asked.

Dee took a deep breath then, and her eyes widened reflexively. "Yes," she said quietly but uncertainly.

He laughed a little. "This last February, I took my old toboggan up here one night, when the moon was out, and spent two hours sliding on the hill here."

She let out the breath she had been unconsciously holding, put a hand to her breast, and joined him in another laugh. "The next time, you *must* invite me," she said.

"I will," he answered simply.

The tension left her as she laughed, and she patted the stone beside her. "Sit down," she said, though it was his land she was sitting on.

He hitched a thumb over his shoulder. "I have to get back," he said, though he hesitated after saying it. "Old Hank will wonder why I left him with only three shoes."

"Is that the big fellow you brought back from the fair?" she asked. She had admired the tall, gray horse the first time she had seen it pulling Olin Bell's old carriage through the village.

"Yes," said Olin with a rueful expression. "He could pull a coach from here to Boston, but he wouldn't stoop to plow a field for me. I don't know why I keep him."

"Oh! He's *so* beautiful!" Dee was pleased to see the man blush at this exclamation. Other farmers might think it the height of foolishness to keep an animal strictly for its elegance, but here was a man who had been sledding only last winter. "I haven't been for a drive since last summer," said Dee, suddenly preoccupied with the thought.

Olin stood a little longer, looking uncertain. He had already given his farewell speech, as it were, and now he hemmed and hawed a little before saying, "Well, it's good to talk to you, Dee," while he looked at his boots.

"Thanks for coming up," she said as he walked off. When he was some yards away, she shouted after him, "Collect me next February when you toboggan again."

He turned, smiled, and nodded. She thought he might have wanted to look back as he descended the meadow, and just when she decided he wouldn't he turned and waved. She waved back, quickly enough to signal to him that she had been watching.

"Oh, be more careful," said Dee aloud to herself. She had almost asked him to come by for dinner some evening, then wasn't sure if she was glad or sorry that she hadn't. She turned back to the Eastern rather than continue watching him, which she had been doing almost without thinking. The top of the hill seemed solitary, of a sudden, but she stayed for a while waiting out the sensation. Her finger hurt a little.

✿❀✿

Ezra Porch had almost followed Dee when he saw her go up the field, but he was comfortable where he sat. The lilacs were leafed out and a tiny patch of sunlight had been traveling up his side with the progress of the afternoon. He fell into a nap but snapped awake sometime later at the sound of her returning footsteps.

Dee picked her way back down the road; past the Baptist Church, she saw Mrs. Wellington pruning her roses. "They're an awful sight," said Mrs. Wellington. "But the rheumatism has been acting up, and I didn't have the will to do it till this morning."

"They're always so beautiful, Mrs. Wellington," said Dee from the road.

The woman dismissed this with a wave. "They smell pretty," she said.

Amos Beachum went by on his wagon and tipped his hat. A sense of well-being filled Dee. The road was less muddy nearer the village and she walked more briskly. The few people in town stood on the porch at Labarge's General Store or down by the green. There was no one in the post office but Mrs. Stroller, the postmistress, who was having a cup of tea. She got up for the letter Dee took from her skirt pocket.

"How are your cousins?" asked Mrs. Stroller. She had seen the return address on the letter that arrived that morning; it was not inquisitive to ask, only polite. "That Billy does make me laugh," said the postmistress. "Always with a grin. Three cents," she said, and Dee dropped the pennies into her hand. "I suppose you'll be leaving for Portland soon."

"The end of the month, I guess."

"Ah, well," sighed Mrs. Stroller. "It must be fine by the water in the warm months. All those ships, though. I might feel strange just seeing them clutter up the harbor."

"They do want to lure a body off," said Dee with a playful squint.

Mrs. Stroller shuddered. "It's enough to read about them. My brother went up to Bangor with no intention but to see the city. He signed on the first ship he saw and went to China!"

"Your brother Amos?" asked Dee, though she knew the story.

"Yes, you've met him. He lives over to Belgrade, you know. He came last Thanksgiving and said grace in *Chinese!* if you will."

"That's wonderful," said Dee.

"I *think* it was grace, at any rate. How's a person to know?"

"Have him write it down," said Dee without really thinking, "and I'll have a Chinese man I know in Portland translate it for you."

"Oh, go on with you," said the postmistress with a laugh. "You're as bad as your Cousin Billy," she said delightedly.

⚜

Back home, Dee stood at the gate for a while. The day was warm and she pulled the shawl from her shoulders. She could see the top of the rise, on the other side of which she had talked with Olin Bell. She wondered why he had come up to see her; perhaps only for the novelty of it—a farmer stopping in the middle of shoeing a horse to walk up a field and chat with someone.

But Olin Bell? she wondered to herself again. The thought made her smile and she laughed a little, quietly. She remembered when they were children. He'd been a likeable fellow, typically adverse to female company till he reached a certain age. ("Didn't know any better, I guess," he had said.) He left town after school, and Dee had seldom thought of him. People said he'd lived in New Hampshire for a while, that he'd been married and that his wife had died very young.

Strange that she couldn't be any more certain than *people said.* Most people in town knew most everything about most everyone else. Things had changed some during the past half a century, but they really weren't so very far from the days when you might rely on your neighbor for your life, when it was of signal importance to know just who that neighbor was and what he was capable of, good *and* bad.

Dee wondered about Olin Bell alone on his uncle's farm. The thought made her almost sad, so she took a breath and sighed the melancholy out of herself. She passed through the gate and ambled up the walk to the front door of the little Cape, pausing long enough to say, "I see you in the lilacs, Ezra Porch." Perched in the bush, Ezra Porch widened his eyes for a moment, then closed them down to unfathomable slits and turned his face away.

17. The Ominous Card

Speaking above the noise of the crowd (but politely), Matthew Ephram said, "It is a splendid evening," to the cab driver.

"The day came off pretty fine, if a little tardy," agreed the driver. He held the carriage door and excused himself to a couple who were moving past him on the sidewalk.

"Continued fair tomorrow, with possible thundershowers mounting by evening," said Christopher Eagleton as he stepped down, adding, "Seasonable to warm temperatures expected."

"High tide at 9:33," said Thump, close behind Eagleton.

"Setting sail, are you?" wondered the driver.

Thump looked mystified.

"It is forty-seven minutes before . . . the curtain," announced Ephram when he joined them at the outskirts of the crowd, and this departure from his usual phraseology surprised his friends, then made them laugh. Even Thump forgot the driver's peculiar inquiry and chuckled deeply.

There was a whir of excitement outside the Portland Theater. Men were dressed in their best hats and tails and the women wore elegant gowns beneath their coats and jewelry upon their necks. Laughter rippled among them, and friends greeted one another with merry voices.

Eagleton paid the driver, then craned his neck to look over the heads of theater patrons before the door. A large bill, decorated with the comely image of Miss Ethel Tucker, stood before the queue, but he could only see the words BACK BY POPULAR DEMAND! and part of the actress's fashionable coif. "It was a marvelous idea coming to the play," said Eagleton to Ephram.

Ephram said something modest that was lost in the hubbub.

"It was a wonderful notion," insisted Eagleton. "Wasn't it a wonderful notion, Thump?"

If they had learned anything from Mister Walton it was that there is honor in fleeing melancholy. They had not planned on visiting their chairman over the next few days and yet the news that he was to be "out of town" affected them with a touch of gloom. Ephram was inspired to suggest that he and his fellows attend Miss Ethel Tucker's celebrated return to the Portland stage. They felt a little giddy with this new adventure. It was stimulating to stand in the crowd before the theater and join in the *"Hurrah!"* when the doors were opened. Without actually eavesdropping they were privy to snatches of conversation around them, and they were much enlivened by the voices of women in the crowd.

Ephram had come down to the theater earlier in the day and purchased tickets for the mezzanine, and it was not long before they were installed by the rail enjoying the prospect of the seats filling below them. The lights dimmed when the time came for the owner of the theater to step onto the proscenium and make a speech, the gist of which few could have recalled when the evening was over, though he did invoke the name of Miss Ethel Tucker which roused a warm round of applause.

As promised, the evening began with renditions of some old favorites, as well as current popular tunes, by a double male quartet, who finished their performance on the rousing notes of the "Battle Hymn of the Republic." Men in particular joined with this song in a spirited and even martial enthusiasm. Ephram, Eagleton, and Thump almost stood, they were so moved, and the atmosphere in the theater was charged with emotion and expectation.

The lights dimmed and the curtains raised upon the first act of *While She Waits in Silence* and the scene of the palatial home of the heroine and her family. Wrote the *Daily Advertiser* on the morrow:

> From the very first moment, the tale was a spellbinder, and if the audience could see the writing on the wall when Wanda McCintyre (as played by Miss Ethel Tucker) threw off her fiancé for the imagined honor of her family they suffered all the more from agonies of suspense. Throughout the scene in which she told her brave lover that she could see him no more there were gasps from the audience and even a cry of "No, no" from someone in the balcony.

Many in the audience stepped out for a breath of air after that breathless moment when the curtain fell upon the first act. Ephram, Eagleton, and Thump were a little shaken by Wanda's and her beau's "final parting," the more so since Wanda's family had already shown their true colors; the members of the club remained seated throughout the first intermission.

The second act only complicated matters as the full villainy of the McCintyre family was revealed. Eagleton thought his hair would stand on end during Edward McCintyre's monologue, in which the blackguard admitted his willingness to imperil even his own daughter for worldly gain! The air in the balcony grew close and warm, but if Eagleton had not been so rapt in the unfolding drama he would never have tugged at his collar in public.

As the second act came to a close, Wanda began to suspect, and finally to understand, the magnitude of her family's perfidy. But it seemed too late; her relations watched her closely and kept her from speaking to her former beau at a crowded social gala. All seemed lost until the final speech before the second intermission, when she revealed how she had written her name upon a card—she had only that much time—and slipped it into her former beau's pocket in prayerful hope that he would "rightly characterize its otherwise unexpected appearance as a silent cry for rescue!"

The curtain fell, the crowd applauded, people below the balcony turned to one another with excited expressions and eyes filled with wonder and hope for the story's third and final act. Eagleton was again stricken silent and immobile; he was shocked at the very *idea* of such treachery as was exhibited by Edward McCintyre and his clan; he was filled with anxiety for the fate of Wanda and anticipation of her beau's return to the main plot.

Eagleton shook himself from his meditations long enough to turn to his left. Ephram sat there in much the same straits; his mustaches had taken on an arrhythmic twitch, and Eagleton thought his friend might sneeze.

Eagleton turned to his right and discovered that Thump had left his seat. "Thump," said Eagleton, looking along the aisle and back to the stairwell, but his friend was gone. "Thump," he said again, and then, "Thump? Ephram, did Thump tell you he was stepping out?"

"I beg your pardon?"

"Thump has left his seat."

"Has he?"

"It seems unusual."

"Didn't he say anything?"

"I turned to him, just now, and he was gone."

"It does seem odd. It is warm in here, however. Perhaps he went out for some air."

"Perhaps we should look for him," considered Eagleton aloud.

"Perhaps we should," agreed Ephram.

They excused themselves as they stepped past the people in their row, and nodded politely to the women fanning themselves in the aisle and said "Good evening" to the gentlemen talking business in the stairwell. The lobby was filled with people and chatter and Ephram and Eagleton were charmed by the sight of so many ladies in their jewels and finery and most trifling manners.

The breeze coming through the open door was indeed refreshing, but they stepped into the cool May night with only the slightest pause to consider the invigorating air before looking for their friend. Eagleton stood on tiptoes to see over people; Ephram leaned to see past them. Women looked content as they held on to their fellows' arms; clouds of smoke rose from cigars and pipes and even cigarettes; there was laughter bubbling from one circle or another.

"There he is!" said Ephram.

Eagleton followed Ephram's gesture but only caught sight of Thump after he had weaved some distance through the crowd. "Thump!" he called as he neared the man, but Thump's great brown beard was tucked into his chest as he contemplated a small article which he held in his hands. "Thump," said Eagleton again when he reached his friend's side. Ephram was close behind, and he lent his own rendition of Thump's name to the general air of inquiry.

Mysteriously, the only indication that Thump had heard them, or that he was even aware of their presence beside him, was that he lifted the object of his scrutiny so that his friends might better see it.

It was a calling card—a plain beige card, like those used in society for introduction or invitation. Eagleton noted that there was a feminine signature upon it. He reached for the card, hesitantly at first. Thump extended his hand. Eagleton took the slip of paper and gave it his close and fascinated inspection, while Ephram peered past his shoulder. They moved their lips in puzzlement, and even astonishment, as they read:

Mrs. Dorothea Roberto

Thump absently considered the street some paces in front of him.

"Mrs. Roberto!" said Eagleton. He looked from Ephram to Thump and back to the card in his hand. He read what he saw aloud. "Mrs. Dorothea Roberto!" It was extraordinary to be holding not only her card but a hand-*written* card at that. "When did you see her?" wondered Eagleton quite naturally.

The previous summer, at the Freeport Fourth of July Picnic, they had *all* seen her, though Thump from a rather unique perspective since he had unintentionally looked up while refereeing a boxing match between two political candidates to discover that the renowned parachutist (and widow) Mrs. Roberto was within an ace of landing on him (in her attractive suit of tights). Thump's head, in fact, did collide with her boot heel, and when the parachute was lifted from them he was regaining consciousness with his head resting in that extraordinary woman's lap.

He may have regained consciousness but he had never quite regained his equilibrium. Waking with that soft pillow beneath his head, looking up past certain notable endowments and into her warm brown eyes, Thump was stricken in a manner that is as common as it is difficult to explain. That evening at the Freeport Fourth of July Ball he had danced with Mrs. Roberto, and what was common in his stricken nature rose into the realm of the *un*common.

But as far as Eagleton and Ephram understood, there had been only a single, faraway glimpse later in the summer when she repeated her daring descent (in her attractive suit of tights) at Deering Oaks.

"I didn't," said Thump in answer to Eagleton's query. "That is just the matter. I found it in my coat pocket this past New Year's."

Eagleton passed the card to Ephram, who held it with great care. Thump may have been struck in some uncommon way, but they each had been greatly impressed by the lovely woman. "Mrs. Roberto!" said Ephram quietly.

"New Year's, you say," said Eagleton. He found a handkerchief in his coat pocket and dabbed at his forehead.

"New Year's Day," said Thump.

"Did she give it to you last Fourth of July?" wondered Ephram.

"I never knew it. And I found it in my winter coat. I was never wearing my winter coat in July."

"No," said Ephram, looking at the card again. "Mrs. Roberto."

"It is very strange," said Eagleton.

"I have thought so ever since I discovered it," agreed Thump, but he did not venture the reason for showing them the card that night.

"She has very nice handwriting," said Ephram.

"Thump!" said Eagleton suddenly.

"Hmmm?" said Thump.

"Ephram!" said Eagleton.

"Yes, my friend?"

"The card!"

"Yes?" said Ephram.

"The card, Thump!"

"Yes, Eagleton!" said Thump with more volume than was natural to him. "Yes! It was what brought me out here."

"What?" said Ephram.

"The card, Ephram!" said Eagleton. "Wanda McCintyre!"

"What?" Ephram was startled. Something in him almost resisted the logic of his friend's thinking. "Wanda McCintyre!" he said. "Good heavens!"

"It was what brought me out here," said Thump.

Eagleton thought back to the last words of the second act of *While She Waits in Silence*. He spoke them aloud. "'. . . *and rightly characterize its otherwise unexpected appearance as a silent cry for rescue!*'"

"My word, Eagleton!" declared Ephram.

"Yes, indeed!" replied Eagleton.

"Thump!" said Ephram.

Thump looked grim.

"Since New Year's Day," said Eagleton, almost breathless. Then with horror, he looked into Thump's eyes and added, "Or before!" He felt an absolute chill clutch at his heart and could only guess at what Thump was experiencing.

But Thump's grim expression was taking on the rigid steel of determination. "I must find her," he said simply.

"Yes, my friend," said Ephram. He placed a hand on Thump's shoulder and gripped it. "But we are with you."

Eagleton took a deep breath. He thought last night's fog had returned; it was hard to see of a sudden. He nodded emphatically, but was not able to speak, and so he took a few steps down the sidewalk and away from the crowd.

"Looking for someone, dear?" came a melodious voice.

Eagleton was startled from his short reverie; a woman was walking toward him from the edge of the crowd. She was not dressed as finely as the other women standing about, but she had a way of carrying herself that marked a high degree of self-confidence and a look in her eye that rather dissolved Eagleton's. "Looking for someone?" he said, making the words mean something quite different.

"Some folk think I look a bit like Miss Tucker," said the woman with a wink that made Eagleton jump.

"They do?"

She was very close to him, and he very nearly tugged at his collar again. She looked up at him with peculiar and potent interest, and he was taken by her sharp blue eyes and her wide and oddly attractive smile. She had a small upturned nose and expressive dark brows. She smelled rather nicely, too. He couldn't imagine that the temperature had risen so quickly.

But why had the woman invoked the name of *Miss Tucker!* He had read enough books to know that covert signals and messages can be sent in many forms, and here he had just watched Miss Tucker play a role in which she surreptitiously slipped a card to the hero in hopes of rescue, just as Mrs. Roberto seemingly had slipped a card to Thump. Now there was a woman asking if he were looking for someone even as she spoke Miss Tucker's name. Clearly Mrs. Roberto was in jeopardy, and this woman was like unto many an agent he had read about—speaking in vague phrases, but offering help to a complete stranger. She had been sent, he was suddenly sure, to lead him and his friends to Mrs. Roberto's deliverance.

"Yes," said Eagleton. "I *am* looking for someone!"

"Consider her found," said the woman, surprised at his sudden decisive nature, and perhaps impressed with it. Her manner had dimmed slightly while she watched Eagleton's confusion but now it blazed again. She glanced over her shoulder at the crowd and back to him. "*Miss* Tucker knows just what you're looking for."

"She does?" wondered Eagleton. He glanced about them for the actress.

"I mean me!" growled the woman.

"Oh! Of course! Shall we . . . I . . . follow you?" he asked. He did not want to frighten her away if she weren't expecting the entire league.

"In a manner of speaking," said she. "But give a lady some time."

Of course! he thought. *She doesn't want to be seen leading me if she is being watched!*

"Danforth Street," she pronounced carefully. "Two doors down from the Weary Sailor. The brown house. 12A." She gave something like a cautious glance about her, then moved off with an odd swish to her walk.

"Danforth Street?" said a horrified Eagleton under his breath. "Good heavens! Is Mrs. Roberto in such dire peril?" He turned back to the crowd and searched for his friends. "Thump!" he called. "Ephram!"

18. Mr. Parkman's Bones

Following the afternoon chores and sometime before the call to supper, Mister Walton and Sundry were left to their own devices for an hour or so, during which interval they acquainted themselves with their rooms and dressed for dinner. Having put on a fresh shirt and trousers, but yet to don his tie and jacket, Mister Walton sat down at the desk in his room and began to compose a letter to Phileda McCannon. There was a surprising amount of news to relate, considering he had seen her off at Brunswick Station only that morning.

> *Dearest Phileda,*
>   *I seem to have accumulated some knowledge regarding pigs since I saw you last, if one is to judge by expectations of folk here in Bowdoinham, where Sundry and I will be staying until tomorrow.*

Mister Walton proceeded to tell of his day, hoping that Miss McCannon would not consider that he had run counter to her directive regarding the fellowship of interesting people. It was of particular importance that he communicate the dismal state of the patient in question and the insistent attitude of the Fern family.

There was a knock at the door and Sundry poked his head in. "Hello, Mister," he spoke, and the rest of his long form entered after.

"I am writing Phileda," said Mister Walton, looking up from his work.

"Best to confess up front, I always thought," opined Sundry.

"Yes," drawled the portly fellow, the spark of humor in his eyes lighting an otherwise dull expression. "It is difficult to communicate the serious nature of Hercules's case," he confessed.

"A glum pig is something best heard about in person," agreed Sundry. He wandered Mister Walton's room, readying his employer's bed and laying out his nightclothes.

Mister Walton sighed, returning to his letter. "I was not cognizant of the four temperaments as manifest in barnyard creatures before this morning."

"I once knew a cow that had a very refined sense of humor."

Mister Walton waited to hear more, and, when he didn't, he asked, "Is that your uncle's cow that could tell the weather?"

"No," said Sundry. "I don't think that cow was funny at all."

Mister Walton let this go with a small chuckle, but wondered about this droll bovine at supper while stories went round the table. He and Sundry quite amazed and delighted their hosts with diverting renditions of the adventures they had shared in the past ten months, and Mister Walton even forced a great whoop of laughter from the seemingly staid Aunt Beatrice with his remembrance of Maude the bear and how she caused an uproar by attending, unannounced, an indoor concert in the town of Damariscotta.

"What a marvelous supper," said Mister Walton when the party had adjourned to the parlor.

"I dare say Mrs. Fern has met the challenge since I first flinched at eating one of our animals," said Mr. Fern with some pleasure in the claim.

"I dare say it hasn't harmed you," said Mister Walton.

"I am fortunate to be able to entertain such eccentricity, Mister Walton. If not for a considerable bequest from my uncle, I would be forced to feed my children in accordance with societal norms."

"You seem to have used your inheritance for other people's children as well," suggested Mister Walton.

"The school, you mean." Mr. Fern waved this intended praise away. "Once a pedagogue, always a pedagogue," he said with a rueful laugh. "Truthfully, I have always believed that I must aspire to good works with my inheritance, as my uncle's wealth was earned in the service of a base master."

"Oh?" Mister Walton was startled to hear it.

"My uncle ran a tavern."

"It isn't a dishonorable trade," said Mister Walton.

"My husband is a follower of Neal Dow, Mister Walton," said Mrs. Fern, meaning that he was a member of the Temperance Movement.

"Ah," said the portly fellow, remembering Johnny Poulter's characterization of the farmer. "But your uncle and his tavern were not."

"He was a bit of a rogue, Mister Walton," said Mr. Fern. "A scoundrel."

"Percy was an honest taverner, Vergilius," said Aunt Beatrice with some stiffness. She and Mrs. Fern were embroidering, and the old woman looked up from her work, peering over her glasses at her nephew. "You shouldn't bite the hand that has fed you," she advised.

"Yes, well, God rest his soul, he did right by me, it's true."

"There have been great men in our history, besides," continued the aunt, "who weren't afraid to take a drink."

"I dare say, they would have been great men if they *hadn't* tipped a bottle," said Mr. Fern.

"Vergil," chimed his wife in a musical, if definite note. Clearly this was not the first time that the subject had been raised in the Fern parlor.

"I beg your pardon, Auntie," said Mr. Fern, catching himself, with his wife's help. "Mister Walton, Mr. Moss, forgive an obsessive dislike on my part. Some will think me fanatic." He chanced a look in his wife's direction but Mrs. Fern was back to her needle and thread.

"I wouldn't refer to my late brother as a scoundrel, Mister Walton," said the elderly woman.

"Of course not," said Mister Walton, a little embarrassed to be in the middle of these semantics.

Mrs. Fern gave her husband a quick glance.

"Percy was a rascal, certainly," said the aunt.

"Oh?" Mister Walton laughed with gentle surprise.

Mrs. Fern looked up from her work again, and other heads in the room came around. Madeline, who had conscripted Sundry's assistance while she wound a skein of yarn into a ball, fell off her task, and they both watched and waited for Aunt Beatrice's unexpected pronouncement to bear fruit.

"You've probably never told anyone about Mr. Parkman's bones, Vergilius," said the old woman.

Mr. Fern cast an eye about the room. "I don't think I have," he said.

Mrs. Fern had altogether left off her work now; she folded her arms and considered her husband with an expectant expression. Sundry did his best not to look too inquisitive but cast a glance over his shoulder.

"I venture that I will have to now," added Mr. Fern, and there was a noticeable sense of relief throughout the room. Mr. Fern stared with some energy into his hands. "My grandfather, who indulged in tobacco, Mister Walton, would say this was a 'two pipe tale.'"

"You intrigue me, Mr. Fern," replied Mister Walton.

Mr. Fern took a long breath. To begin with, he did not look very interested in telling his tale, but he soon warmed to it. Mrs. Fern smiled at Mister Walton and would later express her gratitude to the portly fellow for distracting her husband, however fleetingly, from his worries.

Mr. Fern said, "My uncle conducted his business on the Phippsburg peninsula some years ago. His tavern was the Oak and Dory, as he had brought his worldly possessions to that place in a wagon, the body of which had been fashioned from an old boat. The wagon was stationed beneath a grand old oak, beside which he built his tavern, and the two devices were made plain upon the sign above his door. He was a canny businessman, my uncle, but circumstances were thus that a few years after he opened the Oak and Dory he was in danger of losing much of his business to another house.

"From the hamlet of Winnegance, there are two roads that will take you past Phippsburg to the village of Sebasco, one to the east, one to the west. It was on the western side that my uncle built his tavern; another fellow, by the name of Benjamin Crate, offered rest and sustenance to the wayfarer at his ordinary, the Elm and Eagle on the eastern road.

"My uncle's difficulties began with the arrival of the railroad in Bath, several miles inland from his establishment. It was decided among the town fathers that the roads needed improvement; and, to be specific, that a single route from the extremity of the peninsula to Bath should be widened so that the people of Sebasco and Small Point might have easier access to the railway. Have I proved accurate, thus far, Aunt Beatrice?"

"I will tell you if you veer," she promised.

"So you see the problem, Mister Walton," said the host.

"It seems to me," said Mister Walton, "that your uncle was in rivalry with the Elm and Eagle to have the widened path pass his own door."

"That is exactly so, sir, and very perceptive of you."

"But Daddy," said one of the little girls, "who is Mr. Parkman?"

"You will see," said the father. "Or hear, at least."

"And what about his bones?" asked Madeline.

"In time."

"Will any of us be able to sleep after we've heard this?" wondered the mother.

"Will any of us be able to if we don't hear it?" revised Madeline.

Mrs. Fern returned to her embroidery, smiling softly.

"As it happened," continued Mr. Fern, "there was no obvious choice between the two roads. If you looked at the map you would see that the road to the east is straighter and even a bit shorter; look at a census and you would see that the western road was the more populated.

"The town officers attempted to solve this riddle and when they debated themselves to a standstill, they held a special meeting and the townspeople debated themselves to a standstill. Finally, they decided that they should put the question to a vote, and, by a slim margin, the eastern road won out."

"It must have," said Mrs. Fern, "or there is no story."

Mr. Fern waggled a finger in the air. "Now, my Uncle Percy," he continued, "had a cousin, by the name of Arthur, who had, several months previous to this historic vote, set up his practice as a physician in the town of Topsham, not far away from either ourselves or Uncle Percy. Uncle Percy, in fact, helped Arthur settle in when he arrived from his schooling at Harvard, and was rather taken with a human skeleton that his cousin had brought with him in a trunk. Arthur had named the skeleton Mr. Parkman, after a professor who, according to the young doctor, had slightly less personality than these remnant bones, and he regaled my Uncle Percy with several amusing anecdotes concerning the mischief one may cause if one is in possession of such a thing."

"I am sure that these anecdotes were instructive," said Mister Walton, hoping perhaps to hear one or two of them. The children were aghast at the thought of these bones, and one of the little boys shivered, which made everyone but his father laugh.

"It was in the midst of June," said Mr. Fern, "that work commenced upon the eastern road. Uncle Percy truly feared that his custom would dry up if the wider way did not pass by his door, and since the very hour of that vote he had been wracking his brains for a way to turn the course of improvement in his direction.

"My uncle surveyed the eastern route one evening, when the work had not progressed very far, and he found, not an eighth of a mile from the place where the gang had left off that day, a stretch of road confined by two low but rocky hills. Here would prove the hardest labor; great boulders would have to be broken up and rolled away, with high ledges on either side that left just room enough to accomplish the deed and no more.

"The next day, my uncle visited his cousin the doctor; and that evening, after supper—and subsequent refreshment, I don't doubt—the two of them went for a pleasant drive down the peninsula. And anxious that he had grown lethargic in his trunk, they took Mr. Parkman along with them."

"Oh ho!" said Mister Walton. Sundry positively beamed with the possibilities. The children looked amazed and mystified. "Oh, dear," said Madeline. She and Sundry had lost all sense of what they were doing, and she had made a terrible mess of her winding.

"The doctor realized, of course," said Mrs. Fern, "the importance of exercise."

Mister Walton almost shouted, he liked this so well.

"The next day," continued Mr. Fern, "in the middle of the afternoon, work on the road came to a complete halt. The gangs stood about, scratching their heads, gazing down at what several overturned rocks had revealed. It did not take long for the word to spread up and down the peninsula, but the doctor had evidently not heard of the road crew's discovery when he appeared from around the bend. He was not on an emergency call, so he climbed down from his carriage and let himself be led to the site.

"It had taken two fairly strong men to move the rocks up the slope and back from the widening road, but when the stones had been rolled away the well-preserved skeleton of a human being was revealed. The doctor, of course, was as surprised as anyone, and he knelt down to inspect the remains with great interest.

"It was the skeleton of a man, he declared, long buried in this strange place. They were pleased to have his expert opinion, but was there a cemetery nearby? Or a single grave site recorded?"

"'Did you send someone to ring the church bell at the mills?' asked the doctor.

"'No,' replied the gang leader. 'We only raised this poor soul an hour ago, and have been standing here talking about it since.'

"'Yes,' said the doctor pensively. 'It was about an hour ago that the church bell rang.'

"'Do you know,' said one of the men, 'I thought I heard something when we turned that last stone over.'

"'That *is* strange,' insisted the doctor. 'And no one went to ring the bell and alert the town?'

"'Upon my word,' said the foreman, shaking his head.

"'Strange,' said the doctor again.

"Now, several of the workmen were sure, upon reflection, that they had heard the church bell peal at the very moment of the skeleton's exhumation. Two of the men crossed themselves several times over, and several, *not* in the habit of that gesture, thought it best to attempt it just this once for caution's sake.

"The town officers were sent for, but they were stumped; then the town elders were called upon and driven to the sight, but they stood over the melancholy remains and shook their heads. It was evidence of a murder, said some. No, said others, it might be a British soldier from the raiding parties of the War of 1812. Someone had heard tell of a strange man, found dead years ago; where had *he* been buried? An Indian, insisted another, but artifacts common to Indian grave sites were not to be found with the bones.

"The one thing that many of them did agree upon was that they had heard the church bell peal a single time, though nobody could be found who was responsible for tolling the bell. Someone—perhaps the doctor—had heard of a similar instance when the tolling of a bell had indicated that some long-passed soul took exception to his bones being disturbed.

"My Uncle Percy, like everyone else, visited the site and was just as amazed. But no, he hadn't heard the bell, though the church was only a little ways down the road. 'Good heavens, Percy!' they said. 'You must be deaf as a haddock!' He shrugged and laughed; sometimes his wife did used to speak to him, God rest her soul, and he didn't hear her.

"It was Uncle Percy who suggested that a casket be sent for and that the skeleton be given a proper burial in the churchyard. This seemed the only answer, but dusk was settling by now, and nobody exactly wanted to be carting strange remains in the gloom of night. Time enough on the morrow.

. "And so, they rolled the stones back into place and everyone went home with something new to discuss over supper. And wasn't it strange about the bell tolling all by itself?"

❧≋❧

How was it, when the setting sun had not drawn with it the warmth of day and the lamplight was just as bright as it had been a half an hour ago, that the air seemed a degree or so cooler, and even darker, of a sudden? And how could it be, though knowing their origin, that the vision of those anonymous remains yet gave Mr. Fern's listeners some sense of All Hallows' Eve lurking in the spring evening? Aunt Beatrice had a shawl in her lap, which she drew about her shoulders. Mister Walton leaned from his seat as if the story might reach his ears more quickly the closer he was to the man telling it.

"In the middle of the night," said Mr. Fern, "at midnight, to be sure, that same bell rang out again like a peal of thunder or cannon shot. People for miles around heard it, and men leaped from their beds in alarm, tossed on their clothes, and found themselves gathering uncertainly before the church at Phippsburg.

"The parson had already gone inside, and he seemed more than a little baffled with what he had to tell them. Hardly believing him, they went inside and found that the bell rope had been snapped off, almost to the bell itself.

"What could it mean, they wondered? Such a sign seemed impractical without some obvious purpose behind it, but there was little sleep that night, you can be sure . . . and less the night that followed.

"For when morning came, the townspeople gathered to witness the re-covery of the skeleton. They got a bit more than they bargained for, and some hurried home when the stones were rolled back again. There, in the grave, beside the nameless remains, was the bell rope from the church."

Mr. Fern leaned back in his seat and crossed his long legs; Mister Walton thought the man would have done well to have a pipe just then. Some story-tellers Mister Walton had known would have puffed on a pipe or quaffed a glass of beer by way of swearing to the authentic nature of what was told.

"The rope was in the grave?" said one of the children.

"The point of which was," ventured Sundry, "that the skeleton did not want to be moved." He, too, seemed a little awed by the tale.

"Ah," said Mr. Fern softly. "You have grasped the nugget of my story."

"And since the skeleton could not be moved," said Mister Walton, "and since no one would willingly cut a road over a grave, the crew must back up to their starting point and widen the western route instead."

"Some might have wondered," said Mr. Fern, "if the person whose remains the road crew found had not been a good friend of my uncle's. Cer-tainly Uncle Percy used to speak of an invisible partner in his business—a Mr. Parkman. Besides my uncle, only the doctor had ever met this investor, it seems."

"And your Uncle Percy's business prospered," said Mrs. Fern.

"It was not hurt by circumstances."

"And Mr. Crate's business?" asked Mister Walton, not one to celebrate anyone's misfortune.

"Did not suffer either, happily enough. His tavern was not far from the strange grave, and the story of it drew many curiosity seekers."

"And the grave is still there," said Aunt Beatrice.

"There is a small marker, with the single word: UNKNOWN."

This satisfied Mr. Fern's audience for a moment; Sundry and Mister Wal-ton consulted one another silently. Sundry was first with an opinion. "Most definitely rascals—the both of them."

"I agree with Sundry," pronounced Mister Walton. "Rascals, yes; but cer-tainly not scoundrels."

"It is unanimous, Vergilius," said Aunt Beatrice with evident satisfaction. "Unless there are worse secrets, our family is free of scoundrels."

"Ah, well," said Mr. Fern, with all due irony. "We will not lose hope."

"Who sells liquor in *these* parts?" asked Sundry quite unexpectedly.

There was a moment of silence. Mrs. Fern looked up from her work and over her glasses. Madeline, who was in the process of restoring her ball of yarn, paused to gape at Sundry, as horrified as if the tether of wool between them inculpated her somehow in his depraved interest. Aunt Beatrice looked almost frightened. Even Mister Walton was taken aback, and Mr. Fern, having expressed his distaste for liquor and its peddlers earlier in the evening, was hovering near the cautious border of affront.

"I don't imbibe myself," said Sundry, recognizing the consternation he had provoked, "but there can be few towns anywhere in the state that haven't someone ready to run round the law."

"There's Jacob Lister," said Mr. Fern quietly.

"Jacob?" said Sundry. The name appeared to please him for some reason.

"So I've heard," said Mr. Fern.

"A young rapscallion, no doubt," said Sundry.

"Not at all," said the host. "He's as old and rumbustious a codger as you could ask for."

"To be sure?" said Sundry, who was surprised by this information.

"If he's so old," snapped Aunt Beatrice, "perhaps you should speak of him with more respect!"

Mr. Fern was about to say something else, presumably with a good deal *less* respect, when he stopped himself. The whole family was startled by the aunt's outburst, herself included, and she quickly excused herself on the grounds of weariness. Polite good nights were exchanged and Mrs. Fern began to gather up sleepy children for bed.

"I do beg your forgiveness, Mister Walton, Mr. Moss," said Mr. Fern, when all but his older daughter had gone up to bed. "It is not seemly to demonstrate familial dissension in front of guests."

"It seemed only a mild sort of disagreement, Mr. Fern," said Mister Walton, with a mild sort of expression.

"Thank you, but my aunt, of late, has altered in her view of things, and I have not kept up with the change, I fear."

"It might be considered admirable that a person of her years is willing to modify her views at all," suggested the portly guest.

"My own views are a little stiff, perhaps." He glanced to his daughter, but Madeline, who might have said something in a less occupied environment, only considered her hands folded in her lap.

"I thought nothing of the kind," said Mister Walton.

"I should take a more Christian view of Mr. Lister."

"I apologize for bringing it up in the first place," said Sundry.

"Not at all," said the host, though he was less sure of this dismissal, perhaps, than he liked to betray.

"Mr. Lister is at least *seeking* to be more respectable," said Madeline. She caught the glances of each of the men but settled on her father, who looked doubtful despite his recent retraction. "He's lived in the next thing to a shack all these years hoarding his money, people say; but lately he's been building quite the grand house."

"Has he?" said Sundry.

"Yes," drawled the father. "The Lister Estate," he added wryly.

"That's interesting," said Sundry.

Mister Walton was interested in Sundry's interest.

"After all," said Madeline, "the local schoolhouse was built on a tavern's trade."

"Have you any children, Mister Walton?" asked Mr. Fern.

"I do not have that pleasure."

"Ah, well," said Mr. Fern. He cast an indulgent look at his oldest daughter before he thought of something else and let out a sigh of renewed sadness. "Shall we go out and take another look at Hercules?" he said, shaking himself from the previous moment.

Mister Walton agreed to this and Mr. Fern went in search of a lantern. Madeline went to change her parlor slippers for proper shoes.

"I am thinking that Hercules could do with a dose of birch-bark tea," said Sundry when he and Mister Walton were briefly alone.

"Are you?" said a bemused Mister Walton.

"Birch-bark tea," said Sundry with particular emphasis upon each of the three syllables.

"I have been endeavoring since this afternoon to understand your thought processes," said Mister Walton.

"I don't know if *that* is a worthwhile pursuit," said Sundry.

"Experience tells me otherwise," said Mister Walton.

19. The Woman in 12A

Danforth Street was rather more subdued than when last visited by the Moosepath League, but the comparative silence was almost more nerve-wracking to Ephram, Eagleton, and Thump than the clamor of the night before. They heard a piano from somewhere playing "In the Sweet By and By"—presumably *not* the instrument that Gillie Hicks had pushed off the balcony of the Weary Sailor.

They were surprised how near Danforth Street was to the theater; their carriage had only turned a corner or two before it stopped and the driver asked *where* on Danforth Street they needed to be. They got off at the crossing and paid him, and as the cab dwindled into the night they wondered if it would have been wise to keep quick transport near at hand.

Ephram questioned if the police should have been notified about Mrs. Roberto's speculative peril, but the police were seldom notified in any of the tales of imperiled women they had read, and it did seem that more should be known of Mrs. Roberto's situation before involving the authorities. All too soon they passed by the Weary Sailor, pausing only to consider the spot where the piano had landed on Thump's wallet.

"Could the thief have been involved?" said Eagleton. The card with Mrs.

Roberto's name had been in Thump's wallet. Could there be a connection? He shivered at the possible intrigues of Mrs. Roberto's persecutors. "Two doors down, then," he said. "We'll have this soon solved, Thump, don't you worry." He considered his broad-bearded friend, who stood hunched and expectant before the brown house, then Eagleton looked past Thump to Ephram, who looked back, each hoping to see certainty in the other's eyes.

"Did you say 12A?" said Thump.

"Yes," said Eagleton. Now that he thought of it, the brown building didn't look as if it could house a 12A. It consisted of only two stories, with perhaps a half a story beneath the eaves. There was a light behind the front door and at a window to the left. Another light emanated from a gable end, shimmering a faint glow against the building next.

"Do we knock?" wondered Ephram.

Thump looked from one to the other of his friends and with sudden resolve advanced to the door and did just that. After a second series of raps the door swung open and a small elderly man peered out at them, saying, "Yes, yes?"

The Moosepathians were suddenly alert to a social difficulty. It hardly seemed proper to inquire after a lady—so late at night, in such a place. *Why, we don't even know her name!* Eagleton realized with a start.

Thump made a grumbling sort of sound that often signals a preface to speech, and the old man leveled the whole of his gaze upon him, but nothing else was said for a moment or two. Thump turned to Eagleton for help.

What *had* they been thinking? Eagleton said "Ah" several times, and finally added, "There was a lady."

This appeared to surprise the elderly man.

"12A?" said Ephram.

"She spoke of only *one* man," said the man.

"Ah!" said Eagleton, as this indicated that they were in the right place. "These gentlemen are my fellow members," he said. "I do nothing without them."

This caused the old man to look a little wild-eyed. "I don't know what Winnie will think of this!" he said, clearly amazed.

Thump was considering the weeks and months that had passed since New Year's Day, when he first found the card, and of all weeks and months that Mrs. Roberto might have been in terrible peril before that; suddenly this small delay was untenable to him and he said in his deep voice, "Perhaps you had better let us in, sir." He took a step forward and the old man retreated from his post, backing into the small front hall till he stood opposite the three of them at the foot of a narrow stairway. There were closed doors at either hand, and the members of the club could hear low conversation coming through one of these.

"Which one of you is she expecting?" asked the old man.

Eagleton had been glancing about. There was an odd painting on the wall, going up the stairs, that depicted a woman on a bed (sleeping, he thought, though she was not cozily blanketed); a single lamp shone from the landing above. Eagleton thought he detected signs of other people there—perhaps a shadow moved or someone murmured. "*I* spoke to the lady," said Eagleton.

"Then you may go up," said the old man. "12A. Your fellows may adjourn to the parlor."

"He is trying to separate us," Ephram hissed into Eagleton's ear.

"What's that?" asked the old man.

Eagleton could not have gone to a woman's room by himself. He could barely imagine visiting a woman's room at all, even with his friends, and he wasn't sure that it was very proper, no matter their number or motive, but he could not conceive of going there alone. "I would not accuse you of anything, sir," he said. "But where one of us go, there go we all."

"Bravo, Eagleton!" said Ephram quietly, even as the old man objected.

"The lady I spoke with might herself be in danger," said Eagleton.

"In danger?" said the old man.

"12A!" said Thump suddenly, and he led the charge up the stairs.

Eagleton snatched a closer glimpse of the painting as he followed and wondered if the woman depicted there was sleeping at all. He came close behind Thump, while Ephram brought up the rear. The old man at the foot of the stairs huffed and hemmed. Eagleton very nearly ran Thump down when they rounded the landing and reached the upstairs hall. The designations 12A, 12B, 12C, and 12D were indeed marked clearly upon the four doors before them. Thump had come to a halt at the first of these, and they looked past him and read the room number silently in unison.

"Room 12A, and on the second floor!" marveled Ephram.

Simultaneously to this statement, the door to room 12A opened and the woman who had spoken to Eagleton outside the theater stood before them in what might be termed a contradictory manner, for her expression looked expectant and even welcoming while her brief attire could not, by any stretch of the Moosepathian imagination, indicate a woman expecting *anybody*, much less a masculine visitor. Ephram, Eagleton, and Thump had nothing in their lexicon to describe her garments (as they had always politely passed over the newspaper advertisements for the underpinnings of the female ensemble) and perhaps less in their experience to lead them through the next few moments.

They were too startled to even look away. Eagleton said something that sounded a bit like "Ooff!" several times over, while Ephram sucked in his breath as if ready to put his head under water, and Thump simply went "Hmmm?" The sound of laughter came from a room down the hall.

The woman from 12A looked at Thump first and appeared more puzzled than dismayed. She caught sight of Eagleton then, and the smile she had employed outside the theater bloomed across her lips till she considered Ephram and the puzzled expression finally won out. "What is *this?*" she said.

"I beg your pardon," stammered Eagleton. "I thought it more proper if I brought my friends along."

Her eyes widened considerably and she said, with a gasp, "That's a different sort of proper than *I've* ever heard of!" She had a wrap of some sort about her shoulders and she pulled it more securely around her.

This relative modesty on her part gave Eagleton enough encouragement to continue speaking. "Anything you can pass on to me you can pass on to each of us," he said, trying to explain. Ephram and Thump thought he was doing extraordinarily well considering the situation.

"I beg your pardon!" she said.

"The card," said Thump in such a low tone that she might not have understood him. It did not help that he was looking into his beard.

"The what?"

"Mrs. Roberto," said Ephram, who appeared to have found something fascinating about the ceiling.

"Where?"

"We always stay together in these situations," said Eagleton.

"I can't imagine it!"

Eagleton was sorry to hear this, as it seemed to indicate that she lacked friends. Clearly they were out of their depth and it was time to retreat. They heard footsteps behind them and turned to see a wiry blond fellow climbing the stairs three at a time, a strange grin across his face and a truncheon in his hand.

The truncheon dropped and the grin disappeared when he raised his eyes, however. He stopped short of the landing. "What is *this?*" he said, just as the woman had moments before. "The three of them?"

Ephram, Eagleton, and Thump turned on the man with a degree of energetic suspicion. "The gentleman from last night!" said Eagleton.

Suddenly the Moosepathians were subject to all manner of conjecture, and it occurred to them, all at once, that the man—indeed, the *men*—who had been running after Mr. Spark the night before were part of the plot against Mrs. Roberto and that this fellow had come to silence the woman in 12A.

Fuzz Hadley was astounded. Having planned this trap with the woman in 12A, he had expected to find but one of the men who had come to Thaddeus Q. Spark's assistance—perhaps even the one who had rescued Spark's wife's uncle from a life in prison; but here were all three of them, and what did *that* mean? He was further unnerved by the barely concealed disapproval in their furrowed brows. The one with the beard, in particular, looked formidable. Fuzz pivoted on one heel and almost tumbled down the stairs in his retreat.

"Fuzz!" shouted the woman as the man fled, and then, to Eagleton, Ephram, and Thump, "Are you the cops?" She looked ready to shut the door.

Thump stepped forward and laid his hand upon the knob. "Don't be alarmed," he rumbled, though this assurance was perhaps too late.

"It is awkward, of course," said Eagleton in a rush, "but perhaps you had better get yourself suitably arranged, and then you can tell us what you know about Mrs. Roberto. That fellow is gone, but come with us and we will find safe harbor for you."

They might have been complete lunatics, for the expression on her face. A door opened down the hall, and a distinguished gray-haired gentleman leaned his head out and said, "Is it the cops?"

The front door banged open again and several men charged into the hall below. Eagleton all but pushed his fellows through the open door to 12A just as Fuzz Hadley pointed up the stairwell and shouted, "There they are!"

Eagleton fell over Thump, who had tripped over something, and Ephram slammed the door behind them. They were in a small, sparsely furnished chamber dressed in red and gold. The sound on the stairs was thunderous and the harsh voices and vicious-sounding (if mysterious) jargon of the oncoming horde horrified the Moosepathians. With a shout, the lady (Winnie, as they were to understand) disappeared into a further room and slammed the door shut just as Eagleton had caught the glimpse of a garishly bedecked bed. There was a tentative shove at the hall door from without, but Ephram had enough leverage to hold it till he was able to turn the key.

There was a bang, and they imagined a gun had gone off, but it was only the crash of a shoulder against the other side of the door. Another bang followed, and another, in quick succession. A woman screamed from another room, and there were shouts from someone asking for a rear exit. More imprecations made their way through the door. Someone bellowed "Get back!" and another collision shook the door.

Ephram, Eagleton, and Thump were horrified. "Quick! Out here!" came a voice behind them. The single window in the room had been raised, and a young boy was standing on the narrow ledge beneath the gable. He beckoned to them, saying, "Come on!" The door gave a sickening snap beneath the next blow. Thump stared at the boy and said, "It's the Spark lad!"

Timothy's freckled face was stamped with fear and astonishment. "Mr. Thump, please hurry!" he said, obviously near to flight himself.

"But the lady!" declared Ephram.

"The *lady?*" said the boy.

Crash!

"We cannot abandon her!" agreed Thump.

"Winifred?"

"She must be rescued!" declared Eagleton, halfway to the inner door.

Crash!

"She's part of the gang!" shouted Timothy just as the outer door took the penultimate blow with a jarring snap.

Eagleton turned about-face, saying, "What?"

"She's part of the gang!" Timothy helped Ephram out the window. Eagleton raced back to the sash and gave Thump some assistance in clambering onto the roof, then scrambled his own long form through the aperture.

Timothy slammed the window shut just as the door burst open and several cursing, shouting, flailing men toppled into the room that had just been quit by the Moosepath League.

20. The High Road

The steep pitch of the roof and the theater-appropriate shoes worn by the members of the club were not elements to engender confidence, there on the slates, in the near dark, with the strange silhouettes of gables and chimneys and other roofs against the stars and the voices of their pursuers only yards away. They were on the back side of the house, the dim glow from the window fanning into the gloom of a narrow alley, and their eyes needed several moments to adjust. When they were able to see, the gentlemen of the club were each startled by the presence of a small boy atop the gable, straddling its peak like the imp on a Gothic cornice.

"That's Mailon," explained Timothy Spark.

The Moosepathians were doing their polite best to greet Mailon when they heard a woman's scream, then a crash. Presumably the gang thought that Ephram, Eagleton, and Thump were hiding themselves with Winifred, and the door to her inner room had suffered a fate similar to that of the outer entry. They were horrified by Winifred's shouts, and if Timothy could not see their expressions very clearly he yet knew what they were thinking.

"She's part of the gang," he said again.

Eagleton's feet were slipping, and only his grip on the corner of the gable kept him on the roof.

"You okay?" asked the skinny little fellow atop the gable.

"I believe so, thank you very much," said Eagleton. He let go of the gable with one hand long enough to tip his hat.

Mailon indicated with a wave that Eagleton should think nothing of it.

Ephram and Thump were having similar difficulties with the steep roof, and they could only be glad the rain had left off. Voices echoed from Danforth Street on the other side of the house.

"We'd better scoot," said Timothy, though now that he had gotten them out of the room he considered it a little daunting to get them off the roof and safely away. "There's more coming all the time, by the sound of it," ventured the boy. "Can you make the peak?"

If the Moosepathians doubted their ability to achieve this end, another crash from inside, punctuated by still another dire scream, was all they needed for encouragement. They scrambled for the summit, up the shifty slates—slipping but making headway, scurrying three or four steps to gain a single foot. It was a blessing, perhaps, that the men inside were making such a racket, since they did not hear the desperate scuttling above them, and eventually the three men threw their arms over the peak like exhausted mountaineers. Peering over the roof, they could see a crowd gathering on Danforth Street.

Tim and Mailon stood above everything, balanced like goats on the peak. "Where's Bobby?" wondered Tim in a whisper. He looked anxiously down at the street, then across the varied roof levels to the west. A birdlike call warbled from somewhere in the night and Tim said, "Ah!"

There were more shouts from the house, the noise of which rose as the window opened again and someone said, "They couldn't have gone out this way!" and another said, "Where else could they go?"

"Come on!" hissed Tim. He tried to help Eagleton up onto the peak of the roof, but Eagleton had to do most of the work himself. Once perched there, he was able to assist Thump and Ephram. Tim was already halfway along the ridge of the roof, with Mailon toeing just behind; the men half crawled, half slid after them. "Don't let old Fuzz Hadley catch you," warned Tim as they drew near to him. "He's mean as a hurt dog. Come on."

Some men from the house had joined the gathering mob in the street and they were gazing up at the roof just as Eagleton stood, one sliding foot on either side of the ridge. A shingle gave way beneath his shoe, scraping down the slope of the roof and out into space. "There they are!" shouted one of the men in the street, and then, "They're throwing slates down at us!" There were shouts and curses and the crowd scattered.

Feet slipping, arms windmilling, Eagleton took off after the boys. Ephram was close behind. Thump gained his feet only to lose them and sit heavily with a gust and a groan, his legs straddling the peak.

"Quick!" shouted Tim. "Down here!" At the end of the peak, he gave Eagleton a tug and the man found himself stepping into thin air. There was a sickening plummet of a yard or so before he landed upon a shed roof, slid the length of this slope, and met thin air once again, his trajectory carrying him over a narrow alley and onto the short, second-floor balcony of the next house. Eagleton stumbled against a door, which swung open, and he sprawled upon the floor within. He had no more than righted himself, with the help of some unseen agent, when there came a shout of surprise.

Shoes slipped at slates, another shout rang out, and Ephram landed feet first upon the balcony. He took several steps into the room beyond and bowled Eagleton onto his back. Staggering upright, they had little chance of recovery before Thump came rolling after them.

Eagleton had the dazed perception that Tim landed like a cat upon the balcony, Mailon like a bird. Another door opened and a third, older boy (the unseen agent) led them down a steep enclosed stairwell, through a darkened kitchen, and out into a small yard. All the while they could hear angry voices following them through the house and through the alley to the backyard which the fugitives crossed at full speed.

There was a wooden crate before a fence, and Tim used this to vault to the other side. Ephram, Eagleton, and Thump performed this feat with surprising speed, if less grace. Then the older boy handed Mailon to Eagleton, tossed the box over the fence, and climbed after. He was almost over when he was caught hold of by the leg, and he only just shook himself loose by kicking his assailant with his free foot.

They were in another alley. A door opened some yards away and a young woman stepped out and beckoned. Blowing and puffing and wheezing, the Moosepathians offered to raise their hats to the girl as they passed and were startled to discover that their hats were gone.

"Good heavens!" said Eagleton.

The girl closed the door and escorted them down a dimly lit passage. The men were aware of the scent of tobacco smoke and of other pungent smells less familiar. The girl put a finger to her lips as they passed two doors, from behind which they could hear a dull murmur that reminded them of the crowd at the Shipswood. Perhaps there was even the clink of silverware.

They were led onto a small unlit street, and the older boy lingered behind long enough to take the girl's hand and thank her. She had a pretty round face, and she hardly looked into the boy's eyes but smiled before she stepped back inside and closed the door.

The ruckus on Danforth Street sounded distant, and the Moosepathians hoped for a moment to catch their breaths. "They'll be scouring every lane from here to the mills," said Timothy, and he led them down the dark street into yet another alley, and then through a series of confusing doorways and passages, till they came, exhausted by nerves and exertion, to an old, three-story house—the Faithful Mermaid—on the western end of the Portland waterfront.

21. Sight Unseen

"I think it's beautiful," said Cordelia with as much pride as if she had made the gown herself.

Priscilla didn't know if she cared anymore; it had caused a frightful row— or if not a row, exactly, then the sort of unhappy stir that invariably surrounded her mother whenever she felt she had been crossed.

The article in question was behind the door, where Cordelia had hung it. Simply looking at it made Priscilla feel guilty and she wished it had been put in the closet. She hadn't the will to approach it, now that she had prevailed upon her mother, with the help of her cousin and Great-aunt Delia. *Goodness!* she thought, and with very little humor. *Cord is well named!*

Delia Frost had been waiting for them in the parlor when they arrived from Freeport by carriage that morning, and the old woman looked much aged since the previous fall. The winter had been a difficult one for Aunt Delia; she had spent the better portion of six weeks convalescing from a fall on the ice in her yard, only to be struck down by the influenza for almost a month. She looked pale and tired when they arrived but perked up with the presence of the young women, particularly her namesake.

Cordelia may have been saddened to see her beloved Aunt Delia so weary and drawn, but she would not show it. Delia laughed, the redheaded bride-to-be was so lively with news and plans.

"Cordelia!" admonished Grace. "Don't be tiring out your aunt, now!"

"Oh!" scoffed Delia, with a wave of her cane. "Don't talk nonsense! Maybe I'll kick the bucket with a good laugh rather than fade away in a dark room listening to my own snores."

Upon hearing the phrase "kick the bucket," Grace was so shocked she couldn't find it in herself to exclaim her usual "Aunt Delia!"

Cordelia, herself a little horrified (not by the expression but by the thought behind it), said it for Grace. "Aunt Delia!" Priscilla, who had seemed terribly out of sorts since arriving, gasped herself and snapped out of a grim preoccupation.

The old woman laughed again, looking pleased with herself.

And so they had lunch, served in the parlor, and talked about the coming wedding and the June Ball and finally what gowns they would buy. "I expect to see both of you fit to knock several men over at a single glance," said Delia, which did raise the customary protest from Grace.

"Gorgons did that," said Cordelia, which made Priscilla laugh.

"Well?" said Aunt Delia, undeterred. "What's the point in buying a new gown and going to a ball if it's not to spread a little heartache? The night I met Abner Frost, I thought he'd fall dead in his tracks to see me, and I was quite happy with the effect. Never mind that I had to throw him out a few years later. It was worth doing. Cordelia has apprehended one heart, that's clear, but it doesn't mean she can't still be dangerous from a distance; and Priscilla"— here the old woman gestured once again with her cane—"I think your hour of conquest has arrived!"

Priscilla looked startled, as if some secret had been discovered; even Cordelia cleared her throat in order to gain time to think. Grace was too distressed with the general tone of the conversation to notice her daughter's reaction, but Aunt Delia picked up on it immediately.

"We will purchase something very *nice* and *decorous* for both of them," said Grace, taking command of the discussion. Her tone of voice indicated that the subject was tabled.

Delia Frost was willing to cede the last word to Grace but not the gesture. She lent a certain weight to her own inclinations by insisting that everything be put on her own bill at the shop. Grace (who was not stingy with her own money, only *careful*) hesitantly acquiesced to this offer, vaguely suspicioning how the balance of the matter had subtly shifted.

"Now, please me with something appropriate for that young woman," said Delia quietly to Grace, "and not simply *proper.*"

For Priscilla Morningside, the trip to the dress shop was charged with happy anticipation and a degree of wary foreknowledge of how her mother and Cordelia might come to loggerheads. She hadn't expected, however, that the moment of confrontation would occur before they had even entered the store.

The gown was in the window of Beal's Dress Shop on Main Street, and Priscilla was enamored of it the instant she saw it.

"Oh, Priscilla!" enthused Cordelia, and "Oh, Cordelia!" Grace sputtered, one on the heals of the other.

Priscilla may have loved the gown on sight, but she could not imagine herself in it, which was all the more reason, according to her cousin, why she must try it on.

"Most certainly!" agreed the proprietress, Mrs. Beal, when she considered Priscilla's figure, and there was such sincere conviction in the assessment that Grace could not refuse her daughter's right to try it on even if, according to her lights, it was ridiculous to consider buying it.

Mrs. Beal was a canny saleswoman, however, and while she assisted Priscilla in the dressing room she expressed, in no very quiet tones, how much like her mother the young woman was. Priscilla was, in truth, the image of her paternal grandmother—her long dark hair, her faultless complexion and warm brown eyes, the maturity of her figure that was so well served when she appeared from the back room in *the gown.*

Even Grace could not resist a gasp, but more out of trepidation than delight. Cordelia put her hands to the sides of her face and absolutely gaped.

"There isn't an alteration to be made!" proclaimed Mrs. Beal.

Priscilla made a face. Mrs. Beal had taken her spectacles away and she looked vaguely comic as she squinted at the mirror across the room.

"Here, dear," said the shopwoman. "I believe they do suit you."

"Oh, my," said Priscilla when she replaced the spectacles on her nose. The glasses did do something interesting to her face, but it was the gown that startled her—or, rather, herself *in* the gown. She hardly recognized the woman in the looking glass—a comely, even beautiful, vision; mature, and surprisingly confident in the dark, sleeveless bodice with gorgeous beading that hid yet at the same time drew attention to her full bosom. The contours of her lower portions were accented by a sheath of rich blue fabric, and the whole effect was magnificently lifted in soft folds about her feet and ankles. Her arms were frilled to the wrists in lace, and Mrs. Beal had set the entire revelation off with a dark blue velvet ribbon fastened about Priscilla's graceful neck with an ivory cameo at her throat.

"Oh, dear," said Grace with very real sadness for her daughter, "it's much too—"

Tears were in Cordelia's eyes. "Priscilla! You are—"

"—expressive," said Priscilla's mother.

"—beautiful!" said her cousin.

"It's a little vivid, I think," added Grace.

"—stunning!" continued Cordelia.

Grace was almost wringing her hands. "It's very nice of Mrs. Beal to let you try it on, but—"

Cordelia strode up to her cousin and gripped Priscilla's hands, which were cold and damp.

"Oh, I don't know, Cord," said Priscilla. It was one thing, she thought, to carry such a thing off in a dress shop, but quite another in the company of strangers, under the critical gaze of men and among women of much greater wealth and elegance.

"No," said Grace, simply and without being heard.

"After seeing yourself in this," insisted Cordelia, "how could you think of anything else?"

"It's very—" Priscilla considered herself in the mirror again, "mature."

"And why not?"

"No," said Grace again, and her tone, if not the word, sank through the young women's consciousness.

"What, Aunt Grace?"

The older woman hurried across the room and took a pale yellow gown— to be favored, perhaps, by a young girl on a summer day—from its stand and held it before her. "Look at this!" she said a little too emphatically. "Isn't it sweet?"

It was just the thing Priscilla *might* have worn under any other circumstances, but she looked from her image in the mirror to the yellow gown and something like horror showed on her face. Even Grace flinched at what happened to the grown woman in the beautiful gown, and Cordelia stepped back and looked from her aunt to her cousin. Priscilla might have lost two inches of height and several yards of confidence.

Mrs. Beal looked philosophic and unmoved.

Grace Morningside herself drooped so that the hem of the gown in her hands touched the floor. "Is that the gown you want?" she said to her daughter after a long and terrible moment.

Priscilla was not sure, of a sudden; certainly she hadn't been sure before, but for different reasons. "I don't know," she said, but so softly that no one heard her.

"Oh, but you must!" said Cordelia, almost as softly.·

Grace did not look at her niece. "Is that the gown you want?" she asked again.

Priscilla looked like a child, fingering the velvet at her throat, but when she looked back at her mother, her expression changed, as if some recollection had unexpectedly determined her answer. Her jaw stiffened and there were tears in her eyes. She said nothing but nodded.

Grace blinked and looked as if she found it difficult to breathe, or even move.

Cordelia was startled, as well; from the moment they set eyes on it, she had believed the dress to be a lost cause. Now she hadn't the slightest notion as to what had prompted Priscilla's unexpected decision, but Cordelia studied her cousin's face and thought there was, in Priscilla's teary eyes, a brief and quiet anger.

⁂

So the gown had been carefully gathered and boxed, and Grace even purchased the velvet ribbon and the cameo with her own money. Cordelia found a nice gown, relying as much as she dared upon her aunt's advice. It was not a brilliant choice. (Priscilla suspected that her cousin had purposely insisted on something less grand.) Grace, too, found something suitable for a fancy ball that would yet do no harm to her insistent widowhood.

Great-aunt Delia did not seem very happy with Cordelia's selection till she saw Priscilla's. She perhaps understood what Priscilla had suspected and returned to Cordelia's finery with more praise. She was quite pleased with Priscilla's gown, but did not go on about it. "Very practical," she said at one point, and Cordelia almost laughed. Grace frowned at her aunt.

Hanging behind the door in the bedroom upstairs, the gown looked a bit like *traitor's weeds* to Priscilla. Grace had not said very much to her daughter, and only Cordelia's careful chatter kept conversation alive till it was time for bed.

When she was dressed for bed, Cordelia took another look at the gown behind the door and breathed a great sigh. "It is . . . marvelous!" she said.

"*You* should wear it," said Priscilla.

Cordelia made a noise. "*I* haven't the figure." It was true: she was a willow.

"But you have the spirit," added Priscilla.

"Not as spirited as you looked when you came out of that fitting room. By Aunt Delia's definition—or anyone's, I dare say—you'll knock over Mr. Moss, and any number of *other* men in the process."

"Please, don't joke, Cord."

"Why do you think I'm joking? I told you, if you had only once looked up on the train, you might have seen how Mr. Moss was watching you."

"I think he's very kind, is all."

"*I* think he's very smitten."

"He did see us down from the train."

"He saw *you* down from the train. We just happened to be with you."

"Ah," said Priscilla after the briefest hope had touched her eyes. "I might never see him again."

"He's going to the ball."

"He said he would think about it."

Cordelia saw that Priscilla was not ready to be encouraged, so she came away from the gown, went to the edge of the bed where her cousin was sitting, and kissed Priscilla on the top of the head.

For a moment, Priscilla let herself imagine Mr. Moss at the ball, herself in that magnificent gown, and she and Mr. Moss dancing a waltz about Mrs. Morrell's grand ballroom. It was not long before a voice rose up and swept these visions aside—a voice and words she had heard only that morning. Cordelia had not heard them, or had made nothing of them if she had, but that voice—those words—only added to the impossibility of Priscilla's sweet daydream.

It was while they were taking the hired carriage to Aunt Delia's. Priscilla was feeling a little giddy from having seen Mr. Moss. The entire day seemed dizzy when she looked back at it, but on the train, and for a while after, she had felt an unaccustomed pang of possibilities. She had even been brave enough to speak to her mother.

"Mr. Moss was very nice to see us off the train," she said with complete innocence.

Grace was looking out the window of the carriage. She looked a little bored, a little weary, but Priscilla realized that her mother's thoughts were racing. "After all, dear," Grace had said, "he *is* a servant."

Priscilla's giddiness had ended at that moment, and at that moment, as her anger rose above her fear, the gown in Mrs. Beal's window was chosen before any of them had ever seen it.

22. What They Promised Phileda

Sundry thought it polite (and even circumspect, perhaps) to wait for Mister Walton and their host before stepping into the night after Madeline, but the young woman turned and smiled from the front yard—an expression he could not miss in the light that spilled from the hall—and he quickly forgot his brief discretion. The bright scythe of the moon's first quarter was snared in a grove of trees on a hill to the west, and starlight blinked in and out from behind a fleet of clouds. Sundry could smell the lilacs in the yard.

"Don't you love a spring night, Mr. Moss," she said airily, "when summer seems so close behind it?" A feathery breeze caught at certain stray locks of her auburn hair.

"Well—" he began, hoping to think of something wise to say, or poetical, or even lucid, and settled for a simple "I do."

He didn't regret his answer, for it made her smile again. "It's very generous of Mister Walton to help with Hercules," she said after a moment. "Daddy has been so troubled."

"That is an interesting subject," said Sundry, and he was about to make further inroads under this heading when the two older gentlemen arrived on the front steps. The four of them stood in the yard and weighed the evening. "Do you have any thoughts about Hercules, Mister Walton?" asked the farmer as they went looking for the great pig.

Mister Walton decided that now was the time to have it out. "I fear my experience, Mr. Fern, is not—"

"You might want to keep Hercules in tonight," interrupted Sundry.

"Do you think?" said the farmer. Though he regarded Sundry with the smallest degree of caution, his honest and hospitable nature forbade anything but polite replies.

Sundry referred the question to Mister Walton, and Mr. Fern, too, turned to the portly fellow and said again, "Do you think? I told you that we had him penned for three days."

"Not penned, I think," said Sundry, "but in the barn."

A pig in a barn was not a usual thing, and Mr. Fern had to consider it for a moment.

"I knew a fellow once," said Sundry, his hands behind his back and his head up in the posture of one who does his best to recall with accuracy. "He had a cow he would tether before the barn when he milked her. Now, one day, when the cow was in her stall, lightning struck that tether, and afterward, whenever he milked the cow from that tether, she gave sour milk."

"I've read some articles about *electrical dispersement* and lightning storms," said Mr. Fern thoughtfully, "but I've never understood that any effect can linger in an area after the initial charge has dissipated."

"There are other local influences that might have an effect," suggested Sundry. "It's just a notion. And there was the other thing—" Sundry tapped his head, as if he were having difficulty remembering. "What was it we spoke about, Mister Walton, that Hercules should be given."

"Spoke about?" Mister Walton could think of nothing.

"In the house," said Sundry.

"The house?"

"A dose of . . . er—"

"Birch-bark tea!" exclaimed Mister Walton, more from the pleasure of remembering what *Sundry* had been talking about than from any form of conviction. He had, in fact, no conviction at all regarding birch-bark tea, and had hardly heard of it before.

"Birch-bark tea?" said Madeline. She had heard of the drink's powers against headache and rheumatism but would never have thought it a remedy for a melancholy pig.

"Is that what you think, Mister Walton?" asked Mr. Fern.

"I have been meaning to explain," said that gentle fellow, "that Sundry knows a good deal more about these matters than I do."

"Oh?" Mr. Fern spoke the word, but both he and Madeline wore the expression.

"But," added Mister Walton, "a change in venue has often been beneficial to my own state of mind in times of difficulty. Here he is," he said, a little discomfited by the confusion on their faces. "He's on his feet!"

"Yes," said the farmer, recovering slightly. "He often gets up at this time of day, but it doesn't last very long. He seems a little more content in the evening, but tomorrow he'll be sad as ever."

"Could he be eating something he shouldn't, Mr. Fern?" wondered Sundry.

"I won't say he isn't. It's why I penned him up. I'm not a botanist by training, though I know something about plants. But I've had half a dozen taxonomies and the *Farmer's Guide to Destructive Weeds* in hand, as I surveyed the place from corner to corner, and found nothing. There are some birches down in the hollow by the stream, if that's what you think he needs."

Sundry scratched Hercules's head.

Mr. Fern exchanged looks with his daughter. "We could put him in for the night," he said graciously. "What do you say, Hercules? Would you like to stay indoors?"

Mister Walton noticed that Sundry was watching the house; there was a single lighted window on the second floor that spread a dim glow over the yard. Sundry turned away from the house and smiled when he caught his employer's eye.

"Madeline," said the father, "get one of your sisters to go with you down to the birch grove by the stream. How much of the stuff will we need, Mister Walton . . . er, Mr. Moss?"

Sundry indicated some dimensions with his hands, saying, "A couple of lengths like this."

Mr. Fern turned to his daughter and Madeline hurried off. They led Hercules to the barn, his great weight creaking over the ramp, and saw the pig settled into a stall with a trough of slop and water. Mr. Fern's lantern was an island of light in the darkness of the barn; their shadows shivered past timber and post, blotted the walls, and were lost in the rafters. Sundry saw the eyes of an owl shining in the loft, and he had a sense of the great bird swooping over-head as they walked back to the house. Something gave a tiny, frightened squeal in the field beyond.

It was not long before Madeline and her sister were back in the kitchen steeping papery lengths of birch bark in a kettle. "What do we do with it?" asked Madeline.

"Just pour it in with his slops," said Sundry.

After the bark had simmered for half an hour or so, and after the brew had cooled, Mr. Fern himself took it out to Hercules. "Let us hope," he said sim-ply when he came back.

The Ferns and their guests retired, parting in the upper hall, and Mr. Fern thanked Mister Walton for perhaps the twentieth time. Mister Walton blushed and insisted that thanks were unnecessary. Once in his room, he sat on the edge of the one bed and blew a heartfelt sigh.

Lingering at the door, Sundry had a brief glimpse of Madeline; she smiled and gave a hesitant wave, before disappearing through a doorway at the op-posite end of the hall.

"My, but it's a lovely evening!" said Mister Walton when Sundry followed him into his room. "Would you crack a window?"

"I was going to suggest it," said Sundry, and he raised the sash opposite the bed. "I wish we were on the other side of the house," he said as he leaned out the window.

"I don't know how you can tell *which* side of the house we're on," admit-ted Mister Walton. "I was quite befuddled coming up here and will starve for breakfast if someone doesn't lead me back to the kitchen."

"I think I can get you there," said Sundry without pulling his head in.

"My nose might lead me," said Mister Walton with a chuckle. He looked more curious than amused then. "You are filled with interesting questions."

"Am I?"

Mister Walton chuckled again.

"What is it you said last night about spring?" asked Sundry.

"Good heavens! Was that only last night?"

Sundry retrieved the quote, and sent it into the room. "'*A livelier iris changes on the burnished dove.*'"

"Has Hercules been eating irises, then?" said Mister Walton wryly. "And your acquaintance with the cow. Don't I recall Mr. Pue telling us something like it at the Custom House last summer? That wasn't the cow with the sense of humor, was it?"

"Mr. Pue," said Sundry. "Was that who told me? I guess it was."

"But that cow was actually *struck* by lightning." Mister Walton sat upon his bed and began to pull off his shoes.

"I think you're right."

"I wonder if a change in sleeping arrangement will cure Hercules's troubles. That and birch-bark tea."

"It used to do wonders for an uncle of mine," said Sundry.

"Was he sad much of the time?"

"No, drunk."

"Do you really think—?"

Sundry only shrugged. "What I really think is—" and here he pulled his head and shoulders back into the room. "What I really think is—what about this?" He pulled a white flower from his pocket.

"What is it?" said Mister Walton.

"A lilac, I think."

"Yes, but what does it mean?"

"A lilac beneath the hydrangeas."

"And you picked it?"

"I picked it *up*, I should say, *among* the hydrangeas."

"It wasn't growing?"

"They have lilacs in the front yard, but purple ones."

"This is white," said Mister Walton quietly. Hardly conscious of what he was doing, he pressed the withered petals to his nose. "There's little fragrance left to it."

"Perhaps it had been there a while."

"Sundry?" said Mister Walton. "What is this about?"

Sundry cocked his head to one side, and said, "Listen."

Mister Walton froze in a posture of absolute attention, his eyes wide behind his round spectacles. Together they did listen, and Mister Walton thought he heard a distant rumble. "Is it thunder?"

"Not yet, I think."

"Some wild creature?"

"It would depend very much upon opinion," said Sundry. He went to the door and, bearing its weight from the hinges, opened it with hardly a click or a groan.

Mister Walton inched closer to the door, still keening an ear. The noise was louder and more distinct, but it took him a moment or two to place it. "Someone is snoring," he said finally.

Sundry nodded. One finger held in the air, he conducted another half a minute of silence while they listened to the racket. "I hope that's not one of the young ladies," said Sundry as he closed the door again.

"Sundry, do you really believe that pig has been suffering from drink?"

Sundry stood in the middle of the room with his arms folded and said, "It does seem unlikely. But if he has, one must wonder who has been feeding it to him—and why."

"It occurs to me," said Mister Walton, his hands on his knees and his bespectacled gaze fixed upon the floor before his feet, "that anyone involved with hard drink would be an unwelcome guest here at Fern Farm."

"And an unwelcome suitor to any of Mr. Fern's daughters."

"But why intoxicate the pig?"

"He *was* a 'watchpig,' they tell us."

"Of course," said Mister Walton, then: "The young man who drove us here was quite definite on the subject of Mr. Fern's temperance. Did you notice a certain nervousness between him and Miss Fern?"

"Madeline?" Sundry nodded. "Johnny's smitten and no mistake. I hardly blame him, but I wonder what else he might do besides blacksmithing."

"I was ready to lay my head down and sleep, my friend," said Mister Walton, "but I have revived."

"You did promise Miss McCannon we would stay out of adventures," chuckled Sundry.

Mister Walton considered this with all due gravity. "A melancholy pig seems tame enough."

"If that's all it amounts to." Sundry nodded philosophically. "Perhaps it will turn out in the morning."

"Ah, well," said Mister Walton with another sigh. "I will just have to make it up to her."

23. More Things in Heaven and Earth

From the backdoor of her late aunt's house, Phileda McCannon could see the light in a window on the opposite bank of the Narramissic reflecting off the rushing stream. The gates and sluices commanding the little river were still; only weeks before the water in these locks swarmed with the dark backs of the mysterious alewife, and the shores of the river likewise were crowded with fishermen and onlookers by day and lamplit night.

To the south there were more lights down in Orland Village, and more than a mile to the east, just ahead of Phileda (where she leaned at the doorpost), the black mounds of Great Pond Mountain and Cave Hill rose out of the bed of the land like half-wakeful heads.

Phileda was tired, though she didn't think she had done very much. Her cousin had been here last December and accomplished most of what needed doing to close the house. This afternoon Phileda had gone straight to work, packing away some things left in the shed, wrapping kitchen glasses and plateware in newspaper. Tomorrow she would go to Ellsworth to talk to the banker and meet a prospective buyer. She would have liked to have kept the house, but it was foolish enough for one middle-aged woman to occupy such a large place in Hallowell—her parents' old home. What would she do with two houses?

And as beautiful as it was here in Orland—as cozy and snug—it was that much further from someone. *He will be in Norridgewock, by now*, she thought. There was an old map of the state, dated 1872, in a room upstairs, and earlier that evening, by lamplight, she had peered at this chart, tracing the line formed by the Kennebec till her finger met the name of the town where she imagined Mister Walton to be spending the night. The contours of geography, the name Norridgewock, the map itself, did not tell her nearly enough.

All evening Phileda had sensed that she was on the verge of losing something, as if Toby might vanish into thin air were she not there to watch him. The thought did make her smile, though in a contrary manner; with his portly frame, it would take a little more vanishing than with some people.

The house had worked its recent history upon her imagination, that history being of an unmarried schoolteacher, long retired. Aunt Katherine had been the very model of a spinsterish schoolmarm. Phileda herself, visiting Aunt Kate in the summers of her youth, had seldom seen beyond the expected surface—a kind heart wrapped in practiced severity, a flinty curiosity concerning her neighbors, a list of aphorisms and object lessons as long as your arm.

Aunt Kate wrote formal letters to her nieces and nephews and signed them in a lovely hand beneath the words *With great affection*. Her dry sense of humor was often evident, but Phileda was always surprised to be reminded of it. She was a capable cook and though not an excellent one, Phileda's father always said "she had gingerbread to a standstill." Phileda could almost smell it now. There was always some waiting in the warming ovens when Aunt Kate brought one of her visiting nephews or nieces back from the station. You could smell it from the street, and entering her house was as warm and comforting as sinking into one of the down mattresses in the rooms upstairs.

Looking out over the river toward Great Pond Mountain, Phileda was gripped by a chill, and she came in from the dark to the dimly lit kitchen, poked at the small fire in the stove, and turned up the lantern. Her cousin had left some things in the parlor—personal items in a single box—and Phileda brought these into the kitchen and put them on the table.

It was a strange thing to be picking through another person's life; Phileda felt sadness but also curiosity, which is *not* a sad emotion. The sadness is most of all for ourselves, she knew, when we see the small objects that make up our lives and how very common most of them are; everyone with a home has dishes and chairs and framed portraits on the wall. The things she took from the box seemed too unsubstantial to represent a life; she had felt the same way about Aunt Kate's funeral service. What a rich thing a single moment can be; perhaps you are only standing at your front door watching a chickadee flit in the rosebush, or you stop singing long enough to hear the rest of the congregation and wonder at the disparate voices joined together, or you laugh at something no one else would understand. But when a life is done, you must wonder what all those moments have amounted to.

The first thing Phileda pulled from the box was a small diary; the year 1896 was written in pen on the first page. It would be unfinished, of course; Aunt Kate had taken sick in November, Phileda had come to take care of her at the beginning of December, and she knew her aunt had not been well enough then to write. She thumbed through the diary's pages to the last entry—November 21, 1896—and found references to the neighbor's boat, early snow, and an item in the local newspaper concerning a white deer sighted on nearby Verona Island, but no mention of illness or hint of what was soon to come.

Phileda experienced no ambivalence about reading the diary; there would be nothing very revealing, certainly nothing shameful, and there was a trunk filled with previous years in Aunt Kate's bedroom upstairs. If a life's moments were to amount to something, what better place to find them out? But there would be no secrets to uncover, Phileda knew—nothing that was not proper and demure for an unmarried schoolteacher of forty-two years and retired twenty-two more.

Next she found a deck of *bishop's cards*, which contained no faces or suits. Aunt Kate had not been unusually religious for her time or her generation but had contracted a suspicion (almost a superstition) regarding face cards from a minister uncle when she was young. Phileda had pleasant memories of playing with the strictly numbered deck (never on Sunday, of course) games that resembled whist or hearts.

Next there came half a dozen fine lace handkerchiefs—marvelous, delicate things, ivory white. They had the monograph *K. P.*—Katherine Pitcher—in one corner, hand-sewn in a pale blue by Aunt Kate's own Aunt Kate, who had made them as part of a trousseau. The first Aunt Kate had lived and died on Prince Edward Island, having come from the south of England. The handkerchiefs were treasures of the most precious sort, and Phileda was touched that her cousin had left them for her. She put them on the table and softly pressed her hand upon them before peering back into the box.

There was a locket watch, dangling upon a gold chain; a little key to wind the watch hung like a tiny sparkling pendant from the middle link.

There were some old photographs—one of Phileda's mother, Aunt Kate's older sister, sitting sidesaddle on a small, dark horse. Helen Pitcher looked satisfied, and even a little wry, not quite regarding the camera. She was very young. Dim and losing its detail, the picture was from before the war. Phileda had to guess at the people in the other pictures, and she looked in vain for something written on their backs. *I must remember to write on the backs of all my photographs*, she thought to herself.

In the box, there was a Bible and a hymnal. There was a small sheaf of newspaper clippings, including one (Phileda could read most of it without undoing the ribbon that tied the bundle) that reported the victory of one of Aunt Kate's students at a countywide spelling bee.

John Burton, thought Phileda, silently mouthing the student's name. She undid the strap and unfolded the piece of newspaper. When she found a reference to the boy's parents, she laughed delightedly. John Burton was the present warden of the alewife stream she could see from Aunt Kate's kitchen window—a lean Yankee fisherman short on talk and long on studied silence. He was a son of the rocky shore, with a fierce reputation for the letter of the law, when it came to his stream, and checkers. He kept a *bachelor's hall* outside the village, and each year, during the month of hunting, disappeared to some interior forest.

And he was, according to this yellowing piece of newsprint, a master of the language—a champion speller. Who would guess that the gray-headed fellow barking orders by the sluice gate in alewife season had the intricacies of the English tongue and its wayward spelling harbored in his brain or that he had friends to this day (Phileda did *not* know this, of course) who still tested him with outrageous words, of which English has plenty.

It made Phileda smile, thinking of Aunt Kate glowering over her class as she called out the week's words and young John Burton, born with native genius, soaking in what Aunt Kate so dearly hoped to give all her pupils. This was the moment bestowed upon Phileda in the nearly silent kitchen (a clock ticked in the parlor and a little wind pulled at the northeast corner of the house), a moment that might be lost someday with John Burton himself—Aunt Kate's moment, and what a life might honorably amount to.

"There is no such thing as wasted knowledge," Aunt Kate used to say, and the old woman had firmly believed, Phileda knew now, that any life was enriched by knowing where to find Calcutta on the globe, or how to divide by a fraction, or how Hamlet described the formidable state of being human.

Phileda wished Toby were near enough to tell this to.

A small plaque, writ with John Burton's name and the magnitude of his accomplishments, came out of the box like continued revelation. There was a handwritten note attached to the corner of the award, and Phileda pulled the lantern closer to read the small, finely crafted letters.

"Miss Pitcher," said the note, *"you should have this. John."*

Then curiosity overwhelmed all sadness, and, with the date of the newspaper clipping committed to memory, Phileda took the lantern to Aunt Kate's bedroom and sorted through the old chest at the foot of the bed till she had found the corresponding diary.

What she found was that Aunt Kate's diaries of her teaching years recorded every triumph and every sadness she experienced through her pupils, and on the date following the spelling bee there was an entry for February 20, 1869, that said simply, *"Found John's award left upon my stoop this morning with a note from him that I should have it. It made me cry."*

Phileda cried herself, there in Aunt Kate's room, but didn't feel sad, somehow, except for the absence of Toby Walton.

24. The Fallacious Extremity

Fuzz Hadley waited in the back room of the Crooked Cat, questioning his gang as they straggled in from the back alleys of the waterfront. The brown house on Danforth Street was abandoned, for the moment. Patrons had been the first to bolt at the first sign (or sound) of trouble; the ladies of the establishment were close behind, once Fuzz and the boys had knocked down the door to room 12A.

The Moosepath League and their rescuers had escaped, and Fuzz was pretty sure where they had gone.

"They were waiting for me," said Fuzz, lifting a beer. He'd been properly startled to find three men instead of one at the head of the stairs; and they'd been a serious-looking trio. Spark's bearded relative had seemed especially grim and dangerous. "Right on my own street," he said, more to himself than to the *boys* who waited with him for the cops to clear out. They could still hear the occasional shrill whistle or shout, and several officers of the law had tromped into the Crooked Cat, but Percy Beal had handled them nicely. Percy's business ran counter to the law, but elections were over and the police had their hands full with more important matters—like busted down doors and women screaming in the night.

Percy stuck his head into the back room and said, "They're gone, Fuzz."

"Another beer," was about all the thanks that Percy got. "Right on my own street," said Fuzz again.

"*'And dar'st thou then, To beard the lion in his den?'*" said Peacock Hope, sitting at the other side of the deal table.

"I didn't know lions had beards," said Jimmy Fain.

"They knew their way around," said Fuzz, who continued to be baffled.

"It was one of the Spark kids with them, I'm dead sure," said Harmon Blunt when he and Tony Sutter scuttled in through the backdoor. "Tony had him by the cuff, but he shook himself free."

"I had him, but he kicked me in the chops," said Tony, coming up behind. He had a hand to his face. "Knocked a tooth loose," said Tony, and he didn't look very happy about it.

"They must have flown over those roofs," said Harmon.

"I didn't know lions had beards," said Jimmy.

"It is not a true beard, I believe," said Peacock, "and Scott refers to it in the most figurative sense."

"What?" said Jimmy.

"*I* can't figure what they wanted," said Fuzz. There was a faint knock and Winnie Peel almost fell into the room when Harmon Blunt jerked open the door. "I guess they didn't want you," said Fuzz to Winnie, when she had dusted herself off. Only Peacock rose to offer her a chair.

Winnie made an unhappy sound and crossed her arms before her. "They were expecting *more* than me, I guess."

"They were expecting *me*," said Fuzz.

"I believe your *modus operandi* has lost its power to surprise," said Peacock, and, as usual, most of them didn't know what he was talking about.

Winnie said, "I *mean* they were expecting another girl."

Fuzz grunted.

Hankie blew his nose loudly. "Sorry," he said afterward.

Winifred said, "That fellow looked plenty interested when I talked with him outside the theater."

"'*Vain as the leaf upon the stream,*'" pronounced Peacock, "'*And fickle as a changeful dream—*'"

Jimmy Fain started to say something a good deal less genteel to Winifred but had not taken the precaution of stepping out of her reach, and he caught the back of her hand across his ear. "Ow!" said Jimmy.

"They were asking about some *Mrs.* someone," said Winifred, who seemed to think this query more insulting than curious. "Roberto. Mrs. Roberto. They mentioned her twice. I don't know who *she* is."

"Ah! Mrs. Roberto!" said Peacock, sounding rapturous.

"You know her?" asked Fuzz.

Peacock was ready to tap his endless storehouse of gaudy words till Fuzz gave him *the look*. "I do," said Peacock simply. It was the shortest sentence they had heard from him for quite some time. "She is the ascensionist!" he informed them.

This sounded like more fancy speech, and Fuzz said, "Now, look, Pea!"

"The parachutist!" declared Peacock Hope, his hands up, as if to prove he was unarmed. "The balloonist!"

"The woman who jumps from the balloon?" said Tony, nursing his jaw.

Peacock nodded in agreement. "The same," he said.

"Oh!" said Winifred with a gust. "She's grand!"

Hankie gave another sad honk into his ever-present handkerchief.

"I saw her once," said Jimmy, and he was taken with the recollection.

"Mrs. Roberto!" said Peacock. It cheered him just to say her name. "She drops in beauty, like her flight."

"The lady in the balloon," said Fuzz. "Why were they looking for her?" he wondered aloud, then to himself, *What were Spark's boys doing here tonight?* And what was Spark's bearded relation doing here with *his* gang? Fuzz was of a suspicious nature, and he had been working on a major suspicion regarding Thaddeus Spark for some time now. "Where's she from?" said Fuzz, and when this garnered only expressions of curiosity he said, "This Mrs. Roberto?"

Jimmy shrugged.

Winifred said, "She's foreign."

"She keeps her gear over Bergen's place," came a voice not previously heard from that evening.

"What's that, Skelly?" asked Fuzz.

Skelly Wilson came out of his corner like a little rat. "Those rich fellows," he said. "I bet they were looking for where she has her gear."

"Why would they?"

Skelly shrugged elaborately. "Something there must be worth something to someone. That coot keeps about a dozen locks on the door."

"Old Nick?"

Skelly nodded. "He's keeping something from someone, and that's for certain. Tossed me out the window."

"The window?" said Jimmy.

"He did. But I did some asking around and found out, finally, that it was that woman's place where she keeps her gear. I didn't have but a minute to see for myself. It was dark, too. Lots of books and clothes and her parachutes, I wager. Big silk things."

"Silk things?" said Peacock with great interest.

"Thaddeus must be keeping his rum there," said Fuzz.

"Thaddeus doesn't sell rum," said Tony.

"He must be keeping *something* there!"

"But why would this relative of his," said Peacock, "be asking after Mrs. Roberto in *your* establishment if Spark himself is using *her* rooms to conceal distillates?"

"I don't know!" growled Fuzz. "It doesn't make sense. If I knew, I'd know what Spark was up to." The very backward nature of it all was what troubled him so. "That relative of Spark's had *some* reason to come down here, and clearly it wasn't you," he said to Winnie. "He brought his gang with him, as if they were ready for a fight, but skedaddled the moment we headed up the stairs."

"Perhaps," said Peacock, "we are considering this impasse from the fallacious extremity—wrong end to, as it were."

"I think I knew what he was saying that time!" said Jimmy, a little amazed at his own wisdom.

"Wrong end to?" said Fuzz.

"It's quite obvious, now that I think of it," said Peacock Hope. "They thought that *we* have possession of this Mrs. Roberto, or of something associated with her."

"Yes," said Fuzz. This was a little too obvious, he thought.

"And if they want this . . . *whatever*," continued Peacock, "and if old Nick is keeping it behind barred doors—"

"Then it must be worth having," said Fuzz. "Or at least keeping it out of Spark's hands."

"Right end to," finished Peacock, as if he were demonstrating a mathematical proof.

"Boys," said Fuzz, "let's go and visit Old Nick."

They were all curious now, Winnie included, and she was not happy to be left behind. She hovered at the backdoor and watched them leave. The men moved quietly, and Fuzz, too, just as if he didn't own the street, or just as if they were sneaking up on some poor unsuspecting soul already in sight.

The door to the tavern room opened, startling Winnie, and Percy Beal poked his head in. "I've got Fuzz's beer," he said, looking around for the man. From outside somewhere there came the doleful sound of Hankie's nose.

"Fuzz is gone," said Winnie. "Give it here."

25. The Fateful Reinforcement of the Family Spark

On Friday night, the twenty-eighth day of May 1897, the regular patrons of the Faithful Mermaid were in the tavern room—among them, tall Jefford Paisley, whose ham-sized fists were blessedly attached to an amiable nature and whose often glowering features masked a placid temperament; retired Captains Broad and Huffle, whose combined trove of lore and fable regarding their adventures among the coasters would exhaust volumes; the Todd *brothers* Tom and Patrick (who weren't related) and *Catcher Gowdy*, all three of whom worked the west docks; and Emry Pinbrock, who ran the mail stage from Portland to Portsmouth. There were others besides and a small cadre of respectable laundrywomen nursing *small beer* in the corner. The tavern room was cheery with friendly voices.

That evening, the older members of the Spark family were at their customary chores. *Mother* was in the kitchen with Minerva rolling biscuits for tomorrow's breakfast. Betty and Annabelle were seeing to customers while Davey poured the beer and ale and stout. Timothy was overdue, and Bobby, who had been sent to look for Timothy, was nearing a similar state of absence. Thaddeus paced about abstracted by worry.

Thaddeus himself had come from a large and largely unstructured family; he had been a fairly autonomous soul by the time he was seven or eight. He knew some of what his boys were up to and didn't know if he wanted to know the rest. Portland was not a very dangerous place for a kid who kept his brains about him and looked before he leaped, but things did happen, and Thaddeus was fretting some. He went to one of the front windows of the Faithful Mermaid and frowned at his own reflection. It was seven minutes before the hour of eleven, as we have reason to know.

"That'll be the boys," said Thaddeus with some relief at the sound of the backdoor and Mabel crying, "Watch your dirty feet in my kitchen!," then, "Good gracious sakes alive! I thought you were Thaddeus!"

Thaddeus keened an ear. A different sort of commotion rose from the kitchen. There was the voice—the rumble, really—of a grown man, and Mother sounding uncertain as she asked a question. Thaddeus exchanged glances with Davey as he moved to the back of the tavern. The kitchen door swung open suddenly, almost striking him, and his middle son, Bobby, almost ran into his father's arms.

"Whoa there, Newt! You're heading for the woodpile!" declared the father with a short laugh.

Bobby came almost to Thaddeus's shoulders. His face was red with exertion and excitement, and he held his father at arm's length and spewed forth a torrent of words, all resolved to catch Thaddeus with the same agitation. "You told Timothy to watch Mr. Thump and he and Mailon have gone and saved him and his friends from Winnie Peel's and I found them following Mr. Thump and I went over with them and we got Mr. Thump and his friends down through Hemple's kitchen and Fuzz Hadley and his boys came within a fleabite of catching us—!"

"What?" said the father in his high-pitched voice. His voice, in fact, had almost left him at the thought of Fuzz Hadley within thirty yards of his boys. "What?" Thaddeus picked his son up and set him aside, then barreled past the door into the kitchen. "Timothy!" he almost shouted. "I told you to keep an eye on the man, but I thought you knew enough not to—"

Thaddeus fell silent. Minerva stood with a rolling pin poised over tomorrow's biscuit dough, and Mother, with flour up to her elbows, had her hands on her hips; they peered from Thaddeus to one of the men standing at the back of the room. Timothy looked more delighted than daunted, and, behind him, Mr. Thump and two other gentlemen (by their clothes, if not the *state* of their clothes) looked only daunted and dazed. Mailon, somehow, had gotten himself inside Mrs. Spark's kitchen.

"Jumping Jehoshaphat!" said Thaddeus. "What's been happening?" The three gentlemen jumped at the sound of his voice. Their clothes were spattered with mud, and even torn in places, and they hadn't a hat among them. "Good Godfrey! You gentlemen look like three weeks and a gale."

Thump and his companions were visibly shocked to hear it.

"I did what you told me, Daddy," said Timothy before anyone else could speak (and, in fact, everyone else seemed speechless).

"And what's this about Winnie Peel?" said the father. He glanced to his wife; she would not be happy to have *that woman*'s name invoked in her kitchen.

"They were upstairs already," explained Timothy, pointing at the men behind him, "the three of them, and Bobby went over to Hemple's and snuck up the balcony. Fuzz and his gang were on their way, so I climbed up the back shed at Winnie's and got round to the window."

"Timothy!" said his horrified mother.

"Why didn't you come and get me?" demanded the father.

"There wasn't time. Bobby and Mailon were with me," finished Timothy, as if this answered for everything.

"However did you get them out?" wondered Betty, who had come into the kitchen with Davey and Annabelle.

"I took them over the roofs," explained Timothy, "down through Hemple's, and Bobby and I led them out the alley, through Missie Burns's, and roundabout from there to shake Fuzz's gang."

"Well, there," said Mr. Spark, looking pale. "'*All's well that ends*,' they say." His wife looked as if she considered the situation neither ended, nor all well, and that she would have *plenty* to say before long. Thaddeus scratched the top of his head. "Well, Mr. Thump—" he said.

"Thump?" said Mrs. Spark.

"It was a close thing, from the sound," said Thaddeus, "Winnie Peel has a reputation for luring men to her rooms, where Fuzz Hadley waits for them. They're likely to be found down on the wharf, those men, next morning, in a heap with a headache and not their wallet, if you see what I mean, and not many a man will go to the cops to tell them where he's been."

Thump did not entirely appear to *see* what Thaddeus meant.

"Mr. Thump?" said Mabel Spark again. Though she had never met the man, she held him in great esteem for having rescued her Uncle Gillie from a life in prison, but she was struck with disappointment to hear of his patronizing an establishment like Winnie Peel's.

"I beg your pardon," said Joseph Thump, and he introduced himself and his friends to the woman of the house. "We are the Moosepath League."

"Well," said Mabel, instead of "Hello" or "Glad to meet you." She suspected that Messrs. Ephram and Eagleton had led the good Mr. Thump astray and declined to shake their hands.

"When Timothy and I visited you this morning, Mr. Thump," said Thaddeus, "I couldn't have guessed that we'd venture to reciprocate before the day was out. I don't care to have my boys over there to Danforth Street, but I'm glad everyone is back in one piece."

"We are very grateful, sir," said Thump. "And what an extraordinary thing that your son was at the window!" It seemed a terrific coincidence.

"And this little fellow," said Ephram. He indicated Mailon, who would liked to have gone unnoticed. No one made him go outside, however.

"It was a curious business," Eagleton was saying.

"Clearly those rough fellows were attempting to get between us and our purpose, Mr. Spark," said Ephram. The family was astonished that he would mention such *purposes* before them. Mabel Spark made a choking sort of noise.

"Yes," said Thaddeus, and, red to the ears, he looked at his feet. His wife would have a conniption fit.

"How were you all climbing out the same window?" began Annabelle indelicately, though her voice trailed off as the thought coalesced. "If one of you—" she said, and she fell silent.

"Annabelle!" said the mother under her breath. She waved a flour-covered arm and was going to usher all the children from the kitchen or Mr. Thump and his friends out the door.

"The three of them were up there all at once," said Timothy, the very image of innocence with his broad, freckled face and tousle of blond hair, but the declaration stopped everyone.

Mabel lowered her arms and betrayed a less than seemly curiosity. "The three of them?"

"It did seem proper," said Ephram quietly.

Thaddeus's eyes went wide, and his wife's mouth hung open. Annabelle let out something like a laugh. Bobby thought an explosion was pending, and he looked over his shoulder to see how close he was to the door.

"Unfortunately," said Eagleton, "we never got what we came for."

"She may have had no intention of giving it to us," said Ephram wisely.

One could have cut the encircling silence with a knife, but Ephram, Eagleton, and Thump seemed unaware.

"It has occurred to me, Ephram," said Thump.

"Yes, Thump?"

"Eagleton?"

"Yes, my friend?"

"That the lady did not *have* what we were looking for."

From what he had heard about Winnie Peel, Thaddeus was pretty sure that she did, and almost said as much. He clamped his mouth shut. He didn't know that he'd ever been within a street's width of the woman, but the eye is long and his ear was good. A man did not run even a respectable tavern and not get wind of people like Winifred Peel.

Eagleton had gripped his friend's shoulder. "We will yet find Mrs. Roberto, Thump," he said. "Perhaps the police can help us."

"The police?" said Davey, who had just entered with a tray full of mugs.

"Mrs. Roberto?" said Thaddeus. The name rang familiarly in his head.

Ephram looked to Thump for his friend's consent, then with arms behind his back he stated, "It was our object, you see, to discover the whereabouts of Mrs. Dorothea Roberto. We have reason to believe that she is in some danger. Miss Peel approached Eagleton outside the Portland Theater during intermission and intimated that she knew where we might find the lady."

"Now, hold on, there," said Thaddeus. He scratched the top of his head again, so that the Moosepathians had the impression that he was encouraging thought by these exertions. "Do you mean to tell me that you went to Winifred Peel's to find out about this . . . Mrs. Roberto?"

"Yes," said Ephram, as if he thought this had been apparent from the beginning.

"Mrs. Roberto!" said Davey, and respectfully. Bobby tugged at Davey's sleeve and queried his brother with a look.

"We are quite concerned for her," said Eagleton. "And I must say, the events of this evening have not gone far to relieve our minds."

"By some means," said Ephram, "those . . . gentlemen suspected our suspicions. I would not speak ill of anyone, nor harbor misgivings of people not properly met, but I must wonder if the entire business weren't—" and here the thought seemed so dire that he almost whispered, "deliberate."

"The balloonist!" said Davey.

"What?" said Annabelle.

"The balloon woman. Mrs. Roberto."

"Mrs. Roberto!" said Thaddeus, his high voice carrying over the general murmur. He was struck by sudden visions of a summer day and bright blue skies and white cotton clouds, gay crowds and laughter and cannon shot and fireworks, and, of course, the lovely, almost regal Mrs. Roberto dressed (as advertised) *in her attractive suit of tights*, leaping from the basket of the ascended red, white, and blue balloon, and her magnificent red, white, and blue parachute blooming above her, and her graceful form floating some thousands of feet like an angel to the grass and the band and the cheering people below. "Mrs. Roberto!" he said again.

"Fuzz Hadley's gang?" wondered Davey aloud.

"Oh, the dear woman!" said Mrs. Spark, horrified.

But Thaddeus had to have the entire business put straight before him. "Are you telling me, Mr. Thump," he said, "that you and Mr. Ephram, here, and Mr. Eagleton didn't go to Winifred's in search of—well, er, favors?"

Thump considered the question but didn't get very far with it.

"Didn't you hear them, Father?" said Mabel to her husband. "They were searching for Mrs. Roberto, having realized she was in trouble, and Winifred Peel led them to believe that she could help them find her, and Fuzz Hadley and his gang set upon them, and it's clear as day that Fuzz has the poor woman somewhere, or plans to put her in dreadful circumstances!"

It was an extraordinary speech and might have come from one of the books that Ephram, Eagleton, and Thump had read in recent months. (As it happened, Mrs. Spark had read some of them herself.) The members of the club were riveted; they themselves had hardly dared put the situation in such definite terms.

Understanding that a crisis was nigh, tall Jefford Paisley had poked his gloomy countenance past the tavern room door and now he stepped into the kitchen to listen. No one realized he was there until he let out a low whistle. Thaddeus exchanged glances with Jefford. Neither of them would put such doings past Fuzz Hadley and his gang.

Thaddeus wouldn't put *much* past them, in fact. "Some kidnapping scheme," he said. "Or blackmail, perhaps. It's terrific! Mr. Thump, you are a knight. *And* your friends."

"The dear woman," said Mabel again, piping a tear. "To perform before royalty, and now this." It made the gentlemen look aside.

Betty wiped the flour from her hands. Minerva rolled up her sleeves as if she were ready to tangle with someone.

"We should go to the police," said Davey.

Ephram, Eagleton, and Thump had been considering this, and there was a general stirring among them.

"Have you any evidence?" asked Thaddeus.

"We have our suspicions," said Ephram. "Though it seems obvious now that she is in danger."

Thump looked fit to burst.

"What led you to think it in the first place?" asked Annabelle, who was a wise girl.

"Thump found her card in his pocket," said Eagleton. He leaned forward to stress his next remark. "It was very mysterious."

"We had our doubts," said Ephram, "but then Miss Peel approached Eagleton and said she knew where Mrs. Roberto was."

"Actually, what she said—" began Eagleton, but Thaddeus was already thinking aloud.

"Why else would they have lured you to Winnie Peel's with the promise of bringing you to Mrs. Roberto? Suspicious is what suspicious was. Clearly, that was an attempt to get you out of the way. It's a wonder you weren't murdered outright." This caused some gasps, not the least from the three gentlemen. "But the police won't touch it unless you have some hard sign," said Thaddeus, who seemed, to the Moosepathians, anxious to leave the authorities out of the matter. "They've no love for Fuzz and his men, but it's their word against yours. And though I hate to say it, going to Winnie Peel's will not put you in a favorable light with the cops."

"Thaddeus, we have to do something," said Mabel.

"Yes, yes." He waved a finger in the air to indicate that he was *on the case*.

He paced the floor and everyone watched him, Ephram, Eagleton, and Thump following his movements as if they were keeping track of a tennis match. "We'll ask around," he said, speaking to himself.

"I'll go with you!" said Timothy.

"You will not!" declared Mabel. "You'll go upstairs." She gave Timothy a swat on the posterior that was wholly inappropriate for such an adventurer. "And *you* be careful where you *ask around*," she said to Thaddeus.

"We can't wait till morning," he said. "Jefford?"

"To be truthful, Thaddeus," said the tall fellow, "you might ask no further than your own ordinary." He hooked a thumb over his shoulder. "Captain Huffle knows her, I'm sure. He was her pilot, last Independence Day, in Freeport, dressed as Uncle Sam."

"Captain Huffle," said Mabel Spark simply. She was picturing the man, who sported a fine white beard, as Uncle Sam in Mrs. Roberto's balloon.

They all hurried into the tavern room and surrounded the table where sat Captains Broad and Huffle. "Were you really Uncle Sam?" asked someone, and another said, "Where does she live?" and finally Thaddeus vocalized a birdlike stutter in his high pitch that grew louder till everyone else went quiet.

The two old salts looked no more dismayed than might be implied by squinted eyes and exceedingly straight postures. Captain Broad, by his own report, had been surrounded, at distinct moments in his life, by all manner of pirates, headhunters, and deadly creatures. Captain Huffle was not far behind on this count and was purported to have talked himself out of being executed by a Chinese warlord without so much as raising his voice above the level of polite conversation.

The old seamen were naturally curious, of course, to be encircled in this fashion; Jefford Paisley and the Spark family were watching Captain Huffle with great fascination, and behind them were three fellows dressed in fine, if hard-used, attire. One of these looked remarkably like their host, and all three hung upon the moment with expressions of extraordinary suspense. Further back in the ranks were the Todd *brothers*, Tom and Patrick (who were not related), stage driver Emry Pinbrock, and the other late-night patrons of the Faithful Mermaid.

"Boys, howdy!" said Captain Huffle.

"It does remind me of the time I sneezed a gold tooth out of my head on Penalty Street down at Bangor," said Captain Broad.

"Did you?" said Captain Huffle, though perchance he had heard the story before.

"Sneezes often come in threes, you know," said Captain Broad, "and there were some who gathered about to see what I would produce next." He was explaining this without taking his eyes from the crowd.

It was a comfortable place, the tavern room of the Faithful Mermaid; the ceiling was not high so that the smoke of pipes and cigars fogged the upper atmosphere and muted the light of the lamps; certain corners of the room looked dark and remote enough to encourage a satisfactory drowse. Ephram, Eagleton, and Thump might have spent some moments taking in these strange surroundings had they not been so intent on Captain Huffle and his purported knowledge of the endangered Mrs. Roberto.

"Jefford says you know Mrs. Roberto," Thaddeus said to Captain Huffle.

"Mrs. Roberto?" said the old salt, as if he must run through an entire catalog of like-named women.

"Mrs. Dorothea Roberto," said Thump with more emphasis than could be answered in a casual manner.

"The parachutist," said Thaddeus. "Mrs. Roberto."

"I have a small acquaintance with the lady," admitted Captain Huffle with an odd mixture of pride and circumspection.

"We have reason to believe, sir—" said Thump, bending his stocky frame over the seated Captain Huffle. "We have reason to believe that Mrs. Roberto is in some hazard."

Someone let out a gasp. The laundrywomen had risen from their seats and they closed in upon the Captains Broad and Huffle from behind. The Todd *brothers* had already reached the outskirts of the small crowd. Looking grim, Thump straightened to the limit of his concise stature. A second collective gasp followed close upon the first.

"Ahem!" said Ephram, and Thump wondered if he had spoken out of turn. Eagleton said something like "Ooop!" and finally Mrs. Spark said, "Oh, dear!" which Thump considered strange since she had been apprised of Mrs. Roberto's unfortunate situation in the kitchen.

The bearded Moosepathian glanced back at the Spark family and was dismayed to recognize the target of their gaze. Had he not been so intent upon the imperiled state of Mrs. Roberto, he might have been conscious, before that moment, of an unaccustomed draft from somewhere in the area of his trousers' back pockets.

"Good heavens, will you look at it!" declared one of the laundrywomen with a cluck of her tongue that affected Thump like a poke in the ribs. She shook her head. "And the coat torn, too."

26. The Ubiquitous Imprint

A low-lying fog prowled the waterfront, a cold damp breath that followed the men from the Faithful Mermaid as they wound through a series of alleys, and less than alleys, till they faced the back of Winter Street. Captain Huffle, who had once wrestled a dozen or more roughnecks in a Bangor saloon for a gold tooth, was yet a little cautious of waking old Nicholai Bergen.

Thaddeus and Jefford were there, as well as the two old salts. Ephram and Eagleton were in the middle of this troop, and Thump, who was newly decked out in clothes borrowed from Mr. Spark, strode in the van. The Todd *brothers* Tom and Patrick, had requested to come along, as Fuzz Hadley was somehow involved in this business, and Tom in particular had expressed interest in modifying Fuzz's appearance.

If Captain Eban Huffle was not keen to rouse the proprietor of the house before them, he was yet a man to do his duty and with speed. He led the way along a narrow place between buildings till they came to Winter Street, where the dim lamplight was bright and glaring after the preceding dark.

"Now, you understand," said Captain Huffle to Thaddeus, "she doesn't live here, not at any time of the year."

Thaddeus nodded. "If you knew where she did live—" he began.

Captain Huffle shook his head, and, without further exchange, he advanced upon the steps of Bergen's place till he realized that a dim light spilled across the stoop. "What's this?" he wondered aloud. The front door of the house was wide open.

Thaddeus walked several paces past Nicholai Bergen's house; he stopped and listened, catching the sound of human feet scurrying into the surrounding dark. Something banged inside the building, and already Jefford Paisley and the Todd *brothers* were charging up the steps.

With each passing moment, the Moosepathians felt more at sea. Attending the theater without the guiding presence of their chairman had seemed adventure enough, but then there had been the card in Thump's pocket, Winifred Peal, the gang at the brown house, and the chase over roof and fence. Still the extraordinary events of that May night were not finished, for they must pursue once more the continuing hints of Mrs. Roberto's unspecified peril. Now their odyssey took them to Winter Street, where it appeared *breaking and entering* had recently transpired.

It was not simply the open door and the banging from within that foreboded ill doings, though these were strange enough; the front hall was littered with debris, as if a great wind had blown through. A door to their left opened and an old woman peeked out before she slammed it shut and shot the bolts. Gaslight burned dimly at the other end of the narrow hall, shivering with the pounding vibrations. A second door opened, and an elderly voice called out, "I'll call the cops! I'll open a window and shout!"

"It's all right," piped Thaddeus. "We're here to help," but that door slammed shut as well.

The house seemed right enough, aside from littered halls, but it was strangely partitioned, so that they had gone from one to another to still another corridor before they found a bald fellow in nothing but trousers and an unbuttoned shirt leaning over a struggling figure. The bald man let out a frightened cry when the first of the Faithful crowd rounded the corridor.

"We're here to help," said Thaddeus again, almost in a squeak.

"Mr. Spark?" said the man, staring first at Thaddeus and then at Thump. Not only did they look alike, but now they were similarly dressed.

Thaddeus looked past the bald fellow at the wriggling figure on the floor—a gray-bearded man lay there, bound and gagged and clearly not happy about it. "Nicholai!" declared Thaddeus.

The bald man was working at the knot behind the bound man's skull, but with little success. "I'm a clerk, Mr. Spark, not a knotsman," he said.

"Nicholai, lay still," said Thaddeus. "We'll get you loose."

Captain Broad stepped past Eagleton and Ephram, a large knife suddenly appearing from a sheath beneath his coat. Nicholai Bergen went quite still at the sight of it, and in a moment his gag and bonds were cut away by an aged but steady hand. Suddenly, the air was filled with language that was highly mysterious to the Moosepathians. Mr. Bergen was upset, and rightly so, but his manner of expressing his mood was so curious to the members of the club that they were sure he must be articulating a foreign tongue.

It was Ephram who noticed the open door. A single lighted lamp stood upon the floor of the room beyond, and there was such a scatter of debris about it that he wondered the house wasn't on fire. Dutifully, he retrieved the lamp, lifting it by the bale so that the shadows about him sunk into the lower corners of the room. Behind the door, which was swung partway closed, was an advertisement that tugged at his memory.

"What are you doing in there?" came Nicholai Bergen's growl, but Ephram was already reading the bill: NEWLY ARRIVED FROM EUROPE! EXCLUSIVE TO PORTLAND'S DEERING OAKS THIS SATURDAY! "Get out of that room!" Nicholai said as he stormed past Eagleton and Jefford Paisley. He stopped in midsentence, however, and took in the wreckage.

"Was it Fuzz Hadley, Nicholai?" Thaddeus asked, but the gray-haired veteran didn't seem to hear.

"Biscuits and barnacles!" said Captain Huffle, coming up behind.

"They shouldn't have done this," said Nicholai, and there were almost tears in his eyes. "First Skelly Wilson and now—"

"Skelly Wilson?" said Thaddeus.

"Yes," said the graybeard. "He came in by that window, maybe two weeks ago, and I stuffed him back through it before he knew which end was up."

Thump was in the doorway now; he had a strange look upon his face. He and Ephram blinked at one another. Eagleton and Jefford Paisley peered in past Thaddeus and Thump.

Nicholai Bergen righted a pair of high-button shoes. He patted the silk material on one of the lower shelves. "I think they took one of the parachutes," he said quietly. "But what were they in here for?"

Other folk appeared in the hall, and the Faithful crowd pushed a little further into the small room. There were shoes and articles of clothing and books and other oddments strewn about.

"What were they looking for?" said Nicholai Bergen. "And why would anyone take a parachute?"

"Mrs. Alvina Plesock Dentin," said Ephram.

"Yes?" said Eagleton, astonished that Ephram should pronounce that name just then.

Ephram picked a book from the floor. "Why, it's *Arabella's Winter Home!*" he declared, as if he had discovered an old friend. "Here's another. *Wembley Upon the Hill!* Good heavens, Thump! The noble lady has a very keen taste in literature!" Thump leaned into the room to look at the scattered books. Nicholai Bergen was assessing the disorder and had ceased to notice the other men. "Here is one by Mrs. Penelope Laurel Charmaine!" continued Ephram. "And another!"

Thump stepped past the open door with an odd sort of caution. Having discerned that here was the room containing Mrs. Roberto's effects, he was struck with a fearful and fearfully pleasurable sort of pain. He found it difficult to breathe of a sudden. What was Ephram saying?

"Here's one I haven't read!" said Eagleton, who had joined Ephram in retrieving the scattered books and placing them on the shelf beyond the door. "It's by a favorite of yours, Thump—Mrs. Rudolpha Limington Harold." He held the book up to the light that Ephram still carried. *"The Misery of Millicent Babbington,"* he read aloud. "My, that sounds gripping!"

Ephram came to a pair of boots, absently picked them up, then said, "Oh," as if not sure what they were.

Nicholai Bergen came to life just then and abruptly took the boots from Ephram. "What are you doing here, all of you?" he demanded. "What's brought you here?"

"Was it Fuzz Hadley?" asked Thaddeus again.

"What?" said Nicholai. "Fuzz Hadley? Did *he* do this?" He leveled a dark glare on Thaddeus. "I wish I knew, believe me. They had me trussed up like a Christmas goose before I was half awake. But Fuzz Hadley, you say?"

"Here's *The Rose Beneath the Street,*" said Ephram. "That was a fine story."

"What has Fuzz Hadley to do with anything or anyone in my house?" demanded Nicholai Bergen.

"Do you know where Mrs. Roberto lives?" asked Thaddeus.

"What about Fuzz Hadley?"

"Mr. Thump and his friends," said Thaddeus, "believe she might be in some sort of danger."

"Danger? Mrs. Roberto?"

Thaddeus nodded, and soon a concise form of the tale was laid before the old man. Nicholai looked dark and gloomy. "Really," he said when they were done. He rubbed at his beard, concern clouding his face. "And this Winifred said she knew where Mrs. Roberto is?"

Eagleton thought a moment, then said, "Actually, what she said was, 'Looking for some—?'"

"Why haven't you gone to the police?" said Nicholai impatiently.

"We only had what Mr. Eagleton heard," said Thaddeus, "and wouldn't Fuzz deny it! And what were they doing here, if they haven't some plot afoot?"

Nicholai turned away. "I'll have to take stock and see what they got away with," he said. "Can't understand what they'd want with a parachute." Then he looked back at Thump. "Her card, you say?"

Thump nodded. He reached into his coat pocket to produce the article and a look of absolute horror fell across his face. He frantically patted at his pockets and searched through every corner of his habiliments. "It's gone!" he said in his deep voice. "The card is gone."

"Your wallet, Thump!" said Ephram.

"It's gone," said Thump. "They're gone."

Nicholai Bergen's face took on a fresh shade of misgiving. "Did you see the card?" he asked Thaddeus.

"I didn't think to ask," said Thaddeus.

"They must be in your coat, Thump," said Eagleton.

"Of course," said Thump, though he continued to look lost, patting his pockets absently. He said, "The important thing is to find Mrs. Roberto."

Still unconvinced, Nicholai swung his glance around the room. Jefford Paisley shrugged unhappily. The Todd *brothers* shook their heads.

"*Some*thing is going on," said Thaddeus, gesturing toward the room.

"And I'd like to know what it was," said Nicholai. "Now, get out!"

"Could you tell us where Mrs. Roberto lives?" asked Thaddeus.

"I couldn't," said Nicholai, which, they realized later, might have meant either one of two different things. "But *I'll* talk to the police if you won't, and woe betide *any*one with the wrong hand in this business."

Ephram had gotten the last of the books in some sort of order on the shelf. There were thirty or more of them, looking almost like a set of matching volumes though they were from several different authors, all but one of them women. The resemblance between the books stopped him for a moment. Nicholai was impatiently herding everyone from the room, but Ephram had halted, more out of sudden inspiration than willfulness.

"Look, Thump!" he said.

"Hmmm?" said Thump.

"Eagleton!"

"Yes, Ephram?"

"Look at the books!"

They did. Even Nicholai Bergen stopped to peer at them. "What's the problem?"

"I don't believe there is a problem," said Ephram. "But the imprints."

"Imprints?"

The rest of the crowd could not see how a shelf of books could help them and they stood shuffling in the hall, but Eagleton suddenly said, "Why, yes, Ephram!"

"Hmmm!" said Thump with specific gravity.

"What is it?" demanded Nicholai, almost fearfully. Now he wouldn't *let* them leave until he knew.

"They are all the same," said Ephram.

"The publisher," said Eagleton.

"The imprint on the bindings," said Ephram, and he pulled one of the books to show the old man. "They are all the same."

"And so—?" said Nicholai.

"It is unexpected, is all," said Ephram, taken aback by the old man's indignant manner. "Seven or even eight authors—nine!—and all from the same publisher." Ephram's own library was gleaned from a profusion of publishing houses, and unless a given shelf was occupied by a set of matched volumes—an encyclopedia, say, or a multi-volume memoir—there might be a dozen different imprints upon the bindings. He opened the book in his hands and read aloud from the title page. "*Bangor, S. Siegfried and Son, 1894.*" He considered this, then he said simply "Bangor."

Thaddeus had moved back into the room to consider the shelf of books. He peered at the *imprints*. "What does that mean?" he wondered.

"Perhaps there is some connection between them," suggested Eagleton.

"Siegfried *is* an exotic name," said Thump in his deep bass. *Mrs. Roberto*, of course, was a *highly* exotic cognomen, quite in keeping with both the woman and her occupation.

"Bangor," said Ephram again. Detectives in books often solved a case on such enigmatic hints.

"Yes," said Eagleton with special emphasis. "Bangor."

"You're going to Bangor?" said Thaddeus. He still did not understand their logic and he stood scratching his head and staring at the books.

"We will to old haunts," said Eagleton. "What do you say, old friend?" he directed to Thump.

Clearly Thump's mind was miles ahead. "To Bangor," he said quietly.

"To Bangor!" declared Ephram.

"To Bangor!" echoed Eagleton.

27. Pig in the Loft

Even into the late nineteenth century, the natural disposition of an owl to rid a barn and fields of rats and mice was often translated by farm people into something like a good omen. The silent flight, the white face and wide eyes that never seemed to sleep, the ghostly voice were easily imagined into something from the spirit world. Hercules himself respected the owl in the loft, though he might ward against the shadow of its wing for the sake of the ducks, who feared it. Flopped upon his side, the great white pig might have looked, from the barn rafters, like a ghost himself.

Hercules heard the owl touch its perch, and it was strange to the pig, experiencing the presence of that great bird from inside the barn; but it was already strange to feel the barn floor beneath him, drumming when he moved his feet, groaning under his weight. The ducks had wandered the barnyard till they found the wall by Hercules's stable, and when he grunted they quacked and muttered conversationally on the other side. The cows and horses clumped and shifted, a yearling calf *blatted* itself to sleep. There were cobwebs at the windows, and flies, desultory in the cool of the night. Starlight hardly pierced the dusty panes and the moon was low. The barn was dark.

Hercules had been feeling ill since morning (for days he had been feeling ill *since morning*), but the very thing that afflicted him also called to him and he would have eaten it, or drunk it, if it had been at hand. He did not truly understand this contradiction in his behavior, but he sensed it on some porcine level and it troubled his heart.

The slop he'd been given tonight had been peculiar; it put him in mind of the white trees down by the pond. Being a pig, he had eaten it. He lay on his side now and closed his eyes, though the dark of the barn was itself a balm to his aching head.

He was hardly aware when he began to feel better; even as the dull throbbing fell away, *he* fell away into sleep. Hercules dreamt he was in the loft with the owl and also that there was nothing unusual in this. He had wings on his feet. He could soar above the roofs of the farm and see the light in Farmer Fern's bedroom window. He could hear the man's snores rumble through the night. Hercules grunted as he slept and the ducks on the other side of the wall woke briefly and muttered back.

He was conscious in his dream of the owl's great gray wings, and it was impossible to say if they flew together or if he and the great bird were one and the same. The riddle troubled him only for a moment, for soon he was marveling at the hills and fields, the groves and stone walls, and then he was aware of a carriage stopping on the other side of the hill toward town and a foxlike presence stealing close to the house.

"He-e-e-re, pig, pig, pig, pig, pig," came a man's voice through the dark. "He-e-e-re, pig, pig, pig, pig, pig. Her-r-rcule-e-e-es."

He had a full bottle of rum with him, tucked in a pocket. Hercules could almost smell the stuff.

"He-e-e-re, pig, pig, pig, pig, pig. Her-r-rcule-e-e-es." The man was more cautious now. Where was the pig? What had changed? They hadn't killed the creature, had they? One more time, he called out softly, "He-e-e-re, pig, pig, pig, pig, pig. Her-r-rcule-e-e-es."

In the barn, Hercules grunted in his sleep and the man started at the sound. Where were the ducks? Hercules heard them, but from a distance.

"Hssst," came a voice from above. "Hssst."

"Ah, my love!" came the man's voice in a stage whisper, but further endearments were cut short.

"The pig is in the barn," came a woman's voice. Hercules had heard them many a night before in a dull and besotted haze.

"In the barn?" said the man.

"Come back tomorrow night—"

"Of course, but—"

"I'll have my things packed and ready."

"Do you mean it? Do you promise?"

"Yes, yes! Not so loud! We have guests, and I'm not sure why they're here."

"What do you mean?

"One claims to know something about pigs, but I don't believe it for a minute. They may be detectives or something."

"What?"

"Hssst. Tomorrow night."

"Oh, let me climb up for one brief kiss!"

"No, no. Tomorrow night, I'll be packed and ready."

There was the sound of a kiss, blown across the dark yard, and a man's voice muttering, "Yes, my love, yes!" Then he was gone, over the hill to his carriage, and then the carriage was gone. The window was closed. Mr. Fern's snore reoccupied the night.

Hercules grunted. The ducks muttered. Then the pig woke with a start. It was like losing the wings on his feet and plummeting to the ground with the sudden weight of a three-hundred-pound rock. The pig said something fearfully and the ducks came awake with loud squeaks and quacks. Hercules found himself on his feet, as if he had landed on them. He had to separate what was real, the darkness of the barn, from what was not, his owl-like flight, but the presence of the man in the yard crossed the borders of his dream and in the end he couldn't parse it out.

His headache was mostly gone and his supper had settled comfortably, but these things hardly occurred to him. He was worn out from weeks of indulgence not meant for man or pig. He flopped back onto his side, shaking the barn to its rafters, and fell asleep. The owl, itself startled by this tremor, lifted from its perch in the loft and vanished against the stars.

BOOK FOUR

May 29, 1897
(Morning)

28. "... Sleep in Spite of Thunder"

There was only the one Pullman car on the *Dawn Express* leaving Portland for Bangor at 4:12 on the morning of May 29, 1897. Mail and freight occupied the other twenty-seven cars, so that the engine and the coal car, the caboose and the single Pullman, made for a moderate train of thirty-one cars, two hundred and forty-eight wheels, and a single lonely whistle announcing the crossings along the first twenty or thirty miles of the coastal route before the sun topped the rim of the cold Atlantic.

Mr. Pottage, the conductor, indulged in a cup of coffee in the caboose, and joining him was the mailman, Mr. Pale, from the next car, as well as a retired brakeman, Mr. Clive, who was taking the trip to Bangor to see his latest grandchild. The east was just pinking when the conductor remembered he had some passengers, and he left the caboose's little stove and convivial railroad gossip to see to tickets. He moved without difficulty through the mail car and crossed the rattling gap to the Pullman with hardly a look down; though he was known to weave a bit when treading solid ground, Mr. Pottage's legs were as accustomed to the shimmy and vibration of these particular rails as an old salt is to the shift and sway of a ship's deck.

It was not unusual for passengers to sleep on the *Dawn Express*, but, as a rule, Mr. Pottage had but to clear his throat or say "I beg your pardon" and they would rouse themselves long enough to produce their tickets for his inspection.

There were only three passengers in the Pullman this morning; in one seat there was a long, well-dressed man with blond hair and no hat, and a shorter, stockier man with a massive beard and dressed in rougher clothes and a bowler hat; opposite these two was another well-dressed fellow, again without a hat, but with black mustaches. They were sleeping, and not only were they sleeping, but they were sleeping in a most profound and impenetrable manner. They were propped in their seats, chins upon their chests, hands dangling at odd angles or resting on their laps, and the constant shiver of the rails and the occasional pull around a sharp turn seemed only to serve them as a mother's rocking chair might her drowsing infant.

Mr. Pottage cleared his throat and they never quivered, though the man with the great beard let out a sawlike snore.

Mr. Pottage said, "I beg your pardon," and they did not stir. This time, however, the blond man gave a heartfelt sigh.

Mr. Pottage cleared his throat *and* said, "I beg your pardon," with considerable more volume, the result of which was that the man with the black mustaches produced a high-pitched whinny.

While Mr. Pottage contemplated this trio, the blond man let out another snore and the bearded man gave another sigh and the man with the black mustaches whinnied again. It was then that the conductor saw that they were holding their tickets, and without taking any great care he lifted one hand at a time, located the proper spot on the ticket gripped thereby, and applied his punch.

The three men snored, sighed, and whinnied—each very politely waiting his turn—and Mr. Pottage didn't know when he'd seen three individuals so thoroughly insensate. It was heroic, really, and he observed their slumber as one might some natural phenomenon, like an eclipse of the moon or a rainbow that will evaporate in the next minute.

The spectacle did not evaporate, though it did alter somewhat. (Rainbows fade and brighten again sometimes.) The bearded fellow's snore lessened in volume, or the mustached man raised the pitch of his high-noted whinny. The blond man left off sighing altogether and said something inarticulate, but eventually he recommenced his sighs with redoubled effort.

Mr. Pottage was fascinated. He wondered what extraordinary triumphs or failures had worn them out, and he suspected an indulgence in liquid spirits, though he could smell no telltale fumes. Mr. Pale raised an eyebrow when Mr. Pottage returned to the caboose. "Any problems?" asked the mailman. He and Mr. Clive, the retired brakeman, had got out the cribbage board, and Mr. Clive was just dealing out another hand.

"No, no," said Mr. Pottage. "Sleeping like babies." He sat in the berth opposite the game and poured himself another cup of coffee. He wasn't a young man, and there was the slightest nip in the air this morning that had gotten into his bones. The caboose was toasty enough, but he intended to stand by the stove till it would be a relief to step out on the back platform and get some fresh air. "Sleeping like babies," he said again absently.

"I've never slept aboard a train," said Mr. Clive. "Can't do it now." There were few occupations in the railroad business as filled with peril and inclement conditions as that of the brakeman.

"These fellows are doing it for you," said Mr. Pottage.

"I knew a fellow who always slept with his pillow under his feet," said Mr. Clive.

"Did you ever know Maynard Eliot?" wondered Mr. Pale. "He's a gandy dancer up the line. We were laid up just below Bangor two years ago come June and he happened to be coming through with the rest of the line crew and offered me a place to sleep. He had the howlingest hound I ever heard. That creature bayed at every sound, and then came all over nervous when there wasn't anything to bay at and he bayed some more. Why, he started in howling when we showed up and ran right through bedtime. I asked Maynard if he could keep his dog quiet, and he allowed how he couldn't sleep without it, so I went back to the station and made a bed in the storeroom." Mr. Pale shook his head. "Maynard couldn't sleep off the line without that dog howling."

"I hope his neighbors were deaf," said Mr. Clive.

"What's that?" said Mr. Pale with a hand to his ear.

Mr. Clive began to repeat himself, a little louder this time, before he realized his leg was being pulled.

"Well, these fellows were all in but the buttons," said Mr. Pottage, returning his thoughts to the men in the Pullman. He watched the game for a while, then took on the winner.

The subject of sleep continued to occupy their discourse, and Mr. Pale told of a dream he'd had some years back that concerned a summery day and small flying cows. Mr. Pottage had once read the Kickapoo Indian Dreambook, but he couldn't recall anything about flying cows.

"You wouldn't guess it," said Mr. Pale, "but it was as pleasant a dream as I can recall."

"Do you like cows?" wondered Mr. Clive.

"I like cream in my coffee and butter on my toast," said Mr. Pale, "but I've never given cows much thought."

"Flying cows sound precarious," said Mr. Clive.

The train roared through the first station and Mr. Pale excused himself long enough to retrieve the mail and *re-arm* the mail hook. "They were small things, really," he said when he got back, as if the conversation had never been interrupted. "About the size of a big dog." Mr. Pottage and Mr. Clive understood that he was talking about the flying cows.

"I saw an ostrich once," said Mr. Pottage. "There's not much flight in them, for a bird." He shifted his hat back on his head and concentrated on his hand for a moment. When he had discarded, and they had turned over a card, he added, "They'll lay an egg the size of your head."

"My wife's brother saw an ostrich at the circus," said Mr. Clive. "He considered the creature proof that God has a keen sense of humor."

"Do you think?" said Mr. Pale.

"Of course, there are those might consider my wife's brother proof enough."

Somehow they got to talking about how best to mesmerize a chicken, and it may have been this slant to the conversation, or the recurring image of those profound sleepers in the Pullman, but Mr. Pottage, who was generally known as a canny man at cribbage, mismanaged his hand more than once and so Mr. Pale took Mr. Clive on again. Mr. Pottage used this opportunity to wander back to the Pullman car, thinking the three men there would be awake by now and hoping to realize from them the cause of their deep slumber.

The conductor had a moment of sharp concern when he entered the passenger car. The three men had not moved and their snoring and sighing and whinnying had stopped. Mr. Pottage stood over them for a moment before he ascertained that they were still breathing. It was terrific how very asleep they were. He leaned down and tested the air but could detect no scent of intoxicants. The tickets were still gripped in their hands.

"Well, there!" said Mr. Pottage quietly. The *Dawn Express* was stopping for her connection with the ferry at Bath. The switch toward the river was not the smoothest and the Pullman rocked more than sometimes. Wheels braked against the rails and steam spewed along the length of the train, almost with a bang before the diminishing hiss. The sleepers did not stir, but the bearded fellow snored again, and almost like actors waiting for their cues the blond fellow sighed and the mustached man whinnied.

"They're still at it," said Mr. Pottage when the train had crossed the Kennebec and he returned to the caboose.

"Under the weather, perhaps," said Mr. Clive. He sat back from the cribbage board and filled his pipe.

"I couldn't smell a thing on them." It was the conductor's job to toss drunks from the train and his nose could be trusted, as a general thing.

The mailman and the retired brakeman followed the conductor back into the Pullman and they considered the three sleeping men with the sort of concentration one might render a hunting dog for sale or a beef critter.

"I had an uncle," said Mr. Clive, who seemed to have quite a few relatives. "He always fell asleep in the parlor and rarely got to bed. Set himself on fire with a cigar so many times that his wife kept a bucket of sand next to his chair."

"That one with the beard has some rattle in him," said Mr. Pottage. Obligingly, the bearded man let out a grinding snore. The sighs and whinnies impressed Mr. Clive, and Mr. Pale as well.

"They sure are sleepers," said Mr. Pale.

"Where are they going?" wondered Mr. Clive.

"Their tickets say Bangor," said Mr. Pottage.

Mr. Clive, and then Mr. Pale, nodded. Mr. Pottage joined them. The whistle signaled the approach to Wiscasset Station. Across the Sheepscott River the sun shone over the saltwater farms and greening fields of Edgecomb.

The whistle blew again. The man with the beard stopped in midsnore and opened his mouth, as if ready to speak. The railroad men halted. The bearded man's eyelids trembled. The railroad men held their breaths and leaned forward. The bearded man let out a furious sneeze and his two companions started in their sleep. (The three onlookers jumped themselves.) The whistle up ahead sounded louder among the buildings of the Wiscasset shoreline. They were charging through the station and could see the bag of mail on its post fly by on its way to the hook. Mr. Pale would have to retrieve it, but he was fascinated by the three slumbering men. They had passed through Wiscasset before the man with the beard closed his mouth again and recommenced his powerful snores. The sigher and the whinnier kept time.

"That's all for now," said Mr. Clive philosophically.

"What do you suppose you snore for?" wondered Mr. Clive, after he and Mr. Pottage had watched Mr. Pale get the Wiscasset mail and the three of them had gone back to the caboose.

"I don't know that I *do* snore," said Mr. Pottage. He got a few drops from the coffeepot, then peered through the spout as if he might scare some more out of it.

"No, I'm saying why do you suppose *any*body snores?"

"I couldn't say." Mr. Pottage looked up from the pot and got a tin of coffee down from the cupboard. "I haven't put much thought to it."

"I read once," said Mr. Pale, "that in the old days it was a means to assure a body's safety against wild animals while he slept."

"While he slept?" said Mr. Clive.

"Scared them away," averred Mr. Pale.

"The animals?"

"Lions and things. Back when people lived in caves."

"In caves!"

"It was in a book I read."

"People will write them."

"We had a writer on the train the other day," said Mr. Pottage. "Wandering up and down the cars. Sort of a nuisance, I thought."

They weren't sure what possessed people, but that didn't discourage them from further conjecture. The journey to Bangor was without incident if one discounts the sleeping men in the Pullman. Mr. Pottage went back to the passenger car every once in a while to take a peek at them, and sometimes the other men would go with him.

"That bearded one may be dressed in labor, but his hands haven't seen much work," said Mr. Clive. It was an astute observation, and his companions were impressed. He had nothing else to add, however, but they all stared a little harder in case some other salient detail had escaped them.

The stations flew past and Mr. Pale gathered the mail. On other trains there was often another man or two sorting as they traveled, but Mr. Pale was only expected to throw the sacks in a heap on one side of the mail car. The three passengers continued to sleep undisturbed.

The sun was almost over the station house when they pulled into Bangor, and the three railroad men were in the Pullman to watch the sleepers wake.

The train chugged into the shadow of the surrounding buildings and veered onto a freight siding before coming to the last stop.

The three sleepers never stirred.

"It's colossal," said Mr. Pale.

"It's epic," said Mr. Clive.

Mr. Pottage felt a little responsible for the slumbering passengers, and so did not like to lade praise upon them, as it might seem like boasting. "I haven't seen much like it," he did admit.

The snores, the sighs, and the whinnies continued.

"Here's a friend, perhaps," said Mr. Clive, looking out the window beyond the blond sleeper.

A rough-looking fellow had approached the Pullman from the station house and he was craning his neck and standing on his toes to see inside. After a moment he mounted the steps and poked his head past the door. "Nobody riding?" he asked.

"They're riding, all right," sid Mr. Pottage, "and that's just about the size of it."

The man at the door made an odd gesture, shaking his forefinger in front of his face, before he entered the Pullman. He saw the three sleepers, after a moment, and seemed startled.

"Thaddeus?" he said, and then: "Goodness' sakes. Won't they wake?" He was a fellow of medium height but burly as a bear; his hair was a red-brown and his face had not seen the edge of a razor for several days. He wore a green cap cocked over one ear, and he squinted when he wasn't talking. His nose looked as if it had met with accident more than once, and his large bristly knuckles bore the scars and warps of a fighter. He had a way of watching a person, as if he were *sizing them up*, which was not designed to put the object of his focus at ease.

"I was just going to nudge them," said the conductor. Mr. Pottage thought the newcomer looked like mother's own rogue.

"My word, Ephram!" declared the blond sleeper as, without warning, he sat bolt upright with wide eyes. "Where are we?"

"What? What?" said the man with the black mustaches. He produced a watch from one of his pockets and announced: "Thirty-two minutes past the hour of eight."

"Clear and fair," said the blond man. "Seasonable to warm temperatures expected. Wind shifting to the southwest."

"High tide at three minutes past ten," said the bearded man, even as he wakened. "That's Portland, of course. I must recall the adjustment for Bangor. We are in Bangor?"

"Gory!" said the burly redheaded man. He made that small gesture before his own face again, saying, "I thought you were Thaddeus!" Clearly he was amazed at the likeness, and when he let his mouth hang open he revealed a great gap between his upper front teeth. "Are you Mr. Thump?"

The bearded man turned about and looked at the newcomer. "I am," said that worthy in a deep voice.

"I could hardly miss you, could I," said the unshaven man. "I'm Thaddeus's cousin. He wired me and said I was to do what I could to help you. Couldn't imagine what was up when I got a telegram! I thought someone had died! It must be *some*thing doing. I haven't heard from Thaddeus in three years. He said I'd find someone that looked like him, but I never imagined. I never imagined." He passed Thump a piece of yellow paper. The blond man and the man with the black mustaches leaned forward and considered the telegram. Messrs. Pottage, Pale, and Clive crowded closer themselves.

PORTLAND TELEGRAPH COMPANY
Office: Grand Trunk Depot

MAY 29, AM 3:45
SYDNEY STREET 5A
MR. LEANDER SPARK

MR. THUMP MR. EPHRAM MR. EAGLETON WILL BE ARRIVING BANGOR ON 8:24 FROM PORTLAND. IMPORTANT YOU HELP THEM AS YOU CAN. MR. THUMP FAVORS ME.
THADDEUS

"You are Mr. Spark?" asked Eagleton.

"What's that?" snapped the burly fellow. He glanced from face to face as if he'd been suddenly threatened. Mr. Pottage guessed that the local constabulary had put that very question to him more than once.

"Leander Spark?" said Eagleton.

"Well, yes—" said the fellow, his voice trailing off on an unfinished note. "They call me *Sparky*," he added after a moment of silence. The railroad men gave the brute a collective squint, and with a gapped-toothed smile and a bashful swing of the head the broad fellow admitted (and with all due humility), "I'm a bit of a hand with the women, you see."

Mr. Thump nodded, though he perhaps did not quite understand what the man was expressing. Thump considered the telegram once more, then glanced at the railroad men, who each in turn looked as if he should be doing something besides looking over his shoulder.

"Everything in order," said Mr. Pottage. "I hope you gentlemen enjoyed your trip."

"Yes, yes," assured the blond man.

"Did we?" said the man with the black mustaches. "Yes. I am sure it was very nice, thank you."

"Siegfried," said Mr. Thump darkly, and he stood; one could almost see the sense of mission filling him.

The blond man stood; with only the smallest of creaks and groans, his companions followed him onto their feet and down the aisle. It seemed unfair to the railroad men that these three would leave just as the nature of their business might be revealed. Broad as a barn, Sparky lumbered after them (pausing at the door to perform his finger-shaking gesture), and the four men conferred by the siding (and very seriously) before striding in the direction of the station house and disappearing among the traffic on the platform.

"They're as purposeful awake as they are asleep," said Mr. Clive.

"Mr. Thump," said Mr. Pale. As a reader of books, he would have occasion to see that name in print one day.

"I don't mind admitting to great curiosity," said Mr. Clive.

"I suppose we'll never know," said Mr. Pottage. He'd seen many a slice of other folks' dilemmas pass through his passenger cars between here and Portland in the past twenty-two years.

29. Hercules Unbound

Sundry surprised himself and Mister Walton by sleeping so soundly. Mister Walton had to shake him, finally, and even then Sundry sat up feeling dull and sluggish. He yawned magnificently and did his best to concentrate on what his friend and employer was saying. "Excitement?" said Sundry. It was the only one of Mister Walton's words that he had properly understood.

"Yes," said Mister Walton. "I heard a terrific thumping from outside, and then a man's shout. There have been footsteps and running all through the house for the past five or ten minutes. I am sorry to wake you but I fear something terrible has occurred."

Sundry swung himself out of bed and cast about for his shirt and pants. Mister Walton was already dressed, though hastily; what is more, his face was unshaven and yet he was contemplating going out into the day. Sundry rubbed his own chin, which was considerably less fertile of beard. "I'll get dressed and see what's happened, if you want to wash up and shave."

"Oh, yes!" said Mister Walton, suddenly horrified at the thought of meeting people in his present state. "Thank you, Sundry. But if you would like to tend to your morning toilet—"

"I am *that* curious that I will put it off," promised Sundry, pulling on his boots and hastily lacing them.

Growing up outside of Mister Walton's realm of city and society, the

154

thought of appearing before the world unshaven did not distress Sundry as it did his friend; perhaps, too, he thought it amenable to arrive in the midst of whatever excitement while it was yet at its height. He did not encounter anyone in the hall, nor on the stairs. The parlor and the kitchen were empty, and yet he had no premonition of disaster or peril. He did hear some excited voices rising from the barnyard, and he followed these directly.

What he discovered when he came around the small shed was anything but terrible. The children were leaping and dancing and shouting with laughter; Mrs. Fern almost danced herself, she was so happy, and Madeline was clapping her hands. None of them had taken any more time than Sundry in pulling on their clothes or organizing themselves for the day, so that the children were barefoot, and Madeline was in her slippers, her hair unbound and flying.

During all of this giddiness Mr. Fern was laughing and scratching the ears of Hercules. Hercules himself sat up like a giant dog, looking happy, if not completely recovered, and someone had gathered a bunch of dandelions and placed these about his head so that he might have been a porcine Caesar returned from victory.

Sundry let out a laugh, and when Madeline realized he was there she ran over to him and threw her arms about his neck.

"Oh, Mr. Moss! You've done it! You've cured Hercules! Daddy hasn't been so happy for weeks!"

Sundry's heart performed several significant somersaults, but he cautiously patted Miss Fern's shoulder rather than return the hug in all its sweet splendor. She kissed his cheek then and he was all but done in; any native wit or power at his command left him and he gazed down at his feet like the rankest clod.

Madeline took Sundry's hand and pulled him toward the celebration. "Daddy!" she shouted. "Mr. Moss is up!"

"Mr. Moss!" shouted the father; the features that were by nature so long and dolorous had lifted into the peaceful expression evident in the portrait in the parlor. Mr. Fern gripped Sundry's hand like a vise. "I must confess I had my doubts about you and Mister Walton when I laid my head upon the pillow last night. I must ask your forgiveness for a lack of faith in what seemed a feeble prescription. Mister Walton must explain to me what has been remedied here." The farmer swept a hand to indicate the feted pig. One of the boys returned from the cellar with an apple, and when the oinking ungulate *scoffed* this into him, the family erupted in renewed cheers and gales of laughter.

The farmer thumped the pig affectionately on his massive white side. Hercules grunted contentedly—a low, earthy sound that carried through the human gaiety. Sundry meanwhile had hardly recovered from Madeline's gratitude.

Mister Walton arrived among them, and, truth to tell, he might not have tended to his morning rituals as cautiously as was his custom; there was a spot

of alum on his chin, and Sundry thought the grand fellow had not quite leveled the growth of beard beneath one ear. To say that Mister Walton beamed,
however, would hardly have described his expression. Madeline hurried to his
side, but she did not quite throw her arms around their portly guest as she had
with Sundry, nor did she buss him on the cheek.

Mr. Fern greeted Mister Walton, pumping his arm and thumping the
man's shoulder so that the guest's spectacles joggled down his nose.

"You must speak to Sundry," insisted Mister Walton. "It is his remedy.
He's a farm boy himself, you know."

"You are too modest," declared their host.

"He will be too *hungry*, if we don't supply some breakfast," said Mrs.
Fern. "Imagine a guest getting up in the morning without so much as a soul
in the kitchen or a cup of coffee to greet him." She may have thought it proper
to make up for her daughter's recent neglect, for she pecked Mister Walton's
cheek on her way back to the house.

Mister Walton accomplished an admirable shade of vermillion, and he
threw attention away from himself by laughing as the children danced a ring
around the giant pig. Hercules lifted his snout, his tiny eyes squinnied into
delighted slits, and he grunted with such a smile that one could imagine that
he was laughing, too. Sundry and Mister Walton could hardly conceive of the
family leaving Hercules now, and they might have wondered if he would come
in to breakfast with them, but he looked ready to lie down, after a little more
celebration, and it was agreed that he needed a rest.

"He appears tired but not forlorn," said Mr. Fern before returning to the
house. "Aunt Beatrice!" he announced when they came into the kitchen and
saw the elderly woman at the table. "Hercules has recovered!"

"Great day in the morning!" she replied. "You'd think he was going to
save us all!"

"He did save Homer from that stray dog, Auntie," said Madeline.

"Save one of us and you *do* save us all," declared the father.

"I'm not sorry he's better," said the old woman grudgingly. "The lot of
you have been walking about like condemned men." Aunt Beatrice was the
only one among them that appeared to have taken the requisite time and effort to ready herself for the day. Her hair was in a practical bun, her bonnet
was on straight, her clothes were neat, and every button was hooked.

"What was the matter with him?" asked one of Madeline's sisters.

"What was the birch-bark tea for, Mister Walton?" asked the other.

"That was Sundry's remedy," said the bespectacled guest.

"I don't honestly know," said Sundry before the question could be put to
him. "It is a remedy for glumness in pigs, is all I can tell you."

"I didn't realize that pigs were famous for being sad," said Madeline. She
glowed beautifully this morning, and her hair was still undone and a little
reckless. Sundry's head swam to be the focus of her happy regard.

"*You* said it was a cure for headache and arthritis," he offered. "He may have suffered from one of these."

"It worked," said Mrs. Fern, indicating that they should not badger Mr. Moss for an answer; either he did not know or was unwilling to tell. Conjurers were to be granted their secrets.

"Should we give him another dose tonight?" asked Mr. Fern. "Will he get worse again if we don't?"

"I would keep him indoors at night for a while," said Sundry. "And I shouldn't wonder if he *was* eating something wrong for him he won't eat it again once he's improved, don't you think so, Miss Beatrice."

The elderly woman looked completely startled at first but then recovered herself, put on a frown, and said, "Great day in the morning!"

30. The Former Mailon Ring

Mailon couldn't tell what time of day it was from his corner of the tiny room beneath the remains of the old shipping agency off Sturdivant's Wharf. He sensed that he had slept late; it was his stomach, perhaps, that told the hour. The room was pitch black, having no windows, and the walls themselves were black with coal dust. Years ago this had been the coal room for the Chalmers and Holde Shipping Firm, though presently it was the tentative residence of Burne Ring and his one surviving child. Above them (and unknowing of their presence), Pearce Eddy ran his flophouse *of the last resort.*

Burne Ring was beyond the last resort; he had fallen upon hard times, but that was years ago, while Mailon was still a baby. The child's mother was dead, and the child's recollection of the mother pale. Life was a hand-to-mouth proposition for Mailon, but he had landed on his feet the day he met Timothy Spark. As he survived into his sixth year—largely due to his meals at the backdoor of the Faithful Mermaid—Mailon's principal goal was to please Timothy Spark and, by extension, Timothy's family.

His father had not met anyone of equivalent virtue, but Mailon sometimes snuck some of the food Mrs. Spark gave him back to Burne, who sometimes ate it. Burne's primary concern came out of a bottle, the very instrument that had led him and his boy—by way of a twisting and muddled path—to this blind compartment. Burne was not an unkind man, even when drunk, and there were days when his predicament and that of his only living child weighed heavily upon his besotted heart, whereupon he simply grew quiet and remorseful.

Now Burne was breathing quietly on a plank he had dragged in from the wharfside some weeks ago; Mailon could hear him from the pile of rags in the corner. Sometimes Mailon heard other things, too, and not just the footsteps and general commotion from the flophouse above but the chatter and scuttling of other creatures endemic to the waterfront. Mailon hardly knew enough to be afraid.

It was cold in the old coal room, and damp. Sometimes, at the full of the moon, Mailon could hear the rim of high tide lapping only a foot or so below their door, and the one time that men came down to investigate strange noises they were turned back by the nearness of the water. Some folks who frequented the flophouse thought there were ghosts of drowned men below, and no one ever came down again.

On the alley side of the room there was an old coal chute that Mailon could clamber up and down, and he found this a swifter means of egress than the door and the series of ledges and plank switchbacks beneath the wharves that his father used. Mailon could scramble up this narrow passage like a spider, and, as he neared the tin cover at the top, he received his first real indication of the hour and weather; lifting the cover, he peered out like a rat from a drain. Often as not, he could slip into the alley without so much as a cat taking notice.

A narrow length of blue sky glowed brightly above the shadows and dank brick; it hurt Mailon's eyes, and he hurried up the hill toward Brackett Street with his head down and his shoulder barely grazing the corner when he turned onto the busier thoroughfare. He crossed the street, darting among the rigs and cabs, with more instinct than awareness, and hurried to the back door of the Spark family's tavern.

Things were not in their usual order at the Faithful Mermaid that morning; the door was opened wide, and the kitchen seemed more hectic and less organized. Mrs. Spark was not at her counter—hands kneading dough or cutting vegetables, arms covered with flour, and her gray-speckled hair tied back beneath a calico scarf. The older children were moving with unwonted quickness and determination in the absence of their mother's industry.

"We need more sugar," said Annabelle.

"The second cupboard," came Mrs. Spark's voice, and Mailon realized that she was seated on the other side of the room. He could just make out the top of her kerchief as she looked down once again.

Mailon waited for some time to be noticed, his stomach grumbling. He even waved at Minerva as she rushed past but didn't obtain so much as a glance. Not thinking about what he was doing, Mailon stepped inside the kitchen as he had done the night before, and, when this raised no objection, he wandered across the room and stood for a moment at the door to the backstairs. From this vantage he could catch a glimpse of Mrs. Spark meticulously sewing the rent seat of a pair of trousers. Tim's brother Davey shouldered his way in from the tavern, a stack of well-cleared plates in his hands.

Just as if he'd done it many times before, Mailon opened the door to the backstairs and climbed to the second story. Here the paying residents and guests of the tavern kept their rooms. The child peered from the landing at the comfy-looking hall, marveling at the dark carpet upon the floor, the brass sconces on the walls, and the foreshortened sight of a bucolic print hanging in its false-gilt frame on the right-hand wall. Mailon knew that the family rooms were on the third story and he recommenced his ascent.

Soon he paced the close-walled, low-ceilinged hall that bisected the third floor, peering past half-opened doors at neatly made high-posted beds and short piles of newly folded laundry on low dressing bureaus. The rooms and their furniture would have appeared simple and even crude to someone used to Mr. Thump's apartments, but the sense of permanence, the tidy warmth of these surroundings, affected the child with a hushed amazement.

Mailon stood at the threshold of a small bedroom and looked past the open door at the figure of Timothy Spark curled insensibly in his bed. It was a moment before Mailon noticed someone's feet on the floor, pointing at the bed, and when Mailon leaned a little to one side his eyes followed those feet to a pair of trousered legs, and those legs to the thickset form and bearded face of Mr. Thaddeus Q. Spark.

Mailon had some moments to observe Mr. Spark, and he thought the man appeared troubled as he watched his son sleep. Mailon stood at the threshold, and finally the man looked up and greeted him as if it were not unprecedented to have the dirty little urchin inside the house.

"Mailon," said Thaddeus.

"Good morning, Mr. Spark. Is Tim still asleep?"

"He's been stirring," said the man.

"That was *some* business last night," conjectured Mailon.

Thaddeus nodded. In retrospect, it had been a little more business than he was ready for when it came to his children, and he had been sitting in this chair thinking on the matter between dozes since he came upstairs early this morning. He hadn't rested much and looked a little billowy around the eyes.

"Good morning, Daddy," said Tim.

"Good morning, Chief," said Thaddeus.

"Good morning, Tim," said Mailon.

"Mailon?" Tim rubbed one eye, as if he might be seeing incorrectly. He sat up. His father, too, considered Mailon as if for the first time. So deep was everyone's concentration that no one heard Mrs. Spark's purposeful tread along the worn carpet of the third-story hall till she was at the doorway, mended trousers in hand and peering down at Mailon as if at a drunk in church.

"I want you to try these on," she said to Thaddeus, shaking the trousers at him. "Mr. Thump put a sturdy rip in them and I just hope I haven't shortened the seat too much."

"Is it late?" wondered Tim.

Thaddeus caught the trousers in midair and midyawn.

"And you, young man—!" said Mrs. Spark to Mailon Ring.

"I am sorry, ma'am," said Mailon.

"Be happy you're not the child of Thaddeus Spark!"

Mailon's eyes widened. He couldn't think of anything that would have made him happier. Thaddeus let out something like a growl.

Mrs. Spark said, "He refused a sum of money for his son from those gentlemen last night, but I wouldn't let him refuse it for someone else's." Mailon's expression was proof that he understood very little of this. "But I'm not giving it over to you just so it can be put into a bottle for Burne Ring," she continued despite Mailon's opened mouth.

"They were going to give me money?" asked Tim.

"Chief, you be quiet," said Thaddeus. His wife's opinions were not new to him, but her conclusions were, and he wanted to listen carefully.

"There's a corner room down the hall," she was saying, "and you can stay there, if your father lets you. I wouldn't consider *that* if I weren't ready to toss you in a tub and see what's left once you've soaked all morning."

Mailon's expression altered appreciably from wonder to trepidation.

"Timothy."

"Yes, Mom."

"They'll be needing you downstairs. If you can clamber around rooftops and rescue gentlemen from precarious circumstance then I guess you can wash dishes and sweep floors." Timothy looked a little like Mailon, his eyes wide, his mouth turned down at the corners. "Show a leg!" said his mother.

Timothy leaped from bed like a shot and scrambled into the clothes that hung haphazardly over the low footboard.

"You come with me," said Mabel Spark to Mailon, her voice noticeably softer. She laid a hand on the shoulder of Mailon's greasy coat and marched the child down the hall. "I'll have one of the boys haul water up, and you can wear some of Timothy's old clothes."

Tim pulled his shirt over his head and leaned into the hall. His small friend looked uncertain of Mother Spark's intent, and Tim (a sympathetic fellow) shouted after them, "Don't worry, Mailon! It doesn't hurt much, after she stops scrubbing!"

The socks Tim had draped over the foot of his bed early that morning were still wet, and his sneakers were stiff and damp, but he found dry socks in a dresser drawer and he yanked his shoes on with a series of squeaks (from the shoes) and grunts (from himself). He had tied his sneakers and was ready to race downstairs when his father spoke up. "Tim," said Thaddeus. He still held Mr. Thump's trousers and hadn't risen from the chair. "Come here."

"Yes?" said Tim as he approached his father. The morning had already supported more than its share of surprises and he looked doubtful about what would come next.

Thaddeus leaned forward, clutched his boy by the arm, and pulled him onto his lap. The tousled and towheaded seven year old looked only slightly put out to be treated so and knew better than to fight it. Thaddeus leaned back with his arms around Tim and held him there for the length of several long breaths. Then the father said softly, "That a boy," and let his son go. Tim raced out without a look back, only to stop and peek back into the room.

"Mr. Thump and his friends were going to give me money?" he asked.

"Go!" said Thaddeus.

"Tim, send Davey up with the tub and some soapy water," called Mabel.

Thaddeus grunted. He had spent the morning pondering the reality of people like Fuzz Hadley in relation to Tim and the rest of his family. Thaddeus had managed to keep out of reach of Adam Tweed, the former gang leader on the western end of the Portland waterfront; he had never considered knuckling under Fuzz Hadley, who had yet to secure his position now that Tweed was in jail. Thaddeus had understood the possible danger to himself but had never imagined that his children might be put in harm's way. Certainly he had never imagined that his suggestion to Tim that he *look after* Mr. Thump could end up on the roofs of Danforth Street with two of his sons (and little Mailon Ring, for goodness' sakes!) being pursued by Fuzz and his gang.

Thaddeus's first thought was to wring Fuzz's neck, and he could probably do it; but the truth was that Fuzz hadn't a notion he was chasing anyone other than Mr. Thump and his friends. Thaddeus was a practical man besides, and there was too much chance of landing in jail and too little chance that anyone better would step into Fuzz's place.

Thaddeus was more angry with himself than anyone else. There had been something of a game about his dealings with Fuzz till his sons were caught up in it; now the whole business must be *put paid* somehow.

He was still in his chair, thinking how to deal with Fuzz Hadley's strong-arm tactics, when Davey came puffing down the hall with an empty washtub slung over one shoulder and a pail sloshing in hand. "Another?" Thaddeus heard Davey say when the young man reached the corner room.

"Yes," said Mabel. "And see if your father has tried on those pants."

"Yes, yes," said Thaddeus, when Davey stopped at the door.

"Is Mailon staying with us?" Davey asked.

"Go get some more water," said Thaddeus.

The taverner stood up, when his older son was gone, and surveyed the mended trousers. They were certainly made of fine stuff, and Mabel's sewing was next to invisible. Thaddeus wondered where Mr. Thump's coat was. (The man had lost his hat.) Mabel had brushed and blotted the whole suit, and, with the seat of the trousers mended, it would be like new. Thaddeus held the waist of the trousers up to his own and considered what he would look like in them. Suddenly, he was anxious to try them on, and the coat and vest with them.

"Thaddeus!" came Mabel's voice.

"Yes, yes," he said. He had gotten out of his own trousers and was only putting a leg into Mr. Thump's.

"Thaddeus!" Mabel's voice came from the hall now.

Thaddeus Spark hopped to the door and peered out. His wife was pale, her eyes as wide as had been Mailon's only minutes before. "Mabel?" he said.

"Thaddeus," she said. "It's Mailon."

Thaddeus was struggling with Mr. Thump's trousers now, hopping on one foot while he ran the other out the cuff. "Mailon? What's wrong with him?"

"It's Mailon," she said again. "He's—He's . . . a girl!"

31. Though It Was Saturday

It was Thump's clever idea to look for the address of W. Siegfried and Son in the telephone directory at the clerk's desk in the Bangor station house. Thump was abashed at the praise that this notion inspired from his friends, and he insisted that it was got from Mr. Moss, who similarly found a haberdasher for Mister Walton several weeks ago.

The clerk at the station house was accommodating and he poured through the ledger himself, Ephram, Eagleton, and Thump looking over his shoulder and Sparky peering from the back row, as it were. Sparky admitted to having picked up a phone once or twice and turning the crank; he had listened to the voice on the other end inquiring what help it could be, but he had never attempted to put one to use. He was disappointed that his new acquaintances weren't actually going to make a call, but he thought it interesting that a person could find someone's address in this manner.

"Some months ago," said Ephram to Sparky, when they were riding in a hired cab for an address on Union Street, "I cut an item from the *Eastern Argus* that concerned the finer points of telephony etiquette. I have found it to be of immense comfort when I employ that instrument and would be more than glad to copy it out and send it to you." He expressed this with a mild smile.

Sparky received the offer with an open-mouthed sort of expression that seemed to indicate he hadn't heard Ephram properly. The Bangor man was fiddling with the cracked molding around the cab window and managed to extract a sliver of wood by his labors. Without taking his puzzled gaze from Ephram, he picked his teeth with the splinter, which activity occasioned a similar expression on the Moosepathian faces. "I've picked one of them up once or twice," said Sparky again, which seemed circuitous to them. The cab was pulling up before their destination, however, and the subject of telephones and their proper usage fell by the way.

The Moosepathians had been to Bangor once before, but that visit had been a brief one, rendered hectic by the transportation and sudden loss of a mysterious chest and cut short by pursuit of a gang of latter-day pirates. Bangor's South Station stood beside the historied Penobscott River and boasted among its sights a panoply of masts and hulls, restless upon the deep water.

They were quite pleased with it all, though the eastern aspect of the sky, as they looked over the river and the ships, was that of impending storm. It was not common to see weather looming from the east—the prevailing patterns of Maine's climate arise from western precincts—but sometimes the winds back up and the ocean pushes dark clouds back over the mainland. Eagleton thought the weather strange, and it made him thoughtful.

Traffic was brisk on Union Street; the avenue was filled with wagons and rigs, and the trolley was climbing up the hill. Stepping from their hired carriage, Thump tipped his hat to an impressive matron as she walked by, and Ephram and Eagleton also attempted to doff their missing *chapeaus*. Enough concentration was needed for this courtesy that they lost track of their feet, but after Sparky helped them up again and they had dusted themselves off they were ready to present themselves to the publisher.

There was actually a bookseller on the first floor, and they pressed their noses to the window in order to consider the stacks of publications and well-ordered shelves before entering the little door to one side and climbing the staircase to the second story.

At this threshold, as at every threshold they had passed together, Leander Spark paused to raise a forefinger before his face and shake it. Eagleton had taken note of this ritual when they got into the carriage and also when they got out, but he unconsciously displayed his curiosity at the door on Union Street.

"Doorways are very chancy places, you know," said Sparky.

"Are they?" said Eagleton.

"No place more obliging to the evil eye," said the big man, and just mouthing the words *evil eye* he was compelled to repeat the gesture.

"Really?" said an astonished Eagleton. He shook his own finger before his face just to try it out before he followed Ephram and Thump up the narrow staircase. Sparky lumbered after.

A similarly narrow hallway bisected the upper portion of the building, and they leaned back from the doors as they passed them, considering the names on each, till they came to one that announced the presence of W. Siegfried and Son: Publishers of Fine Books. Several gentle raps at this portal did not elicit any response, and the members of the club would have left the hall to discuss further possibilities on the sidewalk had Sparky not grumbled something under his breath, reached for the knob, and turned it.

The door swung open with a shudder and a creak. Ephram, Eagleton, and Thump had imagined a publisher's office to be filled with banging presses producing hills of books and bustling workers—like gnomes in an old fairy tale—with stacks of paper in their arms and pens over their ears.

"Perhaps they are closed on Saturdays," said Eagleton as they peered into the room beyond.

The atmosphere that greeted them was silent and desiccated; piles of books (not all orderly) and desks lost beneath stacks and spills of paper seemed to have drawn all moisture and life from their surroundings. Light from the windows on one side of the room spilled over the dark floor. One shadow flickered past Thump's line of sight and he started, but it was only that of a pigeon soaring between the windows and the sun. On the other side of the room stood another door.

"They appear to be closed," said Eagleton. He could see a grand bookcase to their left, and, even at this distance, he recognized the many instances of the very imprint that had instigated their journey. His eye followed the line of shelves to a desk, a conch shell precariously balanced atop a listing stack of papers and a pair of spectacles reflecting some of the light from the windows opposite.

Eagleton flinched and leaned further into the room. Past the glimmer from the windows and through the glass of those spectacles, Eagleton detected two eyes glaring in his direction. Slowly, above the spectacles, a round, balding head seemed to form itself out of the shadows, and, below the lenses, there appeared a frowning, jowly mouth and chops. The face simply stared, and Eagleton wondered if he wasn't actually looking at an extremely successful portrait of an exceedingly cheerless man.

"Good morning?" said Eagleton.

"Yes?" said Ephram.

"Good morning?" said Eagleton again.

Thump then saw the man behind the stack of papers and said, "Hmmm?"

The eyes behind the spectacles did not blink. The mouth beneath frowned a little deeper. "It's Saturday," said the mouth in a tone similar to that of a child who finds overcooked asparagus on his plate.

"I beg your pardon," said Eagleton.

The inner door opened at this juncture, and a small, bent, gray man came into view. "Mr. Mullett?" he was saying. "Did I hear a knock at the door? Oh." This last remark was made in the direction of the men in the hallway. "Good morning," said the elderly fellow. He adjusted his spectacles in an attempt to see the imaginary hats that Ephram and Eagleton were holding to their chests. "Mr. Mullett, we have guests," he pronounced.

"It's Saturday," said the voice from behind the desk.

"Certainly it is," said the older man, "but that fact does not excuse inconsideration. Come in, gentlemen. You must forgive us. We don't often take business on Saturday and habitually use it as time to catch up on correspondence and bookkeeping."

Still pressing his nonexistent hat to his chest, Eagleton stepped into the room and said, "Good morning, sir. We are the Moosepath League."

"Are you?" said the older man, his eyes wide.

"We have come from Portland," said Ephram.

The gray head nodded agreeably.

"It had never occurred to us till last night how very many of your authors we have read," continued Eagleton.

"Oh?"

"Or, rather, how very many of our *favorite* authors are published under the aegis of your company."

"It is very good of you to say so, sir."

"Not at all. We are great admirers of your imprint."

"We are searching for someone," said Thump, who was quick to get to the heart of a matter.

"Very good, Thump," said Eagleton.

"How can we help you?" said the elderly man. "I am William Siegfried." He encouraged the three men (and Sparky behind them) to come into the room. His hand was shaken diligently by each of the Moosepathians as they introduced themselves and given a puzzled sort of press by Leander Spark. (There had been an unmistakable urgency to the telegram that Sparky had received from his cousin that seemed at odds with the scene before him.) "This is Mr. Mullett," Mr. Siegfried was saying.

They greeted Mr. Mullett with polite nods.

"It's Saturday," said Mr. Mullett. It was difficult to know what he was doing before the interruption; when they left, Sparky would opine that the man had been sleeping.

"Mr. Mullett seems to think it is Saturday," said Mr. Siegfried with a quiet smile.

The Moosepathians looked concerned. They had understood that it *was* Saturday.

"May I inquire who it is that you are looking for, gentlemen?" asked Mr. Siegfried, before the day of the week could be positively identified. He was not palsied, and his eye was bright, but he might have been a little infirm; he rested himself against the desk opposite Mr. Mullett. Mr. Mullett, for his part, only continued to stare and look cross.

Thump stepped forward. He clasped his hands behind his back and raised his bearded chin. "We are in search of Mrs. Roberto, sir," he said.

"Mrs. Roberto," said Mr. Siegfried musically. He cocked his head to one side, as if assessing the name.

"Mrs. *Dorothea* Roberto," amended Thump.

"*Hmmm*," said Mr. Siegfried, which *hmmm* was very different from Thump's *hmmm*s. "Have you ever heard of a Mrs. Dorothea Roberto, Mr. Mullett?"

"I have not," said Mr. Mullett, and he finally seemed to blink.

"She owns a very many of your books," Eagleton informed the publisher.

"Oh?"

"If the collection we saw answers for her possession," said Ephram, "she owns nothing *but* your books. Or, rather, the only *books* she owns are yours." He wanted to be accurate.

"Is that so?"

Ephram nodded.

"And you say that many of *your* favorites are published by us. It is quite gratifying."

"Perhaps she is a subscriber," said Eagleton, "and you might have her address."

"Oh," said the elderly man dubiously.

"It is a long story," said Ephram. He had read this phrase in a book—in fact, in several books.

"We specialize in them," said Mr. Siegfried pleasantly.

"I found her card in my pocket," said Thump.

"Her card?"

"With only her name," said Thump.

"We fear that she may be in danger," said Eagleton.

Mr. Siegfried did look concerned.

"You see," said Ephram, "the presence of her card in Thump's pocket was mysterious."

"There was a play," said Eagleton.

"I discovered it on New Year's," said Thump.

"The play?" asked the elderly man.

"The card."

"It *occurred* to us during the play that she might be in danger," continued Eagleton.

"The woman placed a card in the fellow's pocket as a signal of distress," explained Ephram.

"Did she?"

"Why, yes! We saw it!"

"I thought you *hadn't* seen it. You said it was mysterious."

"To *him*, it might have been. We didn't stay for the third act."

Mr. Siegfried looked pleasantly confused.

Ephram tried again. "There was a woman outside the theater who looked a bit like Miss Ethel Tucker—"

"I hadn't heard of *her* yet," said Mr. Siegfried.

"She gave us the idea," said Eagleton.

"The woman outside the theater?"

"No, sir. Miss Ethel Tucker. The woman outside the theater said she knew where Mrs. Roberto was."

"She gave you the card?" asked the elderly man.

"The woman outside the theater?" said Eagleton.

"No, Miss Ethel Tucker," said Mr. Siegfried.

"No, Mrs. Roberto gave it to Thump," said Ephram. "Or some agent in her employ. Miss Ethel Tucker had a card, but she gave it to her erstwhile fiancé."

The elderly fellow continued to be amazed, saying, "I hadn't heard of *him* either."

Ephram looked extremely serious and said, "A noble fellow, I promise you, sir."

"I am glad to hear it."

"He works secretly for the police," said Eagleton. Having not seen the end of the play, he was still thinking of it in the present tense.

Throughout this discourse, Mr. Siegfried nodded and betokened the most profound interest. Mr. Mullett hardly moved, though his eyes darted from speaker to speaker, and his frown, if anything, deepened. At the mention of the police, Sparky looked highly consternated.

"Are you with the police, then?" wondered Mr. Siegfried, with a puzzled glance at the burly Leander Spark.

"Not at all," said Eagleton. "Our evidence is intuitive, except for the woman who said she knew where Mrs. Roberto was."

"But she didn't, I take it, since you are still searching for her. Mrs. Roberto, I think I mean."

"We don't know whether she knew or not. There was a large group of men who attempted to knock down her door."

"Good gracious!"

"Our thoughts exactly, Mr. Siegfried," said Ephram.

"We thought they were after the woman," said Eagleton.

"Mrs. Roberto?"

"No, the one who looked a bit like Miss Ethel Tucker."

"Who gave her card to her former fiancé. Miss Ethel Tucker, I mean."

"My word, Mr. Siegfried!" declared Eagleton. "You understand so well!"

"I'm not sure that I do. Was the large group of men indeed after the woman who looked a bit like Miss Ethel Tucker?"

"We were assured by the young boys who led us over the roof that they were not."

"Young boys? But they knocked down the door."

"The large group of men did, yes indeed!" said Ephram. "It was a good thing we went out the window."

Mr. Siegfried was no closer to understanding a word of what the three men were talking about, but he seemed to be enjoying it more every minute.

Eagleton heightened Mr. Siegfried's confusion—as well as his pleasure—by saying, "Thump bears a strong likeness to the father of one of the boys."

"Does he?"

"I should say he does!" announced Sparky. They had forgotten that the strapping fellow was standing there. "I thought it was Thaddeus himself! *Or his ghost!*"

"Is that a clue?" wondered the elderly man. He looked about till he found a chair and sat down. "The resemblance to the boy's father, I mean."

"And my cousin!" added Sparky.

"I don't believe so," said Ephram, answering the elderly man's question.

"Well, he *is!*" said Sparky, thinking that Ephram had been responding to his addendum. In a quieter tone he said, "Unless it's true Thaddeus's mother jumped the fence." He suddenly looked abashed that he had presented this theory concerning a family member and fell silent.

Wide-eyed, Eagleton said to Mr. Siegfried, "Thump saved his wife's uncle from being crushed by a piano."

"Your wife's uncle?" said the old man to Thump.

Thump looked perplexed.

"The uncle to the wife of the fellow whom Thump resembles," explained Eagleton.

"Mr. Spark's cousin," said Ephram.

"Well, I *thought* he was," said Sparky glumly to himself. There was a brief and general silence.

It did seem the moment to recapitulate, and Mr. Siegfried said, "So you are not looking for the woman who looked like Miss Ethel Tucker."

"Not at all," said Eagleton.

"We found her, actually," said Ephram, "but she was affiliated with the men who broke down her door."

"And you are not looking for Miss Ethel Tucker herself."

"We are quite sure we know where to find her," assured Eagleton. "At least, of an evening."

"You are looking for—"

"Mrs. Roberto," said Thump. "Mrs. *Dorothea* Roberto."

"And she is—?"

"A balloonist," said Eagleton.

"A balloonist?" said Mr. Siegfried.

"An ascensionist," added Ephram.

"Really?"

"A parachutist," said Thump.

There was another brief silence.

Eagleton said, "She parachutes from an ascended balloon."

"I can understand why you would be sorry to lose her," said the older man. "Mr. Mullett?"

"I didn't understand a single word," growled the man.

"I must say," agreed Mr. Siegfried, "I haven't quite placed this Mrs. Roberto, or understand exactly about the card, or Miss Ethel Tucker, or the woman who looks a bit like Miss Ethel Tucker, Miss Ethel Tucker's former fiancé who works secretly with the police, the men who broke down the door, the boys who took you over the roof, the boy's father whom Mr. Thump so resembles, or the uncle of someone who was saved by Mr. Thump from being crushed by a piano. I would ask you to begin at the beginning, but I have the vague apprehension that you already have. Perhaps you could recommence by explaining the connection between this Mrs. Roberto, for whom you are searching, and ourselves, who are your humble servants and will do for you whatever is in our power—and—or—legal."

Mr. Siegfried had proved, for an elderly man, to have astonishing powers of thought and retention, and the members of the club were themselves swimming with this itemization. They considered one another for several moments before Thump took the fore and said, "We hoped you might be able to furnish us with Mrs. Roberto's address, sir."

"And you thought I would know her address because—?"

"All her books were from your publishing house, sir."

"But if you have seen all her books, then you must have been to her address."

"Not her address, but the address where she keeps her parachuting equipment."

"Someone tied up the landlord and broke the locks," added Ephram.

Mr. Siegfried raised his hand and silence fell upon the room. "What were these books?" he inquired.

"There were a good many," said Eagleton. "And several authors."

"Nine," said Eagleton. "Nine authors. All with your imprint."

"Mrs. Alvina Plesock Dentin," began Ephram.

"Oh?" Mr. Siegfried clearly recognized the name.

"Mrs. Penelope Laurel Charmaine," said Ephram.

"*Oh?*" said Mr. Siegfried. He frowned thoughtfully.

"Mrs. Rudolpha Limington Harold," said Eagleton.

Mr. Siegfried sat up in a way that indicated real surprise.

"And there was a *Miss*," said Ephram. "Miss Marion Elfaid Plotte."

Mr. Siegfried folded his arms. "Were there any *male* authors?" he asked.

"There was the one," said Ephram.

"Mr. Wilmington Edward Northstrophe?" queried the elderly man.

"Good heavens!" said Eagleton.

"How did you know?" said Ephram hopefully.

"A lucky speculation."

The Moosepathians were impressed. "I suspect you do yourself an injustice, sir," said Eagleton.

Mr. Siegfried waved away this praise with a thin hand. "The obstacle, you understand," he said mildly, "is that even if we were to have this Mrs. Roberto's address it would not seem proper to give it out to even such well-meaning gentlemen as yourselves."

"Yes," said Eagleton slowly.

"Of course," said Ephram. They hadn't thought, and this embarrassed them a little.

"Hmmm," said Thump. It was a quandary—an ethical conundrum.

They had reached an impasse.

"I *am* sorry," said the elderly publisher.

Eagleton held up his hand. "Please, it is *our* difficulty," he assured the man. "*And* our impropriety for asking you in the first instance."

"Thank you," said Mr. Siegfried. "Perhaps if the police were involved."

"Goodness!" said Sparky, almost in a shout. "Don't do that!"

Mr. Siegfried looked from Sparky to the three Moosepathians as if he were trying to add something up. "Perhaps, if I had your cards, I could let you know, should I hear anything, that I am at liberty to pass along."

"Why, yes, of course," said the three men, in unison, and they handed the man the requested articles.

He looked at the one card after another, then said, "The Moosepath League." He rather liked the sound of it.

"At your service, Mr. Siegfried," said Ephram.

They all shook hands once again, and even Mr. Mullett was drawn into the exercise, however involuntarily. Sparky stood back from this conviviality and was the first out the door.

"What do you think, Mr. Mullett?" asked Mr. Siegfried when their callers were gone.

"It never pays to answer the door on a Saturday," said the frowning man.

"But what do you think of our friends, the Moosepath League?"

"Crazy as bedbugs!"

"Hmmm. I don't know." Mr. Siegfried went to the desk opposite Mr. Mullett's, found a piece of paper, a pen, and a bottle of ink, and began to write. "I want you to take this for me, Mr. Mullett," he said as he put the final flourish to his work. He held the paper up and waved it in the air so that the ink would dry.

"Never get anything done," said Mr. Mullett. He glowered at the piece of paper before rising from his chair and retrieving his coat.

32. Dollars to Doughnuts

Arriving streetside by the narrow stairs, Ephram, Eagleton, and Thump were conscious that the day had darkened. Eagleton pondered the clouds. It was not at all what he had expected, or, rather, what yesterday's *Portland Daily Advertiser* had predicted. He wondered what the paper had said this morning; he always felt peculiar when he was out of its reach.

"We are little better off than when we began," lamented Ephram.

"Mr. Siegfried was a very nice gentleman," said Eagleton.

"He was, wasn't he," said Ephram. The thought cheered him somewhat.

"Mr. Mullett did seem concerned about the day of the week," said Thump.

"I couldn't help but notice," agreed Eagleton.

"I would not be sorry to have our chairman's ear at this moment," said Ephram, and all three of them nodded solemnly. "And Mr. Moss's."

"I'd stand across the street, were I you," said Leander Spark. It was odd how he could all but disappear behind the fog of their concentration.

"Oh?" said Eagleton.

The husky fellow pointed. "Behind one of those carriages."

"Would you?"

For reply, Sparky walked into the street, hardly troubling to look for traffic. An oncoming horse and wagon pulled up suddenly and he patted the animal's nose as he passed by. The Moosepathians looked inquiringly at the driver, who gave them a growl and waved them on. Hanging on to their hats (or their missing hats), they hurried after their guide; the street seemed uncommonly wide and filled with horses and rigs, and their path described a good deal of weaving and bobbing before they accomplished what Sparky had managed in a straight line. The brawny fellow waited for them behind a carriage, and it was a moment before they saw him beckoning. Eagleton still held his hand on top of his head. Sparky peered at him.

"Here we are!" said Ephram breathlessly.

Sparky peered through the carriage windows at the entrance to W. Siegfried and Son across the way. "I don't *bout*, these days," he said, applying a rough sleeve to the near piece of glass.

"Don't you?" said Ephram.

Sparky thumbed his nose with his left hand and jabbed softly at Ephram with his right. "I don't fight anymore, you see."

"That's very good," said Eagleton.

"I lost my wind." A well-dressed man paused on the sidewalk to regard them with suspicion. Sparky grinned savagely at the fellow, and the well-dressed man flinched and hurried on his way. Other passersby cast glances at the four men. Sparky said, "My legs don't hold up. Don't ever let anyone tell you that the legs aren't the first to go."

"I certainly won't," said Ephram. He and his friends vaguely understood *what* the man was imparting to them but not *why*. "Thump mediated a boxing match last July," Ephram informed their guide.

"Did he?" Sparky seemed surprised. "Well, I don't *bout* these days. But I do take on collections for certain parties to whom money is owed. And I've learned something about people who owe money."

"Oh?" said Ephram.

"Aye. And that's that none of their friends or relatives ever know where they've gone to."

"That is troublesome," said Ephram. "What could have happened to them?"

"That's just it, you see," said Sparky with a wink and a toothy grin. "They haven't a notion where he is, but they'll quickly lead you to him."

"They will?" said Eagleton.

Sparky nodded and flashed his grin again. "When you're a collector, you see some interesting sights." He reached into a pocket and produced what looked like a small piece of fur.

The members of the club looked at one another, hoping that one among them had grasped what Sparky was attempting to explain, or that collectively they might somehow decipher his words. "How do they lead you to the person if they don't know where he is?" wondered Ephram.

"You just wait outside their place for a bit and, dollars to doughnuts, some friend or family of the fellow who owes money will hurry off to tell him that *someone's* been looking for him." Sparky then pointed at his own breast, and they considered his buttons for a moment.

"Extraordinary!" said Eagleton. "And without knowing where they were!"

"You wait, now," said Sparky with a wink. He was rubbing the piece of fur with his thumb. "Something was up with that old dodger."

"Old dodger?" said Ephram.

"Those names you were giving him," said the brawny man. "He was more surprised with each one."

"Mr. Siegfried, do you mean?" said Eagleton.

"And *then* he guessed that man's name."

"Mr. Wilmington Edward Northstrophe?"

"But he didn't say that he *didn't* know where these people were," said Thump. "It was simply improper for him to tell us."

"It's the same thing, ain't it." Sparky let out a chuckle that was almost a growl. "Oh, he's a canny one, he is. If I'm wrong, I'll go back up there and he'll talk before I'm through."

"I beg your pardon!" said Ephram.

"This Mrs. Roberto," said Sparky. "Does her old man owe you money?"

"Good heavens!" said Eagleton.

"She's a handsome piece of work, I warrant," said Sparky with a wink.

"Mr. Spark!" said Ephram, and Thump was straightening to his not considerable height with growing indignation.

Sparky had spotted his quarry. "Look here!" he said.

There was a hollow *thock* as Ephram, Eagleton, and Thump attempted to look through the carriage window at the same time. Rubbing their noggins, they watched a morose figure pause outside the publisher's front door. The man glowered at the street, at the traffic and the darkening sky, put his hat on his head, adjusted his spectacles, and marched up the hill.

"That was Mr. Mullett," said Ephram.

"Aye," said Sparky.

"He did seem concerned about the day of the week," said Thump again.

"Come with me," said Sparky, with a finger aside of his nose to indicate the need for clandestine movement.

"Oh?" said Ephram, but Sparky was already stalking up the sidewalk, across the street from Mr. Mullett. And so they followed Sparky in what they considered to be attitudes of absolute secrecy—crouching and skulking. It did not occur to them that they appeared to be hiding behind tree and bush when there was no cover, or that they were gathering all sorts of stares from people who passed them on the sidewalk.

Ahead of them, on the other side of the street, Mr. Mullett paused to consider something in a storefront window. Sparky stopped, and Ephram, watching Mr. Mullet with wide eyes, ran into their guide's broad back. Eagleton and Thump, too, added something to this small collision, which caused Sparky to look back with amazement at their tense and furtive postures.

"Look careless, will you!" he said.

"Careless?" said Ephram.

"I lost my hat," said Eagleton looking around him.

"You didn't have a hat," muttered Sparky.

"Yes, of course," said Eagleton. He had been touching the top of his head. "Right you are!"

Realizing that Mr. Mullett had continued on his way, Sparky let out a low sound and hurried after. The opposing pedestrian traffic parted for the former prizefighter like water before the bow of a sailing vessel, and the Moosepathians fared on in his wake. There was a certain simian quality to Sparky—his broad, broken nose and wide smile with the space between his upper front teeth, his long arms and bristle-covered knuckles; his eyes were small, peering brightly above round cheeks.

It would be a mistake, however, to equate these apelike characteristics with any lack of wit or ingenuity. Leander Spark found the members of the Moosepath League a little mysterious, to be sure, but in his own element he was as quick and sharp as a fox. If Mr. Mullett, some yards ahead and on the other side of the street, stopped to considered a window display or greet an acquaintance in his gloomy manner, Sparky anticipated him; the one man would hesitate and the other would already have paused beside a carriage or have turned about to watch his quarry's reflection in a shop window. Ephram, Eagleton, and Thump did their best to imitate him, and eventually the stares they drew were only vaguely curious.

Mr. Mullett rounded the corner of Union and James Streets, walking in a westerly direction, and Sparky let out a dark chuckle. James Street was itself busy, and much of the activity there was due to the telegraph office. People came and went and newspaper boys and street hawkers occupied their self-claimed turf, advertising the enticements of the news or their wares in competing voices. It was not the first time that Leander Spark had followed someone to this place of business.

"Wait here," he said, and then, "No, go across the street and admire the shops there so he won't eye you when he comes out." Then Sparky stuffed his green cap in a pocket, exchanged a couple of pennies for a paper from one of the nearby vendors, and gestured against the evil eye before stepping inside the telegraph office. He found a corner of the office and looked occupied with some front-page item while watching the reflected images of several customers in the highly polished brass of a wall sconce. The ticking and tapping of the telegraph and the murmur of private conversation underscored the public business of the place.

While Mr. Mullett had his turn with the clerk, Sparky went to the raised counter on the other side of the room and fiddled with a telegram form and a broken pencil.

"What's this?" the clerk inquired of Mr. Mullett.

"*People-in-pen*," said the gloomy fellow.

"Yes, well, dashes or not, I'll have to charge you for three words there," said the clerk.

"It's all one to me," said the customer indifferently.

"It's all *three* to me," retorted the clerk. "I count thirty-two words, including your *people-in-pen*. Sixteen cents."

Mr. Mullett looked as if he thought this was steep, but he might have worn the same expression if the clerk had offered to pay *him*. Mr. Mullett laid some coins on the counter and left the office.

The *tick* and *click* of the telegraph sounded in sporadic bursts as each message, in its turn, was sent up or down the line. Sparky had caught sight of Mr. Mullett's contribution to this chatter—a single piece of paper, like a dozen others, passed between the clerk and the telegrapher—and just as a man might keep track of the cup that holds the ball in a magician's game, the *collector* marked that particular piece of paper as it was processed from one man to the other, till it had been read and sent and placed on a spike with scores of its brethren.

Sparky leaned over the counter and whispered to the telegrapher, "Do you know what the time is?"

"What?" said the man at the telegraph.

"Do you know what the time is?" Sparky showed his gapped teeth in a broad grin to the customer who was then dealing with the clerk. The grin was somehow unsettling, and this customer and several others turned their heads or found something of interest in a newspaper or the charts on the walls. Leander turned back to the telegrapher, who had paused in his duties to nod in the direction of a wall clock behind him. Sparky shrugged, indicating that he was unable to read the time and a little embarrassed to admit it.

The telegrapher managed not to look too put out. He glanced over his shoulder and considered the clock behind him. "It's twelve minutes before twelve," he said, turning back, but the brawny man was already shouldering himself out the door.

33. Pants and Trousers

"Now, clear the decks!" declared Mabel Spark. "This isn't a sideshow." She waved a hand at the faces peering round the doorframe. Only Annabelle, who stood near to the bed in the corner room, seemed exempt from this dismissal.

Bobby hung for a moment at the threshold, looking uncertain and timid—not of his mother but of circumstance. "Are you sure he's a girl?" he asked.

"I guess I know the difference," said Mabel. "Or you had better hope I do. Now go!" Mabel was not a cross person, but recent events had *ridden out of rule*, and she had sensed even before this latest revelation that a firm hand was required to set things right. She listened to the last of the footsteps disappear down the hall; then she turned back to the room and the small person on the bed.

The child known to them as Mailon sat with her vigorously washed hair glowing in the light from the single window, her shoulders hunched and her eyes downcast. Small bare legs dangled beneath the hem of one of Timothy's nightshirts—what might pass for a shift—and narrow, scarred feet twisted against one another. There were red welts on the girl's limbs where she had been bitten by fleas or lice.

But their eyes and minds came back to the girl's hair; her light brown locks were cut short and uneven so that no amount of soap or grooming could tame the shaggy spikes that remained. Her face appeared (to them) to have taken on a softer appearance—an impression due partly to the removal of dirt and partly to the eradication of their former ignorance. It seemed that if one looked past that boy's shorn hair, one *could* imagine a girl of six years.

Thaddeus was as amazed (and disconcerted, to be sure) as he had been when, as a child not much older than Tim, he'd seen a bearded woman at the circus. His understanding of gender did not leave much room for indecision, and the sight of what had been a scrappy little boy transformed into an apprehensive little girl affected him with nearly as much consternation as it had his youngest children.

The former Mailon Ring looked like a prisoner in the dock expecting some terrible sentence, hardly daring to move, to breathe or even look up from the floor.

"Dear," said Mrs. Spark to the child on the bed with absolutely nothing behind the word but a kind of sad acknowledgment.

The little girl did not look up.

"Dear," said the woman again, more as address this time than comment. She did not think to sit, or to scooch down, or otherwise put herself at a level with that small, down-turned face. "Do you understand that you're *not* a boy? That you *are* a girl?"

"A little," came a small voice. It was a moment before they understood what she had said.

Mabel looked to her husband, but Thaddeus was staring at his own feet. Annabelle stepped in, leaning down just a bit and saying, "How long have you been—? I mean, how long have you—?"

The blue eyes looked up, though the girl's head hardly moved. "As long as I remember."

"But why?" said Mabel.

"Dad says boys aren't hard put like girls," pronounced the waif.

"Well!" breathed the mother.

Thaddeus cleared his throat and raised his head.

"He says," added the child, "that if something happens to him, I'll more likely make it if I were a boy."

Mabel sat down on the bed, only to relieve her shaken frame, but the effect was to make her a shade less daunting to the child.

"Was that a bad thing to do?" asked the little girl.

Mabel patted the bony knee and said "Shush." She had tears in her eyes.

"I think," said Annabelle, "when she grows her hair out, and we get some of Betty's old dresses from the back closet, she'll be pretty as can be."

This pronouncement was meant as comfort, but the child's face revealed a confused aversion. "I've never worn a dress," said the little girl, equally astonished and frightened.

"You can't dress like a boy any longer," said Mabel firmly. "Certainly not if you're going to live here."

The little girl looked out of breath and ready to cry. "I can't climb a tree in a dress."

"I should say not," said Mabel.

Thaddeus cleared his throat again, and his wife looked up to invite his opinion, but he had only been reacting to a sudden understanding, and that was of how much a girl, or a woman, gave up by putting on a dress. He'd been rather fond of climbing trees in his youth, and might be climbing them still if his age and girth (and, ostensibly, his dignity) hadn't stopped him.

"Annabelle never climbed trees," stated the mother in a quiet tone.

Annabelle looked as if she might have something to say about this but remained silent.

"I won't be able to play with Tim anymore," said the girl.

"Nonsense."

"He doesn't like girls much. He told me so."

Annabelle let out a noise that was part disgust, part amusement.

"He'll like them if I tell him to," said Mabel. "He may not be playing a great deal himself in future if it means I have to worry about him chasing over roofs in the middle of the night."

The memory of that adventure altered the little girl's face the slightest particle. "That was *some* business," she said.

Mabel had been complaining all morning about "what boys get up to!" but this assertion from the little girl rendered the matter in a separate blush. Suddenly, she was proud of the waif, and this sensation left her almost as confused as Thaddeus. "Good heavens," said Mabel. Her husband cleared his throat a third time, and she said, "Thaddeus, will you stop grunting and say something?"

"What do we call—" he began before finishing a little weakly with "her?"

"You have something there," said Mabel. "What do we call you, dear?"

The former Mailon looked down at her feet again. She was receiving more attention than she could ever recall, and she was finding it a mixed blessing.

"Your poor departed mother must have given you a name," said Mabel. "She didn't call you Mailon."

"Melanie," said the little girl, looking the slightest bit defiant of anyone who might dare laugh.

Mable and Annabelle looked at one another, then at the child before them. "Why, that's beautiful!" said Annabelle.

Melanie reacted to this particular praise about as happily as Timothy would have. "Do I have to wear a dress?" she asked as if she had been condemned.

"You had better get used to it, Melanie Ring," said Mabel Spark. "Particularly if you're to live—"

"Not yet," came Thaddeus's high-pitched voice.

"What?" said Mabel, the snappishness in her voice rising more from surprise than anger.

"Not yet," said Thaddeus, his hands behind his back. He had been thinking, among many other things, that he might have treated Mailon Ring more gently if he'd known her as Melanie Ring, and it disturbed him. He'd never been unkind to the child, it was true, but he had seen the little boy as simply another peripheral character in the life of the tavern—a character who would probably vanish as quickly as he had appeared, with no explanation given, and none asked. A little girl he might have looked after more closely, which distinction was the other side of the coin but also part and parcel with her own father causing her to disguise herself in the first place. "It will do her good—and us, too, I think—if we get used to the idea a bit at a time."

Melanie looked as if a great weight had been lifted from her. Annabelle winked at the little girl.

"I don't know, Thad," said Mabel. She was a woman of proper upbringing, and the idea of knowingly allowing a girl to dress in boy's clothes seemed highly inappropriate.

"Not yet," was all he said, and the subject was closed for the time being. "Chief!" called Thaddeus. "Tim!" The father had not heard his youngest child's footsteps among those leaving some moments before.

Guiltily, Tim poked his head in from the hall.

"Come in, now, and say hello to your friend," said Thaddeus, sounding more sure of the situation than he felt.

Tim cautiously stepped into the room. His parents had wondered if he had ever suspected (or perhaps even known) about his friend's secret, but they could see now that he had not.

"Are you a girl?" he asked. He might have been asking an apparition if it were a ghost.

"I guess so," said Melanie quietly.

"Oh," said Tim, then to his father, "Can she still climb trees while she's dressed like a boy?"

Thaddeus almost chuckled, though he did his best to look solemn.

Mable decided to ignore the question—in fact, to derail it, so to speak. "Those trousers fit, I see," she said.

Thaddeus considered Mr. Thump's pants.

"My sewing hasn't suffered," said his wife with audible pride.

Thaddeus peered down at his own backside. "Can't see it from here."

34. Something Past the Hour

The wagon bumped and joggled over the fields behind the Ferns' roan mare, riding the green ridges and near to plummeting into the little dales where streams ran among the poplar and the willow. Behind the wagon ran the children, and behind the children strolled Madeline Fern and Sundry Moss. Mister Walton rode alongside Mr. and Mrs. Fern and in front of Hercules, whose celebratory picnic this was. The pig sat up, when he could keep his balance, and grunted at the children who ran and shouted behind. Aunt Beatrice had seemed pleased to be left off at the neighbor's.

May is famous in the State of Maine for blackflies and impatience, as spring enlivens the least of creatures to pester beast and human alike, and summer often stands just out of reach but tantalizes a body with a sweet breath now and then and a modicum of buds to dot the waking fields. May of 1897 was more summerlike than some, and since the wind had seen fit to come around to the west and display enough life to keep the bugs clinging to shelter, the Ferns deemed it a propitious day to venture an outing.

From certain heights they had glimpses of the Abagadasset River and, further on, the broader reaches of the Kennebec and the crest of Swan Island.

With the wind at their back, the climbing sun in their faces, and a happy pig among them, the world seemed unhindered and simple to grasp.

Sundry had the ability to entertain a crowd or a single person by way of the stories he told, and he had Madeline laughing about his cousin, who, at the age of thirty-eight, was nearly shot for a woodchuck in the act of sneaking with a May basket through the garden of a querulous spinster, and then Madeline was gasping at his rendition of his father's near legendary (at least in Edgecomb, Maine) battle of fisticuffs with half the Blamey clan of Mount Hunger. In short, he had risen above his earlier fit of cloddishness and thoroughly charmed the young woman.

By the time they caught up with the front of the party, the linen was spread upon a knoll above the river, the children had gone with Mister Walton to the water's edge, and Hercules had trundled down the board ramp that Mr. Fern laid out for him. The pig quickly found the shade of a crabapple tree, where the winy remnants of last fall's decaying fruit encouraged him to root the ground and toss dirt over his shoulders.

A sweet, almost doleful, note sounded the clear air. Mr. Fern stood upon the flat height above the water with a flute to his lips and piped a gentle melody as the sun glanced from the instrument. He had his eyes closed—his features sad with the beauty of the song he produced—and his wife, too, listened from beneath a lowered gaze. After a time, a single voice rose up to meet the graceful notes.

> "*Oh, wherefore did God in His power so wise,*
> *Occasion a pasture like Bonniekell Rise,*
> *And impart such a blessing with His gracious hand,*
> *As Bonniekell Brook to water the land?*
>
> *What were His thoughts, and what was His notion,*
> *That took me to Bonniekell, far 'cross the ocean?*
> *What was His reason? Why did His grace*
> *Shine like the sun on this sinner's face?*
>
> *Oh, wherefore did God, in His wisdom so great,*
> *Render me power to raise an estate,*
> *To harrow the earth and raise up my bread,*
> *And fashion a cottage to shelter my bed?*
>
> *What were His thoughts, and what was His notion,*
> *That took me to Bonniekell, far 'cross the ocean?*
> *What was His reason? Why did His grace*
> *Shine like the sun on this sinner's face?*

Oh, wherefore did God, from His throne up above,
Raise up the maid who accepted my love,
Who waits by the door, and sees with her eyes,
The flourishing glory of Bonniekell Rise?'"

The flute and Madeline's voice carried over the knoll and even as far as the water's edge; the children slowed in their tracks and looked up the slope of the shore to see their sister singing with the clouded sky behind her. Mister Walton looked up as well, but then gazed down at his feet as if this were something too intimate for any but the nearest family.

If such compunctions visited Sundry, other sensations transcended them; he watched Madeline, herself like a figure in song, as she mingled her voice with the flute's music in the most natural and candid manner. She, at least, had no compunctions about being watched—she hardly understood that she was—and the very act of singing seemed as true to her as it would a lark or a robin, or a bluebird perhaps, as she was dressed in blue and her hat was wide with frills of white and blue.

The ensuing silence was only broken by the wind in the grass and the sound of Hercules grunting his satisfaction. Mr. Fern's long face beamed, and his wife reached up to take his hand. Madeline flashed a brilliant smile at Sundry, who was not prepared for such a blow.

⚜

Earlier in the day, Mister Walton had sidestepped Mr. Fern's questions regarding pigs, intending all along to find the proper moment to confess his ignorance and to apologize for anything he might have done or said to cause such a misconception. The Ferns, however, had interpreted his gentle evasions as professional reticence; or perhaps (they wondered) his history with pigs was wrapped in some untold tragedy. Nothing if not polite, they decided to talk about anything *but* pigs, and Mister Walton's opportunity of making a gracious confession seemed to grow ever more remote. They all took turns visiting with Hercules, however, and the great pig lay in the shade and ate very well from the plate that Mrs. Fern made up for him.

Mister Walton was a little lost in the day, as it progressed, and Sundry was not sure if he needed to be pulled from reflection or allowed to bask in it. The bespectacled fellow joined in the conversation and food happily enough, but he grew thoughtful, and it did seem too bad that Phileda McCannon was not there to share the day.

Sundry felt a pang of concern for his friend, though he suspected that seeing Miss McCannon again would set the man aright quickly enough. After their picnic, Mister Walton was content to sit in the sun with his back against a wheel of the wagon and listen to the chatter of the family and the ripe notes of Mr. Fern's flute.

The wind that riffled the grass and chopped the surface of the river, paused, like a strange and dreamy portion of tide between ebb and return. Mr. Fern put down his flute, and the company grew silent without the awkwardness that often attends a lull in conversation. After some moments, Mrs. Fern said, "It's either twenty past the hour or twenty before."

"Is it?" said Mister Walton. It seemed an odd assertion.

"When everyone goes silent, and conversation dies, it is usually twenty past the hour or twenty before."

"I never knew," said Mister Walton.

"Do you mean," said one of the Fern daughters, "that it might be either twenty past or twenty before, or that you can't remember which it's supposed to be."

Mrs. Fern looked doubtful. "I'm not sure," she admitted. "I only know that's what my mother used to say." She considered the question some more. "I'm not sure which *she* meant, now that you ask."

"It's twenty minutes past, I think," said Sundry. He had been interested in the contentment around the picnic spread. The Ferns were not *simple* people, but they had been made happy by simple means. Hercules was more like his old self, and they were pleased to celebrate. It seemed obvious to Sundry that some agency had been behind the pig's recent gloom; the Ferns did not seem to consider it, or to consider it worth fretting about. Sundry imagined that someone nearby had wished poor Hercules ill or wished him out of the way and that the symptom had been dealt with but not the cure. The young man looked placid, however, and offered his own theory about the recent *silence*. "It was when Lincoln died, wasn't it?" he said. "Twenty minutes past the hour?"

"I have heard of something like it, now that you tell me," said Mister Walton, who had seen the shadow of something pass over his friend's face.

Mr. Fern then spoke.

> "'And people all across the land,
> Have grown, of late, to understand,
> That silences will sometimes last,
> Whene'er the clock meets twenty past;
> Since Lincoln lingered till that time—
> The mind so keen, the heart sublime—
> Was stilled, and by God's leave,
> Half-knowingly the people grieve,
> Or maybe simply sense the essence,
> Of Uncle Abe's consoling presence.'"

He finished this bit of verse with a small chuckle.

"I've never heard that," said Mrs. Fern.

"It's in the children's primer."

"It is a dear thought," said Mister Walton.

"And who belongs to it?" wondered Sundry.

"The poem?" replied Mr. Fern. "I can't recall who wrote it. Not a distinguished bard, and not a great piece, though the sentiment is worthy. One of the boys at school suggested that it was well we hadn't *many* great men like Lincoln, else we'd be silent all the time."

"Vergilius!" admonished his wife, as if this were a bit of sacrilege.

"It is now seventeen past twelve, by the way," said Mr. Fern. "Though my watch may be slow."

Mister Walton coughed once, and quietly; he had resisted looking at his own timepiece.

"And I believe," continued Mr. Fern, "that Lincoln died at twenty-*two* minutes past the hour, but the clock at that house might have been fast."

35. A Bully for Jasper Packet

"Here we are, now!" came a low growl, and the Moosepathians jumped and shouted as one. They had been taking their guide quite at his word and were attempting to admire the shopwindows on the other side of the street. Sparky squinted at them. "What'd I tell you?" he said, and held out a piece of paper without further comment.

The members of the club were then quickly immersed in studying a telegram form that had been filled with a close, pragmatic script.

BANGOR TELEGRAPH COMPANY
James Street Office

MAY 29, AM 11:36
DRESDEN MILLS, MAINE
MRS. JUDD PILICAN

FOUR MEN VISITED THIS MORNING, ASKING AFTER YOUR NINE PEOPLE-IN-PEN COLLECTIVELY. REFUSED THEM INFORMATION AS TO ANY WHEREABOUTS, BUT THOUGHT IT STRANGE AND THAT YOU SHOULD KNOW. LETTER TO FOLLOW.
WILLIAM SIEGFRIED

"Whatever *that* is," Sparky added, pointing a blunt forefinger at the hyphenated phrase.

"Good heavens!" said Eagleton.

"People-in-pen?" said Ephram. Sparky squinted at him as if he'd cursed.

"Nine of them?" said Thump, counting on his fingers.

"Dresden Mills?" said Eagleton. He was attempting to read a map in his mind that did not, as it turned out, include a Dresden Mills.

"Nine of them," said Thump. He looked up from his hands.

"Good heavens, Mr. Spark!" said Eagleton. "How did you come by this?"

"Good heavens!" declared Ephram.

They gaped at the husky Mr. Spark, who flashed his gap-toothed smile; then they looked at one another, hardly able to articulate the fear that this communication was got to them by less than honorable means.

"It hardly seems right to make use of it," said an astonished Eagleton.

Leander Spark's smile began to fade.

"You are right, of course, Eagleton," said Ephram, who was amazed that Sparky could have done such a thing. "And yet, if Mrs. Roberto is—"

"If she is in peril," finished Eagleton.

They looked to Thump, whose dark expression found its way through the beard before it. "Dire circumstances oblige us to dire means," he said in a dark and dire voice. A moment's silence followed this pronouncement. "We must return someday and make this right with Mr. Siegfried," said Thump.

"What?" said Sparky.

Eagleton put a hand upon Thump's shoulder. "Of course, my friend."

"And we will make it right with Mrs. Pilican, whoever she may be," said the bearded Moosepathian.

Ephram seemed to grow larger with the thought. He, too, gripped one of Thump's shoulders but said nothing and only nodded and blinked.

"To Dresden Mills!" declared Eagleton.

"Hold it there!" declared Leander Sparky in a threatening tone. The members of the club turned back to him, but he was spying something or someone else down the street. "What's the trouble?" wondered Eagleton, craning his neck.

"I just spotted a liability," growled the burly fellow. He did not wait for the passing crowd to part for him but reached with both hands, as if he were opening a double-hung gate, and shoved several men aside.

"A liability?" said the three friends, hurrying after, weaving among the oncoming traffic, and even begging pardon as they helped one fellow back to his feet and dusted off another gentleman's coat. When they caught up with Sparky on the busy corner of Union and James Streets, he was looming over a man who regarded the thickset collector with an uncertain frown.

"I was told you were out of town," Sparky growled, as he caught himself a handful of the man's back collar.

"Well, I was, Sparky, I was," said the man, and though he appeared sensitive to the immediate situation he did not seem at all like a man near panic. "I just got back in, thank you," he said. He had an old brown cap that he tipped gallantly while Sparky lifted h'm onto his toes. His lanky, brown hair needed cutting, and his clothes begged repair or retirement. He was a singularly un-prepossessing fellow, with sleepy eyes and large teeth. He wore spectacles, the lenses of which were as spotted as his clothes; they sat a little crooked on the bridge of his nose as Leander hoisted him by the collar. "I came back to settle up," the ragged man was saying.

Sparky gave the man a little more lift with a sudden jerk and growled, "Which is why you sprung like a cat, the moment you caught sight of me."

"No, no!" declared the fellow. "You only startled me, is all!"

Sparky grinned unpleasantly. "What? Little Leander Spark?" The grin went out as suddenly as a candle. "Look at you! I don't know how you gulled even a *penny* out of the boss."

"I thought it very liberal of him, to be sure," said the man, and Sparky shook him again.

Ephram, Eagleton, and Thump watched in astonishment. A few other people stopped to see what was amiss, but on the whole, men and women alike hurried past with their eyes averted.

"*You* come with *me*," said Sparky, and, dropping his catch, he urged the man back down James Street with a shove and a shoe.

"Good heavens, Ephram!" said Eagleton.

"Yes, my friend!" agreed Ephram.

"Thump!"

But Thump had walked around Sparky's broad form to insinuate himself between prey and predator. "I beg your pardon, Mr. Spark," he said, "but what is the meaning of this?"

"What are *you* doing here?" declared Sparky. "You got what you wanted!"

"But what do you intend to do with this man?" demanded Thump. Ephram and Eagleton each strode up to one of Thump's shoulders and appended serious expressions to this question.

Sparky was not tall, but he could stare right over Thump's head at Ephram and Eagleton, and as broad as Thump was he looked like a calf to Leander Spark's bull. "Thaddeus asked me to see after you fellows," explained Sparky evenly. He nabbed the ragged man's collar once again. "I've done my part, but now you're interfering with business."

"*Business*, sir!" said an affronted Eagleton. "What *sort* of business we might ask!"

"Very good, Eagleton," said Ephram.

"Thank you, Ephram."

"It's my business, if you must know," stated Sparky flatly, "to wring five dollars from Jasper Packet here, or take him with me so he can explain to my boss why not."

"Yes, please!" said the man in Sparky's grip with sudden and surprising passion. "Take me to the boss! Anywhere but here! Please!"

Sparky's brow furrowed.

Without really thinking about it, Ephram reached up and laid a hand on Sparky's arm; Eagleton stepped closer to the scene, but it was Thump who spoke. "Mr. Spark," he said. "You will put that man down, or I will be forced to strike you!"

"What?" said the astonished Sparky.

"Please, take me with you!" Jasper Packet was saying to Sparky in a low but fervent manner.

Something else occurred to Ephram, and he said, "Five dollars, Mr. Spark?" He was going through the contents of his wallet and producing the requisite bills. "It seems little enough reason for rough behavior. There. That's the amount you quoted, sir?"

"Yes," drawled Sparky. He considered the funds held out before him, but suspiciously.

"You *must* take me with you!" hissed Jasper Packet. He was tugging at Sparky now, and looking more desperate than ever, which seemed very odd. Passersby could not hear what he was saying, perhaps, but they noticed his agitated expression as he clutched at the burly fellow.

"What?" said Sparky. He cast another frown at the ragged man, then snatched the money from Ephram's hand and began to count it. "You're daft as a mole, Jasper. You'd better thank this fellow before he changes his mind, and *I've* a mind to give him the opportunity! And *you!*" he said to the others.

"What is it, sir?" said Eagleton.

"You'd do well to stay out of business that doesn't concern you."

"Business?" said Ephram, sounding much as Eagleton had. "Does your *mother* know what sort of business you're in?" His chin was up, his chest out, and his mustaches were terrifically agitated.

"*Mother?*" growled Sparky. He registered the most extraordinary surprise. With a great huff he swung his head away and proceeded to follow it with the rest of his brawny physique. His former captive, however, was not be let go so easily.

"Sparky!" declared Jasper Packet, clutching at the man's arm. "Don't leave me here! Please. Whatever you do, don't leave me!"

"What?" snarled Sparky. He glared down at the man and shook him off.

"Take me to the boss, Sparky! I'm in awful peril!"

"Peril?"

"That man!" said Jasper Packet in such a tiny, fearful voice that the members of the club could barely hear him. "That man! He's after me!"

"What man!" Sparky craned his neck and gazed about them. Ephram, Eagleton, and Thump were almost dancing with splintered nerves as they looked for the man who was after Jasper Packet.

"That man!" said Jasper again. He pointed with a shivering finger down the street, but as there were any number of men at several distances from the present scene, it was impossible to say which one he meant.

"Which?" demanded Sparky.

"Him!" said Jasper, and for a moment he seemed a little unsure. Then a particular fellow crossed the street corner to walk in their general direction and Jasper shouted, "Him! With the brown bowler and the gloves!"

"Him?" said Sparky. The man looked like nothing more than an average citizen, and a singularly unthreatening one. "He doesn't look like he's after you." Sparky eyed the oncoming fellow with his trademark squint.

"That's just it," said Jasper, grasping onto Spark's sleeve. "He wouldn't! He's a dead man, Sparky!"

"Dead man?" said the burly collector. His face blanched with the notion and he pulled from his pocket the bit of fur that he had been rubbing earlier in the day.

"I killed him last night!" declared Jasper.

Ephram and Eagleton let out odd, birdlike sounds, and Thump said, "Hmmm?"

"You're crazy!" said Sparky, vigorously rubbing his piece of fur.

"I did!" asserted the ragged man. "I didn't mean to but I did! It was an accident, I promise you, but before he died he said he'd get me! It was horrible, Sparky! Horrible! Look at him!"

With this outrageous proclamation ringing in their ears, Sparky and the Moosepathians could indeed see something sinister about the approaching fellow; the man had little or no expression on his face, and his progress hardly seemed to deviate for traffic, or alter in its pace. Sparky glanced up at the sky, which he thought grew darker even as they spoke.

"Take me with you!" pleaded Jasper. He pawed at Sparky's sleeves and coat. The big man inched away. "He'll kill me!" the ragged man was shouting. "He said he would! It'll be terrible, horrible! His cold breath! His hate-filled eyes! I buried him with my own hands, but he rose from his grave to kill me and anyone in his way!"

Sparky was swatting at Jasper's hands the way one would swat at a swarm of bees. The big fellow backed away a step or two, then, leaping a third step, he turned, charged down the street, and ducked into an alley. Jasper did not pursue him, but he shouted after Sparky, "Don't leave me!" Strangely the fear had left his face.

Ephram, Eagleton, and Thump were backing away from the mysterious figure. The crowd that had gathered watched the scene with interest, and a little apprehension, but the man, whom Jasper Packet claimed was pursuing him for postmortem revenge stopped briefly to glance in their direction, then carried on down the street—whereupon Jasper Packet looked remarkably complacent and said, "That's that."

"That's *what?*" said Eagleton.

Jasper let out a short laugh. "Oh, your faces!" he declared.

"I beg your pardon," said Eagleton. He and Thump put their hands to their cheeks.

"I don't think that man was after you at all," said Ephram.

"He didn't appear," agreed Eagleton.

"Gentlemen, gentlemen," said Jasper Packet. "How very kind of you to take my part against that great ape! And you, sir!" he said. "My hearty thanks." He held out several dollar bills to Ephram, who peered at them as if they were some previously unreported specimen of life. "I think it's all there," said the ragged man.

"All there?" said Ephram.

"Your money."

"But that man," said Eagleton. "You said you'd killed him."

"Never seen him before in my life. He gave me a turn, though."

"Did he?"

"I was afraid *he* was going to turn at the corner, and he did look my best applicant."

Eagleton was the first to understand that the recent clamor had been something of a ruse. "But why did you carry on so, when Mr. Spark had been recompensed?" he asked.

"At first, I only meant to get away," said Jasper, "but then, once he'd been paid, I had to detain him long enough to get these back." He shook the bills at Ephram. "I do cherish the loan, Mr.—"

"Ephram," said that puzzled worthy. "Matthew Ephram."

"Jasper Packet," said the ragged man as he shook Ephram's hand and accepted introductions from Thump and Eagleton.

"What's going on here?" inquired a new voice, and a police officer loomed where Sparky had moments before.

"Only a bully, officer, getting a bit of his own," said Jasper. He took hold of Ephram's hand and pressed the bills into it.

The officer considered the four men—Thump in the clothes of Thaddeus Q. Spark, Ephram and Eagleton in the togs of well-to-do gentlemen, and Jasper Packet in near rags. "You had better move along," he said quietly.

"Dresden Mills!" said Eagleton, suddenly bringing the club's collective mind back to their principal objective. He piloted the way up James Street with Ephram and Thump close behind. It seemed very natural that Jasper Packet should accompany them, which he did, waving back at the officer who watched them dwindle with the sidewalk traffic.

"So that man you indicated was *not* after you," said Ephram, wanting to be clear on this subject.

Jasper Packet let out a short laugh. "I wouldn't have been pawing after *Sparky* for protection if he had!"

"But this money?" said Ephram.

"Yes?" said Mr. Packet.

"You took it from Mr. Spark's person," said Ephram. They had stopped again on the sidewalk.

"Yes?" said the ragged man. "What? You're not thinking of giving it back to him?"

"But he was owed five dollars," said Ephram.

"Go ahead," said Jasper. He looked grim. "Go catch him up. Maybe you can help him throw an old woman out of her house, or take the last piece of bread out of some kid's mouth."

The Moosepathians were horrified. Their mouths hung open and they gaped at one another. "We will follow this up," said Ephram, "when we return to make things right with Mr. Siegfried."

"Yes, Ephram," said Eagleton. "Very good."

They recommenced their progress down the street with Jasper in tow. Ephram gripped the money in his hands, and on the way to Bangor's South Station, he threw it into the collection bucket of a Salvation Army sergeant.

"I am feeling a little peckish," said Ephram.

"Hungry, are you?" said Jasper Packet, taking the lead. "We can do something about that," and he began to sing:

> "*Turnips and taters and carrots for stew,*
> *And dumplings and brisket will be in there, too;*
> *Apples with nutmeg cooked up in a pie,*
> *And heapings of hot-bread as tall as your eye!*
>
> *Oooh! The goose is stuffing!*
> *Oooh! The plum is duffing!*
> *Gather round the table, gents, for so the vittles go!*
>
> *Onions and scallions and sizzled up trout,*
> *Sweet stuff and hard stuff to bring on the gout;*
> *All you can eat is all you can get,*
> *When Maudie's done cooking and table is set!*
>
> *Oooh! The turkey's dressing!*
> *Oooh! The water's cressing!*
> *Gather round the tables, gents, for so the vittles go!*"

In the midst of this rendition, Jasper Packet marched to the fore of their little procession, delighting them with his stouthearted baritone and conjuring visions (which were, alas, visions only) of grand repasts with his verse.

36. Five Tins of Tecumseh

"Drat!" said Deborah Pilican. Her right hand was aching from gripping the pen so long. *Well, I was in the midst of a gripping scene*, she thought wryly as she tried to shake the pain from her old knuckles.

Fale's voice came from the kitchen. "Is it my sister I hear begetting such language?" He'd been banging at something in there, and she was half curious to know what he was up to.

"Yes, it is," said old Mrs. Pilican. She sounded about equal parts irritated and amused, but not very contrite.

"I wouldn't put that in your next book, if I were you," called Fale. "You'll consternate your readers."

"It's my hand," said Mrs. Pilican. She rubbed her swollen knuckles.

Fale came through the pantry and stood in the doorway. He was three years her senior and subject to his own bouts of rheumatism; it was not like Deborah Pilican to complain, however, and he viewed her with concern.

"And my handwriting!" she exclaimed, before looking up and seeing him. "These days it looks worse than hen scratch!"

"Maybe Dr. O'Hanrahan has something for it," he ventured.

"Something to put me to sleep," she replied tartly.

He made a short, low sound—sort of a chuckle—and said, "Old Dad used to use the hot wax treatment," more by way of reminiscence than advice.

"I don't remember."

"Many's the cold morning he stood out at the backdoor with a lighted candle dripping hot wax over his hands. I used to watch him from my window, wondering what he was up to. He saw me once and called me down, whereupon he lectured me on the power of hot wax and how he got it from his grandfather—Old Stout Paul, he used to talk about—who'd come over from Bristol."

"It sounds painful," said Deborah.

"That's what I thought. I told him it was like pinching yourself to stop a toothache, and he drove me off."

The image made Deborah laugh.

Deborah Ann Field Pilican was a button of a person, no bigger than a kitten when she was born (her father had claimed) and struck with poliomyelitis (as the affliction would later be termed) when she was nine years old. She had been sent to the country—the village of Albion—where her mother's cousins might watch over her recuperation in the country air. Her mother died before she came home, and she was more or less adopted by her relatives, making occasional trips to Portland to see her father and siblings.

The young Miss Field regained her feet, after many months, through much struggle and heartache. The doctors had said she would never walk again, but Cousin Deborah, for whom she'd been named, wouldn't hear of it. The girl became a young woman, limping only slightly when she met Judd Pilican at the harvest fair; she had regained her feet as a child only to be swept off them as a woman. She and Judd were married, and he took her to Dresden, where he built and repaired wagons, mended harness, and assayed related work among the locals. There were five children, four of whom survived an epidemic of influenza twenty-nine years ago. The lost child, their next to youngest, was up in the cemetery with Judd, who had also succumbed to the disease.

That was 1868, the year of the epidemic; her brother Fale had been home in Portland for three years, following his service in the Union Army, but he had yet to settle upon a steady trade. He had always been something of a dreamer, and though the grimness of war had not entirely changed him he came north to Dresden and struggled with his late brother-in-law's trade till he nearly mastered it. *Sticktoitiveness* and the tolerance of local farmers for sometimes rough work, carried the family through lean years.

Deborah's old sickness revisited her, and without her Cousin Deborah or her beloved Judd for inspiration and devotion she eventually lost her ability to walk. For years now she had lived in this house and in this wheelchair. For almost as long she had been writing—first for the local newspaper and then the *Ladies' Home Journal* and the *Country Gentleman*, and finally for Siegfried and Son, in the guise of nine different pen names and, until recently, for the *St. Nicholas* magazine for children.

Deborah never tired of her work; each book was, if not like a child, then like a well-loved pet. Her pseudonyms had taken on lives of their own, too, so that she imagined Mrs. Alvina Plesock Dentin to be patrician, highly starched, with large teeth. Mrs. Rudolpha Limington Harold had a gorgeous mane of dark hair (not unlike Dee's) and an evocative look in her eyes. *Mr.* Wilmington Edward Northstrophe had been one of her favorite disguises; a man could say things (or write them) that a woman never could. Mr. Northstrophe (she imagined) was a world traveler, dismissive of his own work, and wealthy enough so that it represented nothing more than a means to amuse himself between his jaunts to the wilder borders of the known world and beyond.

She sometimes talked to her family about these personages as if they were real women (and one man); to other folk in the village she rarely said a thing about her writing. Most people in Dresden hardly guessed that she had so many names. It was all something more than a lark, having kept her family in comfort for many years now, but she hoped also that she thought of her writing (just a little) in the manner of *Mr. Northstrophe*.

Once, when being castigated for telling a fib, five-year-old Dee had scrunched up her face and asked her mother, "Why don't *you* tell the truth about who you are?"

Deborah had been astonished at first but quickly recovered herself and promised Dee that someday she would reveal herself to the world.

"Oh," Dee had said, and it was *her* turn to be astonished, "I don't think you should do *that!*"

Deborah thought of this conversation rather often these days while she considered using her own name beneath a title for the first time. Thinking of Dee's amazed expression made her laugh, and the laughter made the pain in her hand diminish. She flexed it to be sure of this interesting phenomenon; it was not the first time she had experienced it.

"You want me to get you a candle?" asked Fale, who looked half serious.

"No. But if I wasn't almost sixty-eight years old, I'd teach myself to write with my other hand."

Fale grunted. "That Stockbridge boy out by the corner throws a ball left hand and bats from the right."

For some reason, this made her laugh again. "Where's Dee?" she asked. Mother Pilican had been so in the grip of her writing that she hadn't the slightest notion where her daughter was.

"She's up the neighbor's," said Fale, "explaining what that cat of hers was doing chasing their dog."

"The poor dog," said Deborah. "It must embarrass him terribly."

"Don't worry," said her brother, not forgetting their original subject. "No one but me heard you swear."

Deborah was about to protest against this accusation when Dee came bustling in. She held Ezra Porch a little carelessly in the crook of one elbow. "I don't know how Mrs. Burns knows who was chasing whom, when they were going around in circles!" she said, even before the door was closed.

"Dee!" said Mother Pilican. "She might hear you!"

Dee didn't seem to think it was likely. She set the cat down in the hall and he slunk upstairs. "Are you feeling well?" she asked her mother.

"What?" said the old woman. "I'm fine."

"You're looking peaked."

Mother Pilican waved a hand, but it ached when she did.

"Your mother's been swearing," said Fale with a straight face.

"She has?" said Dee. Uncle Fale's mock solemnity made her laugh.

"Go on with you," said Deborah.

"She said 'Drat,' " he informed his niece.

Dee laughed again, but something else followed close on the heals of her amusement. "Is your rheumatism bothering you again?" She came up to her mother and took the delicate, knob-jointed hand in her own. She gently pressed her mother's old knuckles, then rubbed them. "You remember what Dr. O'Hanrahan said about the farmer with rheumatism in his shoulder?"

"I'm not a farmer," said Mother Pilican.

"A day's scything will aggravate it."

"I'm not going to do any scything." The old woman waggled her hand experimentally. "Fale thinks I should drip hot wax on it."

"Ouch," said Dee. "Wouldn't a bowl of warm water do as nicely?"

"He thinks you have to pinch yourself to get rid of a toothache."

Dee didn't entirely follow it all, but she was used to this sort of *roundabout* between her mother and her uncle; they were as close as brother and sister could be, though they liked to tease one another. "If you want me to stay home this summer, Mom—" Dee began, lending a surprisingly serious note to the proceedings.

"Not go to Portland?" said Deborah. "You look forward to it all year!"

"I can go to Portland anytime, but if you're not feeling well—"

"Don't be ridiculous!" said Deborah. "I'm fine!"

"It's just Portland."

"Don't be silly. You spend most the year doing for Fale and me. Your cousins will be here, and I'm fine." Dee had the healing touch, it seemed, for Dorothy's hand didn't ache while her daughter rubbed it. The old woman would never have said as much, however, as this would have given Dee more reason to consider staying.

Fale only shrugged when Dee appealed to him with a look.

They were suddenly aware of a skittering from upstairs. Fale squinted up at the air register that communicated to Dee's bedroom. A dark form shot past his line of sight and there was a renewed scuffle.

"What is that cat up to now?" declared Dee, and she hurried up the stairs. Soon they could hear her scolding Mr. Porch as she marched across the floor above. Fale laughed quietly.

Mother Pilican shook herself from a brief reverie and turned back to her work, marveling at the vanished pain in her hand. She considered the page before her, half filled with handsome letters (no matter that she thought her handwriting had failed). She couldn't remember where she had left off and read a paragraph twice without taking it in. Fale was back in the kitchen, banging at something, and she hadn't thought to ask him what he was up to.

Of course she would have liked nothing more than to have Dee stay home. Mother Pilican's other surviving children had scattered to the winds, one as far as Ohio, and she knew that she might not see any of them again, though they were dutiful when it came to writing.

She wondered (and not for the first time) what Dee did during her summers in Portland. Dee wrote when she was away, and her letters were filled with the day-to-day incidents of city life, with friends and social events; but Deborah had suspected for a long time that something else lurked beneath or beyond the safe and homespun prose of her daughter's correspondence—or perhaps the old woman had simply been writing romantic notions too long.

Traffic was not exactly rare along the main street of Dresden, but outside of certain regular hours—often representing the arrival of the mail or the stage—the sound of a horse and carriage brought people's heads up. Living so close to the road, the Pilican house was privy to every rider or set of wheels that trundled past, and Mother Pilican was still thinking about Dee when she heard the clop of hooves and the jingle of harness not only nearing the house, but pulling up before it.

"Who's that?" she wondered. From her chair, she peered through the window and the stand of lilacs beyond but could only see that a rig had pulled up at the gate. "Someone's here," she said.

Fale came out from the kitchen again. He had an old bucket in his hand, and still Mother Pilican hadn't a notion what he was doing.

"Is someone here?" Dee was saying as she sailed down the stairs. There was a knock on the door when she reached the downstairs carpet, and for some reason they were all startled. Dee pulled the door open, which in turn startled the man who was standing there with his hand raised to knock again.

"Oh," he said.

"Oh," said Dee.

"Good morning," came the man's voice. "I was on my way to Pittston."

"Olin," said Dee simply. Her hand went up to the back of her head, as if to test how wild her hair had gotten since she got up this morning. It was indeed a little disorderly and entirely pleasing in a windblown manner. Dee had stepped backward, more as an act of retreat than actually inviting the man inside, but he entered the hall and saw Mrs. Pilican and old Fale Field.

"Good morning," said Olin Bell, and they exchanged pleasantries. "I was on my way to Pittston," he repeated. "A fellow up there owes me for a cow, and he's got a plow he'll let me have." This explanation suddenly shifted its focus to Dee, who looked perplexed and wide-eyed. "You said you hadn't gone for a drive in some time, and though it's a wagon and not a carriage I thought you still might like to—"

"Oh, thank you, Olin," Dee interrupted before he was caught without anything more to say. "But I don't think today—"

Olin was nodding almost before she began. He lifted his hat, as if to say good-bye and shifted his feet.

"I've gotten so behind in my—" Dee continued, adding one unfinished sentence to another.

It was his turn to speak before she ran out of something to say. "Just thought, as I was passing by—" Olin said. He was red to the ears.

"You know, Dee," said Uncle Fale, "old McGoon up to his general store stocks my Tecumseh shag." This was Fale's favorite pipe tobacco, and he often complained that the local grocer couldn't find it in his heart to carry it. "If you *did* go up, I'd be obliged were you to buy me a tin or two."

"Oh, well—" said Dee. Uncle Fale had put her in something of a bind, and she looked a little helpless. It was clear, however, that she wouldn't fail the old man.

"I'll pick it up for you, Mr. Field," said Olin. "I'll be going right by McGoon's." He said this with an easy sort of expression on his face and a nod to Dee. "Can I get anything else for you?"

Quite without thinking, Dee put her hand on Olin's arm. "No, Olin," she said, "I'd like to go."

"What?" he said. "No, really, it's no problem at all. I'll step into McGoon's for a tonic and a little gossip, anyway."

"*No*, Olin," said Dee again, with quite a different emphasis. "I would *like* to go." She touched his arm again and smiled.

If Olin's ears could get any redder, they did. The older folk in the parlor relaxed, and there was a collective breath before Dee asked the blond farmer to wait a moment. She had an odd expression on her face as she hurried up the stairs. Olin stood in the hall with his hat in hand, shifting his feet. Fale said something about the weather, and Olin seemed to agree with him without really thinking about it.

"It's a beautiful day for a ride," said Mother Pilican.

"I hope so," said Olin. "Mr. Mooney says rain is coming back, but not till late tonight."

"It's going to be a fine day," assured Fale.

Dee came back down more quickly than any of them had expected. She had a pretty shawl around her shoulders, and was still in the process of pinning her hair back, which matter most women would have finished in private. There was nothing studied or premeditated in her behavior—it was just Dee; but this small domestic and very female sort of activity appeared to strike Olin Bell firmly.

"There!" announced Dee. She raised her chin and smiled, her eyes sparkling with her own brand of dissident amusement. She took the man's arm. "I've given Mr. Porch very strict orders to behave himself," she called back to her mother and Uncle Fale.

"Mr. Porch?" they heard Olin say as he and Dee went out the door.

Dee pulled the door to behind them, saying, "My cat."

Mother Pilican and Fale did their best not to be too obvious as they watched Olin help Dee onto the wagon's bench, then climb up on the other side and shake the reins. Hank, Olin's tall, gray horse, looked grand enough to pull royalty.

"Olin Bell," said Mother Pilican.

"Pretty smart, aren't I," said Fale, peering after the wagon.

"Oh?" said his sister.

"I already have three tins of Tecumseh in the kitchen cupboard."

"You had better hide them."

"He's younger than Dee, isn't he?" wondered the old man.

"It doesn't make a skiff of difference," she replied. Judd Pilican had been seven years older than Deborah Field, and had died too young.

Her brother chuckled.

"Fale!" said Deborah Pilican. "*What* on earth are you doing with that bucket?"

The old man considered the object in his hand, looked up at his sister, then back at the bucket again. Finally he looked back at the pantry door, as if some answer might be evident there. "Well," he said, "I can't remember."

"Pretty smart," said the old woman with a small laugh.

37. Fern and Moss

The Ferns and their guests had whiled away a further hour with peach pie, pound cake, and small talk when Madeline declared the need to walk off a drowse and Sundry offered to accompany her almost before she had finished the thought. He was wise enough, after this readiness, to inquire if anyone else would like to join them; the parents' doubts concerning his intentions were thereby allayed, and the children rose up as one with renewed excitement.

Madeline might have been disappointed to have a crowd escort them, and Sundry sorry that his invitation was so happily accepted, but they bore circumstance bravely and off they went across the field. Sundry was of farm stock himself and used to children and family at his elbows, so that the laughter and commotion was hardly more distracting than the call of birds or the breeze in the stand of birch they passed along the bank of the river; little could dissuade his pleasure in the company of such a pretty woman.

Before they made the top of the nearest hill, he guessed that the oaks and maples upon it, the crowns of which he'd seen from the picnic sight, cast their shadows past rows of gravestones. It was not strange to come here; cemeteries along these riverside towns often occupied the finest views, and a sentiment among Yankee folk holds the graveyard as part of the community's conscious life. Lovers might tryst demurely in its quiet and children play hide-and-seek among the stones. If those departed souls were close enough to hear, how much better might they like the sound of children's laughter than silence.

Madeline picked some wildflowers at the edge of the cemetery and brought them to a pair of graves some rows away. "My mom's people" she told Sundry. "I never knew my grandmother, but Grandfather I remember from when I was small." There was something sweet in the way she divided the flowers between the two memories and considered the pair of names and dates. "He was a very short man," she said. "My mom grew up on the farm, though it was smaller then, and Granddad had a little shop, that burned years ago, where he made fences and hurdles."

"Did your father come from Bowdoinham?" asked Sundry.

"He's from Chelsea. He schooled at Bowdoin, but his father lost all the family's money, and Daddy was left without room or tuition, or even the fare to get back home. I don't know how he lived—sweeping storefronts for a penny, I imagine. If he'd found the job here a few months earlier, he would have been teaching Mom. They both say it's a good thing he didn't. They met at church."

"Your father never went home?"

"His father drank, which was the beginning of *my* father's hate for the stuff, and, I dare say, he was never too fond of his father to begin with. There was a terrific sum of drinking at Bowdoin in those days, and he doubly despised the practice by the time he had to leave."

"Your Aunt Beatrice doesn't despise it quite so much."

"I don't know what to think. Until a few months ago, she echoed every curse Daddy laid upon drink, and more. Mom says that old folk sometimes grow tired of strict rules and perhaps we could learn something from that."

The little boys played tag along the further slope, and some rows away the two middle sisters earnestly read the stones as they walked arm in arm. Madeline and Sundry had reached the less tended border of the graveyard, where their boots kicked up last year's leaves. One low piece of granite caught Sundry's eye, and he scooched down to brush away the grass and scratch at the lichen that covered the single word—*Unknown*.

"It puts me in mind of your father's story," he said.

"I had heard it before," said Madeline. "Two or three times, though Daddy doesn't remember telling it."

Sundry hardly heard her. His mind had left the hilltop, and the beautiful young woman and the laughter of children from over the further slope, to delve beneath the loam and soil at his feet and consider, not the remains of some forgotten member of the species, but the person himself (he imagined a man), and to know a brief wonder and concern that was not unlike a generative act. His mind did not construct a particular face, or a specific heart, but something of his own perceived self, akin to that which was, here, *Unknown*. He did not forge particular deeds, or thoughts, but had a crisp realization of all the moments and every breath that amounted to a lifetime, whether well used or wasted.

There was something more compelling about that single inexplicit word—*Unknown*—than all the names and dates and accolades that might cover the tallest stone. A soul like Sundry's could breath something like life into ancient clay.

While he considered the nameless stone, Madeline said, "Mom can tell you about this."

Sundry looked up and around them, at the fields and the rock-strewn hills, like ripples in a vast counterpane. Great tracts of Maine had long ago been cleared of those ancient forests that greeted the European. Now where farms were given up for other ways of life, or abandoned for less rocky soil out West, the groves were beginning to return to the glaciated hills and river valleys. Below this small, well-tended graveyard some seventy years of straight pine rose up like guardians to watch the approach by river.

Sundry and Madeline went down a short, steep slope to sit beside one of these lofty trees. He held her hand as they went and reluctantly let it go when they found a spot with a clear view of the river. A chipmunk scolded in the branches above them and a blue jay flitted among the trunks, cocking his crested head at the pinecones as he turned them over.

"This is my favorite place," said Madeline.

Sundry could believe it; there were three worlds within a stone's throw—the fields and meadows behind, the river before, the shadowed grove between. Sitting there, he had the first intimation of weather on the way—a subtle shift in the density of the air, a doubling back of the wind; the scent of a darker front brought his head up and sent his gaze among the breaks in the trees, where a patch of blue, or a tatter of cloud, could be seen.

There was something enlivening about those places in between—the pines, the turning point of weather they occupied, that brief experience of thought and apprehension at the *Unknown* grave as contrasted with the presence of Madeline Fern. Sometimes, thought Sundry, a person is gifted with a moment of absolute clarity; Madeline was speaking, and he was thinking less about her words than about the song he had heard her sing, as it was now and continually evident in her voice.

Their hands were propped beside them, his right hand within a finger's width of her left. Her knees were up, and he could see a hint of stocking between her short boots and the hem of her blue dress. Her head was rested against the bark of a pine; there was a single brown needle in her hair above her ear. She was laughing about something, and Sundry grinned (stupidly, he was sure) as she spoke.

"And I would have rolled all the way to the river if that tree hadn't stopped me," she finished, pointing down the slope and laughing.

Sundry laughed with her as the import of her story came to him *from behind*, as it were. He thought, however, what it might be like to sit with another young woman (Priscilla Morningside, to be exact), and though there would be those who thought Madeline the more beautiful, she was transcended somewhat—not dimmed but transcended—in his mind.

Something else occluded the tension of the moment, the sense that a love was as sacrosanct as a mate, and that, by being there first, even an *unspoken* love had certain rights and expectations. Most important, Sundry was not staying in Bowdoinham, and though Priscilla Morningside lived in Ellsworth (and Sundry wasn't staying there, either) he felt something very different about the two equations.

"You have a great admirer," he said to Madeline, without even a warning to himself.

She lifted her hand from the floor of the grove and pulled it away from Sundry, almost as if he had said something insulting (which he hadn't) or intrusive to the moment (which he certainly had).

The awkwardness Sundry had experienced beside this pretty woman left him, and he was his old, engaging self. "Well," he added to his previous statement, "aside from all the other admiring fellows you meet." Madeline smiled, but tempered this bit of light with a wryly cocked eyebrow, which—and he had to be completely honest with himself—made him a little sorry he'd spoken. "I guess you know," he said.

"I guess I don't," she replied. She might have said that she hoped—or, rather, imagined but didn't hope. "Say something!" she demanded when he did not.

"There's only the one fellow I've met around here," he answered.

Madeline looked a little cross. Her jaw set determinedly. "You can't mean Johnny," she pronounced carefully.

"Why can't I?"

"Because he hardly talks to me."

"He's hardly able."

"All he does is play with the children."

"All he talks about is you—when you're out of earshot."

Sundry didn't know if she was embarrassed or angry or simply confused. Madeline pulled her knees closer to her and folded her arms on them. Sundry was startled to see something glistening in her eye. "What am I supposed to do if he won't so much as speak to me?" she asked. "Last Sunday I went right up to him and said good morning and he hardly knew I was there."

"I'm pretty sure he knew you were there," said Sundry. "I guess he thinks the same about you."

"How could he?"

Sundry laughed. He scratched his head. "It is something, isn't it?" He laughed again, but regretfully. "I'm sorry," he said. "I guess I put my oar in where it wasn't wanted."

Madeline put her hand on his—something she might never have dared to do a moment before. "What can I say to him? It's not proper for a woman to speak up to a man!"

"Oh, I don't know—" He thought of Miss McCannon and Mister Walton.

"Some beautiful girl in town is just going to take a look at him one day and decide she's got to have him, and I'll just be *ruined* the rest of my life!" Madeline was in absolute tears now.

"No, no," he was saying. "No, no. Don't think it. He just has to know how you feel about him, and . . . well, *I'll* tell him first thing!"

"Oh, no, you daren't!"

"I daren't?"

"My parents would be beside themselves. If he thought I sent you to tell him, that would be as bad as if I spoke up first."

"*That's* a little refined," said Sundry.

"Do you think so?" She looked at Sundry for the first time since she began to weep, and he couldn't understand how her eyes had gotten so red so quickly. "Good heavens!" he said, sounding a bit like Mister Walton. "How did our parents ever marry? Do you suppose they just tripped over each other one day?"

"I don't know! It's all seems very simple once it's done with, I suppose."

This made him chuckle, but he realized that he had been lacking in basic chivalry and produced a handkerchief for Madeline's tears.

Sniffing, she thanked him, took the handkerchief, and began to dab at her eyes. "It's even worse if you say he likes me, too."

"Of course he likes you," said Sundry—the implication being that any fellow would, himself included.

She looked down at her boots and the needles and roots of the grove and Sundry was struck by the sudden change that *she* had undergone within *him*. Only moments before, he had experienced that potent swirl of emotion spoken of in Mister Walton's remembered verses about irises and doves; his senses were filled with Madeline's beauty: his eyes with her features—her auburn hair and the freckles across her nose; his ears with her voice; and his nose with a kind of perfume that naturally followed her. His hand had reveled at the touch of hers as he helped her down the slope. Now that reel of sensation was focused and still, though just as bright, as he thought it might be, were she simply a friend.

It was a very *nice* thought, in all the primary and overused worth of that simple adjective. Madeline perhaps experienced something like it, for she said to him, "You are a very *nice* man, Mr. Moss."

"Sundry, please," he said, and he laughed, which was a means to fend off embarrassment. "There's something to be said for a man being bashful," he said. "Speaking of Johnny," he added hastily.

"Is *bashful* something you know about?" she asked with a portion of her previous wryness.

He laughed again.

"Well," she said. "I will simply have to wait." Emotions were flying through her like clouds over the sun, and now she felt sad again.

"I don't think it has to be a problem," he said easily.

"But you mustn't say anything to him!"

Sundry promised nothing. "If some girl in town decides she has to have him," he cautioned, "don't say *you* didn't say so."

Madeline's sad expression broke as she laughed softly. "You do have a funny way of putting things," she said. She smiled again, though her eyes were still red. She glanced back at her sisters, but they were concentrating on the ground as they helped each other down the steep slope of the grove. Madeline then leaned forward and kissed Sundry on the cheek.

The wind had risen another degree by the time they returned to the picnic; those dusky clouds, having hung in the east all morning, now advanced against the pale blue half of the sky. When the young folk returned, the older members of the party had packed most everything away, and Hercules, of his own volition, was ensconced in the back of the wagon once again.

"It seems that we are expected to spend another night with the Ferns," said Mister Walton quietly without seeming secretive.

"I think we must," said Sundry.

Mister Walton adjusted his spectacles. "I don't want to keep you from visiting your uncle."

"Once we start a job, we should be sure to finish it."

Mister Walton chuckled.

"Or be sure that it *is* finished," amended Sundry.

The children were already running ahead and shouting something about a shortcut. Madeline lingered beside the wagon, trying to look nonchalant, but was obviously waiting for Sundry.

"You and Miss Fern are getting along well," said Mister Walton in that same quiet tone, but there was a touch of pleasure, and even mischief, in his voice. He had watched with *great* pleasure as the younger children came charging across the meadow to the picnic spread. The middle sisters twirled and skipped, laughing, and Sundry and Madeline came behind, walking and talking, he had noticed, with the ease of seasoned friends. "She is a very lovely woman," said Mister Walton. The playfulness had left his demeanor.

Sundry, by his expression, agreed. "I think I'll go to that ball after all," he said before joining Madeline on her way back to the farm.

Mister Walton was both mystified and relieved to hear it. "Phileda will be very pleased," he said, more or less to himself.

❧ BOOK FIVE ❧

May 29, 1897
(Afternoon and Evening)

38. How to Be Two Places at Once

T he weary sailor had been cobbled back together, more or less, since the "Danforth Street Pianoforte Demolition." It had taken several men to drag the bar back to its previous station, and a ship's carpenter was hired to reaffix it to the floor, though it was unfortunate he took his pay in ale and in advance as when he was finished the bar was out of level and patrons discovered new sport in laying their glasses on one end of the counter and rolling them down to the bartender. Much broken glassware was the immediate result, and the proprietor of the Weary Sailor had more reason still to curse Gillie Hicks.

The famous piano (or what was left of it) was piled on the tavern porch for the inspection of the curious, and a sign was hung from one corner of the inharmonious heap that said flatly, if not with literal accuracy: *This is the instrument of Gillie Hicks's destruction.*

It was just past noon on Saturday when Fuzz Hadley straggled down the sidewalk of Portland's Danforth Street with Tony Sutter and Jimmy Fain. Fuzz was not his swaggering self, which meant that he was a little meaner than usual. He glowered at people, as if waiting for someone to smile or laugh at him. He did not know what Thaddeus Spark's look-alike *relative* and his gang were up to the night before, and he feared that what he didn't know made him look like a fool.

Fuzz turned up the steps to the Weary Sailor, paused only a moment to regard the ravaged piano, and swatted the door open. Things were quiet and dark within. He smelled the sweet tang of a newly broached cask of rum and the not dissimilar scent of fresh wood shavings on the floor. The shadowy crannies of the saloon were dotted with early patrons. Bing, the bartender, a small, bald fellow whose handlebar mustaches seemed wider than his shoulders, wrestled with something behind the counter; his head came up to see who had come in, and, with a cryptic nod at Fuzz, he disappeared again.

Jimmy and Tony followed Fuzz to one of the unoccupied corners of the room, where they set themselves down and expected drinks without asking for them.

Bing appeared above the counter again and came round one end of the bar to approach them.

"You might've saved yourself a trip," said Fuzz quietly, wondering why Bing had not come with the required libations.

Bing gave another nod and this time they saw that he was indicating the other side of the room. Their eyes had grown accustomed to the dim interior, and they descried a lone figure seated beneath a lithograph of the *Lady of the Camellias*. Fuzz narrowed his eyes, then half rose from his seat to gain a better view. Save for the clothes, it was the image of Thaddeus Spark—the remarkable growth of beard bursting over a starched white collar and the fancy vest of a finely tailored suit. The man was short, broad-shouldered, and stocky as a bear; Fuzz could almost believe that this *was* the proprietor of the Faithful Mermaid, except for those fancy duds. The bearded man had a steaming mug on the table before him.

"What's *he* want?" said Jimmy Fain under his breath, and Tony let out a gasp when he caught sight of the man. They had chased the fellow through half the district, and now he was sitting at the very center of Fuzz's turf, as cool as a parson on Sunday.

"He's been there for an hour," said Bing cautiously.

Jimmy Fain let out a low whistle.

Fuzz settled himself back in his seat.

"He's alone," said Tony.

Fuzz cast a suspicious glance around the tavern. "Where's his crew?" he asked Bing.

The bartender shrugged, and, with a jerk of his head toward the front door and the ruined heap on the porch beyond, he said, "Isn't that the fellow who pushed the cop out from under the piano?"

Fuzz grunted for reply. "What's he want?"

"I don't know, but I told him you might be none too happy to see him after last—" Bing was about to say "*night*" but thought better of it.

Fuzz shot a startled glance at Bing. It should have come as no surprise to the aspiring *wharf boss* that rumor of last night's *jinks* had spread.

"What's he want, Fuzz?" asked Jimmy.

"How do I know what he wants?" growled Fuzz. "If I knew what he wants, I'd have expected him, wouldn't I!"

From their expressions one might guess that the boys had trouble following this logic. Bing retreated from the compass of Fuzz's reach.

"Send him over," said Fuzz, though his own nerves jumped at the order.

Some further uncertainty visited Bing's face, but he chose not to share it. Instead, he turned away and crossed the room, his feet *shushing* in the fresh wood shavings.

"What are you going to say to him, Fuzz?" asked Jimmy Fain.

"I'll tell him what's what, is what I'll say."

Jimmy and Tony looked very interested to hear it. They watched as Bing conferred with the man on the other side of the room. The bearded man did not look their way (they were ready to look indifferent if he did), and he hardly deigned to notice Bing himself while the bartender spoke with him. Bing's posture was revealing—he looked like a man who is not sure that he has been heard, then like a man who is equally unsure if he himself has heard correctly. Bing cocked an ear, but the bearded fellow had returned to his mug and his own thoughts. When the bartender returned to Fuzz and the boys, he stood a few feet away from the table and wrung a corner of his white apron in his hands.

"He's says he's comfortable where he sits," said Bing.

"What?" snapped Fuzz.

"He says if you're interested in fair warning you had better come over and have a talk with him." Bing was quick to add, "Those were *his* words."

"He did, were they!" uttered Fuzz, responding to the two sentences at once.

Bing frowned with concentration. Jimmy and Tony were wide-eyed. "What are you going to do, Fuzz?" wondered Jimmy.

"I've a mind—" sputtered Fuzz, and he started to rise, only to sit down again. Bing and the boys were waiting to hear what he was of a mind to do, and Fuzz knew that if he hoped to maintain his reputation of cool authority— or the reputation of cool authority that he imagined he possessed—an immediate response was necessary. "What's he drinking?" he wondered.

Bing seemed almost ashamed to say. "Tea," he said simply.

Fuzz looked as if he'd been personally insulted. He sprung from his seat so suddenly that Jimmy let out a surprised gasp. Bing jumped aside as Fuzz strode past, and they watched him with the avidity of deeply committed gamblers at a horse race.

"I'm Fuzz Hadley," he said when he stood at the bearded man's table.

"I know—" came a high-pitched voice before the well-dressed fellow cleared his throat and began again in an odd tone that wasn't exactly deep. "I know who you are," said the man. He took a sip from the steaming mug before him, then condescended to lean back in his seat and look at Fuzz.

Fuzz shifted his feet and gave the bearded man his best glower. After an awkward moment, he shifted his feet again and said, "You've got something to say to me?"

The man at the table folded his arms complacently and, considering the man before him as a forbearing teacher might a fractious student, he said, "Something by way of a friendly warning, in fact."

Fuzz glanced over his shoulder, not knowing what made him angrier—the superior demeanor of the bearded *gent* before him or the numb-as-a-pounded-thumb expressions of Tony and Jimmy behind. "A warning, eh?" said Fuzz with impulsive fire. "Well, I've got a warning for you!"

"I would stay away from Brackett Street, if I were Fuzz Hadley," said the bearded man, unruffled by Fuzz's sudden pique.

Fuzz was reduced to sputtering, "You would, would you!"

"Adam Tweed crossed the Moosepath League and paid the price."

Fuzz had heard the story of how Adam Tweed was run down by the law and the Moosepath League and how he'd been shot by that club's chairman, though, of course, he did not have the slightest notion of the dire circumstances involved, nor how unwillingly Mister Walton leveled the crosshairs of a rifle upon even so great a villain. By a remarkable chain of events (and, to Mister Walton's thinking, by the grace of God), Tweed had not been killed but was serving an extended term in the Lincoln County Jail. Tweed had been much feared along the waterfront, somewhat as a mad dog is feared, and the name of the Moosepath League, by their involvement in his capture, had become a mysterious, if daunting, byword among his former gang members.

Fuzz flinched and said, without thinking, "How much do you want?"

"How much do I want, Mr. Hadley?" said the man at the table.

"What sort of piece do you think you're going to get?" Fuzz replied, refining the thought.

"Piece?" said the bearded man, that odd, high pitch revisiting the air. For the first time he looked uncertain as a separate light reached his otherwise bland eyes, and Fuzz could believe that the man at the table was calculating a measure of profit to be realized from this conversation. The gang boss felt less daunted in that moment, but then the bearded man shrugged and sighed and returned to his mug of tea; as quickly as it had appeared, the light of avarice was gone from his expression and he said, "Stay away from Brackett Street, Mr. Hadley."

Fuzz was quivering now—shaking with equal parts apprehension and resentment. "You've got sand, coming in here and telling me what to do."

"Not really," said the bearded man. "You don't imagine, do you, that everyone, from my lawyer to the chief of police, is unaware of where I am."

Of course! Fuzz was thinking frantically. *He and his gang helped the police nab Tweed, and just the other night, he rescued Calvin Drum from getting his cop's head stove in!* "Oh, you're right tight with those folk, I can see," said Fuzz, with a measure of disgust.

"Keep clear of Brackett Street," said the man once again. "And don't otherwise be getting in the way of Mr. Spark's business."

"*Mr.* Spark," said Fuzz. "I guess he's 'Thaddeus' to his relations. What are you, cousins?"

"That, Mr. Hadley," said the man at the table, "is for Mr. Spark and myself to know and you to wonder about." He stood, and, in the realm of physical imposition, his stocky frame made up for his lack of height. He might have been a burly quayman, or the poet's own blacksmith, if not for his expensive attire, but the bearded man's air of social preeminence, as much as his muscular frame, encouraged Fuzz to back off a step or two. The man tossed a coin on the table, gave a simple nod with a final "Mr. Hadley," and walked to the door.

Peering around the casement of one of the Weary Sailor's front windows, Fuzz watched the figure of Mr. Thump pause in the midst of the street to consider the neighborhood. Fuzz thought the man's gaze lingered on Winnie's house before he put his hands in his trouser pockets and strode in an easterly direction—perhaps to his home on India Street. Peacock Hope was strolling up the sidewalk, and he stopped to lift his hat and chat with the man.

"The idiot!" said Fuzz under his breath. He noticed then that the bearded man had no hat, and that seemed strange, but he forgot this detail when Jimmy Fain and Tony Sutter came up behind him.

"What did he want, Fuzz?" asked Jimmy.

"What did you say to him?" wondered Tony.

Fuzz snorted scornfully. "I told him that he and his relatives better keep to their business over on Brackett Street and be grateful for it!"

"Did you, Fuzz?" said Tony with a low whistle.

The man was out of sight now, and Fuzz straightened up. He rolled his shoulders, hooked his thumbs in his pockets, and strode up to the bar. "Where's the drink in this place?" he demanded of Bing, who was making a show of wiping down the counter.

"On the house, Fuzz," said Bing. He snatched a tankard from a shelf behind him and bent to the keg at the bar.

"He's not too smart, coming in here, was he Fuzz?" said Jimmy.

Fuzz Hadley took the sloshing tankard from Bing and considered his own reflection therein. "Yes, he's not too smart," said Fuzz, "but I guess he's lucky I'm in a charitable frame of mind."

39. The Sudden Command of Big Eye Pfelt

It was odd how the Moosepath League *didn't* find themselves at Bangor's South Station. Eagleton noticed it first, and his friends stopped to see why he had fallen behind. Jasper Packet marched along, the subject of his song altered, if not his enthusiasm; unaware that his following lagged behind, he sang:

> "'Calico covers my darling by day,
> Dimity does so by night;
> One hiding her various charms so gay,
> The other her blushes so bright!'"

"This is the waterfront," said Eagleton to his friends while Jasper's voice dwindled.

"The waterfront?" said Ephram, and he looked about him.

"Hmmm?" said Thump, blinking.

"We're on the waterfront," Eagleton called to Jasper Packet.

Jasper ventured upon another verse, extolling his "Darling in Dimity," and it took a few bars and a few steps before he realized that the others had halted their progress. "You said you were hungry," he shouted back.

By all appearances, they were somewhere along the less reputable section of Bangor's wharf district. There was a chill in the air; clouds nipped at the sun and a breeze came off the water. Downriver, nearer the center of commerce, ships moved upon the current, tugboats labored the Penobscott, and along the dockside landsmen plied their trades; but there was less noise and traffic where the Moosepathians stood. Gulls wheeled overhead or hopped the planks; water lapped at the pilings. The members of the club peered up and down the wharves to *gain their bearings* (in both the physical and metaphorical connotations of that phrase).

"Where do you suppose the station has gone?" wondered Ephram.

"I can smell it," said Jasper.

"The station?" wondered Ephram. He didn't know if he wanted to smell a station.

"Dinner," said the ragged fellow, and he recommenced his journey down the length of dilapidated wharves.

"We had really intended to dine on the train," called Eagleton. "We are in a bit of haste, to be perfectly honest."

"Never does to hurry while you eat," said Jasper.

"I don't suppose," said Eagleton.

"*Haste and a meal, will make you unweel,*" the fellow called back to them. "That's what my mother always said."

"Oh," said Eagleton. He wouldn't want to contradict someone's mother.

"I *do* smell something," said Thump, but it was not evident, from his expression, whether his nose had detected something pleasant or foul.

"We must be off, Mr. Packet," said Eagleton when they had caught up with the man. "There is a woman who may be in peril, and we intend to go to Dresden Mills with the hope of discovering her whereabouts."

"A woman in peril?" said Jasper, taking several backward steps. "A wife? A sister? Who is she?"

Eagleton looked at Ephram, who looked at Thump, who looked at Eagleton. "Mrs. Roberto," said Eagleton finally.

Jasper frowned. "You had better come with me," he said, and he continued along the wharfside. "Ho, Beau!" he declared, quite unexpectedly, and the Moosepathians realized that they were passing a ragged man who sat on an old crate and looked out at the water with an expression of deep philosophy.

"Ho, Beau," said this fellow without otherwise varying his study, until the three friends passed by. He nodded when Thump tipped his hat and Ephram and Eagleton tipped what *would* have been their hats.

A pile of refuse atop a bit of ledge rose above the level of the wharves, and Jasper Packet led them over this till their line of sight broke the rise and a small shantytown hove into view. Ironically, they could also see, beyond and above the roofs of improvised huts and the crooked chimneys and the wraiths of smoke, a southbound locomotive pulling two passenger cars and a line of freight. Three men were running along the tracks above the hobo village. Like limpets, they caught hold of the ladders on two passing freight cars and were yanked along for the ride. The train and its *freeloaders* passed behind a row of wooden tenements and out of sight.

✺

As well as heroes, the American Civil War (like all wars, it is to be supposed) produced its share of those who wearied of one cause or another, or balked at not getting paid, or disagreed with the length of terms in the contracts they signed when they joined up. Many of these departing fellows—"deserters," according to their armies—hardly dared return home, or perhaps they had learned to love the wanderer's life, if not being shot at.

When the war was over, the ranks of these wanderers were augmented by weary soldiers *ho*meward *bo*und, and some believe these to be the first *hoboes*—a prideful class of men who were not unwilling to work their way home. Some never reached their destinations. Some never stopped traveling *some*where, or *any*where. The war had revealed to them, in shared stories and personal experience, the diversity and breadth of the continent, and the railroad took them there, however unintentionally.

By the 1890s, hoboes still classified themselves separately from *bummers* and *tramps* (an old English derivation), and many a *man of the road* still plied his hand at migrant farmwork in the South or the West and transient jobs in the mills and cities of the North. But whether they wanted to be or not, they were forgotten men, unknown (and largely unseen) by many who only knew the word *hobo* from newspaper items and idle gossip.

Ephram, Eagleton, and Thump had read about hoboes in their respective newspapers; they understood there to be a small hobo enclave on the northern end of Deering Oaks in Portland; they may even have seen, a time or two, a stray, ragged character who fit the description (or their concept) of such a person; but they had never seen such a place as Bangor's little shantytown. By 1897 hoboes recognized themselves as part of a concise society, but they were greatly infiltrated by all types of men, and all ages—*bummers* and *road-kids*, *punks* and *bindlestiffs*, *gay-cats* and *prushuns*.

The shantytown on the sparse end of Bangor's waterfront was a glomeration of huts and lean-tos fashioned from rotten planks and ancient canvas sails and whatnot and populated by a tribe of ragged and largely unwashed men in various attitudes of languor and industry. Here one fellow lay with his barely shod feet near an open fire, and there another mended a pair of trousers with a needle and a wisp of thread. Somewhere, an old fiddle sawed out "Bangor Belle," and a dog barked from across the way. The air was filled with talk and the smell of *slumgullion* from half a dozen pots.

Entering the periphery of the shantytown, Jasper Packet raised a hand and shouted out, "Ho, Beaus!" and the nearby crowd answered in kind with a great "Ho, Beau!" and several other less polite usages.

"What do you have there, Jasper?" called one fellow in an old top hat. "Is that the mayor, or the governor and his friends?"

"I have some *real* gentlemen with me today, Greasy," said Jasper. He led three uncertain Moosepathians into the midst of the little village while a crowd gathered around.

They were a motley group and Jasper was as well decked out as any of them, that is to say, their clothes were much mended, if not in tatters, and none of them wore what could be called a matching suit. These habiliments were dulled besides by the dust of the road and the toil of field and factory. There was nothing threatening about this crowd of almost two score—there was, in fact, a certain bonhomie that accompanied the curious faces and variegated fragrances—but Ephram, Eagleton, and Thump were private men and not used to this sort of interested press. One hatless fellow, with several days' growth on his face and the stub of a cigar in his mouth, hefted a small dog on his shoulder and said, "They do look the real herb, and that's a fact."

A long-limbed fellow with a long nose and exceedingly long ears moved his mouth for a moment before words began to form. "Where'd you meet them, Jasper?" he inquired.

A shorter, plumper sort of fellow beside the long-eared man piped up immediately. "Henry says, 'Where'd you meet them, Jasper?'"

"They just rescued me from Sparky, if you must know." Jasper hooked a thumb over his shoulder to indicate that this deliverance had been actuated in recent history and not too far away.

"Go on with you!" shouted one bearded hobo, waving his broken-crowned bowler before him as if he were swatting flies.

"Sparky?" said a thin man who seemed to have been interrupted with his laundry. He held a wet shirt before him like a plucked goose. "Leander Spark, you mean?" There was a general noise of incredulity and several of them laid their eyes on Thump as the most likely candidate for tangling with Leander Spark.

"Paid off my debt, just like that," said Jasper with a snap of his fingers. "And never laid eyes on me before in their lives." He explained the scene—how Thump had offered to *poke* Sparky in the eye (which he hadn't, or at least not in such detail) and how Jasper's debts were absolved and of course how Jasper had reimbibed (in his words) the debt while playing upon Sparky's superstitious nature. Jasper made a good tale of it, and it was considered a triumph all around. Someone kept shouting "Go on with you!" and the Moosepathians were slapped on the shoulders, their hands were shaken, and their ribs poked good naturedly. Eagleton let out a little *whoop*, as if he'd been tickled.

"That was some kind of you," said the long-eared hobo while he pumped Ephram's hand.

"Henry says 'That was some kind of you,'" said the plump fellow when it came his turn.

The members of the club looked serious when they were offered bowls of stew from a nearby pot, their hunger mysteriously dissolving as they leaned over the proffered meal; the viands did appear a little suspect but, beyond that, it would do no one any good to describe the *hobo chowder* or to conjecture upon the nature of its ingredients. The members of the club very politely declined, and, though they were affected by the necessity for dispatch, they did their best to mind the jolly gathering about them.

An old *trailblazer* rigged out in overwide trousers tied at the waist with a thick length of rope and a coat several sizes too small and bursting at principal joints urged Thump to go to Brownville Junction with him by rail, whereat (he promised) they would find the fishing conducive to an easy life. Meanwhile, Ephram was paralyzed with astonishment by the hatless and cigar-smoking fellow's tale, which related salient events in the history of his dog named Puddle.

"You've never seen such an animal for killing a rat!" declared the man, who seemed to be wearing the remnants of a Federal Army Coat. "He's a sincere fiend for putting hares in the pot!" The man had one eye that grew wide when any large emotion entered him, which seemed to be often.

"I wouldn't have guessed," said Ephram.

"Previously owned by a man who was targeting geese when the discharge from his shotgun knocked him off the barn roof!"

"The man?"

"Indeed."

"My word!" said Ephram. "Did it hurt him?" He didn't even get around to asking what the man was doing on a barn roof with a shotgun.

"I don't know if it hurt him," admitted the old wanderer, "but he was killed pretty thoroughly."

"I am so sorry!"

"Never met him myself. But I was in the vicinity and had a crick in my neck."

Ephram wasn't sure where the crick fell in the narrative of the dog and the man who was knocked off a barn roof by a self-induced shotgun blast, but the narrator was off to other things.

Eagleton, meanwhile, was attempting to explain to Jasper Packet and several others among the crowd that he and his fellow club members must be off, and quickly.

"Who is this woman you're after?" wondered Jasper, which question brought others into the conversation.

"I beg your pardon," said Eagleton. "We aren't *after* Mrs. Roberto but certain nefarious individuals who may have already imperiled her."

"We hope to rescue her, if need be," said Ephram.

"Mrs. Roberto?" said someone.

"What's that?" said another, and the name as well as the gist of Eagleton's and Ephram's words wafted through the gathering of ragged men like a breeze among trees.

"Mrs. Roberto?" said the man with the dog. His eye grew wide. "The woman in the balloon?"

"What woman is that?" said the long-eared man.

"Henry says, 'What woman is that?'" said his plump companion.

Ephram, Eagleton, and Thump nodded or shook their heads at one question and another, and did their best to put in a word edgewise, till someone came out of his hut with a handbill advertising the accomplishments of the woman in question as performed two years before in the heart of Bangor itself.

Thump removed his hat when the bill was unrolled before him, and Ephram and Eagleton stood with their hands awkwardly at their sides. The image of the parachuting woman was, necessarily, a failed attempt at portraying the original, but it was enough to bring the crowd to complete silence, and, beside this reverent quiet, the noises common to the waterfront and the train yard above the shore seemed common indeed—uncouth and even rude. Every face was grave and every hat doffed.

Jasper stepped forward and pointed with great respect to the image of the woman with the parachute. "Do you mean to say that this lady is in danger?" he said.

Ephram, Eagleton, and then Thump opened their mouths but no sound issued forth. They considered the train of events and evidences that had brought them to this shoreside hobo village on the rough end of Bangor, and they closed their mouths again.

"It's a long story," said Thump finally.

"We have every reason to believe," said Ephram, "that Mrs. Roberto is the victim of some diabolic threat."

"Though we have no idea where she is," added Eagleton, "or where she would be under ordinary circumstances."

"We are the Moosepath League," summed up Thump.

The mood of the crowd grew dark. Brows creased, eyes glimmered meaningfully. There might even have been a flicker of recognition in one face or two at the name of the Grand Society, but other concerns overshadowed questions regarding the club.

"So where are you heading if you don't know where to find her?" wondered the man with the dog.

"It is little to go by," said Thump quietly, "but we have the address of a person who may know something about Mrs. Roberto." He had difficulty referring to the honored lady as simply *her* or *she*. "In Dresden Mills," he pronounced with all due solemnity.

"Dresden Mills," said someone.

The man with the dog nodded, then said, "Boys! Pack your trunks! We're heading for Dresden Mills!"

A great cheer rang out and hands and hats waved in the air. The commotion was terrific. Pots of stew were emptied for a quick *slurp*, fires were kicked out, blankets and bedrolls were rolled up with small possessions, and some fellows simply stood where they were as everything they owned was at that moment occupied upon their persons.

"I sure do hope we find her," said the lengthy hobo to Eagleton.

"Henry says, "'I sure do hope we find her,'" informed his echo.

"Thank you," Eagleton was saying, when someone shouted "Wait! Wait!" and they could see one hobo dancing up and down with his hand in the air. "Wait! Hadn't we ought to have a word with Blind Po?"

The unexpected cessation of noise that followed this declaration was almost as alarming as the commotion itself, and the Moosepathians gaped as if they had suddenly lost the virtue of their hearing.

"What?" said the man with the dog.

"Blind Po!" said one of the hoboes, marching forward through the crowd in order to be heard. "We should speak with Blind Po."

A low, communal muttering greeted this statement, and the mob parted so that the attention of the man with the dog and that of the three friends was directed toward a semipermanent hut that leaned against a half-broken, freestanding remnant of brick wall. The lead hobo ambled in the direction of this shanty and the Moosepathians were pulled after him, partly by the obvious expectations of the crowd and partly by their own curiosity. With the dog perched on his shoulder, the fellow who seemed to call the orders parted a curtain that answered for a door to the shack and called inside.

"Blind Po? Are you awake?"

"Yes, yes," came an aged voice, and the man at the curtain stepped back to make room for a bald-pated, gray-bearded wreck of an ancient human being with pale, sightless eyes. "I hear you," he said, and he reached up with a wavering hand till he touched the muzzle of the dog. He scratched the creature's head and laughed when he received a grateful lick in return.

"We're on a tear, Old Po," said the dog-bearing fellow. "These fellows here saved Jasper's hide today, and they say as how Mrs. Roberto the balloonist is in some distress."

"We're going to Dresden Mills!" said someone.

"Yes, yes," said the old man. He lifted his face and sniffed the air. There was quiet, save for a train whistle from the north. He pulled at his fingers and muttered to himself like a man doing sums, then he turned his sightless gaze back to the hobo with the dog and said, "A mighty storm will come behind you! A great thing of fire and wind, and the trees themselves will clutch their roots into the ground!"

This communication moved through the crowd like a careless body, stirring men uneasily as it passed. The man with the dog turned to Ephram and said in a near whisper, "He talks poetical sometimes. By *storm* he'll be meaning some awful battle or something." Then he said, "Po, this storm you're talking of—what sort of calamity are you seeing?"

"*You* know!" said the old fellow. "Clouds and rain and such!"

"Oh," said the hobo leader; then, after an indeterminate pause, he ventured to say, "Well, there are those of us could use a bath."

"You won't find her!" declared the ancient suddenly.

"We won't?" said the man with the dog, echoed quickly by Thump, Eagleton, and Ephram—and in that order.

"Not in Dresden Mills!" declaimed the blind man.

"Well," said someone, "there's no sense in our going."

"For certain, it's someone's death if you don't!" asserted the seer.

"What?" came the general cry.

"Death and loss of property! I can see no more." He lowered his face, took a breath, and said, "I will go with you."

They heard the train again, and some of the hoboes were hurrying in the direction of the yards.

"Do you have passage?" the man with the dog asked Ephram.

"Why, yes," said Ephram.

"Well, that's a good thing. The quickest job of it is to train down to Wiscasset and take the *slim rail* north to Head Tide, and from there it's but a smart jog by the Rabbit Path to Dresden. It'll be a chore for all these boys to find a place to catch hold on the narrow-gauge, but we'll knock down that pine when we come to it. I'm Big Eye Pfelt," he finished, placing on his head a black hat, which he had produced from somewhere on his person, and shaking Ephram's hand. "Puddle you've met."

"Matthew Ephram," said that worthy, and he presented his two friends. They were amazed to see old Blind Po scamper off for the yards with a cane swinging before him.

"Proud to make your acquaintance," said Big Eye Pfelt.

"That old gentleman will harm himself," said Eagleton.

Big Eye looked about but didn't see any old gentleman. "We'll have to watch after Old Po," he admitted, however. "Do you know him?"

"We don't," said Eagleton.

"The police are looking for him."

"Goodness' sakes!"

"I fear that goodness had nothing to do with it."

Simultaneous to this colloquy, the hobo village was emptying as might a military camp on the morning of a long awaited conflict. The members of the club had never seen anything like it, but they could believe that men of few possessions were able to travel on short notice and with such speed. They, too, were carried along by this unexpected migration and found themselves treading a series of damp, dark alleys.

"The police?" said Ephram. For all their speed, Blind Po had outdistanced them.

"It's his poetic charm the women can't ignore."

"Can't they?" wondered one or another of the Moosepathians.

"But he has no constancy in him. There's a *breach of promise* suit, up Rockport way, and a kid somewhere he claims isn't his." The thought may have elicited some pang of melancholy in the man for he sighed, shook his head, and his one odd eye grew very wide.

"Can't they?" said one of the Moosepathians again. They had not gotten past the earlier assertion regarding Blind Po's poetic charm.

Suddenly they came out of shadow and into the midst of the freight end of Bangor's South Station. Big Eye Pfelt was hopping over tracks with one hand on his hat and the other tucking the little dog into his shirt.

"It's two minutes past the hour of two," said Ephram. Eagleton was considering the sky, and Thump scratched his head.

40. Rescued Before Drowning

"I'm afraid I interrupted your afternoon," said Olin Bell when they were under way.

"You didn't interrupt anything," promised Dee. It was not the highest example of a spring day, but it was fine enough and she took a luxurious breath. "I had just returned from next door," she said to Olin then, "making peace with the Burns' dog."

"Is he mean?" asked Olin with a frown.

"Not in the least. Mr. Porch has been menacing him."

"Your cat?" Olin let out a short laugh, then looked perplexed. "The Burns have that great monster, don't they?"

"They call him Rex," said Dee, and Olin laughed again.

"That would be worth seeing," he said. "*I* just had a litter of kittens at the farm."

"Oh?" she said with dissembled innocence.

He cast her a sidelong glance and added, "Well, the barn cat did."

"Do you suppose that is where Mr. Porch disappears to now and again?" wondered Dee. "He was gone for most of a week the last time."

Olin was a farmer, born and bred, and not one to flinch at any aspect of animal husbandry, but this was perhaps a little too earthy a conversation to be having with a woman, no matter that they were talking about cats. "Your mother and Uncle Fale seem to be doing well," he said.

"The winter was a little hard on their rheumatism, I think."

"My Uncle Tim used to say he creaked like an old gate from November to April," said Olin.

Before the road turned left they had a view of the wooded mound of Blinn Hill, a mile and a half away, and of the fields and slopes between. Olin took the wagon through the village, toward the river and Pittston. Mrs. Alley was in her yard hanging out clothes. She wore thick spectacles, and she shielded them with one hand against the blue of the sky to look down from the bank at the passing wagon. When she knew who she was looking at, she raised her other hand and waved. Dee called to the woman and they exchanged pleasantries about the weather.

"Mrs. Mooney says it'll rain tonight," said Mrs. Alley. "Mr. Mooney has a weather elbow."

"She gets her forecast from the same place you do," said Dee when they were out of Mrs. Alley's hearing; what Dee was thinking, however, was that there would be some talk in town now that she and Olin had been seen together.

"Beats the almanac," said Olin, who was probably thinking the same thing.

The wagon rumbled over the wooden bridge that spanned the Eastern River, and soon they climbed the hill beyond. There was a beautiful farm near the top of this slope—a long, red barn, recently stained, and a grand rambling house with bright white clapboards. A golden horse at the top of the barn told the wind. The rail fences were regular, and the animals within their jurisdiction looked fat and healthy. Old Mr. Chalk, who owned this grand estate, sat in the sun on a stool, just outside his barn doors, hard at work on something, but he looked up and waved as they went by.

There followed a considerable stretch of road with nothing for the eye but the occasional tree guarding hilly meadows or for the ear but birdsong and the rattle of the wagon.

"You'll be heading south pretty soon, I suppose," said Olin.

"Yes," she replied without really thinking about what he had said. She was in an almost mesmerized frame of mind; the suddenness of Olin's arrival, the awkwardness of it, along with the unaccustomed movement of the wagon, had disrupted her nerves, then wearied her a little, and finally lulled her into this almost sleeplike state. The day, too, had its effect, and she had always been prone to the *fever* of the season. It was the space of a breath or two before she realized what he had said, and she answered him again. "Yes. In a few weeks, I think."

He nodded without looking at her and Dee felt a sudden sinking of the heart, the cause of which was difficult to unravel. Some of this emotion was not unfamiliar. She had always left Dresden, even as summer arrived, with mixed feelings, but the breadth of this unexpected sadness surprised her. With this handsome man riding beside her, she was more than a little sorry to be thinking about leaving town so soon. She sensed disappointment in Olin as well, though he never showed it in any material way; Uncle Fale always said that if someone else fell and scratched their knee, Dee would feel it worse than they did.

But it was plain to her the sort of courage and resolve it had taken Olin to come and invite her for a ride; rather impulsively, she liked him very much, and her own personal distress and his (as she perceived it) were tangled inside of her somehow. "The summer always goes very quickly," she said.

"You must enjoy Portland." To prove his words held no trace of bitterness, he looked at her with a mild expression of interest.

He was right, of course—the summer would not pass swiftly if time in the city weighed heavily upon her. She *did* love her summers away from Dresden, among her friends in the city, the anonymous bustle of the streets and the crowded events, but it *was* after the rest of the year at home and months of quiet during which a solitary life might stand out in one's heart.

"I do enjoy it," she said.

"You have friends there."

"I do. And cousins, too, who are like friends."

"And your cousins who come and stay in Dresden all the summer."

"Theodora and William, my mother's sister's children. They always come in June, just before I leave."

"I've met them," he said, unconsciously emphasizing his words with a shake of the reins. "They come to the dances down at the grange."

"Theodora is a marvelous dancer," said Dee, and quite unexpectedly a series of peculiar associations led her to wondering if Olin's sudden interest and attention was a roundabout way of approaching her cousin, who was some years younger than Dee and (to Dee's mind) a good deal prettier. Dee's face reddened with something akin to shame, and her heart fell like a stricken sparrow. She had been courted, won, and cast aside all in the space of a few minutes and a mile, and she wondered that she could be so foolish at her age.

With his eyes fixed ahead, Olin said simply, "They're very nice people, but I'm not sure it's a good trade."

The part of her that she imagined had gone down for the last time suddenly came to the surface again for air; in fact, she almost gasped when she spoke. "Olin, what a nice thing to say!" It was remarkable with what speed that horror of foolishness, that near shame, had scattered, and she had to make sense of her emotions all over again.

"You must attend the theater, and the like, down in Portland," he said, which turned the conversation for his own sake and (not inconsequentially) gave her room to regroup her thoughts. There was nothing critical or accusatory in his tone; he seemed wistful, as if he might like to see the city and go to the theater himself someday.

"I don't so much really," she replied. "To be truthful, my life in Portland is nearly as quiet as it is here. But the sense of *other* people doing things and hurrying about their business is a wonderful distraction. I always *feel* as if I'm doing something just strolling the sidewalk."

He nodded. Olin, as it happened, had an imagination, and he could picture things he hadn't seen or feel things he hadn't experienced.

"I would like to go to the city someday when it's winter," she said. It was an old daydream of hers. "Perhaps even for the holidays. Everyone bundled to the chin, rushing about with packages, and wishing one another Merry Christmas."

Olin smiled. "That sounds nice. Do you suppose it's like that?"

"I don't know. Perhaps I shouldn't go and be disappointed."

"I'm guessing you wouldn't be. Christmas is the sort of thing one brings with them." He looked at her. "It's something you learn, I think."

"I think my Mom and Uncle Fale *did* teach me." Dee had a brief image of how this bachelor might spend the Yuletide—a presentiment of the vast space and quiet and darkness of one person alone in a big farmhouse on Christmas Eve. "You must come and have Christmas dinner with us!" she declared.

He laughed. "That's a long ways away."

Then she laughed, too, and the snow and the hurrying people with their glittering presents and the boughs of evergreen and bright ribbons vanished in the reality of the moment and the green fields and trees of May.

The sun rushed from behind a cloud and bathed them in warmth. Dee closed her eyes and raised her face to the light. Olin watched her for just a moment before turning back to the road. They came to a wet place and he nickered at the horse and veered the wagon up the short bank. Another farm appeared in the distance. Hank did not tire in his pace or fall off his elegant stride. He was a beautiful horse and kept his dignity even while pulling an old farm wagon.

"I might take you up on that," said Olin, this time without smiling.

"We'll go tobogganing after," said Dee.

41. Rescued After the Fact

The disguise was off. It mattered not that Melanie Ring was still in a boy's shirt and trousers; the scrubbed face, the shining hair, short as it was, and, most of all, everyone's knowledge picked her out for a little girl—even a pretty little girl. The Spark family did their best to remember what she had been like as a street urchin and a boy, but ignorance, like innocence, is a difficult thing to recapture. Some of the family tried to understand how they could have been fooled for so long into thinking she was a boy, it seemed so obvious to them now that she was a girl—now that she *was* a girl.

The disguise was off, and soon word got about the tavern, and then the street, that the dirty waif in ragged clothes was not what *he* seemed. These whispered tidings bred rumor, of course, and soon the former Mailon Ring was the long-lost daughter of royalty and wealth.

Sitting at his customary place at the Faithful Mermaid that afternoon, Tom Todd, one of the Todd *brothers* (who weren't related), wondered if the former Mailon wasn't the Dauphin himself, who was said to have escaped from a dungeon in France.

"The Dauphin *was* a boy," said Captains Broad and Huffle at the same time.

"That's what they told everyone," said Patrick Todd (the other Todd *brother*), his wide eyes meant to indicate how much *they* could be trusted.

"You might have something there," said Captain Huffle with a philosophic nod and a puff on his pipe. He blew a cloud of smoke and added, "If the child was about a hundred years old."

"We weren't yet a *state* when that fellow was lost," Captain Broad informed the *brothers*.

Tom and Patrick Todd looked as if they might invoke the untrustworthy *they* once again but finished off mumbling into their mugs.

Most people were content to construct castles of wealth for the child, uncomplicated by celebrated bloodlines, but some watched for her in hopes of divining whether she really did take after her father Grover Cleveland, who had once, purportedly, admitted to having sired an illegitimate child. (In this case she would only have to have been about *fifteen* years of age.)

Rumors continued throughout the afternoon, waxing and waning with the inspiration and credibility of the teller. Some unimaginative soul suggested that everyone knew the girl's father, and that he might be seen most nights prowling the streets and saloons of Danforth Streets, so the tale demanded further assembly, and it was decided among the sager heads that this purported father had actually worked for a wealthy individual (to be named after subsequent deliberation) who paid this man to abscond with an unwanted child. Perhaps he had even been ordered to "do her in" (in one of the laundresses' colorful manner of speech) but he hadn't the heart. The whole sordid business, of course, had driven him to drink, so there you were!

"She might have stayed a boy, for all the ridiculous stories going around!" Annabelle stood in the kitchen with her fists on her hips and looked like her mother of a sudden.

Mrs. Spark stopped rolling dough long enough to look distressed.

"People will talk," said Minerva.

"The poor child had reason enough to be confused when she got up this morning!" grumbled Annabelle. "Daddy should be out there telling people how foolish they are."

"Where *is* your father?" wondered Mabel Spark.

"I haven't seen him," said Minerva.

Annabelle shook her head. Mabel looked about the kitchen as if Thaddeus might be lurking in a corner somewhere. Things had been topsy-turvy of late, what with Fuzz Hadley chasing people over roofs and children altering their gender.

"Bobby!" called Mabel, and, after two or three similar vocalizations, the boy came rushing in through the backdoor. "Where's your father?" she asked.

Bobby shrugged. "I don't know," he said with an odd look on his face. "He went out with Mr. Thump's clothes."

"Oh," said Mabel, then, frowning, she added, "But Mr. Thump won't be home," and, finally, "It doesn't matter, I guess." She had hoped that Thaddeus would deliver them directly to Mr. Thump so that he might hear the fellow's praise of her mending.

"I'd like to see him when he comes back," said Bobby, still with that odd expression.

"Mr. Thump?"

"No. Dad." Bobby was peering at a stray bit of uncooked pie dough.

"And why is that?" said his mother, swatting his hand away.

"Because he was wearing them," said Bobby, who'd gotten hold of the dough, popped it into his mouth, and was now chewing on it.

"Get away!" said Mabel Spark. "No. Come here. What do you mean 'wearing them?'"

"He was wearing them. I thought it was Mr. Thump had come back when I saw him in the hall upstairs."

"What are you saying?" asked Annabelle.

"Daddy was in Mr. Thump's suit. And he never looked more like him."

There was a moment or two of silence while the women of the household took in this image. "What in the world is that man about!" said Mabel Spark, and she threw off her apron. "Goodness' sakes alive!"

"Mom?" said Annabelle, who only vaguely understood what her mother had so quickly apprehended. She stepped around the counter, and Minerva, too, was rushing toward the door.

"Put the pies together!" said Mabel as she hurried out the back and disappeared down the alley. Bobby hurried after her, but the girls heard Mabel shout, "You get back inside!" and he came dawdling back, glancing over his shoulder before he returned to the kitchen looking puzzled and uneasy.

"'*The apparel oft proclaims the man*,'" Peacock Hope said to Thaddeus when they met outside the Weary Sailor. Thaddeus was yet a little shaken from his brush with Fuzz Hadley, and he would have appeared shocked if Peacock had been able to see past his beard. As it happened, Peacock had the notion that the hirsute face before him was filled with sudden offense.

"I beg your pardon, Mr. Thump," said the ne'er-do-well with a tip of his hat. "I was simply noting that despite a certain resemblance to Thaddeus Spark, your raiment shines forth to announce your separate self."

Thaddeus frowned while he thought on this. He cleared his throat as a means of testing his voice but decided not to press his recent luck by speaking to Peacock. Instead, he nodded, grunted, and walked away. Thaddeus had the distinct sensation that Peacock watched him as he went, but he did not look back, and he ambled away as if he hadn't a care in creation.

Thaddeus may have been overdressed for Danforth Street that afternoon, where canvas trousers and workmen's aprons were *de rigueur*. People watched him pass, and occasionally a hand was raised in a tentative wave. Most everyone had heard and talked of the gentleman from India Street who looked so like Thaddeus Spark and they were interested to have a peek at him. One entrepreneurial young lady gave Thaddeus a wink and attempted to engage him in conversation. Thaddeus moved on, though it was tempting to simply (and just for a brief moment) bask in this woman's attention.

Ah, well, thought Thaddeus, *Mr. Thump's reputation has taken beating enough*. Thaddeus did not want to cause the good man any more difficulty.

Strangely, he felt invisible. It was himself, of course, hidden beneath unaccustomed clothes, and he peered out from them like a spy. He saw people with a particularity he had never experienced before—their rough hands and rugged garments. A man spat on the sidewalk, a woman laughed uproariously at another woman's ribaldry. The streets on this end of the city were cobbled for the ease of traffic and business, but they were uneven and unwashed. Scrubby sailors and toughs blinked in the sunshine, recently roused from the drunken riots of the night before. Thaddeus knew with a sudden and unexpected conviction that the young woman who had chanced a wink in his direction, thinking him stout and wealthy instead of simply stout, was wearing an old dress that had once belonged to someone else.

But there was a sturdiness about some of these unpolished folk—the shopkeepers and laborers, the sailor come home to family instead of drink, the craftsman practicing his art in a shopwindow. (Thaddeus did not know it, but Mister Walton himself, the very chairman of the Moosepath League, could trace his Portland origins to an old shoemaker's shop not a block away!) There was good cheer along the street; there was hard work *and* wry good humor, on the whole. Thaddeus moved like a spirit among them, watching and almost understanding that here was the main strength that drove the tangible wheel of life, here was the rudimentary foundation of more prosperous men and institutions (who had better deserve it!), and here was the vital pool that flag and country would call upon in times of war and need.

Thaddeus was actually moving away from the Faithful Mermaid. He wanted to be sure not to give himself away, now that he had fooled Fuzz Hadley, and he must look as if he was strolling home "to India Street." He paused now and again, ostensibly to consider the wares in a storefront window or to spot a bird in a tree but actually to glance back down the street to be sure he wasn't being followed, or perhaps he was simply taking in the street with these newfound perceptions.

It was during one of these profound glances that he was startled by the sight of his wife stalking up the sidewalk. Thaddeus gaped momentarily, not sure if she had actually spotted him, then he ducked into a sweetshop and bent over a display of colorful meringues.

"Good afternoon, sir," said Hadley Schmidt from the other side of the counter. Thaddeus knew Hadley just a little, so there was *just a little* confusion on the shop owner's face when the bearded man glanced up briefly to grunt his reply. "Is there something I can help you with?" asked Mr. Schmidt as he studied Thaddeus's downturned features. "Mr.—?"

"Mr. Thump," came a voice at the door, and Thaddeus froze.

"Thump?" said Mr. Schmidt.

"Mr. Thump," said the voice again, manifest with the sort of note that only a husband might decipher.

Thaddeus turned slowly and said, "Mabel," which in hindsight was not well considered.

"Thump?" said Mr. Schmidt again.

Mabel was quick, however. "I thought that was you. Mr. Schmidt, have you met my husband's cousin, though, I dare say, if you haven't you could still pick him out."

"Ah, Mr. Thump!" said Mr. Schmidt as the pieces came together.

"You remembered," said Mabel to Thaddeus with an odd smile.

"Remembered?" He wished she wouldn't move so swiftly from one startling thought to the next.

"How much I love meringue!"

"Ah, Mr. Thump," said the storekeeper, "you cannot let your cousin do without!"

"No, no," said Thaddeus. He realized with great relief, and then an even greater weight of love and reverence, that his wife was not angry or perturbed but only relieved herself to find him safe and sound. She had discovered his intent and rushed after him. He could conceal nothing from her, and this was, in large part, because he never wanted to.

Thaddeus cleared his throat, modulated his voice as best he could, and said, "Do I recall that *orange* meringue is your favorite?"

"Mr. Thump, your memory is wonderful!"

Thaddeus laughed.

Mr. Schmidt might have thought it terribly formal for Mabel Spark to be calling her husband's cousin "*Mr.* Thump," but she was, perhaps, being jocular.

Thaddeus purchased a bagful of meringues, and some chocolates besides, and soon they were back on the street, wandering without obvious purpose in the direction of home. There was nothing untoward that he would offer her his arm, and that she would take it, husband's cousin though he might be; it was, in fact, his duty to offer protection in the most ancient and approved manner.

But he was not invisible anymore. He was transformed by her presence, by her touch, as Scrooge by his visiting spirits. As they walked Danforth Street, he was addendum to Mabel Hicks Spark, a codicil to her intent and whatever she had inspired him to be. He didn't care *who* he was as long as he had her hand upon his arm like an anchor.

Thaddeus Q. Spark was an easygoing man, and so he was wont to travel the days easily and wander from thought to incident without expressing how he felt about it all. But if the well was covered, it was yet a deep well. On those rare occasions when he thought to lift the trap and peek below, he was himself always a little surprised by what he saw.

"I look a sight, walking alongside such a grand specimen," said Mabel, and he might have thought she was being entirely wry if she hadn't brushed at her hair and then at the dusting of flour on her sleeve.

Thaddeus said, "The governor might wish he were Thaddeus Q. Spark or Joseph Thump, whoever's arm you were on."

She squeezed his arm. "Did you fool Fuzz Hadley? Or did I catch you in time?"

"I did," said Thaddeus, having recaptured his customarily high-pitched voice. "And you didn't." There was a silence of several paces' length. "Fuzz Hadley will steer clear of the Faithful Mermaid, I warrant," he said.

"I rather wonder what Mr. Thump will think of it," she said with the smallest hint of reproval.

"I rather wonder what he will think of being my cousin?" he replied.

"I rather wonder he wouldn't be pleased," came her quick reply. She was as much addendum as he and perhaps had thought about it a little more. She'd been very frightened when she understood what he had set out to do and had almost gone into the Weary Sailor looking for him. Then she had caught sight of Mr. Thump's fine suit.

They walked past interested folk. They nodded and waved to people they knew. "I hope Mr. Thump and his friends have found Mrs. Roberto," said Mable when they came to the corner and the roof of the Faithful Mermaid was visible down Brackett Street. "Or found that she is safe."

42. Angels Unaware

Thump peered out the window of the Pullman car, but he could see nothing of the battalion that presumably accompanied them. Ephram and Eagleton also kept their eyes upon the passing landscape. They had seen Mr. Pfelt waving from a siding as the train left the station and they wondered if he had changed his mind. Thump watched from his window seat, pressing his face against the glass, till the train went round a corner and Big Eye's cheery face and the dog on his shoulder disappeared.

"They were very enthusiastic," said Eagleton. He rather liked the idea of having the hoboes along as he imagined them to be capable when it came to practical matters. "But I am a little concerned about Mr. Po," he admitted.

Ephram nodded. He wondered himself what the elderly fellow had done to run afoul of the law.

"That goat he claimed wasn't his must have caused some destruction."

"He is perhaps a victim in the fashion of Mrs. Roberto."

Eagleton ruminated upon another mystery. "I was puzzled about what Mr. Pfelt meant concerning Mr. Po and the ladies."

"Yes," said Ephram. "That was odd. What do you think, Thump?"

Thump's stomach growled, which mechanistic signal could be heard above the general noise of the train and its inhabitants. Ephram had been ready to suggest that they withdraw to the dining car, but now he waited a polite interval before forwarding this motion.

The food served on the train was unremarkable, though much appreciated by the hungry members. Thump had fallen into a funk as the day progressed, but onion soup and oyster crackers, potted beef and potatoes and carrots, sourdough rolls, corned hake and potatoes with pork scraps (the crowning achievement of the railroad cook), another roll or two, and apple pie with cheese, all washed down with tea that was more hot than flavorful, lifted him considerably, so that he was filled with purpose rather than distress.

The meal occupied a large portion of their journey that might otherwise have been consumed with worry and perplexity; they sat down to their first course while changing engines at Northern Maine Junction, and pushed the last demolished plate of apple pie away from them as they pulled into Ducktrap Station. Their journey back to Wiscasset was almost half done and, as they did not smoke or chew tobacco, they passed through the car set aside for those practices and found their seats.

Occasionally, one of them peered out a window or wandered to the end of the car and looked out the rear door, but there was no sign of the hoboes.

"I believe they may have taken another train," said Eagleton as they pulled out of Rockport. The three friends found it hard to credit that the hoboes had actually joined them, and, while the coastline swept past, they meditated on the events of the day and compared their impressions, though it seemed that the memory of Jasper Packet, Big Eye Pfelt, and the hobo village would vanish beneath arduous consideration like a pipe dream.

They had very nearly thought the hoboes out of existence when the 5:35 pulled into Wiscasset Station, and it was time to convert the next portion of their plan into deed. They stepped onto the platform, feeling strangely unencumbered, a presentiment that had been growing in them since morning; they had never traveled so far without bags and certainly Ephram and Eagleton were not used to being seen in public without their hats. Thump had grown used to Thaddeus Spark's clothes by now and rather forgot that they weren't his own till he chanced to see himself in a mirror at the Wiscasset station house.

It was an admirable spring day with the hint of summer to come. The Sheepscott River that they had known in darker moods flowed amicably past, and the groves on the opposite shore, in Edgecomb, where they had experienced the crisis to one of their greatest adventures, looked tranquil and inviting. The gravity of their present mission, however, not to mention its admittedly nebulous quality, commanded the greater portion of their minds.

"Mr. Pfelt was of the opinion," said Eagleton, "that we should reach Dresden by way of Head Tide on the narrow-gauge railroad." They walked through the station house and looked up at the ranks of houses, the moderate traffic, and the greening tops of oak and elm and chestnut rustling along Wiscasset's narrow streets.

"Look!" said Thump, indicating the southern terminus of the Wiscasset, Waterville, and Farmington Railroad (the *narrow-gauge* of which they had been informed). Several men were darting among the cars and buildings, but before Ephram and Eagleton could heed Thump's directive these runners disappeared among the clutter of the freight yard. Then, just as Thump had opened his mouth to explain, another swarm of men appeared further up the tracks, like rabbits between hiding places.

"Good heavens!" said Eagleton.

"I couldn't agree with you more, my friend," agreed Ephram.

On the other side of the W. W. & F. station house, an engine backed along the two-foot track, its rear couplings reaching for a line of passenger and freight cars.

"That is, perhaps, the very train we seek," said Ephram.

"The air is very still," said Eagleton while they hastened from one station house to the next. "Conditions were expected to remain fair, but, alas, I am not privy to the day's forecast. I can't help but suspicion that the outlook has shifted."

"High tide at 10:03," stated Thump authoritatively. "That is the case in Portland, of course. Adjustments must be made for our present whereabouts."

"It's eighteen minutes before the hour of six," said Ephram, referring to one of his watches as he hurried alongside.

They had never traveled by narrow-gauge, but they were delighted with the miniature appearance of the engine and its attendant cars; the W. W. & F. was something of a dog cart to the Maine Central Railroad's horse-drawn wagon, but the train itself was handsome and pleasantly run. The cars were finished inside with darkly stained wood and had the ambience, not to mention width, of a fancy carriage. Before they were able to board, however, they were accosted by Big Eye Pfelt, who came bounding out from behind a freight car with his little dog close behind.

Ephram bowed in lieu of tipping his missing hat. "How gratifying to see you, sir," he said. "We were half convinced that you and your fellows had changed your minds."

"Not a bit of it," averred the hobo. "But we mightn't go much further, or not very quickly, from here on in." He nodded toward the train.

"Mightn't you?" said Ephram.

"One or three might ride," came another familiar voice, "but there isn't enough of her to carry the whole of us." Jasper Packet scurried out from hiding and glanced nervously about the yard. "It'll be morning before we're all in Dresden."

"A little weary from the journey, I warrant," said Big Eye. "And not so ready to tangle with these villains of yours."

"Dear me," said Eagleton.

"Yes, yes," said Ephram.

"Hmmm," said Thump.

"I must admit," said Eagleton, "and here I risk speaking for my companions, but I believe we have accustomed ourselves to the notion of your assistance, Mr. Pfelt."

Ephram nodded gravely, and Thump said "Hmmm" once again.

"Perhaps," conjectured Ephram, "Mr. Pfelt, and maybe Mr. Packet as well, would allow us to sponsor their tickets. In this way they could accompany us and we will benefit from their experience of Dresden and other practical intelligence."

"That's very good, Ephram!" declared Eagleton.

"I don't think I could do it," said Big Eye Pfelt. "I'd feel out of sorts, you know, lording it over the fellows. Haven't ridden inside a train since the war, and, besides, I'm not sure I'd be welcome in my present state."

"You would be welcome as our guests, sir!" said Ephram, his egalitarian imagination rankled by the thought of any man with a ticket being turned away.

"They shall all go," said Thump.

"What's that, Thump?" said Ephram.

"Thump?" said Eagleton.

"They shall all go," said that worthy. "Or, at the very least, all that the train will hold. I will make a draft against my bank."

⚘☙⚘

It was marvelous how Thump took "the bull by the horns" (in Big Eye's colorful locution). The hoboes, eager to experience the train from the inside, were only momentarily deflated when Thump's present mode of costume elicited from the ticket seller a disbelief in the size of his bank account. Without their hats, Eagleton and Ephram did not look the well-off fellows either (and their suits were a small bit worse for wear). They might have been stymied if Laura Patterson, the wife of the local jail keeper, had not arrived from visiting relatives in Windsor and recognized the three gentlemen. Her husband had accompanied the Moosepath League on the aforementioned adventure in Edgecomb, and she was able to assure the ticket man that they were of an honorable order and upstanding members of society at large.

The members of the club were duly grateful, but it was only after lobbying her steadfast support that the jail keeper's wife realized they were attempting to purchase tickets for the crowd of hoboes on the platform. Mrs. Patterson left, not exactly scandalized but certainly puzzled.

"Let's do this proper, boys," declared Big Eye Pfelt.

"Can I have a window seat?" came one voice.

"Henry says 'Can I have a window seat?'" came another.

"They're all window seats on the narrow gauge," said the ticket man.

Their difficulties were not finished, as it happened. The conductor was a bristly old fellow, and his word was as authoritative as that of a ship's captain. He took one look at the ragged crowd and refused to let the hoboes board, tickets or no.

"You can do no such thing!" asserted Ephram.

"I have sole powers of discretion when it comes to who *is* and who is *not* fit to ride this train," pronounced the conductor.

Another patron of the narrow-gauge came forward—a well-spoken man who was just returned from a fishing trip up north. He was a lean, good-looking fellow with a straight nose and humorous eyes and cut out heroically in the gear and accoutrements of the wild, a wide-brimmed hat in hand and his red-checkered sleeves rolled up to the elbows. "Section 7, Chapter 140 of the Revised Statutes of the State of Maine," said this fellow as he came up through the shuffling ranks of potential passengers.

"What do *you* know about it?" demanded the conductor.

This contretemps made for a memorable tableau: the small engine chuffing steam into the cool evening, the picturesque mob of fellows in their rough clothes, some with bags over their shoulders or bedrolls under their arms; there were frying pans and pots, musical instruments, and one fellow appeared like Atlas himself with a great ball of laundry tied up with string and thrown over his shoulder. They were an orderly lot, however, and somewhat in awe of the conductor.

They parted for the man in woodsman's clothes, and this unexpected counselor-at-law approached the scene, quoting: "*'An innholder who, upon request, refuses to receive and make suitable provision for a stranger or traveler, and also for his horses and cattle, when he may under the provisions of this Chapter be re-quired to do so, shall be punished by a fine of not more than fifty dollars.'"*

"This isn't an inn," said the conductor flatly.

"Laws in regard to lodging have often been considered useful precedents for passenger service cases."

"I'm not an innholder," insisted the conductor.

"No, but your employer accepts similar responsibility *and* liability. You could explain it to him." The newcomer's manner was cordial.

"A lawyer," said the conductor simply.

The man nodded.

"I don't suppose you'd be interested in a case like this yourself," said the conductor, not without a certain resigned humor.

"It *would* be different," said the lawyer.

The conductor considered a large pocket watch, then shouted up the line of cars. "Flurry!"

The engineer peered out from his cab. "Yes, Captain?" he shouted.

"Back her up to the second siding. We're putting on another passenger car." The conductor called for other railmen, and the hoboes gave out a hearty cheer as the switch was pulled and the train chugged back to a single car waiting some yards away on a lonely siding.

They did not all fit into the newly joined transport, and the conductor sent the *best* of them (as he judged matters) up ahead, while the lawyer watched amusedly from the platform. Ephram, Eagleton, and Thump pumped the man's hand and thanked him profusely for his advice and assistance.

"You gentlemen go up front," said the conductor, though they were the authors of his present trouble.

"We will ride with our fellows," said Thump.

The conductor put his hat back on his head and took a large breath. "As you will," he said and walked down the platform.

"Will there be dining?" Eagleton called after the man.

"What?" shouted the conductor, and, after a moment's apoplexy, he said, "There's *tea* service."

Ephram, Eagleton, and Thump nodded as one.

"We'll take tea," said Eagleton. "Thank you."

"And for our friends," said Ephram.

The lawyer waved from the platform as the train pulled out of the W. W. & F. Station. Years later, at a convention of legal professionals in New York, a handsome, gray-haired attorney would recount his brief experience of the Moosepath League and the troop of hoboes, averring his everlasting regret that he did not reboard the train simply to see the carload of tramps and road-men tinkling their spoons in the W. W. & F.'s fine china cups.

43. The Unrequited

Hercules paused upon the barn ramp and put his snout in the air. The doors looked southwest, but past the eaves he could see the dark rising off the coast miles away. Birds gathered among the oaks and willows, tittering and chirping the twilight as they might the dawn, and the ghostly forms of gulls padded the fields—the surest sign of an ocean-born storm. Hercules was not so familiar with seabirds and would have liked to have investigated, but Farmer Fern stroked the pig's head and encouraged him to enter the barn. The creature was further stimulated by the sound of supper being served, and he clopped over the hay-strewn floor to the little stable where he happily buried his bristly muzzle in the evening meal. There was an odd taste among the slops again, and again he was reminded of the grove of white trees down by the pond.

Hercules was almost his old self as the light dwindled. Madeline stood with her father and Sundry, her arms folded doubtfully, wondering if it were the birch-bark tea or being locked in for the night that brought about the pig's recovery. Behind the grown folk, the children leaped in the hay and took the day's last turn at the swing that hung from the rafters.

Mister Walton wandered in from a lengthy consideration of the weather. "There is a decided glowering in the east," he said.

"I think we're in for it," agreed Vergilius Fern.

"Hercules will be under cover, at any rate," said Sundry.

"Yes," said the farmer. "That will be nice for him." The thought pleased the farmer, and he scratched the pig's great white back.

"That will be nice for him," said Mrs. Fern when her husband repeated Sundry's observation in the kitchen. Bonny and Susan were washing dishes, and James was hurrying out to milk the cows that had come in from the fields.

The teapot burbled on the stove; the scent of applesauce cake and gingerbread spiced the room. It would have been the *proper* thing to serve guests and family in the parlor, but somehow they never made it out of the kitchen. Mister Walton was urged to sit several times, but he beamed from his place at the counter and looked quite at home with a thick slab of applesauce cake in one hand and a steaming cup of tea, heavily laden with heated milk, in the other. Even Aunt Beatrice came in from the back of the house and sat, though she indulged in *pap*—bread soaked in milk and spooned out of a cup—as tea kept her up at night.

The last of the day took on an amber hue so that the window over the kitchen sink glowed strangely, and the girls paused in their work to gaze out at the gloaming. A chicken ran past. Then the light fell away as if behind a fallen curtain or a closed door. Mrs. Fern lit another lamp. "Never sit in the dark," she said with the force of an old maxim.

"I like to sit in the dark," said Aunt Beatrice, who continued to reveal a contrary streak. "I would never look at a mirror in the dark," she stated with a nod, as if to indicate some level of agreement with her nephew's wife.

"Why is that, Auntie?" wondered Susan.

"There are people back there who reveal themselves to a darkened room."

"Back where?" asked Homer, vaguely horrified.

"Behind the mirror, of course."

The thought caused a shiver among the children, but Mrs. Fern said "Nonsense!" under her breath.

"Do you really think?" said Bonny, a dripping dish poised above the sink. "I'll never walk past a mirror in the dark again!"

"*I've* never heard of such a thing," said Ruth Fern (though she had), and Mr. Fern was ready to register his doubt, when Sundry spoke up:

> "*The room within the mir'r appears a twin by light of day,*
> *The image of the room it apes in every single way;*
> *By night, within the looking glass, a separate place is shown,*
> *The mirror's rays of sun are ours, night's shadows are its own.*'

"I beg your pardon," he said in the silence that followed.

"Not at all," said Mr. Fern.

"Do you see?" said Aunt Beatrice. She smiled at Sundry.

"Who wrote that, Sundry?" asked Mister Walton.

"My father," said the young man. "He won't have a mirror in his and my mother's room in case he has to get up at night. He's superstitious, of course." (Aunt Beatrice's smile faded.) It was difficult to know, despite his use of the word *superstition*, whether Sundry himself credited the belief.

"Your father recited a poem about his woodlot to us last fall," said Mister Walton, "and I thought at the time he might have written it."

"He does write about trees, as a usual thing," said Sundry. "Or dogs." He turned to nod at Mr. Fern for some reason. "Once he wrote a poem about a dog *and* a tree."

"Look into a darkened mirror," said Aunt Beatrice, "and you risk the likelihood of seeing someone *unknown* to yourself looking out."

"We saw an unknown grave today," said Sundry. "I thought of your story last night, Mr. Fern."

"Yes, Mom," said Madeline. "Tell Sundry about the grave of the unknown man up at the cemetery."

"What unknown man?" said Bonny, and Homer said, "What grave?"

"I think talk in this house has been decidedly morbid," said the mother, which was a little more than opinion and slightly less than reproof. "Homer, go help your brother with the cows."

Homer looked distressed but stopped short of protest when he saw the firm expression on his mother's face.

"Bonny, you didn't make your bed this morning," continued Ruth Fern.

"Mommy!"

"Upstairs."

"But I'm simply going to mess it up in a few hours—"

"You can *mess it up* right now, if you like."

Bonny huffed, but did so on her way out of the kitchen.

Susan was very quietly scrubbing a plate and stopped altogether as the attention of the room fell upon her. Mrs. Fern must have decided that her second daughter was old enough to hear what came next, for she only looked at Susan for a moment, then turned back to Madeline and Sundry.

"People *thought* they knew him when he was alive," she said quietly. "He called himself Jonah Redbrook, but the town fathers discovered, after he was dead, that he couldn't be."

"Couldn't be dead?" asked her husband wryly. It was remarkable how much the man had changed since the evening before.

"No," she replied evenly. "He couldn't be Jonah Redbrook.

"It was in my grandfather's day—Homer Mason, who built this kitchen, and the small walls around it. Bowdoinham was living as much on the wood trade as farmwork in those days, and strange men were not uncommon, I am told. Often they would work from place to place as they moved inland, till they could disappear in the wilderness and carve out their own livelihood.

"Now, Jonah Redbrook—or the man who called himself Jonah Redbrook—arrived one day in late summer and worked for the people up the road. They were the Billings—very nice folk and churchgoing people. Jonah said he came from Kittery, and that he was the third son of his family and without hope of inheritance. He lived in the Billingses' barn and proved an amiable fellow and a moderate hard worker. He was not good looking, Grandfather said, but he had a manner about him that attracted people and not a few young women among them. Some thought he might find the means to settle down in Bowdoinham and make something of himself, and that he would be welcome.

"There was a widow in town then—Ethel Dale. She was not young, but she had always been beautiful. Grandfather said that middle years only added grace to Mrs. Dale. She was a quiet, melancholy woman who had loved her husband, and loved him still, it seemed, for she offered no encouragement to suitors, lived alone in a large house with a single maid, and lived off her husband's shipping legacy. People were a little proud to have her in their town and pointed her out to visiting relatives at church.

"No one ever knew exactly when the man called Jonah Redbrook first was taken by Ethel Dale's beauty, but of a sudden he was seen bringing little gifts to her door—a bit of harvest, a load of kindling. He was a tolerable good carver, and he made toys for the nephews and nieces when Mrs. Dale's family came to Christmas.

"People had mixed feelings about Jonah's seeming courtship of Mrs. Dale. No one knew how Mrs. Dale felt about it. He was a likeable fellow, but it did seem unjust that he might win the suit that had been lost by so many local men, and himself without two pennies to rub together. After the New Year, he shoveled snow for her, and she even hired him to do some odd jobs around the house. This seemed more proper, as no one could imagine that Mrs. Dale would ever marry a hired man.

"It was in February—*the lost month*, my grandfather called it. Grandfather had a perfect dislike for February and thought its only blessing was that it was shorter than every other month. I don't think I ever knew why he hated it so, but it can be a bleak time of year.

"The man called Jonah Redbrook disappeared in February of 1823. It was after a two-day blizzard, and it was feared he'd been lost in the snow and frozen to death. Grandfather was eleven years old at the time and remembered the distress of the Billings family when they came to town looking for him. A search was made all over the countryside. They sent for a Micmac Indian down to Woolwich to find the man. His name was Jimmy Salmontail, and it wasn't his woodcraft, in the end, that served the purpose, if they had only listened to him. He never found Jonah, though he led the men on snowshoes with some dogs around the borders of the town and among the forests over by Mallon Brook, and even as far as Wheeler Hill across the town line to Bowdoin. He told someone, though, that he'd had a dream of a man suspended beneath a hovering owl, that there wasn't anything holding the man up in the dream and that meant death, but the owl meant a hole in a tree or an old building.

"Nothing was made of this, however, for Mrs. Dale came forward and admitted that the man had come to her house the first night of the blizzard and asked her to marry him. He had been courtly and polite and spoke softly, but he was ardent in his attachment to her. She had been a little shocked (though no one else could say they were to hear it) and listened to more of his lovemaking than might have been proper, with her maid standing outside in the hall in case she should need rescue. But Mrs. Dale had refused the man as kindly as she could and he had left with a bow, an apology for his boldness, and hardly an expression on his face.

"And that was the last she had seen of him."

Mrs. Fern surveyed the faces before her and Mister Walton's seemed most stricken, though Sundry's was not too far behind. She looked almost sorry to have been so effective with her tale, but she could not know that Mister Walton's own troth—if not absolutely refused because it had not been absolutely proposed—had yet been guardedly warded away. He took his spectacles from his nose and, producing a handkerchief from some pocket behind him and began to rub them thoroughly.

"Bonny," said the mother.

"Yes, Mommy," came a voice from outside the kitchen.

"You might as well come in and hear the rest where I can look at you." Bonny Fern meekly came in from the pantry.

"I'm not sure this is a tale for a girl your age, but Susan will be with you if you're awake tonight."

Susan was the picture of *eyes and ears*, and might herself be subject to bad dreams.

"What happened, Ruth?" said Vergil Fern, who meant, really, "Tell us what happened," as he had already heard the story.

"Mrs. Dale had a barn, though she only used it for her carriage. She sometimes rented horses and paid the ostler to drive her around town in the warmer months, but no one ever ventured into the barn during much of the year. It was in April, during a late storm, that the children were having a snowball fight, when one group drove the other onto the Dale property. It was a noisy game, and Mrs. Dale was enjoying the sight of the children creeping about in the snow. One child was peering through a barn window, while another snuck around the corner with plans of ambush. The first child suddenly screamed and ran away and a few minutes later they all gathered at the window, some pointing and others shouting and crying till Mrs. Dale went to her front door and frantically called to them to go away.

"'What are you playing at?' she asked them. 'It's very upsetting to watch you!'

"'There's a man in your barn, Mrs. Dale,' one of the children cried.

"She was shocked to hear it, of course, and she asked what he was doing.

"'He's just standing,'" said one of the children, 'but we can't see what he's standing on.'"

⚹🐍⚹

"Good heavens!" said Mister Walton. He was not the less shocked for having suspected the terrible truth.

Susan gulped, and Madeline, who had heard the story before, unconsciously put a hand to her own neck. Bonny didn't understand what it all meant.

"But you said that he wasn't Jonah Redbrook," prompted Sundry. He thought it odd how cold the kitchen had become of a sudden.

"I did," said Mrs. Fern. The pleasure of telling even such a tale of horror was a little evident in her expression. Her eyes settled upon each of her listeners before she began again. "Some of the children had known immediately what they were seeing and they ran for their fathers or the constable. Mrs.

Dale's house and yard became the subject and scene of investigation, and Grandfather said she was never the same during the short time afterward that she remained in Bowdoinham. The man had hung himself in the barn, it was determined, on the very night of her refusal, and the blizzard had covered his tracks.

"The cold had done much to preserve his remains and he was casketed and put in the unheated attic of the grange till his family could be notified.

"Mail was slow and unreliable in those days, so an adventurous young fellow set out with horse and sleigh to Kittery, and it is only a wonder that they hadn't put the poor dead body in there with him. The strangest business of all was to be had, however, when the messenger arrived at the Redbrook house in Kittery and was informed that Jonah Redbrook, the only man ever known by that name in that town, had been dead for three years.

"The Bowdoinham man spoke to several people—the family patriarch, the town constable, the minister who officiated at the burial—and the story was always the same: there had only ever been the one Jonah Redbrook and he was three years dead. Finally he went to the cemetery, there in Kittery, and saw the headstone for himself.

"Much was made of it, as you can imagine, and the tales grew wilder as the years passed. Some even speculated that Mrs. Dale had known her suitor's intentions and that she had even watched him dig a path to the barn door and disappear within—but it was a cruel story. That and others like it, not to mention the very real tragedy itself, drove Mrs. Dale from Bowdoinham before the following summer was gone.

"And there were those who speculated about the real identity of the man they had called Jonah Redbrook. Some went so far as to suggest that he *was* the very man he claimed to be, that he had been banished from his family and they had performed a ceremonial burial. Great mysteries were woven around this idea, so that Jonah Redbrook became at once a ghost, a hero, and a scoundrel.

"There was great debate over the proper way to bury him. Many did not think it fitting that he be interred in the cemetery with Christian people, but a compromise was worked out and he was interred within the graveyard but in his own secluded corner, till people forgot his story and thought nothing of encroaching upon that plot."

There was a moment's silence, whereupon Aunt Beatrice lifted the plate of applesauce cake and said, "Have another slice, Mr. Moss."

"Thank you," said the young man, and he took a piece of cake from the plate in rather mechanical fashion.

"Mister Walton?" said the old woman.

"Yes," said the portly gentleman, till he realized that he hadn't finished the piece in hand. "Oh," he said, very quietly, then, "In a moment, I think, thank you."

"It will be someone else's turn to tell about a *grave unknown* tomorrow night, I think," said Mr. Fern. He pronounced the subject of this anticipated story in a melodramatic tone and waved his fingers like a conjurer at his daughter Bonny, who let out a small squeal.

"People see him sometimes," said Mrs. Fern unexpectedly. She had given every indication of having finished her tale.

"See him?" said Sundry.

"Yes. People say they've seen Mr. Redbrook, or at least the man they knew as Mr. Redbrook, standing at his grave."

There was a moment's silence. They could hear the boys coming in from the barn with the milk. When they opened the door, everyone in the kitchen understood that the weather had changed. The human barometer that detects these things sensed a subtle drop in air pressure.

Madeline shivered.

Mrs. Fern was the first to speak and to move. She rose and began to gather the tea things from among them. "More tea, anyone?" she asked.

44. Room to Consider a Lack of Happenstance

"Well, he didn't kiss her."

"The idea! Get away from that window, Fale!"

"It might be a *good* idea, were he a'mind," he said.

"It's getting dark out, and, with the light in here, they might be able to see you," insisted Mother Pilican.

Fale chortled as he scurried away from the window; he even disappeared into the pantry before the front door opened. Dee came into the hall, pulling her scarf from around her neck. Olin Bell came in after with a box in hand, looking diffident.

"Good evening, Mom," came Dee's musical greeting.

"Good evening, dear," said the old woman. "We were beginning to wonder if you'd get home before dark. Good evening, Olin."

"I'm afraid I'm to blame for being late."

"Nonsense," said Dee. "I insisted that he show me the fairgrounds."

"Insisted, did you?" said the mother.

They could hear Fale chuckling in the pantry.

"Come in here and stop eavesdropping," said Mrs. Pilican.

"I was not!" said the old man, still with a laugh.

"He was watching out the window," said Dee.

Deborah Pilican had a magazine in her lap and she used this to swat at her brother when he passed her. He darted forward with surprising nimbleness and let out a shout. "It's not safe in here anymore!"

"Olin has your tobacco, Uncle Fale."

Olin held up the box in his hands, and Fale pointed to the stand in the hall. "Thank you, Olin," he said. "Who do I owe?"

"I took care of it," she said. "You can pay me later."

"There's weather coming," said the old man.

"There is an odd look to the sky," said Olin by way of agreement.

"Did you have a nice drive?" Uncle Fale asked Dee.

"Yes, very."

"Dee says you like old-fashioned roses," said Olin to Mrs. Pilican.

"Oh, I love them," said the old woman. "Judd planted one for me over on the south side of the house, but it died two years ago when we had that awful frost in June. It nearly broke my heart to see it go."

"My aunt planted some on the hill above the farm," said Olin, "years ago, when she first came here. But they've spread everywhere. I'll bring you as many as you like."

"That would be lovely, Olin," said Mrs. Pilican. "But just one, planted on the south side of the house, would make me happy as could be."

Dee pulled a face. She thought she saw tears in her mother's eyes. Suddenly the daughter walked across the parlor and hugged her mother. "What's this? What's this?" asked Mrs. Pilican, delighted.

Dee simply straightened up, half shrugged, and said, "Are you going to use your real name for your new book?"

"I'm considering it. It will probably be my *last* book, so I might as well. I can't suffer from the scandal if I'm not here."

"Her last five books have been her *last* books," Dee informed the man in the hall. "Olin read *Wembley Upon the Hill.*"

"Goodness, did he?"

Olin was standing at the threshold to the hall, one shoulder against the casing, his hat in hand.

"What must he think?" wondered Mrs. Pilican aloud. She had never gotten used to the idea that her neighbors might read her books.

"I got quite perturbed with Matilda," he said without irony.

"And well you should," said the old woman. "She was an awful handful. I couldn't get her to do *any*thing I wanted."

"I could have understood Mr. Wembley waiting for her all those years, if she'd deserved it."

"Ah, well," said the old woman. "Love is not always founded in merit."

Olin thought about this. He nodded without indicating that he entirely agreed. "I hope he was happy, in the end." He did not consider that he was speaking of a person grown whole from the mind of the woman before him, nor guess how much pleasure he had given her by evincing his concern for *Mr. Wembley*.

He left with almost as much awkwardness as he had arrived, which is to say quite a bit. His afternoon with Dee might have been like an unfinished conversation, wherein neither participant can quite decide what it was he wanted to tell the other. He dismissed himself suddenly with a wave of his hat and the assertion that he must be going.

Dee felt as if she wanted Olin to stay but could not think of any good reason for him to do so. She thanked him several times over for thinking of her, and for the lovely drive, and he looked more awkward with every expression of gratitude. He hesitated at the door and on the stoop and on the walk, turning to say "Good-bye" and "Think nothing of it." Dee couldn't decide whether to shut the door and let him drive off gracefully or extend the evidence of their sudden friendship by waving him out of sight. She simply waved one last time when he shook Hank's reins, then she shut the door.

"You might have asked him to supper," said her mother.

Dee thought a moment, took hold of the door again and almost yanked it open. She stopped herself, looked ready to open the door several times in a series of fleeting half seconds, and finally let go the black knob. She was a little vexed with herself, but she shook her head, let out a puff to clear her emotions (which tactic was not very successful), and walked into the parlor. "*You* might have asked him," she said to her mother.

"I didn't know if you'd want me to," said Mrs. Pilican.

Dee put her hands out to signify that it was not a large matter. *I asked him to Christmas dinner,* she was thinking. *Perhaps two invitations in one day would be too much.*

"Where've you seen *him* lately?" wondered Dee's uncle.

"Fale!" said Mother Pilican, though she was curious herself.

Dee said, "We just happened to meet yesterday, when I went for a walk."

"And you happened to mention that you hadn't been for a ride for years," said Mother Pilican, who couldn't help herself.

"Not in *years*, and it was simply in conversation that I brought it up."

"He's a nice fellow," said Uncle Fale.

"I hope so," said Dee impishly, "if *you* let me take a ride with him."

"Much I could have done about it," he chortled. He ambled back to the kitchen for his *mad money*. "How much did McGoon *go you* for that tobacco?" he called back.

"Oh, I don't know," said Dee, lost in her own thoughts. She did not want to appear like a schoolgirl come home from her first spoon, but she *did* want to deliberate on what had happened that afternoon, plain and uneventful as it was. "Where's Mr. Porch?" she wondered.

"He got put out when you left," said Mrs. Pilican—meaning that the cat had been out of sorts. She liked the double meaning of what she had said, however, and added, "And then Fale put him out."

"I suppose he'll be chasing Rex again."

"I haven't heard anything."

"I'll go out and call for him," said Dee.

Mother Pilican went back to her magazine with a "Yes, dear" and didn't even look up as Dee went out the door. She was listening, though, and did not hear the cat's name being called.

"What are you brooding about?" asked Fale when he came back in with money to pay back Dee.

"I'm not brooding," said his sister. "I was thinking of Judd."

45. The Inn at Blinn Hill

It was odd how the Moosepath League *didn't* find themselves quartered in a comfortable inn or boardinghouse when day was done and they were ready to lay down their heads. It was Eagleton who suggested that the hour was growing late to intrude upon Mrs. Pilican (whoever she was). She might be sitting to supper, or even readying herself to retire for the night, by the time they arrived.

"Say no more," Big Eye said. The train had taken them almost to Head Tide, and they were skirting a hilly meadow, the smoke and cinders from the engine billowing and ticking at the windows. "We'll advance upon the errand first thing in the morning," said the hobo. "We know a marvelous place to bed up, when we get to Dresden. It'll be two or three miles' walk from Head Tide, but we'll get there before things are very dark."

"Perhaps we should hire a carriage," said Eagleton.

The village of Head Tide, hard upon the banks of the Sheepscott River, was the picture of a snug New England hamlet, with a church spire rising above the roofs and maple tops. From the station, a plank bridge ran across the river to a tidy street flanked by white clapboarded homes. The place is well named, for it is indeed the *head of the tide*, where the authority of ocean currents gives way to the gravity-fed stream of hill and spring. Here, the Sheepscott River, so potent and broad near Wiscasset, takes to meandering among gravel shallows and between banks no further apart than a stone's throw.

When they pulled into Head Tide, the conductor was quick to step from the train and greet the stationmaster; clearly, he wanted to make his excuses for his *species* of passenger this afternoon. Other travelers, getting off or waiting to board, craned their necks and chattered among themselves as the hoboes spilled onto the platform. There was a livery near the depot, and the Moosepathians were quickly outfitted with horse and rig. A wagon was hired as well to carry the burdens of the troop, and the other men drew straws to see who would ride with old Blind Po.

It was late afternoon and a dark sky mounted in the east long before the waning sun should have left such a shadow. Big Eye squinted at the clouds but said nothing. Eagleton sat beside him. In the back seat, and facing backward, Ephram and Thump watched the wagon bring up the rear. Already the small army of hoboes was scattered along the road, and the members of the club waved to the fellows as they went past.

"I hope the vehicles will be able to negotiate a rabbit path," said Ephram, remembering the hobo chief's report of their itinerary.

"What?" said Big Eye. "Ah, well. Not to worry." He executed a reverse nod, drawing their attention to a sign at a crossroad that said: RABBIT PATH. The hobo turned them down this way, which was more of a thoroughfare than the wilderness trail its name might suggest.

"You are very good to join us, Mr. Pfelt," said Eagleton.

After a moment Big Eye said, "I haven't championed a cause since the war, so I might be overdue."

"You fought for the Union?" asked Ephram.

"I *cooked* for it," answered the hobo. "There were some," he said with a wild leer, "who thought I'd have served the cause a good deal better had I cooked for the Rebs." He laughed then till he almost choked, and finally wrestled a flask from a pocket and took a pull from it. He almost capped the flask but remembered his manners and held it out to Eagleton.

"No, thank you," said the blond Moosepathian, though he hardly knew what he was being offered.

Big Eye looked back at Ephram and Thump.

"I beg your pardon?" said Ephram.

Thump said, "Hmmm?"

"I did see conflict before I was done," continued the older man as he returned the flask to his pocket. "We were near Chickamauga, just days before the battle, and one night our corp commander got his hills fouled up. He had us planted securely behind enemy lines, which fact we discovered the following morning when the smoke from my fire drew a battalion of hungry Rebels.

"The first of them came through like a hurricane, but a little louder than that, and they came all of a sudden. I had just enough time to dump over my big old cast-iron pot and climb beneath it. Shot was whining through the encampment like ten nests of aggravated hornets, and soon I understood that some Johnny Reb was using the overturned pot for cover. Every time the lead hit that cast-iron pot, it rang out like a bell. I was pretty near deaf before long and hadn't a notion that the rest of my corp had been driven off the ridge and into the woods beyond.

"When I felt the pot being turned up on its side, I pressed myself against it like a clam in its shell. The sounds around me were less muffled, then, but kind of tinny. My ears were ringing, you see, but I thought I could hear some southern accents. Then I glimpsed a pair of tan pant legs.

"Well, I figured I was for it, and about two second of breathing left before I was taken prisoner, but the fellows who had pulled the pot onto its side had other plans. A handful of my troop was firing from behind a ledge just below the ridge of the hill, and those Rebels were having the devil's own time getting a shot at them. So they propped that kettle up with a grunt or two—one of them did remark that it was heavier than he would have guessed—and they pushed it down the slope, never knowing I was in it.

"A bowling ball never turned so neatly! Why, that pot blasted down the hill like a bad dream, pitching off the ledge below and scattering the last of my comrades-in-arms the way the first shot of the season scatters ducks. I landed between two trees, bounced a couple of yards, knocked down a sassafras bush, and continued down the slope, end over teakettle, caroming off a rock here and clipping a tree there, spinning faster and faster till I was mostly blind as well as deaf and hardly knew to swim to the surface when the whole kit, me and the pot, took a dunk in the Tennessee River."

It was a marvelous bit of news, and Eagleton took a notebook from his coat pocket and jotted down the tale. "Good heavens!" he said several times over while he wrote.

"I stayed well away from the lines, as a general thing," said Big Eye. "Certainly they kept me away from them after that." The carriage was slowly climbing up a hill, and the hobo shook the reins just to remind the horse that he was there. Big Eye wore an expression of great philosophy and finally he said, "I met an old gunnery sergeant a few years ago who maintained that my presence in the pot might have saved those men below the ledge. He was quite sure that my added weight, as I understood him, helped to increase the pot's trajectory so that it carried over the ledge rather than tumble down it."

"Your fellow soldiers must have been very pleased," said Eagleton.

"They didn't give me a medal," said Big Eye.

It was not long before they were passing Pinkham Pond on their right, and a few minutes later there was Dresden Bog on their left. Big Eye spoke of it as the *Great* Dresden Bog and it did seem extensive to the Moosepathians—not to mention boggy; they saw a small brown creature (a muskrat, Big Eye informed them) and a great blue heron fishing the plant-choked waters.

They continued along the Rabbit Path till they came to the Blinn Hill Road, and, on this track, they passed several houses and farms, eventually stopping before one of them. Big Eye handed Eagleton the reins before he hopped down. For a moment the Moosepathians thought they had come to the boardinghouse or inn of which the hobo had spoken, but he only frowned when they asked him, and he went to the farmhouse door.

After some discussion with a man from the farm, Big Eye climbed aboard the carriage once again and took the reins. Soon they were trundling round to the back of the house, down a short hill, and toward an aspect of long, rolling meadows.

"There's no road to this place?" asked Eagleton.

"Thank goodness, no," said the hobo.

Ephram, Eagleton, and Thump grew more curious with every fall of the horse's hooves, wondering what sort of establishment they must reach by way of a series of fields.

"We've nearly boxed the compass, here," said Big Eye. "Some of the fellows will be along pretty quick, as they'll have hiked it cross country."

Soon they were mounting a short, wood-covered hill, at the top of which there stood a clearing that bore the signs of previous occupation. There were crude lean-tos among the trees and several stone-ringed plots upon the ground where fires had once burned. Collectively, the Moosepath League was puzzled, and then amazed, to hear Big Eye announce that they had arrived.

"I beg your pardon?" said Eagleton. He strained his neck looking for some sign of domicile or house.

"What's that?" said Big Eye.

"The inn," said Eagleton. "I don't see it."

"Inn?"

"Well, the boarding house. The place to stay the night."

"Your sitting in it!" declared the hobo.

Again Eagleton looked around, joined this time by his fellow Moosepathians. "Sitting in it?"

Thump looked behind himself. They were all standing and the phrase puzzled him.

"Mother Nature's your landlady tonight, gentlemen!" Big Eye threw his arms wide as if he were sharing his own personal estate. "The forest floor will be your mattress, the boughs your cover, and the moon your lamp—well, if it doesn't storm."

Ephram, Eagleton, and Thump were astounded.

"Good heavens!" said Ephram.

They stared about themselves. The newly leafed trees were tall and glorious, barely shaken by a breeze from the east. The sun was low in the west and the shadows of the forest long and complex. Big Eye took them to the southern edge of the hill and pointed to a village in the distance lying close by a bend in the Eastern River.

"There's Dresden Mills, gentlemen," said their guide. "And, presumably, come the morning, we will meet your Mrs. Pilican there."

"Whoever she may be," said Ephram.

"Blind Po said Mrs. Roberto would not turn up there," said Big Eye, "and he isn't far wrong, as a general thing, but I've an inkling myself now and again, and I've got the feeling you're going to find what you're looking for, one way or another, when we rise up tomorrow."

46. Watchpig on Duty

Anyone who has lived long within weather distance of the coast of Maine will have experienced the ambushlike reversal of the nor'easter, when a storm gathers power above the turbulence of the ocean, amassing itself into something angry and unstable. A weak weather system, lingering behind such a resurgent storm, has no authority to deny it, but if a second powerful front is following the prevailing weather patterns those two can meet like charging bulls over the land. Betwixt such potent elements, and even near to them, weather and life can become strange and unpredictable. People, too, have been known to do surprising things under the influence of such weather, and lightning can strike ten miles from the storm that produces it.

✹❧✺

"Something has halted it up there," said Mr. Fern when they went outside to check on the animals. The sense of impending weather was oppressive somehow but perhaps they were simply feeling the effects of Mrs. Fern's story. Certainly Sundry appeared preoccupied, and even a little wary. The animals, too, were awake and watchful; they started when a person touched them, and even the normally sanguine Hercules grunted nervously at their approach.

"He's not sad," said Mr. Fern, "but he's on the edge of his nerves tonight."

"It's the weather," said Madeline. "It will have us all on edge."

Sundry silently agreed. He had been expecting something—not weather, really, and not anything he could have disclosed like a tale or a specific prediction; the business of the gloomy pig had seemed to him neither beginning nor end but the very middle of something that would come to a simple and unexpected head. He was quite convinced that some*one* had been responsible for Hercules's recent affliction, and he wondered if the pig's recovery, and his and Mister Walton's presence at Fern Farm, were a source of worry for that someone. It was, he would say later, a pretty dire business to sicken a pig.

The outing above the river, the suspense roused by Mrs. Fern's story, perhaps even the relief over Hercules's recovery, contributed to an early evening at Fern Farm. The little boys fell asleep on the parlor floor, while the older folk talked and the two middle sisters were yawning up the stairs soon after. Mister Walton excused himself before it was eight o'clock, and Sundry went up as well. Only Aunt Beatrice was untouched by the general weariness, and Mr. and Mrs. Fern and Madeline left her tatting lace in the parlor when they climbed the stairs.

Sundry said good night to Mister Walton, went to his room, readied himself for bed, and turned his shoulder to the night.

In his own room, Mister Walton lay in bed and looked up at the ceiling.

Light from somewhere gave rise to an amorphous shape among the shadows in the further corner, but he turned his attention from this and thought of Phileda, which led him to think of the coming ball, which led him to think of Sundry's unexpected announcement this afternoon that he would be attending.

The night was uncommonly silent. There might have been the distant call of some night bird to jar the stillness, but not a breath more. Mister Walton thought such quiet might keep a person awake. Then from another quarter of the house, there came the rumble of stentorian snores—the very same he had mistaken for thunder the night before. The portly fellow pulled the covers over his shoulders and smiled as he closed his eyes, thinking wryly that *this* was not the sort of lullaby he would have chosen. Then he fell asleep.

Then he woke with no sense of how long he had been asleep or of what had wakened him and even a brief lack of knowledge concerning where he was. There was lamplight beneath the door and the sound of movement in the hall.

An alarming clamor came through the window—an animalistic babel, fit to noise the *forest primeval* or perhaps a modern jungle but not (thought an astonished Mister Walton) to occupy the gloom surrounding a farm in Maine. It was a savage sort of sound—a long angry grunt, almost a roar—and it was followed hard upon the heels by a similarly savage crash.

With a shout, Mister Walton sat upright. There was a knock at his door and he said, in a gasp, "Come in, come in!" and, "Sundry!," when the young man stuck his head into the room. "What is it? What time is it?"

"It's just by one o'clock."

"But what's the matter?"

"I think Hercules is trying to get out of the barn."

"Good heavens! The watchpig!"

The angry bellow and the crash came again. Now Mister Walton could hear other voices—the uncertain lowing of the animals in the barn. Sundry was pulling on his boots and throwing a shirt over his shoulders, and, for a portly, middle-aged gentleman, Mister Walton proved swift at dressing. There was a bang and a shout from inside the house, and then the bellow and crash from outside again. Sundry threw open the door to look into the hall.

"Mr. Moss!" came a feminine voice in a near whisper. Madeline stood at the other end of the hall with a nightdress clutched tightly about her, her face pale in the light of a candle, her eyes wide and frightened.

"That shout," said Sundry.

"It came from my parents' room."

Sundry strode purposefully down the hall. "Which door?" he said, and Madeline was in the midst of a gesture that would answer his question, when they heard a second, less emphatic shout and one of the doors to the hall flew open. Mr. Fern appeared, half dressed and hopping on one foot.

"Daddy! What is it?" called Madeline.

"I stubbed my toe!" shouted the father.

The next crash that came from outside sounded different and they could imagine that something had broken loose or shattered. There was a piglike squeal.

The children began to appear in the hall.

"Is something trying to get in at him?" Madeline said aloud.

Sundry shook his head. He thought he heard a man's voice shouting angrily. Mrs. Fern appeared in the hall with a "What is it, dear?" and then Mister Walton hurried out from his room, calling, "Sundry! Where are you?"

But Sundry was charging down the stairs, and Mister Walton and Mr. Fern hurried close behind, Mr. Fern casting assurances back to his wife and children, as well as contradictory warnings to stay away. "He's gotten loose!" said Mr. Fern, and indeed they could hear a triumphant squeal and another piggish roar followed by the shouts of both a man and a woman.

"Daddy!" called one of the children.

"Vergil, be careful!" shouted Ruth Fern.

To the north and east, the sky was filled with clouds, but low in the west sailed an irregular moon. As the three men spilled into the yard, a series of startling squeals, human and porcine, pierced the otherwise still night. A buckboard had been drawn up at the side of the house, led by a brace of lively looking horses. A lantern swayed on a short pole at the front of the rig and gave a weird radiance to the scene as an aged fellow attempted to rest a traveling bag from Hercules's jaws. An elderly woman stood in the seat of the wagon and shouted incoherent instructions to the man, which were interspersed with certain descriptives regarding the pig that would do no credit to the verbal character of a dockworker, much less a country lady.

"Aunt Beatrice!" shouted Mr. Fern, upon which astounded identification Hercules let go of the bag and the man tugging upon the bag fell backward.

"Jacob!" shouted the woman, and she snatched up the carriage whip like an old teamster and gave it a skillful snap over the proceedings.

Several voices shouted out, and Hercules gave a happy squeal to see that reinforcements had arrived. The man with the bag scrambled to his feet. Sundry took hold of Mister Walton's arm and backed the portly fellow away. Mr. Fern was frozen in his steps and the pig bounded his great mass behind the wagon, knocking over the ladder that was propped against the side of the house. "Mr. Fern!" called Sundry. "Get back!" With the ladder crashing among them, and Aunt Beatrice whipping up the horses as the man with the bag climbed aboard, it was prudent to follow this advice. Still, Sundry had to drag his host away.

Mr. Fern shouted and shook his fist in the air. Mister Walton gasped in amazement, but Sundry Moss almost smiled after the eloping couple. They had seen a sad Mr. Fern, and a placid, happy Mr. Fern, but now they were witness to a thunderous, shaking, vehement Mr. Fern. The farmer charged after the wagon, and they thought he might catch it and leap on board. He may have used too much of his energy shouting, however (he was shouting still while he ran), for he suddenly lost all speed and came to a flagging halt.

The buckboard reached the road and headed south toward the village, the sound of hooves and wheels rattling against the road and the snap of the whip and the creak of the rig as immediate as thunder in the still air.

"That drunken sot!" Mr. Fern was shouting. "That intemperate rum peddler!" He was shaking his fist again, only adding to the general astonishment of his guests. "That liquorious cornwinkle! Why, I'll—!" He let out an angry shout, arms flailing, and he leaped into the air as if he might snatch the beard from the object of his wrath. Hercules tromped up to the farmer with anxious grunts and Mr. Fern fell over the animal.

"Good heavens!" said Mister Walton, and he and Sundry rushed forward to help the man, while the wagon's single lantern dwindled and finally disappeared over the nearest rise.

"Daddy!" came a shout from Aunt Beatrice's window.

"Vergilius!" came another.

"Oh, Mother!" called Mr. Fern to his wife. "My aunt has run away with a rumrunner!"

"What?"

"Aunt Beatrice has eloped!"

A general noise was heard from the room above, and it might have been made up of as much laughter and delight as outrage; the men could hear the news being handed back to those not immediately at the window and the shrieks and refusals to believe that ensued.

"Gracious powers, Vergilius!" said Mrs. Fern. With the light in the room behind her and her face in shadow, it was difficult to see her expression. "Aunt Beatrice has gone off with Jacob Lister?"

Mr. Fern simply hung his head and moaned. Hercules sat back on his haunches and grunted sympathetically.

"Well, what's to be done?" said the woman in the window, a query that was more philosophic than practical.

Mr. Fern's head came up. "Done?" he shouted. "I'll tell you what's to be done! I'll go after them!"

Mrs. Fern bumped her head against the sash, said, "Ouch!" and then, "Vergilius Fern! Don't be absurd!"

"Absurd?"

Madeline disappeared from the window, and Mrs. Fern leaned further out.

"Vergilius!"

But he was running for the barn with Hercules close behind. One tall door was lying on its side, where it had fallen from the might of the great pig's massive charge.

"Vergilius!"

"What's he going to do?" wondered Mister Walton.

"He's going after them, I guess," said Sundry.

"Good heavens!" Mister Walton would never have imagined that the seemingly mild farmer had such reserves of energy and wrath.

Mrs. Fern disappeared from the window, and in a moment the front door crashed open and Madeline came rushing out. "Daddy!" she was shouting. "Daddy! Mr. Moss! What does Daddy think he's doing?"

"I think he thinks he's going after his aunt."

Madeline rolled her eyes and headed for the barn.

"*I* was thinking," Sundry called after her, "that maybe a ride in the night air might cool him down a bit."

"We had better go with him," said Mister Walton.

Madeline turned back, saying, "Oh, would you?" she pleaded. "Please keep him from doing anything grievous!"

"I will go along to be sure that calm heads prevail," said Mister Walton. It was his specialty.

"Oh, thank you, Mister Walton."

Mrs. Fern came charging out of the house, bypassing these conversants to run for the barn and shouting, "Vergilius!"

"Sundry?"

"I wouldn't miss it for the world, Mister Walton."

Mr. Fern was in the barn, shouting his determination to rescue his aunt and to bring Jacob Lister to justice.

"But the woman is eighty-three years old!" declared his wife.

"Well, Sundry," said Mister Walton. "What shall we do?"

"Let's hitch the horse," said Sundry. "'*The game's afoot.*' Isn't that what Mr. Holmes said?"

The portly gentleman hurried after his friend. There was a great commotion in the barn as Mr. Fern readied the carriage.

"I think that was Shakespeare, actually," said Mister Walton.

47. Philosophy Among the Trees

They had seen stars, of course, and they had been out of an evening, but they had never seen, while stretched upon their backs, the constellations flicker from behind a canopy of leaves; Ephram, Eagleton, and Thump had never experienced a campfire's pleasures—the contrast between the cool night air at their backs and the heat upon their faces, the mesmerizing light flashing among the trees, and the inspired cascade of sparks disappearing into the vast darkness to mingle with the blinking starlight.

There was, as well, a rough camaraderie to the gathering on Blinn Hill that was foreign to the Moosepath League. At first, they were doubtful about spending the night *beneath the stars* but forgot their qualms when the first of the hoboes arrived on foot, greeting them like long-lost friends. It was too jolly for doubt, meeting these men after the day's journey, watching as they raised their tents or claimed a patch of moss for their bedroll. The provender rendered from the hoboes' kits was more appetizing than the slumgullion at the *shantytown* in Bangor (or, perhaps, the gentlemen of the club were more hungry); a sack of potatoes arrived with one fellow, another man appeared with a whole plucked chicken (and no exact account of where he found it), and someone hefted a small keg from his shoulder and rolled it into the middle of the gathering (Thump bent over the keg and thought it smelled curiously like turpentine).

The members of the club had never seen anything like the campfire in the woods. The conflict between the snapping flames and the darkening atmosphere only increased the fire's fascination for them. The east appeared uncertain to Eagleton, whose weather eye was ever watchful. The sun had set but the land was still visible, and he returned to the southern edge of the forest to look out over the stone walls, the fields, and the hills and river valleys.

Jasper Packet went with him and together they considered the strange sky. "Looks like weather," said Jasper.

"Yes," agreed Eagleton. He was not used to the term *weather* being used to indicate *stormy weather*, so he took Jasper's declaration as pleasingly obvious. "Yes, it does," he said. He tried to think of something else to add, but the word *weather* seemed to cover the subject pretty thoroughly. He turned around and appraised the trees behind them. He had not spent very much time near to so many oaks and maples and chestnuts; when taken together, their size and numbers were surprising to him. After a deep and appreciative breath, he said, "Looks like a forest."

Jasper frowned up at the green crowns, wondering if he'd missed something.

"It's forty minutes past the hour of seven," said Ephram when Eagleton and Jasper Packet returned from the forest's edge.

"Hmmm," said Thump. He wished he had his tide almanac with him.

Eagleton, too, was a little lost without a recent weather prediction from the *Portland Daily Advertiser.*

Ephram looked apologetic and put his watch away.

"What did you see?" asked Blind Po.

"Looks like weather," said Jasper.

"It's interested in what we're up to," said one of the hoboes. "It's followed us all the way from Bangor."

"It's kept its distance," said another.

"We'll feel something of it," said Blind Po, "though I warrant we won't get wet."

"I wouldn't welcome getting rained on," came a voice from some yards away.

"Henry says, 'I wouldn't welcome getting rained on,'" came another.

Several of the men about the fire cocked an appraising eye at Blind Po. "It reminds me of *Yellow Tuesday*, back in '81," said one of them. "There were black skies for nearly a week before then, but they were to the west."

"Yes, yes!" said Eagleton. "*Yellow Tuesday!*" He remembered it with a mixture of pleasure and awe—perhaps even a measure of apprehension. He'd been almost twenty-four on September 6, 1881.

"Was that the Tuesday before the Thursday?" wondered Ephram.

"Yes, yes!" said Eagleton.

"Hmmm," said Thump, for that Tuesday before the Thursday, that September 6, 1881, had been, in retrospect, a red-letter day in the marvelous history of their society, though the Moosepath League *per se* would not exist for almost another fifteen years.

"Good heavens!" said Ephram. "*Yellow Tuesday!*"

It had been, in fact, the very day that Matthew Ephram, Christopher Eagleton, and Joseph Thump first met. The Thursday following was remarkable for being the day of their first meal together at the Shipswood Restaurant.

"There *were* black skies, weren't there," said Ephram. Dark clouds had been rising in the west for two days that September, but on Tuesday the sixth people along the northeastern seaboard rose to find the sky suffused with a coppery tinge. Certain jovial spirits said that the world was coming to an end, and many a church was filled to capacity as pastors and priests did their best to soothe their flocks or to castigate them for the obdurate behavior that had led civilization to such precarious ends.

Ephram, Eagleton, and Thump had each gotten up late, only to find, respectively, the Baptist, Methodist, and Episcopalian houses of worship filled to capacity. It seemed then, to each of them (and independently), sensible to visit the waterfront, where a larger portion of the sky could be observed. And so they met.

Ephram was in the midst of recollection now. "Thump was on the sidewalk, looking down the wharf, when I came along," he said. "I was looking at the sky. *You* helped us back on our feet," he said with a nod to Eagleton. "It is fitting," he said to the hoboes nearby, "that the very first memory I have of Eagleton is of his hand reaching out to help."

Eagleton waved a hand, embarrassed.

"No, no," said Ephram. "Credit where it is due."

"Hmmm," said Thump. He was trying to remember the day, fifteen years ago, but after colliding against Ephram's rugged chin with his forehead his mental faculties had, for a while, been a little foggy.

"Ah, what a day!" said Eagleton.

"And it was *very* yellow," said Ephram.

"A volcano in Bali," said Jasper. "It filled the sky with soot. Or a fire in Montana. I can't remember which."

The light beyond the trees had reached an amber hue, as if the sun behind the rim of the earth had turned to brass, and past the trunks of oak and maple the grass shone like gold, so that it might have been the height of summer when the hay is near cutting; but the leaves along the western edge of the woods were lined with a similar yellow and this put the gathering in mind of fall. The air seemed warm and close among the trees, and hardly a breath of wind stirred the branches.

Almost in the space of a thought, the light was gone from the world and stars began to show at the height of the sky, blinking on like the lamps in the village windows below.

The novelty of the Moosepathian's experience continued with the evening meal. It was strange to the members to be dining without silverware. The affair was simpler than any they had known before and more haphazard, but everything was tasty, and it seemed to them that the most elegant and elegantly turned-out meal at the Shipswood Restaurant paled in comparison.

The three friends had come to trust the wherewithal of their new companions, however rustic it might prove, and they were not disappointed when the time came to bed down. Several fellows contributed blankets or offered advice on how best to make themselves comfortable. The night was a continued revelation to Ephram, Eagleton, and Thump. Thump listened, most of all, to the small but increasing stir among the trees, thinking that the rise and fall of the night breeze in the spring foliage sounded a great deal like waves upon a shore. "It's a very beautiful sound," he said quietly, hardly knowing that he had spoken aloud.

"It's very springlike," said Jasper.

"Is it?" wondered Thump.

"Oh, yes," said this philosopher. "The young leaves have their own sort of sound in the wind."

"They do?"

"Not at all like summer leaves. Summer leaves, when you hear them, are much more . . . summerlike."

Thump had never imagined such a thing, but was grateful for this intelligence and took Jasper at his word. He had heard the wind in trees before, of course, and in all seasons, but not in so many trees at once and that rush among leaf and limb had always competed with the sounds of the city. "And in fall?" he asked Jasper.

"You've never *heard* a sound so peculiar to the season. It's very . . . fall-like"

Thump stared up with wide eyes. The movement of the trees was all the more difficult to understand in the wavering light of the campfires. Lying there, he had the sudden awareness that seasons had been passing by without his full attention, or even his . . . awareness.

"I like the fall," came a voice from the darkness, and then, "Henry says, 'I like the fall.'"

Ephram was thinking upon the passage of time. It had occurred to him, out here in the wilderness, that the movements of his beloved clocks and watches were of little import to a tree, much less an entire forest. It was not even a very big forest, to be truthful, but its sense of permanence gave the lie to what his watch might say about the minute and the hour. He was awed, somewhat as Thump had been by the passage of seasons, but also a little troubled. He held one of his watches and rubbed the back of it with his thumb, rather like Leander Spark rubbing his bit of rabbit fur.

Eagleton, for his part, was speculating about the weather, recalling the *Tuesday before the Thursday* in September of 1881, *and* the days that preceded it.

"It was a very *yellow* day," he said aloud.

"There was another yellow day back in '43," came a voice from beyond the fire. Eagleton could not place who was speaking. "My mother was a Millerite, and my father gave Mom her head in most things, so he went along."

"I had an uncle who followed old Miller," said Big Eye.

"Don't know him," said someone. "This Miller."

"He allowed how the world was going to end," said Big Eye.

"Well, won't it?"

"Yes, but he allowed how it would end fairly quick, and even gave it a date. He said things would close shop round about the third of April 1843."

"What happened?" wondered someone further off, whereupon soft laughter and chuckles filled the night air.

"A comet came by," said the first voice, still unidentified by Eagleton and his fellow members of the club. "Then there was a yellow day soon after and a great crowd of folk—not just the Millerites—went to the cemetery to meet their ancestors, who were expected to rise up. Some of them had special white gowns for the purpose, hoping to *look* like angels when Judgment came even if they hadn't behaved like them. Some people went to the graveyards, naked as the day they were born."

"Good heavens!" came three distinct voices.

"My mother," continued the storyteller, "parked her carcass on her first husband's grave, saying she was that anxious to see him again. My father was so disgusted he went back to the house and made himself supper. I was nine years old.

"After a few hours, when a single ghost didn't show, there were those of us who got a little hungry and thought Dad had the right idea. We got back to the house and he met us on the porch. 'Great socks and shoes!' he said to Mother. 'What makes you think he'd so much as poke his head out if *you* were sitting there waiting for him?' He was that disgusted."

"The end of the world!" said someone. "Foolishness!"

"No, it's not," came the trembly voice of Blind Po, who lay so close by the fire that Eagleton thought he might singe his beard. "It's only foolishness to name the hour. '*But of that day and hour knoweth no man, no, not the angels of heaven, but my Father only.*'"

A vast silence followed upon the heels of this quotation.

"I saw a ghost once," said someone. It was Big Eye himself.

"A ghost?" said Ephram. He had been lying on his back, almost falling asleep as he listened. Now he turned half onto his side to see Big Eye's wide orb shining bright on the other side of the fire.

"I thought it was a little person when I first saw her," said the hobo. "She looked about two inches tall. I thought she was close by, but I was seeing her, to begin with, from far away. Leastwise, she was far away in the spirit world walking toward me. I hardly dared move a muscle. She was all aglow, white as Gabriel's wings, and growing as she walked closer. She was pretty as an elf. That's what I thought she was, too, for a bit, and I was ready for her—my hat turned back and my thumbs hitched together. She disappeared, though, before I got a close look, and I was a little sorry."

"Do you think she was a ghost?" said Ephram.

"Oh, well," said Big Eye with deep philosophy. "She was *some*thing."

"We saw an apparition at a seance," said Eagleton.

"Yes, last fall," said Ephram. "Where did you see your phantom?"

"In the midst of a wood, very much like this," pronounced Big Eye.

Ephram rolled onto his back, his coat beneath his head. He pulled his borrowed blanket up to his chin.

"It was very strange," said Big Eye.

Someone yawned and someone else began to snore.

"Good night," came a now familiar drawl from out of the dark.

"Henry says, 'Good night,'" came a second.

The Moosepathians were both wearied and enlivened by their day, and by the promise of the day to follow. They felt the residual movement that sometimes follows travelers to their beds—in this case, either the sway of the carriage or the shimmy of the rails. The snapping of the campfire was of great comfort, as was its light and warmth. Ephram, Eagleton, and Thump listened to the many yawns, and then the snores, and finally the wind rising in the trees. One by one, they dropped off to sleep. Eagleton was the last, thinking about Blind Po's prediction of a storm.

And then that great ripping crash brought them all—hobo and Moosepathian alike—to their feet with a concerted shout.

48. All Something Breaks Loose!

The wagon was quickly wheeled out of the way and the Ferns' Sunday carriage brought into the yard. Sundry took over, and if he did not *dog* the work he did approach it with a degree of moderation that Mister Walton could not mistake. Only once did Mr. Fern object while Sundry was pulling links.

"It's when you hurry," said the young man, "that you forget a strap or a buckle and find yourself in the ditch a mile down the road." Hercules followed Sundry about with interested grunts; Sundry scratched the pig's head, then went on with his business and pointed out what needed tightening as he moved around the horse and rig. It was done with more speed than others might have credited, considering his deliberate manner, and Mr. Fern seemed calmer for Sundry's capable presence.

The children were all out in the yard by now, and Mrs. Fern and the older girls, including Madeline, stood about with their nightrobes drawn about them and their hair tied up. Mrs. Fern wavered between humor and irritation with her husband, and Madeline rolled her eyes as her father stomped about. He realized that he was not entirely dressed and sent one of the boys in for his boots, which were thrown inside the carriage.

"They have half an hour on us!" declared Mr. Fern, his emotion rising.

"Ten minutes," said Sundry. He looped the reins over the foot rail. "Where did they go?"

"South, is all I know, but we'll find them." There, in his stocking feet, Mr. Fern snatched up the whip and handed it to Sundry. "I don't trust myself to drive while I'm in this state," he said.

"I'll get us there," said Sundry, so he climbed into the driver's seat, and the other men boarded as the rig swayed and creaked.

"You *watch* your state, Vergilius Fern!" declared the farmer's wife.

"Yes, Ruth."

"Do you know where you're going?" asked Madeline of Sundry Moss.

Sundry was good humored about the adventure. "South," was all he could hazard.

"She's eighty-three years old!" Mrs. Fern was insisting.

"I know that!"

"Eloping!" said Mrs. Fern. "Who would have thought!"

"Where did she meet him, I'd like to know," growled Mr. Fern.

Sundry peered into the carriage window from his seat. "All in?"

"Go, go!" said the farmer.

Sundry gave a snap to the leads, and in a moment they were out of the yard, bounding down the road and jouncing against the ruts with a single lantern and the lowering moon to light the way. Behind them, and to their left the dark clouds hung—a great blind mass. Sundry cast a glance back and had the picturesque view of Mrs. Fern, Madeline, the children, and the great white pig gathered in an uncertain clump before the house. Madeline waved.

He drove the horses up the knoll, where the moon shone a little more brightly, and only slowed a bit when the road dropped and wrapped itself around a shadowed corner. Just before they came to the mudhole that Johnny

Poulter had skirted two days before, Sundry remembered that boggy place; he stood against the reins and nickered the horses up the bank.

There were some shouts (from Mr. Fern) and rueful laughs (from Mister Walton) as they jolted along the ridge above the road, and Sundry only caught a glimpse of the slough below him and the remnants of a carriage wheel. "Look!" he shouted. There were lights, perhaps a quarter of a mile ahead of them, disappearing down the further side of a slope.

"What is it?" called Mr. Fern, who was half hanging from the window.

"Carriage lights ahead!" bellowed Sundry over the noise of their movement. "Not half a mile. There was a wheel left behind in the boggy place, back there. I think they might have turned over." He admired Jacob Lister if the old fellow had righted a carriage and replaced a wheel in that short time by himself. Perhaps they had only lost the spare wheel that some carriages had strapped beneath the body.

"He thinks they might have overturned," said Mr. Fern when he pulled himself back into the carriage. The news sobered him somewhat. "I only hope she's not injured."

"He would have come back if anything had happened," assured Mister Walton. He had a firm grip on the ceiling strap beside him as they joggled and bobbled along the field above the road.

"If he didn't think I would shoot him," said the farmer.

Sundry was a good driver, but he was not so familiar with the road, and the moonlight, flickering over the hills and through the occasional grove or solitary tree, made it difficult to judge distance and form. Still, he might have urged the horse to greater speed if he'd been alone or this had been a mission more worthy of risk. The wind and noise of their movement, the tension in the reins, and the sense of things falling past them was exhilarating and not conducive to caution in anyone less steady than Sundry Moss, but the young man had not forgotten that his friend and employer was riding behind him.

"The village!" shouted Sundry. They thundered over the West Branch Bridge and he stood again, searching the places between buildings to catch sight of the fleeing carriage. On Front Street, he pulled up to avoid an old dog. The creature trotted out of harm's way, and they clattered through the sleepy town. Sundry suspected that they were not the first noisy passage in the last few minutes, for lights were on in several windows.

"Behind us!" Mr. Fern shouted, half hanging from the window of the carriage. "Behind us! Heading east!"

Sundry turned to scan the way behind and realized that back across the bridge, and some yards beyond, he had missed a road to their left. He saw a flash of light moving into the stillness and the dark.

Their carriage wheels racketed over the bridge again, then the rig leaned to the right and they were back on the trail. Mr. Fern called to Sundry, warning him about a sharp turn—just in time, it seemed, for they barely made the corner without tipping over. Sundry took them through a crossroad at double speed, then hauled back on the reins as they drew up to the mouth of the Abagadasset and a ferry dock. "Whoa! Whoa!" he called.

"Blast! The ferry!" shouted Mr. Fern. He burst out of the carriage before it had fully stopped. "Have they got it?"

"I believe so," said Sundry.

"Blast!" shouted the farmer again, and loud enough to attract the ferry man's attention.

Lanterns shone on the dock and on the ferry. The craft was cast off, but it had barely rendered enough steam to keep it bow first and the pilot looked concerned. An elderly man on board was discussing something with the ferry man, who had looked up at the sound of Mr. Fern's shout. Jacob Lister hardly looked pressed and only offered a casual glance back. Aunt Beatrice stood, arms folded, looking defiantly at her nephew, who shouted once again.

"Aunt Beatrice! You get back here!"

"Vergil!" she called back. "How come you are so hidebound about one thing when you're so even about everything else?"

"Auntie! You can't run off with that rumrunner!"

"Maybe if I live to be a hundred he'll have time to ruin me," she called back, hardly perturbed.

"Auntie! He's driving much too fast!"

"He'd drive slower if you weren't chasing us!"

Mr. Fern had driven *himself* into a state of terrible frustration and he was hopping about the dockyard like an angry rooster.

"Vergilius!" shouted the old lady. "You're going to burst a blood vessel!"

In the midst of this shouting, Mister Walton said quietly to Sundry, "So, the ladder was the clue." They were standing by the carriage like onlookers at an outdoor play.

"With Hercules's mysterious ailment," said Sundry, "and the dirt on the foot of the ladder, I did wonder, but the lilac among the hydrangeas made me pretty sure. There were marks where the ladder had stood among the hydrangeas. I thought it was Madeline or, goodness' sakes, one of her sisters."

"The old fellow had been courting her at the window," said an amazed Mister Walton.

"*And* lacing Hercules's slops with rum to keep him quiet."

"Good heavens! But you would think that *some*one would have heard them."

"With that thunderous noise every night? We could hear Mr. Fern snoring halfway through the house."

"Yes, of course."

"At least, I hope it was Mr. Fern."

"We can't wait for the ferry," said the farmer. He came around the carriage with a new plan. "We'll go back to the crossroad and head north.

There's a road some miles up that will connect us with that peninsula." He nodded to the other side of the river. "It's a little longer by that route, but their way will be harder going."

Mister Walton gave Mr. Fern the slightest shade of an uncertain expression, but the man did not see it.

"What if they wait for us to disappear and come back over with the ferry?" wondered Sundry.

Mr. Fern looked astonished. "I hadn't thought," he said.

"Or what if they have a minister waiting for them in a house, right over there?" Sundry pointed after the ferry.

"Do you think?"

Sundry laughed. "Not really."

Mr. Fern shot Sundry a perturbed glance. "Perhaps we should drive over the next hill," he suggested. "Then we can douse the light and creep back to watch them."

"That's a good idea," said Sundry, but there was something in his manner that made Mister Walton chuckle. Sundry held his hand palm up and looked up at the sky. They followed his gaze. It did feel like rain.

"I am sorry to drag you gentlemen all over creation," said Mr. Fern.

"You don't know how much we enjoy an adventure," said Mister Walton, that previous chuckle still evident in his voice.

And so they turned the carriage about, and Sundry drove them over the next rise. The lantern was blown out and they hurried back to the top of the slope. It was a little while before the ferry made the other side of the water, though it was a short way. The silence of the weather, the absolute stillness in the air, began to play on their nerves now that their initial excitement had spent itself.

"They might douse their own light," said Mr. Fern, who had begun to have all sorts of suspicions since listening to Sundry.

"They might have someone across there to take the carriage for them while they ride the ferry back," said Sundry.

"Mr. Moss!"

Mister Walton said, "Ahem!"

"Sorry," said Sundry.

"I am beginning to think that you'd be rather good at this sort of thing," said Mr. Fern, not without a hint of humor.

"Do you mean elopement?" said Sundry, without looking at the man. "I think I might hire out." Then he did turn and regard Mr. Fern. "I apologize if I seem to be making light of the situation."

"You are very good to come out with me," said Mr. Fern. "And you're driving is not to be faulted."

There was a silence. The carriage light in the distance mounted the hill above the ferry and headed north.

"Perhaps we should head back home," said Mr. Fern quietly. No one else said anything. The farmer kicked at a rock in the road and chuckled ruefully to himself. "Let's go home and have some breakfast before we go back to bed."

Mister Walton yawned involuntarily.

Sundry looked over Mister Walton's head as if he had seen something or sensed something from the starless portion of the sky; that dark sector suddenly flashed with a broad streak of lightning. Mister Walton had turned away from the north, and Mr. Fern's head was down, but the burst lit their surroundings like broad daylight.

The thunder took two or three seconds to arrive, but then it filled the air as had the flash, charging down river and echoing among the hills like an extended barrage of cannon fire. After the great silence, the thunder was deafening and it shook them to their bones.

"I wonder where that hit," said Mr. Fern. The back rumble of a distant echo reached them, then another. A more earthbound explosion of light illumined the cloud cover in the north, and a deeper, longer sort of thunder soon followed.

"Good heavens!" said Mister Walton. The light from below diminished but did not die entirely. It glowed like a giant's hearth against the intervening hills and trees.

"Good Lord!" said Mr. Fern.

"What could that be?" wondered Sundry.

"That's Richmond," informed Mr. Fern. "They have some massive icehouses up there."

"Icehouses?" said Mister Walton. "I wouldn't have guessed an icehouse was subject to *that* sort of fire."

"They're filled with sawdust to insulate the ice, and much of the ice has been shipped out of the upper levels by this time of year so there's nothing *but* sawdust."

Again there was a silence while they recovered from the awful thought.

"Shall we hurry to see what we can do?" said Mister Walton.

"Yes, quickly," said Mr. Fern. "Mr. Moss?"

"Jump in!" Sundry was already running to the carriage. He hopped onto the driver's seat, gathered the reins, and as soon as his fellows were aboard he snapped the leads and turned right at the crossroads. The glow in the north grew brighter and more definite as they rushed along the old post road, and, half an hour later, when they crested a hill overlooking the town of Richmond, they could see the source of the conflagration—a great mass of flames, still a mile away, at the place called Iceboro.

❧ BOOK SIX ❧

May 30, 1897
(Before Dawn)

49. The Crack Before Dawn

To begin with, there was the lightning itself.

At that potent bark of thunder, Ephram and Eagleton jumped with concerted shouts from their rough beds as if tied to the same string.

"Good heavens!" remarked Ephram.

"My thoughts exactly!" cried Eagleton.

Other, less proper declarations were heard as the rest of the camp leaped to its collective feet. Grumbling echoes rolled back from distant hills, and the ground trembled as beneath a succession of heavy footfalls.

Ephram had used his coat as a blanket, and he endeavored now to put his arms in the sleeves. Eagleton was in the midst of a similar undertaking when Thump (still asleep) let out a grunt that startled them once again. Watching the movements of the roused hoboes, Ephram and Eagleton had revolved in different directions (Ephram clockwise, Eagleton counterclockwise, according to Moosepath tradition), when Thump's unexpected outburst caused them somehow to insert their outstretched arms into one another's sleeves.

Ephram and Eagleton found themselves back-to-back, each struggling with an unknown assailant. Eagleton was sure he had been seized by one of the villains who had imperiled Mrs. Roberto and he began to shout, "They've got me! They've got me, Ephram!"

"I am caught as well!" shouted his worthy friend.

Thump wakened, blinked in the darkness, and sat up. In his ears were the cries of his companions; before him were two struggling figures. Thump gained his feet and apprehended the pair of shadows as he imagined an officer of the law might nab a fleeing criminal—that is, headfirst with a great leap. Shouts and grunts came on the heels of this heroic effort till somebody's foot kicked the nearest fire into renewed life and they found themselves staring at one another's grimacing features in the resultant glow.

"Good heavens, Eagleton!" shouted Ephram. "Is it you?"

"Ephram!" declared Eagleton. "You came just in time!"

"Did I?" replied a perplexed Matthew Ephram. "I was going to say the same about yourself!"

Sitting up, they shrugged themselves into whichever coat was left to them. Ephram took note of Thump, who was rubbing his forehead.

"Where did they go?" wondered Thump.

"Good heavens!" said Ephram again. "It was Thump!"

"Of course!" shouted Eagleton. "Old friend, once again you have freed us from the exigencies of dangerous circumstance."

"You have saved us!" said Eagleton. He stood uncertainly. The coat felt strange about the shoulders but he buttoned it against the night air.

"Saved us!" agreed Ephram, peering into the dark. He stood, dusting his trouser legs. "And in the process driven the villains off, it seems!"

Thump looked up from the ground, wild and wide-eyed.

"We must be close upon their trail!" asserted Eagleton. He had read this phrase once in *The Pathway from Remorse* by Mrs. Minerva Blythe Shield.

"Stout fellow!" said Ephram, helping Thump to his feet.

"Ever in the fore!" pronounced Eagleton with an affectionate pat on Thump's back.

This mutual admiration might have continued if it had not been interrupted by a chorus of agitated voices from the perimeter of the wood. There was a distant glow beyond the trees, and the members of the club vaguely comprehended some grave occurrence.

"What is it?" asked Eagleton as he and his fellows peered after the flames on the western bank of the Kennebec. The fire glowed over its surroundings and etched in shadow everything between itself and Blinn Hill. On those distant banks and immediately above a massive burning building stood a small settlement—houses and shops, a steepled church, and two long structures that quartered the workforce of the local enterprise.

"It's an icehouse," said Big Eye darkly, "and half of Iceboro with it if many more than ourselves don't lend a hand."

They could see, even from that distance, a train engine and several freight cars retreating from the adjacent yards. By the broad docks that reached out from the burning building, two schooners were visible.

Big Eye Pfelt, dog in arms, gave the order to harness the horses and many a hobo raced back to the camp to douse the fires and retrieve his gear. When the carriage pulled up alongside, Big Eye took the reins. "Hop on, gentlemen," he said, "the night promises hot work!"

Men crammed themselves into the carriage. Ephram, Eagleton, and Thump climbed inside, excusing themselves to several fellows who had already squeezed themselves into every available nook and corner. The *I beg your pardon*s and *I am so sorry*s quickly declined into rudimentary grunts and *Oops*es as the carriage rocked and ricocheted its way down the meadow. Big

Eye was a wild driver when the spirit moved him, and he seemed undaunted by any inability to see obstacles in the dark. Inside the carriage it was even more difficult to see. Thump was sure they must all be traveling in a vertically transposed manner till he realized, in an unexpected flash of radiance, that he was looking nose to toe at a pair of boots.

Someone else must have taken note of Thump's posture for he was righted suddenly. There were startled yells and grunts as they rattled against the carriage walls; a flash of light had emanated from a wooden matchstick. Some gray-bearded *man of the road* had actually struck a match to light his pipe in that jumbled space.

How Big Eye knew to pull up before the gate was more than the members of the Moosepath League would ever understand, but they felt the carriage bounce to a stop, and, once the gate was opened, they sailed along with a little less speed and a little more stability. When they reached the road, Big Eye had them charging like thunder itself toward the river.

Peering past bouncing heads and the swaying silhouettes of grizzled faces, Thump saw that the west-facing sides of houses and barns and trees were lit with an angry, orange glow.

50. *Deus Ex Machina*

She drew aside the curtain of her bedroom window and laid her face against the pane, where a spot of mist pulsed with her breath. After a moment she could see a glow above the hill across the way.

The terrific explosion had wakened her in an instant; it had confused her, the din of it entering and merging with her dreams even as she sat up and gasped; the shock from without had brought her heart into her throat and made the visions of sleep more real. A moment later, she gasped again— almost cried out—when the echoes of thunder and the memory of something near to a nightmare returned like a wave crashing off the shore.

The sound receded, and, with a hand to her breast, Dee almost laughed. Some further echo barely rattled the sashes as she first looked out and saw the glow rise from above the hill across the way. Then she cast her night things off and began to pull on whatever clothes came to hand.

When she stepped into the hall, the house was quiet. Had her mother and uncle wakened? How could they not have been shaken from their beds by that crash? She closed her door softly and *shushed* down the stairs. She took a coat from the stand by the front door and went into the parlor, where a shadow stood by the window.

"You saw it?" said her Uncle Fale in the near darkness. He turned his head and briefly fixed a glance in her direction.

"Yes," said Dee. "Isn't that in the direction of Olin Bell's farm?"

"It is, but it's further on, across the river. Where are you going?"

Dee had on her coat and she fumbled with the buttons before returning to the hall for a hat. "To see what it is, and if I can help."

"I'll come, too," said the old man.

"No, Uncle Fale. Mom will be alone and not knowing what's happening." Dee paused then. None of the hats seemed appropriate for going to a fire so she took a dark kerchief from its peg and tied it around her head. "I'm going . . . now," she added, almost apologetically.

"I can't keep up with you," he admitted. "I'll speak to Deborah, and maybe I'll be along. They'll probably need every hand they can get."

Dee stepped into the parlor just long enough to buss Uncle Fale's cheek. She heard something from the downstairs bedroom, then, before she had the opportunity to debate her intentions with her mother, she burst from the door and ran down the walk to the street. There was a commotion toward town—someone shouting from the seat of a wagon; she saw several people climbing on board before the horse and rig dashed off in the opposite direction. Dee raised a hand and opened her mouth to shout, but they were well out of hearing. Looking west, she could only see that surging, orange glow above the hill across the road.

Someone's front door closed with a slam. There was a voice in the night calling out, "Be careful!" Dee hurried across the road, slipped over the fence to the meadow beyond, and climbed the slope. A low trilling sound reached her ears and she was startled, then confounded, to be greeted by Mr. Porch, who seemed equally bemused to discover her on his nocturnal prowl.

"Good heavens!" she said and scooped the purring cat into her arms.

The light from afar grew as she neared the top till her line of vision broke the crest and she saw the fire itself. She was shocked by the awful flames against the dark. The sound of the fire carried to the hill—an immense, if distant, rumble—itself like unceasing thunder. She thought she heard shouts and cries within the greater body of noise, but it was the ball of fire encompassing the center of the icehouse that took her breath.

The burning building was enormous, attesting to the thriving ice business along the Kennebec, which river was famous throughout the world for the clarity of its waters. Some six hundred feet in length and four stories tall, the icehouse dwarfed everything in its vicinity—a massive wooden structure filled with sawdust and ice from the previous winter's cutting and a type common to the scourge of fire. From Dee's hilltop the flames seemed to lick the clouds. Iceboro was lit as bright as day, and she descried the tiny forms of people and horses scattering and congesting the roads outside the village. North of the town, a locomotive engine chugged steam, and in the river two ice schooners moved slowly down the tide, their masts sticklike silhouettes against the blaze as the vessels slipped from danger.

On the near side of the Kennebec, the roofs of houses and farms blushed with reflected light. Lanterns dotted the yards and windows. At Olin Bell's place, Dee saw movement near the barn.

She heard pounding hooves behind her and turned with a startled cry as a dark form rose from the shadows below. "Whoa, there!" came a voice, and the animal reigned in a few yards away on the crest of the hill. "Who's that?"

"Dee Pilican."

"Elmer Barnes," said the rider. "They'll never save that icehouse," he reckoned aloud while his horse stamped. "The town itself could go up."

"Was it lightning?"

"I think it must have been." Even from this distance, the man's face was faintly touched by the massive flames. He looked up. Stars were either fading or already gone from three quadrants of the sky. To the northwest, the eye was dazzled by the blaze. "Lightning, but no rain," he said. "I've seen it once before. It's probably pouring buckets over the Sheepscott."

"Will you take me down?" asked Dee, approaching the horse, one hand up to touch the animal's muzzle. Ezra Porch leapt from her arm and dashed away. Dee rubbed her shoulder where the cat had scratched her. "You can drop me by Olin Bell's farm," she said to Elmer. "I see him hitching his wagon."

Elmer Barnes did not stand on ceremony but offered his hand and pulled her up behind him. "Hang on," he said. He was a good horseman, and he may have picked his way a little more carefully down the hill with Dee riding pillion; under other, less dire circumstances, one might have guessed that it was simply too pleasant having her arms about his waist to hurry.

"Olin!" Dee called from her perch, but her voice was competing with the roar of the fire across the river. She could make out the movements in Olin's farmyard more clearly as things stood out in silhouette against the blaze. There was an explosion from the icehouse; no doubt some cache of sawdust had been heated to the point of combustion. A section of roof and wall shot out over the river in a shower of flame and sparks.

Olin Bell was climbing onto his wagon, which he had filled with barrels and casks for carting water. Dee called out again. He would hardly have recognized her in the dark, with her chestnut hair caught up in a black kerchief, but he knew her voice. Elmer swung his horse's flank around and she dropped to the ground, saying to Olin, "Let me go with you!"

"I don't know, Dee," he said above the rumble. "The docks are too close to the fire, so they're landing the boats at a little shelf almost across from us here." He pointed. "The crossing from this side is above the icehouse, and the boats have to drift past the fire. It's a little chancy."

Dee had climbed up next to him. She squeezed his near hand and said, "Go." A carriage clattered by, and several voices shouted out, "Ho!" and, "Hey there, Olin!" Then Elmer Barnes rode off before Olin was able to steer the wagon out of his yard and onto the road leading upriver.

Dee couldn't take her eyes from the snarling, crackling fire till her attention was caught by a clutch of figures running away from a collapsing wall and the abstract perception of flames against the night—monstrous cousins to the comforting blaze in one's parlor hearth—metamorphosed into a tangible demon. Trees along the near shore of the river cast spasmodic shadows across the road, and as the carriage drew near the crossing the people and horses and wagons along the bank appeared to waver in the strange light. The roar was incessant, and, Dee thought, it must be deafening to anyone fighting the blaze.

Half a dozen volunteers were already loaded on one of the boats coursing the river—*over*loaded, according to one voice in the waiting crowd. "I've got some barrels and casks!" shouted Olin, and these were rolled down the bank, where they might be floated behind the next waiting boat.

Dee was surprised by the size of the crowd. Olin took hold of her arm as he pressed his way through. "Can you swim?" he asked her.

"Why?" she gasped.

"If we drift close enough to that building," he explained with a nod, "and the near wall collapses, we may have to bale out."

"Do you think?" she said almost with a laugh.

The look in his eye betrayed a flash of humor. "Do you still want to go?" he asked, which question was both warning and invitation.

"Yes," she said. "Thank you."

Dee bumped past men and women as Olin led her toward the boat. She did not ask why they were breaking through the line or why no one demanded they wait their turn; Olin had a manner about him that she had not seen before—a steadiness and an awareness of where he was going and what he intended to do mixed, perhaps, with a hint of dread that made the first two aspects of his demeanor the more impressive. In another moment, several men almost tipped themselves into the water offering their seats to Dee as she stepped into the next boat. She plunked herself down, opposite Olin and between two somewhat ragged individuals. The boat was filled with unfamiliar faces that had, perhaps, not seen the business end of a scrubbing brush for some time.

"Ma'am," said one of these fellows. She could hardly hear him for the noise of the fire and the babble of conversation, but he lifted his hat. Like a chorus, they all chimed in and hats were raised in descending order down the length of the boat.

"I don't know you gentlemen," she said over the din.

"We were spending the night up Blinn Hill."

Dee's mouth made an *O* silently. They were hoboes, of course.

"Woke me out of a clean sleep, that bolt did," shouted the fellow. "I was dreaming about chickens."

A voice called, "Haul away!" and the boat was briefly adrift before the men at the oars took over.

"Were you?" said Dee.

The hobo nodded. "I had one for supper." Despite this assertion, he looked hungry. Dee's expression was noticeably sympathetic. He lowered his gaze abashedly. "You look familiar to me, now I think on it."

"Oh?" Had she ever seen the man? She searched his face, then glanced across at Olin, who was watching her.

"You didn't feed a road man or two, did you?" asked the hobo. "Outside your kitchen door?" he added, and, finally, "Last Thanksgiving?"

"I remember something like," she said.

The fellow nodded, satisfied that he had identified her. Then he was back to his original thesis. "There was a whole *lot* us of up there," he said. "Tonight, that is. Up at Blinn Hill. Some have gotten across already."

"Iceboro will be glad to have you," she said.

"That turkey and stuffing was some good," he said.

The heat from the fire was daunting as they closed with the opposite shore. The roar of the flames appeared to rough the waters, their light gilding the river. As the boat glided past the burning icehouse, its passengers heard the shouts of firefighters above the awful clamor. Dee reached out and clutched Olin's hand without looking at him. The heat and light were like a weight upon them when they bumped the shore. Horsemen across the river waited to catch a line and pull the boats back to the crossing.

There was a bucket line climbing the bank a few yards away. "Perhaps you want to help over there," suggested Olin, clearly hoping to keep her as far from the fire as possible.

Dee was having none of it. "It's people nearer the fire who'll be needing a rest," she said, and he saw that it was useless to argue with her.

The noise and the heat increased as they reached the top of the bank at the southern extremity of the burning building. The fire was preeminent, but, like strident grace notes, the cries of men and the hiss of steam played beneath the larger uproar. The street was crowded with wavering lines of bucket brigades. Certain lone men shouted orders. Others simply looked lost.

A horse, pulling a wagon loaded with barrels of water, screamed as it reared in the street, and Olin leaped forward to take hold of the panicked animal's bridle, calling out to the driver, "Get this horse away from here! Get him away and put some men between the shafts!"

"We have to do something!" shouted the driver. "The lines aren't working!" Indeed, one of the nearer bucket brigades stood idle as the men at its head argued. The fire at this end had grown too hot to approach.

"The houses across the street are in danger," said Olin to Dee, then he strode toward the center of debate. The roar of the fire was insistent and she could not hear what he was saying to the men at the head of the stalled line, but he was pointing to the buildings across the street from the fire and obviously redirecting their efforts with the steady bearing of command.

There was a single loud bang amidst the storm of the fire and a renewed wave of heat engulfed the street. The horse reared and kicked and the wagon jerked out from under the driver. Dee jumped aside and people scattered as horse and wagon and water careened down the street. The driver was left on the cobbles, shouting in pain over a twisted leg.

"It's broken," said Dee, hunkering over the injured man. It was a relief, in this heat, to take off her coat and stuff it under the groaning man's head. "Go organize your line," she said to Olin, who came bounding over, "but leave me two men to help move him."

Olin simply nodded, spoke to two burly fellows, and began to reorganize the bucket brigade to protect the rest of the town.

The injured driver let out a terrible scream as the two big men lifted him—*None too gently!* Dee thought. "One of these houses down the street," she said and hurried ahead.

An elderly woman met her on the sidewalk. "Mrs. Mulligan will open her house, I know," she said. "Follow me." They had not gone very far before they came upon three men sprawled on the sidewalk, where they had been dragged after breathing too much smoke. The men were still gasping and retching, and the soot and ash and smoke permeating the atmosphere even this distance from the fire only exacerbated their state. "We'll come back for them," said Dee. She was impressed by the old woman's pace, and they were all out of breath by the time the driver was laid, fainting, on a parlor sofa.

"Oh, dear," said Mrs. Mulligan. "Where's a doctor?"

"We'll have to open this pant leg," said Dee. The chaos and roar of the scene without was loud in the parlor, but she had forgotten it.

"I'll get Jacob and he'll find someone," said the elderly woman.

"The men on the sidewalk," said Dee to the bearers, and without inquiring of Mrs. Mulligan if she minded that they use her house as a hospital. "And shut the door!" shouted Dee after them. "Mrs. Mulligan?" she did say then.

"Yes, yes!" said the woman.

"Put a sheet out on a flagpole, or a broomstick or something, so people will know where to come," said Dee.

51. Thump in a Punt

Moosepathian letters and journals extant from the period presently at issue spend much ink in praise of Joseph Thump's nautical understanding, and Eagleton himself wrote how *"Thump's very bearing seemed ennobled by the mere mention of a spar or a mast, and once I have even seen him meet the wind off the water with a tear in his eye. Or perhaps he might have had a cold."* This is the reason some historians are startled to find that Thump had seldom set foot upon a deck by the time he reached the banks of the Kennebec that night.

He had been on a deck, in fact, a grand total of three instances, the last having been in the previous fall when he had been duped into leaping from the deck of a vessel to a dock on Westport Island, ostensibly to secure the boat with a line from its bow. The possibility that the line might not be attached to the boat did not occur to him, and the villains on board had abandoned Thump.

What next occurred is best considered in the light of that previous adventure.

The Moosepathians would each write an account of their journey to the banks of the Kennebec that night, agreeing that they were out of breath with agitation when they reached the river. (*"Rather done in,"* was Eagleton's way of putting it.) The scene itself was breathtaking: the milling crowd on the near shore; the shining, shifting water beyond; and across the water, the fire itself, roaring and spitting from the opposite bank, and the swarms of people in the street attempting to stem the blaze.

"The longboats are coming!" someone shouted on the eastern shore just as the hobo troop arrived. "The ice ships have sent their boats back up," said one of the hoboes.

"Hmmm," said Thump, and Eagleton would later write how his friend's demeanor changed at the mention of these oncoming vessels. Thump's eyes widened and his chin came up (*"quite heroically,"* according to Eagleton).

With Puddle cradled in his arms, Big Eye Pfelt led his troop past the crowd to the edge of the shore, widening his titular orbit and growling to be let through. "Make way!" he shouted. "We've a power of road men here, and we've a mind to put out that fire!"

"Are you going to sit on it?" shot back one farmer who was undaunted by Big Eye's bluster. There was a chorus of laughter, and the hobo himself laughed, but the crowd parted and let them through.

A small square-ended vessel (indeed, an erstwhile punt, its pole having been replaced with oarlocks and a pair of oars) was settling against the bit of gravel beach. The odd little boat was hardly large enough to fit more than its present occupant and Big Eye gave no thought to this craft but waited for the longboats that could be spotted, even now, making their way up the flame-lit river from the safely anchored schooners. A launch from Gardiner was in sight as well, coming round the nearest bend upriver.

Ephram, Eagleton, and Thump were mesmerized by the fire. They had never seen, nor even imagined, anything like it. It seemed all but on top of them, and they lifted their eyes to peer after the columns of smoke and sparks that met the clouding sky.

"Look alive, there!" came a voice. "Take the painter!"

Thump shook himself from the sight of the flames and considered the little punt even as the man in it pitched him the line. Thump caught the end of the rope—the experiences of the previous fall rushing back at him like a sudden, unpleasant wind. He was standing on the dock again, there on Westport Island, holding one end of a line that was fastened to nothing else. The boat was drifting away. The line was spooling out. Amos Guernsey was saying something to him.

Then he was back on the shore of the Kennebec, and the man in the punt stood and hopped ashore. Without thinking, Thump crossed paths with the boatman, stepping from shore to punt. Thump stood unsteadily in the boat, then took another lurching step.

"Hey, there!" called the punt's owner, but Thump's weight in the back of the shallow craft lifted the bow from the strand, and the force of his movement encouraged the vessel to slide, spinning, into the current.

"What are you doing, you fool?" came the punter's voice from the shore.

Objecting to such an epithet being attached to his friend, Eagleton said "I beg your pardon?" to the punter. Several other cries of surprise, and even dismay, rose up from the crowd. Someone laughed.

"Good heavens, Thump!" said Ephram.

"Hmmm?" said Thump. He tottered. An eddy caught the boat's stern and spun him faster. Thump's view of the dwindling shore and the crowd and his friends twirled away into the daunting spectacle of the fire. Then the fire was gone and his friends and the shore had dwindled further still. Thump looked as if he might attempt to walk back. He did take a step in that direction, but the boat tipped disconcertingly, whereupon he did his best to correct this alarming trend by falling in the opposite direction. He landed upon the seat of the punt, squarely between two short oars.

"Ever in the fore!" declared an admiring Eagleton.

"A veritable lion!" averred Ephram.

"*What* is he doing?" demanded Big Eye.

"I'm not sure," admitted Eagleton.

Thump wished the punt would stop revolving.

"Thump!" called Ephram. "Are you all right?"

Thump's reply, if any, was inaudible.

"The oars, man!" shouted the punter. The dog barked, and several others, including Big Eye Pfelt, joined in, shouting, "The oars!"

Thump looked startled. He had never rowed a boat before, but he had some notion as to the mechanics involved. Grabbing one oar with both hands, he gave it a pull that would have done a Viking proud. Unfortunately, this magnificent sweep rather augmented his current gyration and the punt spun like a carnival ride.

A general sound of consternation rose from the crowd on the shore. The punt was not only spinning but steadily drifting across the river in the direction of the burning icehouse.

"I didn't know he knew how to do that!" said Eagleton.

Thump's confusion increased with the speed of his rotation, and he was hardly aware of the heat and flames that mounted overhead.

"Floundering fish in a basket!" shouted Big Eye. "Quick, quick! The boats!" The last boat to cross the river was being pulled back along the shore by horse, and the oarsmen in this craft were shouting as well.

"*A great surge of effort followed Thump's courageous example!*" Eagleton would write in his journal some days later, but the events of the next few minutes were but a blur in the memory of their participants. In their minds, the immensity of the fire had rendered the overall emergency to the level of the philosophic, but the peril of a single man, whose craft was even now spinning beneath the blazing, crumbling walls, was more than could be borne quietly. There were shouts and orders, and Big Eye himself commandeered the arriving launch, dictating the rhythm of the sweeps with a "Pull away, boys!" and "Pull again!"

Thump, meanwhile, caught hold of the second oar and stiffened it against the movement of the punt till his circuitous movement was all but halted. His stomach felt uncertain and the surrounding scene spun in his head. Shouts and warnings reached his ears, but he could make nothing of them. It was very hot, but he imagined that his recent, toplike ordeal was responsible for a rise in bodily temperature. He peered back at the recently quit bank, but it was difficult to see past the intense glare of the burning icehouse.

The icehouse! he thought. He had only to look up to see the tall flames. He smelled something like singed fur, and he took off his hat to fan himself only to see, with a perplexed start, that it was smoking.

"Thump!" came a familiar voice. He looked up to see that a vessel filled with men, Ephram and Eagleton included, coursed the river toward him like a water beetle.

"Get out of there, Mr. Thump!" Big Eye Pfelt shouted from the bow of the launch. A terrible boom sounded out.

Ephram and Eagleton let out a single shout of fear as a section of the icehouse buckled outward in a gout of flame, the crumbling ramparts revealing the white-hot interior. The wall leaned over the river, then let go in a barrage of firelit destruction that fell between the oncoming rescuers and the man in the punt. Ephram and Eagleton gasped as their friend disappeared behind this inferno, and the expert rowers behind them only just veered the launch from the path of a floating, flaming ruin of twisted posts and beams.

Then, a breeze came up—perhaps the harbinger of the weather to the east—and the billows of smoke and steam were wafted back toward the town.

There in the punt sat Thump, rather contrarily (it seemed, at first glance) bailing water *into* his boat with his hat. He had floated past the burning icehouse and was docking rather neatly by the landing at Iceboro.

52. Herald of the *Henceforth*

Elmer Barnes was right, but prematurely: It *would* eventually rain buckets over the Sheepscott River. In Iceboro, the first real indication of the storm (after that single, disastrous stroke of lightning) was a northeast wind that rose in the early hours to blow hot ash and sparks and sometimes flaming debris over the roofs of the town.

"Mister Walton!" said Vergilius Fern. "Mister Walton! You should go further down the line!"

Mister Walton, his face the color of a boiled lobster, lifted his hat and wiped his brow with the back of his hand but looked determined to hold his position in the bucket brigade at the northern end of the fire.

Sundry watched his friend with concern; he could attest that the excitement and labor, as well as the terrible heat, could take their toll on even a *young* man. Mister Walton was neither young, nor built these days for hard work, but fearing to offend his friend Sundry had perhaps waited too long to speak. "Mister Walton," he said now as they continued to pass sloshing buckets up the line, "you should fall back, I think."

"I have no hair to singe," said the portly fellow with candid humor. "I need my hat wetted down, is all."

"We need to wet down the buildings across the street, is my guess," said the man ahead of Sundry.

Another furnace blast of air engulfed them and they all backed away.

"The icehouse is hopeless," called a tall, blond fellow, who was just arriving. "From the river, you can see that the other end is gutted already. We should be rescuing the buildings nearby before they catch fire."

It was during this speech that they first felt the wind from the east; the blaze shifted and the line of men retreated further; the flames pulsed with the wind, and blistering waves of air radiated from the burning core. The firefighters turned their faces, hiding their heads beneath their arms as a burst of sparks erupted from the blaze and scattered over the gables and façades on the other side of the street. A full retreat was in order, and, when they reconnoitered some distance away, it was decided that they must concentrate their efforts on saving the remainder of the town.

Already people appeared with blankets and quilts, which were quickly loaded into a wagon and taken down to the river to be soaked. A line south of them had shifted to the buildings opposite the icehouse, and this organization would hang the bedding from roof and window and keep them damped down.

"Are you all right, Mister Walton?" inquired Sundry.

"Yes, yes. But I fear the town will go up if rain doesn't come."

"I continue to embroil you in trouble, Mister Walton," said Mr. Fern.

"It is Fate, Mr. Fern, that embroils us."

"My aunt has made her escape," said the farmer, but their attention was taken by a series of unearthly wails—high-pitched moans that seemed expressive of terrible pain or sadness. Smaller screams and whines punctured the longer moans, and, all together, beneath the roar of the flames, these sounds had the power to stop men's hearts and raise the hair at the back of their necks.

"Good Lord!" declared Mister Walton. "There are people in there!" and he took a step or two toward the blaze before Sundry caught his elbow.

"No, no!" shouted the tall, blond man, who came up behind Mister Walton and tugged at his shoulder. "It's the fire, sir!"

"The demon in it, at any rate," said another fellow.

The blond man said above the roar of the fire, "It burns out pockets in the wood, and dried sap, and the Lord knows what else. You've heard the chirps and grunts from a fire in the hearth. A blaze like this, burning tons of wood and heating the roofs to bursting, will sound like Hell itself!"

That's not to mention what it looks like, Sundry thought.

A man with drinking water arrived, and they went to him to slake their thirst. They were not meant to rest, however, for a rough-looking fellow with a single wild eye and a little dog perched on his shoulder came running through the lines shouting that another roof was on fire.

A flash of sparks beyond the icehouse had just caught Sundry's eye. They all turned to see where the newcomer was pointing, and more than one let out a gasp of newly revived horror. The roof of one of the boardinghouses, built to room the ice cutters, was smoldering. Many of the firefighters down the street were too involved with their work to see this new danger. The air above the threatened house was filled with ash and sparks, wavering with the blistering heat and light, and the smoke of this new danger curled into the air and around the steeple of a church hard by.

"The church," said someone. More sparks rained upon the boardinghouse roof. The shingles smoldered, but the roof was too high for anyone to easily get water on it. They could imagine the boardinghouse going up in a sudden roar and the spire of the church bursting into flame.

"There's a ladder to the belfry, I'll be bound," said Sundry. "We could run a brigade up inside the steeple and reach the roof from above." He was already leaning in that direction, like a sprinter ready for the starting pistol. The blond man and the man with the dog did not hesitate but scurried up the street to the church. Sundry turned, wondering how to ask Mr. Fern to look after Mister Walton without offending his friend and employer.

Mister Walton had a strange look on his face. The dipper in his hand dropped to the ground and, in an instant that would alter the remaining history of the Moosepath League, the portly gentleman fell like a downed boxer, crumpling to his knees and pitching forward.

"Mister Walton!" cried Sundry as he and Mr. Fern dropped beside the collapsed form. "Mister Walton!"

The eyes behind the spectacles were closed, the recently red face looked pale, even cold. Frightened, Sundry lifted Mister Walton's shoulders into his arms and pressed his ear to the broad chest, but there was too much noise. He could detect nothing. Frustrated by the chaos around them, he leaned close to that round beloved face. The light of the flames flickered in the spectacles. A gout of smoke rolled past, stinging Sundry's eyes.

"This is where my anger has brought us!" said Vergilius Fern.

With one arm still beneath Mister Walton's shoulders, Sundry slipped the other beneath the limp knees and raised the stout form as he stood. "Help me, someone!" he shouted, and Mr. Fern joined him, shouting, "We need a doctor!"

Something loud occurred behind them, but they were oblivious. There was another breath of sparks and smoke, blown like the blast from a forge. Men careened past, unheedful of what was before them. Then a raggedly dressed man slowed his flight and considered the scene. "There's a hospital set up in the building over yonder," he said. "Ho, beau!" he shouted, seemingly to no one in particular, though several fellows halted their retreat. "Help carry this gentleman!"

"I have him!" shouted Sundry. "Just clear the way!"

How long had it been since Mister Walton collapsed? Sundry wondered. How could he have let his dear friend join in the effort to put out the fire, to let him stay so close to the heat and smoke?

The young man was tall and narrow and his burden portly and solid, but Sundry would have carried Mister Walton a mile if he'd had to. Several roughly dressed men organized around them, and the crowd parted before their shouts and prods as if a great hand had pushed it aside. When they reached the house with the white flag, an older woman met them at the door, took one look at the fallen man, and directed them through the hall and into a pantry where a cot had been set up. Concerned faces whisked by. People stood aside to let them pass. A handsome woman in a dark kerchief came out of the kitchen; she carried a roll of bandages and a bottle of liniment, but she handed these to someone when she saw Mister Walton.

"Put him on the bed," she said, but Sundry was already moving in that direction. He laid Mister Walton down as he might the most precious breakable, then put his ear once more to the great fellow's chest.

The room went silent. Mr. Fern stood at the door, his hands folded in prayer. The woman from the kitchen stood by, waiting. The muted crackle and roar of the fire could be heard like the constant movement of the sea or a great wind, but Sundry caught the faint thump of something moving with its own rhythm beneath his ear. He passed his hand over the cold, damp brow, then carefully removed the round spectacles and put them in his own shirt pocket.

Nothing was asked, but Sundry said, "I don't know," to the woman. "He just collapsed. He still seems so pale. So—" He had almost said "So lifeless" but stopped himself, or rather his voice did, since he had, lost, temporarily, the power to speak.

The woman touched Mister Walton's pale cheek, and when she withdrew her hand a soft blush was left behind. "He's overdone, perhaps. But a little start to his nerves might not hurt. If we had a touch of something hard to give him."

"Jacob!" came an older (and, to Sundry, a familiar) voice. He looked over his shoulder to see Aunt Beatrice standing at the kitchen door. "Jacob! Bring that flask of yours."

"Auntie!" said Mr. Fern.

An elderly fellow shuffled in from the other room; he was taken aback at the sight of the farmer, but he considered the impatient hand of his intended bride and pulled something from the inside of his coat. "Well, by gum!" he said to the old woman. "How did you know I had that?"

Aunt Beatrice made a sound that was about equal parts peevishness and humor. She passed the flask to the woman in the dark kerchief, who quickly had the top off and the flask upended over her fingers.

There was something so rare and intimate about the handsome woman's next act that it almost made Sundry flinch. When she had wet the tips of her fingers with the rum from the flask, she very softly knelt beside Mister Walton's unconscious form and touched his lips.

Sundry held his breath and thought he waited an hour before Mister Walton's mouth twitched. The dampened lips retracted, then a tip of the portly fellow's tongue caught the flavor of what had been gently placed there. The round face was clearly startled. Then finally the eyes opened, not with full consciousness at first, but unseeing.

What's happened to him? wondered Sundry with an inward gasp. Every terrible imagining ran through his heart till at last he detected a mounting awareness in those eyes.

Mister Walton blinked, squinted, then raised a hand to feel for his spectacles. He took a deep breath, tasted his lips once again, and said, "Good heavens! That *is* strong stuff!" He turned his head. "Sundry?"

"Mister Walton, I'm here." Sundry gripped the older man's hand.

"Where's Phileda?"

"Phil—? Phileda is in Orland, Mister Walton."

"What? Yes, of course she is. How foolish of me. But where—?" Then the portly fellow took another deep breath, said "The fire!" and sat up, rubbing at the bruise he had contracted by falling on his forehead.

The room drew its own collective breath. "Praise God!" said Mr. Fern.

Sundry stood, cautioning his friend to lay down again.

"Nonsense!" said Mister Walton. "How did I get here?" He glanced around himself, blinking, and Sundry remembered the man's spectacles. Mister Walton put these on, and again he blinked, looking about the room. "I fear I have been some nuisance."

"Nonsense!" said the woman in the dark kerchief, gently mocking Mister Walton's own words and tone. From the moment she stepped in from the kitchen, Sundry was struck by her strength and gentleness; he had been touched by her sweet demeanor when she brushed Mister Walton's lips with the taste of rum; now he was fiercely loyal to her. Beyond her, through the hall and out the open front door, he could see the intemperate glow of the fire and hear the crash of something falling.

"A little extra touch of something?" said the woman. Someone passed her a cup and she dropped a dollop of rum from the flask into it.

Mister Walton caught sight of Aunt Beatrice, looked surprised for a moment, then nodded to her with courtly ease. He looked to Vergilius Fern.

"Please, Mister Walton," said the man. "It will be good for you."

"I think I'm fine, thank you," said Mister Walton with a tired smile.

"For medicinal purposes?" said the woman in the dark kerchief.

"Your kindness has been medicine enough," he assured her. He adjusted his spectacles on his nose and considered the handsome woman more carefully. "You look familiar to me, dear," he said. "Have we met?"

"I am Dee Pilican," she said, offering her hand.

Some might have been embarrassed in such circumstances, but Mister Walton was simply grateful. "Tobias Walton," said he, standing uncertainly. Sundry held his hands out. "Thank you, Sundry," said the bespectacled fellow. "I'm a little shaky, but it's good to be on my feet." He took Dee's hand and considered her more closely. An expression of interest and curiosity touched his face, then he simply smiled and said, "It is a pleasure to meet you."

"Mister Walton," said Vergilius Fern, "I beg your forgiveness."

"Whatever for?"

"For my obstinacy and anger, which has led you to these straits."

The portly gentleman simply raised a hand and chuckled softly.

The farmer turned to his aunt.

"Vergil, Vergil," she said from across the room, not without affection.

He considered Jacob Lister then, and the old man looked wry and philosophical. Further apology was perhaps working within Vergilius, but there was not quite enough of it, in the end, to get it out. He nodded to the room before leaving the house and returning to the larger matter at hand.

Strangers there could see that this was the culmination of some interesting business. The long night, and the battle against the fire, was not yet finished, however. Sundry saw Mister Walton to a chair. Someone came in with a burned shoulder and was laid on the cot. The general commotion in the makeshift hospital reasserted itself.

"Is there water in the kitchen?" wondered Sundry. He was desperately thirsty, and he thought Mister Walton must be in need of something clear and cold. In the room at the back of the house he found a pump and a glass. He was conscious, in the relative quiet of the kitchen, of a distinct change in the noise from without—the roar of the fire and the general din of men and movement had shifted strangely.

"The lower boardinghouse has been put out!" came a shout from the front door, which intelligence raised a chorus of cheers.

Sundry paused long enough to draw Mister Walton a drink and had only glanced out the kitchen window when he saw a ball of flame land upon a roof down one of the backstreets of Iceboro.

53. Thump Was Diligent

Once on shore, Thump made a run at the western bank of the Kennebec. Unused to negotiating such steep inclines, he mounted the first half of the slope with a straight-backed bearing (an admirable posture in most circumstances), his spine describing a line that was almost perpendicular to the ground. It proved difficult, however, to accommodate gravity with his head and feet so out of plumb with one another. Ephram and Eagleton, distracted by an explosion from the burning building, may have missed the sight of their friend as he tumbled back down the shore and bowled over several new arrivals.

"Good heavens!" said Eagleton when he turned back. Thump was making a second attempt upon the slope. "He must have forgotten something!"

When he did make the top of the riverbank, Thump was stunned by the noise and confusion. The bucket brigades that had formed from the shore to the perimeters of the blaze wavered as the heat and flames shifted with unseen atmospheric currents. Store owners and residents cluttered the streets with wagons, into which they piled their possessions, and frightened, sometimes rearing horses added their snorts and screams to the general roar of the fire and the shouts of men.

"I beg your pardon," said Thump to one man running past. "Is there something I could be doing?" The fellow hardly glanced at Thump, though perhaps he hadn't heard. "I beg your pardon!" Thump said again to the next man within reach. "Is there some way I might lend assistance?"

This fellow did pause long enough to say "What?" but hurried off before Thump could repeat himself.

Thump thought his head ached a bit, but he pressed on. "I am sorry to interrupt you, sir," he said to the next man he encountered.

"Then don't!" declared this latest contact.

"Help!" came a musical voice through the commotion. "Help me, please!"

"Yes?" said Thump. He was not tall enough to see over many heads, but he stretched his neck and bounced on his toes.

"Help!" came the voice again.

"Yes, yes?" He saw a woman, who appeared to be wearing her Sunday hat and who wrung her hands as she surveyed the milling street. "Ma'am," said Thump, lifting his borrowed hat. "I am at your service."

"Oh, sir!" she cried. "It's Finney!" The woman laid her hands upon Thump's coat, as if she would shake him, and he looked down at this un-expected intimacy with small alarm. "She's got herself up a tree to see what was about," she was saying, "and cannot get herself down."

"Good heavens!" said Thump, though it might have been in response to a man who sped past, clipping his elbow and spinning him *about-face*. "Good heavens!" said Thump again. "Where did you go?"

"I told her, that, at her age, it was a mistake," the woman explained. Thump was confused by the direction of her voice, and she tugged at his arm to pull him back around. "I told her it was a mistake, but she simply won't lis-ten." Still gripping his arm, she proceeded to weave her matronly form through the immediate press.

Thump bumped into several people. "Is she near the flames?" he won-dered aloud, and when she did not hear him he shouted, "Is she near the fire?"

"The tree is behind Main Street, but you can see the top branches over the roof there." She pointed. "A single stray spark might set the whole thing on fire!"

Thump was increasingly alarmed, not the least at the prospect of climb-ing a tree, and he wondered if he might recruit some help along the way. His "I beg your pardon" and "Is there a ladder handy?" went unheard, however, and soon they were hurrying down a side street. With the immediate clamor of the fire left behind, Thump realized what din had been assaulting his ears, and what cruel heat had brought a flush to his bearded face, rankling his neck beneath a starched collar. He felt, contrarily, as if he were only now reaching the peak of a sudden fever.

The tree that was their immediate destination was wrapped in a strange glow wherever the direct light of the fire reached it. "Finney!" the woman called into the branches. She leaned against the trunk and peered into the leaves. "Finney? You stay where you are! This man will come up for you!"

Thump heard a tiny voice from above.

"No, dear!" called the woman. "You stay right there! This gentleman is quite pleased to come and get you!" She looked at Thump and said, "Mr.—?"

"Thump, ma'am," he said and raised his hat once again. "Joseph Thump, (of the Exeter Thumps), ma'am, at your service."

"Did you hear that?" called the woman into the tree. She looked very plaintive with her hands clasped prayerfully. "He's on his way!"

Thump was momentarily stunned by this emotional tableau, but then he shook himself and scuttled closer to the tree. Even the nearest branches seemed quite high. Peering up, he asked, "Where is she?"

"Finney?" called the woman melodiously.

Then Thump heard the voice more plainly.

"Meeeooooow!"

Thump peered some more. "I believe there's a cat up there," he said.

"What?" said the woman.

"A cat," he said. "I believe there's a cat up there."

For some inexplicable reason the woman swatted him.

Thump looked as if he had been pinched.

"Meeeoooow!" came the voice of the cat. He supposed he would have to deal with the animal while he was up there.

"Ah—this *Finney*," he said. "Is she a Miss or Mrs.?"

54. And Ephram and Eagleton, Too

Ephram and Eagleton felt dizzy and lost when they reached the top of the bank and the full realization of what they were nearing—both the fire and the attempt to control it—was brought to bear upon their senses. They were swept up in the tumult.

The hoboes scattered toward the opposite side of Iceboro's main street, where pockets of firefighters were mounting a defense against the encroaching flames. Men appeared at open windows, across from the burning icehouse, and upon the roofs above, unfurling dampened blankets against the heat. Already there were bucket brigades passing water to these new stations. Men and women came and went from these lines, and others scurried in the places between—some with personal effects rescued from nearby houses, others with equipment to fight the fires, and still some few more who might have had their hands in their pockets, they appeared so ineffectual.

"Good heavens, Ephram!" declared Eagleton.

"My thoughts exactly, my friend," returned Ephram.

"We must find Thump," said Eagleton.

"Yes," said Ephram.

"Where could he have gone?" Eagleton gaped at the blizzard of flame and sparks and smoke. "I do hope everyone got out!"

"I wouldn't want to be in there," came a long drawl.

"Henry says, 'I wouldn't want to be in there,'" came its echo.

Ephram and Eagleton were surprised to find that the long-eared hobo and his shorter, rounder companion were standing at their elbows.

There was a crash from within the burning structure and the nearby line of firefighters retreated. Ephram and Eagleton and the two hoboes ran ahead to avoid being knocked down, and they all reconnoitered some yards away.

Two men—one a small, sharp-nosed fellow with a long-billed cap, the other with a great round belly—stood in front of Eagleton, and the first man leaned close to the second, shouting to be heard above the noise of the fire. "She's going to get loose," he said, which phrase startled Eagleton.

"I don't want to be here when she does," said the larger man.

There came another wave of heat and sparks that scattered everyone. Eagleton found himself huddled in an narrow alley opposite the fire, his eyes temporarily blinded in the relative darkness. "We'd better get to it before she breaks away," came a voice beside his left ear.

Eagleton blinked into the nearby darkness; as his sight returned, he could see a sharp nose beneath a billed cap and two eyes blinking back at him. "Gar!" said the sharp-nosed fellow. He straightened to his feet, looked around, and, locating his big-bellied companion, caught him by the sleeve. "What are you about?" demanded the little man, and he ushered his companion down the alley—a little snarly dog herding a befuddled bear.

"Ephram!" called Eagleton, but it was not Ephram standing beside him. "Henry!" he said.

"My name's Bob," drawled the long-eared hobo.

Eagleton was mystified. Indicating the shorter, plumper fellow beyond the long-eared one, Eagleton said, "Is *he* Henry, then?"

"No, he's Bill."

"Ephram!" called Eagleton.

"Yes, my friend," came the welcome response from further down the alley. They could see Ephram now in the indirect glow of the great fire.

"Those men who went off just now," said Eagleton. "I have reason to believe they may have Mrs. Roberto a prisoner somewhere nearby!"

"Good heavens, Eagleton!" declared Ephram.

"Were *they* the fellows?" said Bob, looking awed and a little fearful.

"Henry says, 'Were *they* the fellows?'" said Bill, looking similarly stricken.

Eagleton considered the two hoboes with an expression of the utmost puzzlement. He said to Ephram, "I overheard them talking about someone—'*she*,' they said—getting loose!"

"Ever in the fore!" said Ephram and truer words could not have been spoken, for Eagleton was, at that moment, hurrying down the alley.

"Come, come!" said Ephram. "No time to gather the troops!" And he, and then Bob and Bill, hurried after.

※⑤⁂

Astride a horse and breasting the hill above Iceboro at about two o'clock that morning, Edward Fischer—a long retired Kennebec County sheriff who had wakened in the night and seen the glow in the east from his bedroom window—was momentarily stunned by the scene before him.

I had smelled smoke for a mile or more, (he would later write to his father in Bath) *and the steady glow over the east had grown in height and intensity as I rode on, but I was not prepared for the sudden view of Iceboro and the fire in its midst when I came over the last hill. Gaping down at the town, I caught glimpses of men and women, ranked in lines, and others rushing about at a dozen missions.*

The orange flames shot against the sky and silhouetted that which was between the fire and myself, so that the outskirts of the town were invisible to me. It was a sight for Halloween and with the roar of the flames and the voices of desperate men upon the wind, there need only be witches on brooms circling above to complete the picture of some corner of the netherworld.

Suddenly, a new shout went up—louder than the others, for it was in concert—and I could see that one of the great boardinghouses constructed for the ice cutters had begun to smolder.

Ephram and Eagleton heard this same cry go up, but they did not waver in their resolve to rescue Mrs. Roberto. The darkness in the alley was far from complete, once their eyes had adjusted; tongues of flame peered over the nearby roofs, and the glow of the fire reflected dully upon the clouds.

Neither of them had very much experience in the art of furtive movement and they tried several modes of tiptoeing before Eagleton hit upon one that seemed appropriate. He had recalled a passage from the novel *Not Without Fondness*, by Mrs. Penelope Laurel Charmaine, in which the hero was described (in the act of stalking the villain) as "*slipping with forestlike stealth upon his metatarsal pads.*" Eagleton had gone to the library to learn where to find his own "*metatarsal pads,*" and here was another instance of life magnified by literature, for otherwise he would never have considered perambulating the shadowed alley in quite that manner. (He wasn't too sure how to *slip*, however and admitted later that he probably did no better than *bob*.) With this unusual gait, and his arms held out in hoops to facilitate balance, he might have given a simian impression, but this, too, was perhaps not an inopportune model for a man attempting "*forestlike stealth.*"

Admiring Eagleton's learned example, Ephram quickly adopted a similar form of locomotion; Bill attempted the same, and, after several experimental steps, even Bob was bobbing.

Reaching the end of the alley, Eagleton looked around the corner, but the two suspicious men were not in sight. Ephram peered after his friend. The clamor behind them echoed in the empty backstreet, and light, too, played strangely upon the roofs and the tops of trees.

Two or three buildings away, a door swung open and the unmistakable form of the big-bellied man hove into sight. They could not know that the sharp-nosed man had ordered his associate to "see if we've been seen"; nor did the sharp-nosed man suspect that he and his confederate would *not* have been detected had he but kept quiet. The big-bellied man leaned out the doorway and glanced nervously up and down the street, then disappeared.

"I believe that is what they call *the lookout*," said Eagleton.

"Very good, my friend!" replied Ephram.

"But what do we do?" wondered Eagleton.

"Do you think she's in there?" wondered Ephram.

"Good heavens!" said Eagleton. It was a startling thought.

"What are they up to?" asked Bob

"Henry says, 'What are they up to?'" said Bill.

"Where is Thump?" Eagleton asked aloud. It was an academic question, but he wished the answer (and the man) were at hand, for he had great faith in Thump's courage and abilities and thought the big-bellied man a little daunting. Thump would be a welcome presence.

"Oh!" said Ephram. "That Mister Walton and Mr. Moss were nearby!"

Eagleton nodded. Another passage from Mrs. Charmaine's engrossing novel returned to him and he said, barely loud enough for Ephram to hear: "'*He could not ask wherefore relief would arrive while some poor soul might look upon his own unworthy brow and say, "Here it is! Here is my relief, my rescue!"*'"

"Very right, Eagleton!" said Ephram, who had read *Not Without Fondness* and recognized the quotation. He patted his friend's shoulder. "Perhaps we should approach the door and view the situation from a closer vantage."

"Yes, yes," said Eagleton. "Very good, Ephram."

"Henry," said Ephram, turning to the accompanying hoboes. "You and your friend may come along."

"My name's Bob," said Bob.

"I beg your pardon," said Ephram.

"Henry says, 'My name's Bob,'" said Bill.

"You're not Henry?" said Ephram to Bob.

"I'm Bob."

"Are you Henry?" said Ephram to Bill.

"He's Bill," said Bob.

"Henry says, 'He's Bill,'" said Bill.

"But he calls you Henry," said Ephram to Bob.

"Yes," said Bob, "he does."

⚹≈⚹

Old Ed Fischer had worked as constable for the town of Litchfield, and then as Kennebec County's sheriff for some twenty-seven years, and if that was all of seventeen years ago, he yet found the habits of his previous employment hard to break; in fact, he didn't try. He still carried a rifle on his saddle, and he still maintained the sort of watchful eye that a person develops when they have spent most of a lifetime nosing out errant behavior.

As he descended the hill above Iceboro, the outlying buildings rose out of the shadows and blotted the fire from view. He rode through the deserted streets, past the houses and businesses; the blaze and the collective noise of the men and women who fought it resounded among the brick and clapboard. The smoke and the acrid smell of overheated metals stung his nose and a freshening wind took billows of sparks over the roofs like fireworks. Emptying into the narrow way that ran behind the buildings on the main street, he felt the shift from country road to hard-packed lane beneath his horse's hooves.

Old instincts pulled him up and he peered into the shadows of this back lane. He sensed movement just north of him. The horse turned its head and shifted its feet.

"Whoa," said Ed quietly, more to himself than to the horse.

The horse blew out its nose.

Ed Fischer could spot furtive movement the way an ornithologist can identify a bird as it wings in the distance against the twilight. Someone was crouching in the shadows up the street, and someone else was skulking by a backdoor. His old eyes were not up to much detail, but gesture was as good as intent, in his mind, and he eased the horse behind a building before dismounting and looping the reins over a porch railing. He wasn't sure the animal should be munching on someone's bushes, but he took the rifle from its saddle sling and slipped down the backstreet with the sort of *forestlike stealth* Eagleton and Ephram would have admired.

He had known looters in his day—all the way from the war to his experiences as constable and sheriff—and they had always proved to be among the lowest and vilest form of men; they were not simply thieves but thieves in an hour of common desperation. To his mind, a looter was almost invariably the worst sort of skulker and the vilest form of physical coward. He liked a looter about as much as he liked a bully, and he despised a bully. Sometimes they were one and the same.

Ed Fischer moved from shadow to shadow. He crouched in a doorway and when he peeked up the street again, he saw two more men standing in the dark. They were conferring, he thought. There was a sign above the door, and Ed could barely make out the word *Emporium*. They were planning a robbery, he realized. The sound and fury of the fire and those battling it had dwindled from his conscious thought, giving way to this secretive tableau.

"Hoboes," he said to himself. He thought he might have to fire a shot to keep them from running, but was there already someone inside? He saw a light at a window.

Ed's attention was distracted then by the beginnings of a fire on a roof some distance up the street. He could see, by the light of the flames, someone rush to the threatened building and throw open a pair of stable doors.

One of the skulkers approached the back stoop, and Ed Fischer had the impression of a well-dressed man, which surprised him. Perhaps, he thought, they would be easier to trap once they were *all* inside. He fingered the rifle's safety. He watched from the shadows as the four men lined up outside the door. The foremost of them reached for the latch, holding it for a long anxious moment. Ed stood.

Without warning, the store's backdoor burst open and a small man in a cap came charging out. It was clear, from his shouts, that he had not expected the men outside, and it was clear, from *their* shouts, that they had not expected his sudden exit. Legs and arms flailing, the whole lot fell over in a shouting, yelping heap. Ed Fischer was momentarily frozen in place while attempting to decipher the relationship between these fellows. Then a larger man came running from the building, his arms full of several items that bounced out of his grasp and fell to the ground.

"Help me! Help me, you idiot!" the first, smaller man was shouting, though he was on the top of the pile of wiggling bodies.

Other shouts of "Good heavens, Eagleton!" and "Metatarsal pads!" and "Ouch!" along with some less genteel locutions, peppered the air.

"Henry says, 'Ouch!'" came a plaintive cry.

It struck Ed that the first four men he had spotted were attempting to *foil* a robbery, and, while he adjusted to this new thought, a horse came charging up the street, took a magnificent leap over the mass of struggling figures, and disappeared into the shadows. Ed stepped from his hiding place, levered a cartridge into the chamber of his rifle, and fired into the air.

55. Where Diligence Leads

Thump wondered how a person got out of a barrel. It *was* troublesome, no matter how he looked at it, and the woman only stood there and said, "Oh, dear!" several times over, once she had gotten past the joy of having her cat safely in her arms again.

It had been puzzling to Thump to discover that he was rescuing a cat, and it took several attempts on the part of the woman to apprise him of this, but no sooner did he understand what was expected of him than he found a barrel that stood at the side of a nearby building and upended it beneath the lowest limb of the tree. Gaining the top of the inverted barrel had itself proved strenuous, not the least because there was hardly enough surface to accommodate him.

As things fell out (or fell *in*, as it were), the durability of the barrel bottom, too, proved insufficient, and Thump plunged straight through to the ground. The barrel staves were a little more dependable, unfortunately, and his broad shoulders were gripped and his arms rendered immovable.

The cat had then seen fit to come down from the tree by way of Thump's head. Now, with the animal in her arms, the lady exclaimed "Oh, dear!" several times, to which Thump's only reply was an increasingly agitated "Hmmm."

"You can come out of there, now," said the woman. "Such a dear!" she said, and she actually leaned forward and bussed Thump upon the cheek.

Thump was astonished.

The woman, meanwhile, was sensible, once again, of the commotion and toil taking place not so far away. The light and sound from the fire spilled down the side street in swells and waves.

Recovering himself somewhat, Thump said, "Hmmm," though he could not expect to be heard amid that clamor. He wiggled himself a little (as well as the barrel) and understood quickly that he was in hazard of tipping over. The slope of the street was not hopeful either, and he thought that he might roll some distance before meeting who *knew* what that would eventually stop him.

As it turned out, *who knew what* was a brick wall at the bottom of the slope. When he hit it, it was with a sudden and startling crash that shattered the constricting barrel like a great eggshell. Thump never was very sure what had tipped him over, though it may have been the act of stiffening at the moment he realized his peril; he was never very sure, either, whether his increasingly rapid progress as he rolled down the hill was improved or worsened by his inability to see exactly where he was going, or to understand that a brick wall was rising up to meet him with like rapidity.

The noise of the barrel striking the building was extraordinary and his ears were still ringing when he staggered back up the hill.

The lady couldn't understand where he had gone. "Sir?" she called. "Sir?"

"Good heavens!" he said, coming up the hill and out of the darkness. "There's another fire!"

"Oh!" she shouted, startled by his voice in the darkness, and the cat leaped from her arms and up the tree.

Thump glanced at the vanishing cat with horror. It was not like him to abandon someone in need, particular a member of the fairer sex, but up the street a roof was catching fire. He saw a woman leading a horse from the smoking building.

"Oh!" said the more immediate lady. "Sir?" she said, pointing up the tree to her newly escaped cat, but Thump was hurrying his stocky frame up the street.

56. Darkness, Fire, and Chains

"A raft of sparks just set fire to the roof of a building back of here," said Sundry as he came back into the pantry.

"Good heavens, Sundry!" said Mister Walton.

"We had better be quick," said Dee.

The old man who had provided the flask of rum scurried into the kitchen and peered through the window at the roof of the imperiled building. Sundry was at the front door, looking for someone to spread this new alarm, but everyone was down the street cheering the brigade that had stopped the boardinghouse from catching fire. He could barely see, through the smokey air and the distance, a bucket line disappearing into the church and someone still leaning out the belfry, dumping buckets of water on the roof below.

Dee knew immediately what he was thinking. "I can go," she said, but Sundry didn't like to ask a woman to skirt the larger fire at the icehouse, no matter that there were women among those fighting it. "If that fire back there breaks loose, you may want to get everyone out of here," he said.

"Jacob's rig is down the street," said Aunt Beatrice.

Sundry would not have trusted many people with Mister Walton, certainly not many people he had just met, but he had an absolute faith in Miss Pilican. He nodded back and ran out the door.

"It's the livery," said the old man as he came in from the kitchen.

"The livery?" said Dee.

"The livery's on fire," said the man.

"Good heavens," said Mister Walton again, and he stood unsteadily from his chair.

"Mrs. Mulligan," said Dee.

"Yes," called the lady of the house from the front parlor.

"Could you find someone to help these gentlemen to Mr. Lister's rig?" asked Dee. Her first steps to the kitchen were brisk; she touched Mister Walton's shoulder as she passed him, and then her steps were hurried. She was running by the time she reached the backdoor.

Across the alley at the back of the house stood the livery. The roof was ablaze, and the leaves of an overhanging elm were curling with the heat. Racing across a small court of packed earth, Dee threw open the stable doors.

Billows of smoke spilled out. She could see nothing inside, but she heard the shuffling of hooves and the frightened whinny of a horse. A spotted dog padded out from the smokey shadows carrying a puppy by the scruff of its neck. There was a crash, one shadow shifted from another, and a horse wheeled out of the smokey interior. The creature plunged past her and galloped up the street.

"Ma'am," came a voice behind her. Jacob Lister was hurrying across the backstreet. "I wouldn't go in there," he said.

Dee almost said, "Of course not," when there came a terrified scream from within. Having deposited one puppy in some safe place, the spotted dog reappeared, balked for a moment at the stable door, then bounded into the darkness. Through the general commotion of fire and the shouts of people on Iceboro's main street, a gunshot rang out, clear and precise. "Now, what is that?" she said, looking up the street. Then she hurried after the dog.

The smoke was not as thick as she feared, but the fire had eaten a hole through the roof, lighting the stables with its orange glow. A dark, wild-eyed horse kicked in its stall, not far from the entrance, and at least one other whinnied near the back of the livery. The dark animal's bridle was chained to an iron ring, which seemed to Dee more than sufficient. *You must be a bad boy,* she thought, and he did have a devilish look to him that she imagined was not entirely due to fear. She had to exercise all her own preternatural calm upon the animal before she dared let it loose and open the stable door. The horse seemed less nervous with her hand upon the bridle, but when it shook its head she was nearly lifted from her feet.

Jacob Lister met her at the door, and when the animal dipped its head the old man snatched a handful of the creature's ear and calmly walked it away. The dog trotted past Dee with two pups in her mouth. Smoke tumbled from the doorway in gouts, and Dee heard a high-pitched whine. The flames on the roof seemed eerily silent; even here, behind the main street, the roar of the burning icehouse drowned everything else.

But where is help? Dee wondered.

There was a low shuddery sound from the horse still left in the livery. Dee made an impatient noise and hurried inside. The increasing smoke glowed with the fire. She was coughing and her eyes watered. The horse at the back of the livery was in a blind panic, crashing against the walls of its stable and kicking as it spun about. Dee felt her sense of direction threatened, she groped forward, her hands out, till she touched a back wall.

"Ma'am!" came the call of the old man from outside. "Ma'am!"

Dee heard a tiny cry at her feet. Blindly, she reached down and touched something soft and shivering. Feeling about in some sort of box, she found three puppies. They were wee, squirming little things, and she gathered them into her arms before stumbling across to the last horse. She heard the stable door burst open and almost stepped out of the way before the horse careened past. The broad side of the animal caught her by the shoulder and drove her against the wall. The puppies whimpered and struggled, but, miraculously, she did not drop them. She staggered back to her feet, then tried dazedly to understand which way was out. Her head reeled from the smoke and the heat and the collision with the wall.

There were shouts outside and she realized that help had come, though perhaps too late if she couldn't find her way out—and quickly.

"Ma'am?" came a voice, close by—a deep voice. "Ma'am?" it came again, and then a hand that she could not see caught hold of her elbow—quite by accident, she was sure—and her unexpected rescuer tugged her through the choking smoke.

57. Everything They Wanted to Know . . .

When the last horse came charging out of the livery, Jacob Lister called after Dee and started in. He was taken by the elbow, however, and pulled back. The young man who had gone to spread the alarm about this new fire had arrived with several others and more were running from the alley with sloshing buckets.

"There's someone in there!" Jacob exclaimed, even as a tall, blond man came up, saying, "Stay back." Olin Bell had shaken a handkerchief from his pocket and was ready to go in himself, the cloth before his face, when a broad-shouldered, stocky fellow with an enormous beard trudged out of the darkness and, without slowing his progress, plunged into the cloud of smoke.

"Quick!" shouted Olin, who still had no idea who was inside. "Form a chain and we'll go in after them." He grabbed one wild-eyed fellow near to him and tugged.

"Ho, beaus!" shouted Big Eye Pfelt, and very quickly a line of men had locked arms in a living chain.

⁂

While hurrying up the street, Thump had seen the woman disappear into the livery, and the closer he got to the burning building, the more sure he was that he was going in after her. He had no notion of the physics of smoke, but it was perhaps a good thing, in the end, that a man of abbreviated stature made the attempt—in such circumstances proximity to the floor is more conducive to breathing.

Nonetheless, Thump entered a choking, pitch-black cloud that set his lungs into rebellion on the instant. It did not occur to him to put his handkerchief to his face, nor would it have done him much good, perhaps. The heat and fumes were thick and strangling; his eyes burned, though he shut them tight, and he felt dizzy as he entered the noxious cloud. There was a great shout from outside, which signal was his only evidence of stumbling in the opposite and (therefore) right direction.

Stumble he did—over a fallen saddle, it was later supposed. He caught himself with his hands and found it a little easier to breath nearer the floor. He scuttled forward—or he thought it was forward—ran into a wall, then shifted direction and scuttled some more. In his hurry, he brushed past something hard. He lurched and staggered against the object again. Groping, reeling like a drunken man, his lungs on fire, Thump caught hold of a portion of someone—an elbow, he realized as he tugged at the woman. "Ma'am," he said, though he was barely able to breathe. "Ma'am." She seemed to be carrying something and was unwilling to loosen her arm from her side. She fell against him, and in his surprise (and having held his breath for an inordinate amount of time) he took a sudden gasp and almost killed himself then and there.

There was another shout—several shouts that sounded as if they came from within the building. There was an awful flash as something burning fell near to him. His eyes weeping, his lungs retching for air, Thump burst into a fit of coughing that only drew more poison into his lungs. For a moment, it wasn't very plain who was being held up by whom. Then he was caught hold of and half led, half jerked toward the broad front doors of the livery, through a surging cloud of smoke and into the sweet, ravishing, resplendent air.

Someone caught hold of the woman from his arms; Big Eye Pfelt appeared and propped Thump up by the shoulders. Thump took one last involuntary breath before he was well out of the smoke, felt his mind darken, and pitched forward onto the hard-packed earth of the livery court.

"Mr. Thump?" came an astonished voice that was familiar to him, and, before he briefly lost awareness, he might have sworn he heard the voice of the Moosepath League's grand chairman speaking his name in similar tones. *If Mister Walton is here*, he thought, *then all will be well!*

When he woke—and, truthfully, it was only moments later—his poor throbbing head was pillowed upon something very soft and warm, and he had the most unexpectedly pleasurable sensation run straight to his heart. The pillow shook slightly as the person attached to it coughed. He took a breath himself, coughed, then breathed again more easily. He relaxed and reveled in the soft place where his head lay, without really understanding what it was.

"My," came a sweet voice above him, "he has a magnificent beard!" Soft fingers delicately brushed the hair back from his forehead. Someone bathed his face in cool water, and a flask of something strange and harsh was applied to lips.

Thump opened his eyes dreamily. He had, for a moment, forgotten where he was, and was thinking of another instance of *coming to*, when he had wakened in the lap of the exquisite ascensionist herself. But that was a bright day in July. It was dark now—a dark punctuated by the occasional lick of flame over the rooftops. But he found himself looking past certain womanly endowments, which were considerable, and into a pair of soft brown eyes that gazed upon him with the utmost concern. The woman's hair was pulled back, but the dark kerchief accomplished something similar to the blue-black tresses he had seen framing comparable features the previous Independence Day.

"Mrs. Roberto!" he said in a gasp and a whisper. His heart flung out of him and tears sprung to his eyes for wholly different reasons. There were small exclamations of surprise all around them—voices, hushed, almost with reverence.

The eyes of the woman betrayed surprise, and then something like humor.

She was about to say something when he said, "You are safe!" which was everything he wanted to know, and upon which tidings he fell into a deep, impenetrable, placid sleep. The stir and excitement of the last twenty-four hours and more had taken their toll. He had eluded a falling piano, and climbed roofs, and chased after nefarious and shadowy individuals. He had got a cat from a tree. He had labored gallantly beneath the highest sort of anxiety. He was done in. "High tide at thirty-seven minutes past the hour of ten," he said, and save for some grand and magnificent snores, this was the last thing to pass his lips for almost an hour.

Everyone within hearing distance watched Dee with great interest. There were whispers and rumors running through the crowd and many of the hoboes doffed their hats, which seemed mysterious to other people.

"We're pleased you're safe, Mrs. Roberto," said Big Eye Pfelt to Dee.

"That's very kind of you, sir, but I assure you—"

"I *thought* we had met before," said Mister Walton.

"And I promise you, we haven't," said Dee, with an odd smile.

"Oh," said Mister Walton. He and Sundry had already exchanged bewildered looks with one another since discovering Mr. Thump, and would pass more between them when Mr. Ephram and Mr. Eagleton next arrived in the company of a retired sheriff and two captured burglars.

For now, Mister Walton simply nodded, calmly accepting this woman's assertion that they had never met. It seemed otherwise to him, but if she were hiding something of herself (as he suspected), and for whatever reason, it was all the same to him as if she told the truth. He would press the business no further. "Miss Pilican," he said with a gentlemanly nod.

It was beginning to rain.

❧ BOOK SEVEN ❧

May 30 – June 2, 1897

from the *Eastern Argus*
June 1, 1897

FIRE RAGES AT ICEBORO

*Volunteers Pour in from
Surrounding Towns.*

*A Night of Heroism Capped
by Welcome Rain.*

*Looters Captured by Retired Sheriff
with Help of Portland Club Members.*

It has been said that there is but one consistent aspect of the Maine climate and that is its unpredictability; surprise does seem our weather's most common element. Still, when a bolt of lightning comes out of a cloudless atmosphere and sets fire to a community's largest building, people have reason to be astonished.

Such a thing occurred in the small hours of Sunday morning in the village of Iceboro, just ten miles or so south of the capital. Citizens of that busy place were long sleeping in their beds when a crash, described by some as "terrific" and others as "the loudest thing I ever did hear," roused everyone from the worst sinner to the highest saint in the same instant. Hardly had the town adjusted its collective nightcap and peered out the window before another awful noise shook the sills— an explosion, this time, from the sawdust-filled icehouse hard by the docks along the Kennebec. The icehouse was on fire!

Some six hundred feet in length and forty feet tall, with a capacity of seventy thousand tons, the icehouse was a formidable piece of building to have ablaze in the midst of town, and, as almost two hours passed before the first drop of rain, it is something of a miracle that more was not lost.

The thunderstroke came some minutes past one in the morning. No sign of storm had arrived as yet, though reports have rain and wind reaching Owl's Head by that hour. Two other buildings caught fire—a boardinghouse built to house many of the ice cutters in the area lost a portion of its roof, and a livery stable in the midst of town was nearly gutted.

Men and women hurried into Iceboro from the surrounding towns, many reaching the fire within half an hour, and much was saved because of their selfless attention to duty. Some forty or more "men of the road" came also, having bedded down the evening before at Blinn Hill—a nearby wood across the river. It was a night of hazard and adventure, and this journal will apprise its readers of the more interesting stories as they are reported to us.

One of the more troublesome aspects of the crisis concerned the presence of looters—some few men intent on robbing their neighbors while all and sundry were fighting for the very existence of the community.

Edward Fischer, a retired sheriff of Kennebec County, rode into Iceboro from the west at about two o'clock when he espied several suspicious figures huddled near the back of Britner's Emporium and Dry Goods. With the skill and cunning realized in more than twenty-five years of service, Mr. Fischer advanced upon these men and was preparing to let his presence be known by discharging his rifle into the air when two more men came running from the store. The four men already outside attempted to capture the two newcomers, and in the resulting melee, Mr. Fischer understood that the first fellows had been in fact laying in wait of looters rather than waiting to loot themselves.

Who did they turn out to be, these self-deputized police, but two "men of the road" and two members of that society which has already gone down in recent local history as harboring men of action—no other order than the Moosepath League itself, one fellow of which, less than a week ago, saved Portland's own policeman Calvin Drum from being crushed by a falling piano. Holmes and Watson could not be busier, it seems!

Mr. Fischer cut short this business by firing a shot in the air, which had been his first intention, and soon the two felons—Clarence Sawtooth and Wallace Poole by name—were caught and collared. The two "men of the road" and the members of the Moosepath League—Mr. Christopher Eagleton of Chestnut Street and Mr. Matthew Ephram of

Danforth Street—were in a great state of excitement but only too glad to except Mr. Fischer's command of the situation. The looters have since been charged and held on bail. They await trial. The participants in this scene were interviewed, and Mr. Fischer reports that he is still looking for someone named Henry who seems to have been involved but has since disappeared.

❧§❧

BANGOR TELEGRAPH COMPANY
James Street Office

MAY 29, AM 11:36
DRESDEN MILLS, MAINE
MRS. JUDD PILICAN

FOUR MEN VISITED THIS MORNING, ASKING AFTER YOUR NINE PEOPLE-IN-PEN COLLECTIVELY. REFUSED THEM INFORMATION AS TO ANY WHEREABOUTS, BUT THOUGHT IT STRANGE AND THAT YOU SHOULD KNOW. LETTER TO FOLLOW.
WILLIAM SIEGFRIED

❧§❧

FROM MR. WILLIAM SIEGFRIED
BANGOR, MAY 29, 1897

Dear Mrs. Pilican,

It is with great anticipation that we, here at Siegfried and Son, await the arrival of your latest manuscript, but more for the continued knowledge that you and yours are happy and well. The spring has been filled with perfect and near perfect days and we imagine with pleasure how you must take the sun of an afternoon when May is at its height.

I must apologize for my strange telegram of this morning and hope that it did not cause you more alarm than was necessary. Four men paid Mr. Mullett and myself the strangest visit today, and I thought it meet to apprise you of them and their purpose.

Three of them seemed quite honest and of the most innocent variety, which made the presence of the fourth man, who seemed anything but innocent, a puzzle. They were very much in a state of agitation—particularly

over the whereabouts and safety of someone with the melodic name of Mrs.
Dorothea Roberto . . .

58. Briefly Ascertaining
the Whereabouts of Several People
(May 30, 1897)

No one really knows what cats think of things, and that is the end of it. Dogs will lay every emotion before you, and sometimes, afterward, they will even show their shame for having done so, but a cat only looks away. A cat will narrow his eyes as if he could not bother to look with his whole sight. When a cat does widen his eyes, the expression is almost always provoked by some perception unknown to us. Ezra Porch would stare with wide, wild eyes when a phantom passed overhead or at the sound of a mouse in the field that you or I could not detect, but the great calamity across the river that night—the roar and sunlike blaze of the fire and the cries of men and women—seemed to merit only his occasional (and narrow-eyed) glance. Mr. Porch hardly moved from his perch atop the hill across from home; surely he was aware of the commotion in the west, but in appearance he remained aloof.

But a field mouse did pass almost under his nose, and several rabbits thumped below him on the other side of the hill. Mr. Porch was, in fact, hypnotized until the eastern sky grew light and the fire in the west lost its preeminence. The early hours of morning had promised rain, and finally rain came just ahead of a false dawn glowing behind an overcast sky.

Ezra Porch turned his head at the sound of a door being opened and closed. He watched with long eyes as the old man of the house hurried down the street and into town. The post office would not be open today, but two fellows were loitering in the shelter of the porch there. The old man stopped before them, cocking his rain hat up and waving his arms till they joined him on the street and followed him to the livery.

Wind and rain met Mr. Porch's face as he turned his pads toward home and down the grassy slope. Even in the wet he barely left a trail behind him. From his perch in the lilacs he watched as a horse and carriage was pulled up before the gate. Two men sat atop, looking philosophical. Their slickers and hats glistened in the half-light. Old Fale Field climbed out of the rig and moved his rheumatic limbs down the walk and up the front steps. The cat could hear everything, though what sense he made of it is a mystery.

"Are you set on this?" the old man was saying.

"You know I am, so why do you ask?" came the voice of Mother Pilican.

"Well, get your hat on." There was a pause, then the old fellow said, "I can find her, you know?"

"I'm not sitting here, fretting by myself. But you're not carrying me out, either."

"No, no. I've got the Sproat boy and the Fallow boy to drive us." The door opened and Fale croaked out to the two atop the rig. "Well, come on. She'll need the both of you."

The two fellows climbed down from the driver's seat, neither of them boys at all but two of Dresden's ne'r-do-wells who had opted to consider the glow of the fire from a distance rather than risk work at closer quarters. Fale had nabbed them, however, and he had exercised all his long-abandoned military bearing to bedevil them into service. He'd left a note at the livery for Maurice Tapperly to the account of a horse and carriage and a pair of slickers he found in the back room for the *boys*. They had done pretty quick work, once they fell to it, and they even seemed a little curious to see what was happening in Iceboro now that most of it was probably done.

Mr. Porch looked a little wide-eyed when the two men came out carrying Mother Pilican, their locked arms like a sedan chair. They were solicitous of the old woman and packed her pretty carefully into the carriage. Fale came scurrying out with blankets, which he tossed inside before climbing after. Ezra Porch watched. He could appear fascinated as long as no one was looking at him. He had seldom seen Mother Pilican leave the house, and never in such weather or at such an hour. He watched the carriage pull away and disappear over the next knoll before he realized he was locked outside the house until someone came home.

It began to rain in earnest. Ezra Porch grew still and inscrutable. He peered through his lilac cover to the top of the hill across the way, but the ascending light of day had obscured the glow in the west.

⚜ ❦ ⚜

Looking for the new day, Big Eye Pfelt peered from under his dripping hat in the direction of the Kennebec River, and the banks and hills beyond, but the smoke and steam had obscured the rising glow in the east.

By the work of man the great fire at Iceboro was contained, and by the vagaries of nature it was quelled. Like a prodigious beast the fire had roared and lay down and died, and, when it was done, the mists of that rainy morning separating from the smoke and steam of disaster, the icehouse itself resembled a ravaged giant. With the rain came wind. Sparks and hot ash flew with the driving wet so that the air about Iceboro was filled with contradiction. The bucket brigades did not leave off their work till the burned-out building swam in ash-choked water.

The firefighters gathered at a respectful distance from the catastrophe, aghast at the randomly spared timbers and posts that thrust blackened from round the core of the original explosion. Some six hundred feet of charred, skeletal ribs and shards of roof and wall had replaced the vast icehouse of the day before, and in the midst of the smoking remains there were great masses of ice—inexplicable and hardly to be believed.

"I've heard of it happening," said Big Eye Pfelt about the surviving ice, "but I didn't expect it." The rain seemed no hindrance to him, pattering in his face and running out of his beard and down his neck. Hoboes are career men when it comes to weather.

"I've *seen* it," said a local man who held his head so that the brim of his hat would guard his face from the rain. "Back in '90," he said, "downriver, at another fire. I've seen it, but I *still* didn't expect it."

"It's a terrible shame," said someone further back in the crowd.

"Henry says, 'It's a terrible shame,'" said another.

"It could have been worse," said one philosopher. He reached out to scratch the head of the dog on Big Eye's shoulder. "We were some glad to see you fellows come across river," he said. "What brought you in such force?"

Big Eye Pfelt was not too sure he could explain the attendance of himself and his fellow road men. Come to think of it, he wasn't entirely sure he could explain the Moosepath League, and the imperiled Mrs. Roberto posed yet another mystery since she arrived on the scene under a separate name, herself rescuing animals from a burning building.

Taken all together, it was perplexing, and certain necessary bits of information under several headings were striking for their truancy.

The Moosepath League itself had seemed perplexed, which perplexed Big Eye further; they had been most particularly astonished that the two halves of their society should meet one another before the burning livery; or perhaps it was merely a feigned astonishment meant to hide deeper purposes. Big Eye Pfelt had been around in his day, but, come that Sunday morning, he was not too sure what he had rubbed shoulders with since yesterday afternoon.

✺

"I am pleased that you are safe, Miss Pilican," said Thump when he opened his eyes and found the kerchiefed woman in a chair beside the sofa in Mrs. Mulligan's parlor. In his mind he referred to her still as "Mrs. Roberto," and he pronounced this new name with some difficulty, but Mister Walton had set a courteous precedent by addressing her in this manner and Thump would follow.

"I have you to thank for it, Mr. Thump," said she.

Thump was speechless. He would have liked nothing more than to simply look at her, but that would have been indelicate, and he stared at the ceiling. He felt dizzy from his ordeal and quickly fell asleep again. Mister Walton, who had felt better himself, was yet fascinated by what it all meant, and Sundry, too, was curious.

"He is exhausted," said Eagleton.

"Clearly, you have had some adventures," said Mister Walton.

"It all started," said Ephram, "when a piano almost fell on him."

"Good heavens!" said Mister Walton.

Sundry leaned back in his chair, his arms folded.

"We were quite amazed, and even overjoyed, to find you here in Iceboro," said Eagleton to the both of them.

"We haven't evaded any pianos," said Mister Walton, "but, to be truthful, we have had some adventures ourselves."

"Have you?" Ephram and Eagleton were hardly surprised.

"Mister Walton cured a glum pig," informed Sundry.

The portly fellow chortled.

"And then we attended an elopement," said Sundry.

Jacob Lister, who sat nearby, grunted at these references and looked uncomfortable. A similar noise came from Mr. Fern as well as Mrs. Mulligan in the kitchen. Sundry cast a baleful eye at the old man, then let it fall briefly on Aunt Beatrice, who stood at the doorway to the pantry. He thought it inferior behavior to endanger a creature like Hercules, and he didn't care who knew it.

Aunt Beatrice looked unrepentant. She returned the young man's gaze with an expression of curdled humor.

And the woman whom they addressed as "Miss Pilican" wondered that the whole lot of them (and the members of the Moosepath League, to be sure) hadn't walked out of one of her mother's books.

Later in the day, Ephram and Eagleton realized that somehow, through all the fire and alarm, they had been wearing each other's coats.

⁂

"She's gone," they told Thump when he woke again. Actually, it was Mrs. Mulligan who gave him the news, and what she said was, "She's gone out to join a bucket line," which was more prosaic than a mere, "She's gone." Thump would always remember the moment, or speak of it (on rare occasions) as if some choral *they* had rendered him the melancholy news, saying simply, "She's gone."

"Of course," he said. *Of course she is gone*, he thought. She was too like a dream—too potent a force (poise and elegance and beauty) to squander herself upon one single being. From a thousand feet above the earth she propelled herself into thin air and caused hearts to leap with trepidation, then to fill with gratitude as she unfurled her star-spangled parachute and drifted like a flower on the wind in her attractive suit of tights! (Thump wrote something like this, and more, in his journal a few days later.)

She was gone, but she was safe. He knew not how she had escaped her captors, nor were any of them very sure how Clarence Sawtooth and Wallace Poole were connected with the affair (the retired sheriff called them "looters" and kept asking who Henry was), but she had rescued herself, only to flee toward danger in the service of those poor creatures at the livery.

Thump hardly stirred. There was less noise from without, but he was conscious that a crowd was gathered on the street. A clock ticked in the hall. He considered a picture on the wall in which Ruth gleaned the fields of Boaz, and there was an old sampler by the door that he could not quite read in the half-light.

Mrs. Roberto! She was gone, but she was safe. Thump was content in a wistful way. He reached up and touched his beard. *She liked my beard!* he thought with cautious pride. Ephram and Eagleton slept in chairs nearby. Mister Walton had been given a bed upstairs in which to sleep, and Mr. Moss spent the remainder of the night keeping watch. Thump heard rain at the windows. He nodded to himself, hardly realizing where he was, then nodded off once again.

59. Briefly Associating the Paths of Several Individuals

Dee would be put out (in her mild way) to find her mother and uncle in Iceboro; she was more apt to give lectures these days than listen to them. She was always telling her mother and uncle to be more careful of themselves, not to overdo, and to stay warm and dry. Mother Pilican would laugh; Dee, who was herself so careless, had listened to many a lecture in her youth.

In the darkened parlor that night, Fale had been the first to fret—an old man who had watched his beloved niece rush through the door toward crisis. Mother Pilican had been about an hour behind in worrying but quickly caught him up. "I wish I hadn't let her go," Fale must have said a dozen times, and his sister would answer, "I don't know what you could have done about it," or, "You didn't. She's a grown woman." Fale had paced the rooms downstairs and they watched the glow of the distant fire shift and brighten and then (they hoped) fade just a bit.

When he stopped pacing, Deborah Pilican knew what her brother was thinking, and, a moment later, what he had decided. "You're not going without me," she had said quite simply, and, "I'm not sitting here by myself," she hastily added when he began to protest. He knew better than to say more.

The rainy drive was long and wearying for them both. They went to Gardiner for the ferry and then rocked down the muddy road south to Iceboro. The Sproat and Fallow *boys* drove well enough, Fale supposed, but the carriage was nothing to boast about. It leaked, and the old folk were weary *and* wet by the time they reached the outskirts of the stricken village.

There was no driving down the main street of Iceboro that morning—the way was choked with people, with rigs and horses and smoking debris. They were surprised that several of the firefighters knew who Dee was and horrified to discover how she came by this notoriety. Their carriage was sent down a backstreet to the home of Mrs. Mulligan, and at her kitchen door Fale inquired after his niece. A building had burned to the ground behind Mrs. Mulligan's, and Mother Pilican wondered if this was the livery from which her daughter had been rescued. The rain grew louder while she waited, and the wind picked up the spray and sent it in sheets against the carriage.

Fale came back to say that Dee had gone home with Olin Bell and that Mrs. Mulligan insisted they come in and warm themselves with a cup of tea. If she hadn't been so very tired and damp and chilled, Mother Pilican would have asked to head straight home, but she allowed the Sproat and Fallow *boys* to carry her into Mrs. Mulligan's parlor, where she was startled to find two well-dressed fellows sleeping in chairs and a third man in more common attire snoring on the sofa.

"I don't think you *could* wake them," said Mrs. Mulligan when the old woman expressed this concern. "The fellow with the beard is the one who went in after your daughter."

"Oh?" said Mrs. Pilican. She had seen only a burly, bearded man stretched out on the sofa—he was perhaps a little rough looking—but now she was sure that he exuded, even in sleep, great heroism and kindness.

"He's a member of the Moosepath League," added Mrs. Mulligan.

"Whatever is *that?*" asked Mrs. Pilican. They were speaking in quiet tones, but she was still amazed that the men didn't wake.

"I don't know for certain. But these other fellows are, too, *and* two gentlemen who are resting upstairs." Mrs. Mulligan pointed to the ceiling.

Fale settled himself in a chair by the window. He glanced over his shoulder at the scene of smoke and ruin outside. "She went off with Olin Bell, you say?"

"I believe so. You should have seen him. He went in right after Mr. Thump, and a line of men guided them all out. It was like something from a book!" Mrs. Mulligan held her hands up before her, as if warding the sight away. "Oh! Oh!" she chirped.

"Mr. Thump?" said Mother Pilican. She liked the name. Mrs. Mulligan pointed out each of the sleeping men as she named them. Mother Pilican liked them very much, and, aside from worrying that Dee would fret when she returned to an empty house, the old woman began to feel less weary and cold. "Thank you so much," she said when a saucer and a steaming cup of tea were put in her hands. She put her palms about the warm china and thought about Fale's hot-wax remedy as the pain in her fingers subsided just a bit.

"Good morning," said Fale, and she looked up to see that the bearded man on the sofa had wakened. There was a series of expressions that ran through his face, brief studies of recall and puzzlement. They could not know what he had been through the past twenty-four hours, nor that he had been searching for a Mrs. Roberto and found a Miss Pilican. The old woman had no notion that she was seated in the very chair occupied by her daughter when Mr. Thump last saw her.

"I beg your pardon," said the bearded man. He stood a little shakily.

The other men, slumped in their chairs, woke of a sudden and rose to their feet, somewhat staggered by sleep. "Where's the observatory?" asked the tall, blond fellow. "What?" he piped. "Oh, here we are! Continued rain, I would suspect, but—" His voice fell off then and he simply blinked at his surroundings.

"Hmmm," said the bearded man. He looked about the room as if he were trying to track a fly.

"Eleven minutes past the hour of seven," said the dark-haired man with the handsome mustaches. He had a pocket watch in hand. Mrs. Pilican and her brother were surprised to see him reach into another pocket and produce a second watch. "Yes," he said, looking from one timepiece to the other.

"Oh, dear," said Mrs. Pilican. "Now we've wakened you."

"Not at all," said the man with the watches. "Not at all."

"Time to be up and about," said the blond fellow, though Eagleton was rarely up at this hour.

"We beg your pardon," said the bearded man again, and the three of them shuffled their feet and bowed and half bowed and nodded their heads to Mrs. Pilican and Fale Field, and the older people were quite entertained.

"Please sit," said the old woman. "You men are deserving of your rest, by all accounts." She smiled upon the bearded man with a degree of solicitous regard that obviously embarrassed him. "And, by all accounts," she said to him, "you deserve our great thanks as well."

"Mr. Thump?" said Fale.

"Yes?" said that startled worthy.

"Fale Field." The older man offered his hand with unmistakable gravity. "My sister and I cannot express our gratitude for your rescuing Dee."

"Dee?" said Mr. Thump.

"My daughter," said the elderly woman.

"My niece," said the old man.

"Deborah," said the mother. "But we call her Dee."

"Mrs. Ro—?" began Mr. Thump, but he paused, quite visibly thought with his hand on his beard, and said, "Miss Pilican?"

"Deborah," said Mr. Eagleton, sounding out the name as if he had never heard it before. "It is a very beautiful name."

"Thank you," said the elderly woman with a renewed sense of gratitude and warmth. "It is mine as well. I'm Deborah Pilican." Putting her cup and saucer on the table beside her, she reached out and grasped Thump's hands in her own, which were cold.

"I beg your pardon!" said Mr. Thump, and he introduced himself and his friends. Handshakes went all around, and the old woman was more delighted still. These three gentlemen were so diffident and yet so gracious that she thought they might have walked out of one of her books.

"Yes, well," said Mr. Ephram. "We are so very pleased to meet you. Your daughter, you say!"

"We are her great admirers," said Mr. Eagleton, who then proceeded to blush. "I mean, we greatly admire her. That is to say, she is admirable."

"You are very kind," said Mrs. Pilican. It seemed that her daughter had won these gentlemen over in a very short space of time.

"Not at all," said Mr. Eagleton.

"Hmmm!" said Mr. Thump.

Mrs. Pilican took hold of his hands once more and said, "I could hardly explain to you, Mr. Thump, how much she means to us, and therefore cannot adequately tell you how very grateful we are."

Mr. Thump seemed to have something in his throat and also his eyes. He allowed Mrs. Pilican to grasp and shake his hands, but he looked uncertain in the light of her sweet smile. There were tears on her face, and soon Mr. Thump was hemming and hawing and blinking and Mr. Ephram and Mr. Eagleton were looking out the windows and making noises as if a billow of smoke had returned to the room.

"Yes, well," said Mr. Ephram. "Ever in the fore, is our Thump!"

"Couldn't want a sturdier fellow in dire circumstance!" added Mr. Eagleton.

Mr. Thump barely found his voice, and then only enough to say, "I wouldn't have been here . . . without Ephram and Eagleton."

"Oh, you poor dear," said Mrs. Pilican unexpectedly, "here I am clutching your hands and mine are simply freezing!" and she let go of him.

"Not at all!" he said.

"Cold hands, warm heart!" she said with a small laugh.

Mr. Thump appeared touched by the thought.

"Could I get you some tea, Mr. Thump? Gentlemen?" asked Mrs. Mulligan, who had been watching this the scene from the doorway. "Toast and jam?"

"Oh, please! Not to bother!" said Mr. Eagleton. The growl of a stomach could be heard, however, and he looked surprised.

"We couldn't put you out," said Mr. Ephram. "You have been so kind."

"Nonsense," said the woman. "I'll be right back."

There was a lingering moment of silence in the parlor. The three men sat down once again, and each of them took on an expression of deep perplexity.

"What is the Moosepath League?" asked Fale suddenly.

"Oh, my!" said Mr. Eagleton. "It is our club, you see."

"Is it?" Fale was interested.

"Oh, yes."

There was another lingering moment. Mr. Eagleton mouthed the words "Moosepath League" silently, then Mr. Ephram did as well. Thump made a low noise. (The truth was, they had several questions for Mrs. Pilican, most of which concerned information gleaned from the *purloined* telegram, but it was an awkward business and they hadn't a notion where to start.) Mrs. Pilican and Mr. Field continued to beam aspects of happiness and gratitude upon them and the Moosepathians seemed to feel the effects of those benign expressions.

"Our chairman, Mister Walton, is resting upstairs," said Mr. Ephram.

"Very good, Eagleton," said Mr. Ephram.

"Thank you."

"Not at all."

This short exchange filled Mrs. Pilican with a strange, almost giddy, emotion that was difficult to index. It had something to do with a great-uncle she had known when she was very young. She did wonder why two of these gentlemen were dressed so expensively (even if their coats showed recent hard use and didn't seem to fit so well) and the third wore the clothes of a laboring man. She would like to have asked how her daughter was rescued, but clearly these men would be abashed to tell her. She was feeling warmer by the minute, though, and the tea was serving her in good stead. "*'What a good cup of tea won't accomplish against the cold and wet may be useless to wish for,'*" she said aloud, quoting from one of her own books.

"Hmmm?" said Mr. Thump.

"Good heavens!" said Mr. Eagleton.

"*How Far the Dawn!*" declared Mr. Ephram, and he stood.

"Good heavens, indeed!" said Mrs. Pilican, for the man had cited the very book. "Do you know it?"

"I have read it three times," said Mr. Ephram, "and have taken that particular bit of wisdom to heart and practice!"

"Indeed!" said Mr. Eagleton. "Mrs. Rudolpha Limington Harold!"

"Hmmm," said Mr. Thump.

"She is a great favorite of ours!" said Mr. Eagleton.

"I am sure she would be gratified to hear it," said Mrs. Pilican, speaking (as she often did) of one of her *noms de plume* as a separate person.

"Do you know her, then?" said Mr. Ephram with great emphasis.

"I suppose as well as anybody does," she said, almost with a laugh.

"*The Atrocious Uncle!*" said Mr. Thump. It was one of his favorites.

"*Gertrude of Aroostook!*" exclaimed Mr. Eagleton. "My, but that was marvelous!"

"And you've read them all?" she wondered, quite astonished.

"Mrs. Pilican," said Mr. Eagleton, "we consider Mrs. Harold a master of—I beg your pardon—a mistress of gripping fiction! I beg your pardon," he said again, looking from face to face. It had occurred to him that the phrase "gripping fiction" was a little unrefined. "I meant no offense."

"I am sure she would take none," said Mrs. Pilican honestly.

"*Kathleen O'Shea!*" breathed Mr. Ephram, and remembering the tale of the Irish lass and her journey from Cork County to the shores of New England gave him great pause.

"*'Who could guess what ancient songs of Erse moved upon the coastal rocks when Kathleen O'Shea explored the granitic shores of her new home or what memory of Ireland not even her own filled her with a faith in greensward and golden sunlight and a faculty for those things that are beyond color and sight, dancing upon the pools of moonlight on a midsummer's eve?'*"

"Oh, my!" said Mrs. Pilican.

It was Mr. Thump, who knew vast passages of Mrs. Harold's prose by heart.

"It sounds very grand, Mr. Thump," said the old woman, "spoken in that wonderful voice of yours."

Mr. Thump looked as if he'd been pinched, but Mr. Eagleton spoke for him. "He is a marvelous reader, Mrs. Pilican! Isn't it so, Ephram?"

"He is indeed, my friend," said Mr. Ephram.

"Mrs. Harold has an earnest following in Portland," asserted Mr. Thump, perhaps in an attempt to veer the conversation from his recitative skills.

"And you say you know her, Mrs. Pilican?" said Mr. Ephram. (He thought he was beginning to make some sense of Mr. Siegfried's telegram, but what was betokened by that odd phrase—*people-in-pen?*)

Deborah Pilican was on the verge of explaining to them just who Mrs. Rudolpha Limington Harold really was, when it occurred to her how disappointed they might be to hear it; she considered herself unprepossessing, and these men seemed so very fond of Mrs. Harold.

"She must be grand lady!" said Mr. Eagleton.

"Oh, my, but she *is!*" said Deborah Pilican. It was then too late to change course. "She's *very* grand, isn't she, Fale?" she said and almost laughed at her brother's expression. "Isn't she grand, Fale?" she said again.

"She's a bit of a handful," he admitted, and that did make her laugh.

"My word!" said Mr. Ephram. The three men appeared puzzled by Mr. Field's statement and by Mrs. Pilican's humor as well.

"Do you remember Miranda Hobbs in *The Atrocious Uncle?*" she asked them.

"We do!" and "Why, certainly!" and "Good heavens, yes!" they said.

Then Mrs. Pilican informed them that "Miranda was certainly Mrs. Harold's most telling self-portrait." The elderly woman had forgotten entirely about being cold and wet and about the pain in her hands.

"I can see it now!" said Mr. Eagleton, as if the book and the woman were both before him.

"Miranda Hobbs, you say!" said Mr. Ephram.

"She is a rare beauty, you know," said Mrs. Pilican. ("And at about that time," Fale would say to her later, "I thought you'd gone clean off the porch.")

"I *am* sure!" said Mr. Ephram. And *he* envisioned Mrs. Harold as plainly as if she were before him—and she was not plain at all.

"She met once, you know, with a Mrs. Alvina Plesock Dentin, on a holiday in Christiania. Mrs. Dentin is an authoress herself."

"We have read a great deal of her!" exclaimed Mr. Ephram.

"Oh, my!" said Mrs. Pilican. There seemed nothing like making matters worse, but she couldn't deny that she was enjoying herself.

"*Arabella's Winter Home!*" said Mr. Eagleton.

"*Wembley Upon the Hill!*" said Mr. Ephram.

"Hmmm!" said Mr. Thump. "*Mrs. Tempest's Tea Cups!*"

"And what did they say?" inquired Mr. Eagleton, who was avid to know. "Mrs. Harold and Mrs. Dentin," he added when Mrs. Pilican did not seem to understand.

Mrs. Pilican had only her old stories, told to amuse her family, to go by. She said, "I am afraid they were not the best of friends, when all was said and done."

"I am so sorry!" said Mr. Ephram, though he could believe, from her writing, that Mrs. Dentin was that much more proper than Mrs. Harold.

"Oh, it was fine, but Mrs. Harold did flirt terribly with Mrs. Dentin's brother."

The very idea appeared to startle the three men. Mr. Ephram touched the back of his neck, as if the hair there had lifted.

"Is Mrs. Harold's—?" Mr. Eagleton could not finish the sentence.

"Her husband has gone to his reward," said Mrs. Pilican. It was news to her, but she could not shock these dear men too much. She must be sure to tell Dee that Mrs. Harold was a widow.

"I'm sure Mrs. Dentin is lovely, too," said Mr. Ephram.

"She is a dear person, if a little formal," admitted the elderly woman. "But"—and here she dropped her voice to a near whisper—"she has very large teeth."

Clearly, the gentlemen of the club did not know what to do with this information.

"But you know these remarkable women!" said Mr. Eagleton.

"As well as anyone, I suppose." Mrs. Pilican felt the slightest twinge of guilt. She might have told anyone else that she was having them on, but these three dear men were so very enthralled that she couldn't bear to disillusion them. "You might say that I represent them."

"How marvelous!" said Mr. Eagleton. (The hyphenated phrase *people-in-pen* in Mr. Siegfried's telegram made sense to him now.) "And Mrs. Penelope Laurel Charmaine?"

"Why, yes!" said Mrs. Pilican, and it was really her turn to be astonished. "How did you know?" She wondered, *Who is having whom on?*

"And Mr. Wilmington Edward Northstrophe?" said Mr. Ephram. "You must tell us about him!"

Fale let out a great "Ahem!" and all three of the gentlemen said, "God bless you."

✤S✥✤

There has been much speculation concerning Mister Walton's appearance in Mrs. Mulligan's parlor at that moment. Many have asked, *What might have been revealed between the members of the club and Mrs. Pilican?* and *What might have been surmised?* Ephram's, Eagleton's, and Thump's litany of her pseudonyms was about to engender a path of inquiry from the elderly woman when the chairman of the Moosepath League stepped into the room with a characteristically cheerful greeting.

"Mister Walton!" declared Eagleton, who was greatly excited by their conversation with Mrs. Pilican.

"Our chairman!" added Ephram, which was both announcement and introduction.

Fale Field rose from his seat and Mister Walton crossed the room to shake his hand. "Tobias Walton," said the portly fellow.

Introductions were made twice, as Sundry Moss entered soon after. The elderly folk hardly blinked at his name.

"We quite admire your daughter, Mrs. Pilican," he said when he shook the old woman's hand, and there was a touch of humor and interest in his face that was not offensive to Mrs. Pilican but only curious.

"How are you feeling, Mister Walton?" wondered Ephram.

"Much rested after a bit of sleep, thank you," replied the bespectacled fellow. "Sundry, however, sat up all morning keeping watch." This was meant to stand for a reprimand but Sundry looked undaunted, if a little pale.

The Moosepathians were adamant that the new arrivals sit themselves down. Mister Walton's face darkened when he had a glimpse, past Mr. Field, of the ruins of the icehouse across the way. "Oh, my," he said softly.

The fire was reduced to not much more than smoke and smolder after the welcome rain, but the crowds had hardly dispersed. It was sad to see the dazed and weary postures and the discouraged droop of people's heads.

"So much ruin and injury," said Mister Walton. "And what it will mean to the town's livelihood, I can't guess." He was not a man to dwell on dark things, however, and he lifted his head again and said, "Your daughter is a courageous woman, Mrs. Pilican."

"It takes my breath away to think of what she did, Mister Walton," said the old woman.

"Ah, well—" he said gently.

"She has little caution," said Fale Field, but he was obviously proud of his niece. "I can't think why I let her out of my sight."

"We can't guess what she gets up to when she's away for the summer," added the elderly woman, almost to herself.

"Does she travel?" asked Mister Walton with a sense of renewed caution regarding the identity of the *Miss Pilican* in question.

"She stays in Portland in the summer," said Mother Pilican. "Perhaps you might see her at the park someday. She tells me she's quite fond of Deering Oaks."

Another entrance had its own effect in ending this singular meeting; Mr. Fern came in, looking wet and dreary. "The clouds are breaking in the east," he announced. "Perhaps it is time to go home and let Mrs. Fern know what has occurred."

"Your aunt—?" queried Mister Walton.

"She and her prospective groom have disappeared once again."

"Hercules seemed much improved," said Sundry recalling the fierce and spirited attitude of the pig when they last saw him.

Then the clouds appeared to break over Mr. Fern's countenance and in the eastern sky at about the same instance. "You're right, of course, Mr. Moss," he said. "Thank you for reminding me."

Sunlight came through the window. The older folk and the Moosepathians knew nothing about a vanished aunt or about someone named Hercules, but it was time for each party to pick up and continue on its way.

"We should be getting back, Deborah," said Fale Field. "Dee will be as distracted as you and I when she finds us away."

"Yes, of course. Where are the Sproat and Fallow boys?"

"If they're not handy, *I'll* drive us home. I guess we might find a strong gentleman or two who would take you out to the carriage."

He was not mistaken. Thump and Sundry carried Mrs. Pilican out amidst many courteous good-byes and words of praise between the older folk and the members of the Moosepath League. The Sproat *boy* and the Fallow *boy*, as it happened, turned up pretty quick.

"If you are ever near Dresden," said Mrs. Pilican to the members of the club, "you must visit us, not a quarter mile from the post office. Anyone in town will point you the way."

"Good-bye, Mrs. Pilican," said Eagleton. "Please send our best wishes and fondest admirations to Mrs. Harold."

"And Mrs. Dentin," added Ephram.

"And Mrs. Charmaine."

"And Miss Plotte."

"And Mr. Northstrophe."

Mrs. Pilican was laughing delightedly, for some reason.

"They'll hear much about it, I promise you," said Fale.

"And your daughter," said Thump. He had not joined in the list of authors to be commended. His expression was almost ardent, and it took Mrs. Pilican by the heart. "Please forward our best to your lovely daughter. And," he added, which was telling to the old woman, "*my* best as well."

The old woman reached out the carriage window and touched his shoulder. She almost said "I will," then almost said "Thank you," but instead she only smiled till the horse was nickered into motion and the carriage taken off.

60. Briefly Back at Fern Farm

"They're back! They're back!" came the cry from the upper hall of the farmhouse, followed by the clatter of two pair of feet half tripping down the stairs. Patient as scouts (and greatly fortified with oatmeal cookies), James and Homer had been watching from an upper window all morning for Father and Aunt Beatrice and their guests, but now the alarm was up. "They're back!" came an echoing cry from the parlor, though Susan and Bonny had seen nothing yet.

"They're back!" said Mrs. Fern more in a gust of relief than excitement.

The girls reached the kitchen first, but the boys were quick on their heels and soon passed them. Madeline practiced a little more dignity in her response, though she was surprised at the stab of pleasure she felt at the thought of seeing Mr. Moss again.

Along with a bit of wind, some heavy rain had come through earlier that morning, but the nor'easter traveled quickly, piling down the coast and inland till it blew itself out somewhere beyond Portland. By ten-thirty, the sun had broken through the clouds, taking command till the day was dewy and bright. Madeline and Mrs. Fern stepped outside, blinking in the sunshine.

Hercules stood at the edge of the drive almost like his old self, grunting happily and letting out squeals of delight when he realized that the family carriage was coming over the nearest rise. The pig could hardly contain himself, trotting circles in the yard before he settled like a footman by the kitchen stoop; the activity wearied him and he blew a great sigh as the carriage trundled up to the house. One of the boys threw an arm around the pig's neck and leaned against him, and they all stood with Hercules in such an elegant group they might have been posing for their portrait. It made Sundry smile to see them.

"Well!" said Mrs. Fern before Sundry had pulled the horse up and stopped the carriage. A breeze accompanied this arrival and the lilacs rustled fragrantly. "Well!" she said again when she thought she could be heard.

The carriage door opened and Mr. Fern stepped out, his face and posture manifesting a great stir of emotions. "We're all home safe, it seems," he announced, though he looked less than certain. "Aunt Beatrice has gone to get herself married to Jacob Lister," he added, almost as a *by the way*. He looked astonished when his wife laughed.

"Oh, Vergil!" she said. The children's reaction was a composite of their parents'—astonishment *and* laughter. "You've been to Iceboro," said Mrs.

Fern amid the sudden hail of questions. "Did you catch her up?" and "Was the fire very terrible?" and "Was Auntie there?" asked the children.

Mr. Fern embraced his wife and managed to nudge or kiss each boy and girl before he hunkered down to commune with Hercules. The pig grunted happily and boxed at the farmer's hand with his nose.

"He's been waiting for you all morning," said Ruth. She could not remain exasperated with Vergil, he was so happy to see his pig on the mend. "He might have gone to Iceboro himself when that bolt of lightning struck, but I called him back."

"Mr. Moss," said the farmer, "I believe your remedy has worked."

Hopping down from the driver's seat, Sundry said simply, "I am glad."

"Is that Hercules, looking so gallant?" came a cheery voice as Sundry held the door. Mister Walton stepped out easily enough, but Mrs. Fern thought Sundry deferred to his friend and employer with more than his usual concern.

The children's excitement had revived, and Hercules, too, had rested up it seemed, for he rose from his haunches and jogged about the yard with James and Homer running at either side and Bonny and Susan performing unladylike somersaults across the lawn.

"How did you know we were at Iceboro?" wondered Vergil Fern of his wife when they got inside the kitchen. He and their guests smelled of smoke.

"I only guessed," she replied. "News of the fire came up the road this morning. We heard the thunder while we waited for you in the kitchen last night. I suppose your aunt and Mr. Lister were there as well."

"We saw them, yes," said Vergil, nodding absently.

"Really, Vergil," said Ruth with sudden heat and not deferring to the presence of guests. "You shouldn't go careening off in such an all-fired huff. Beatrice is a grown woman, if you haven't noticed, and quite capable of making her own mistakes without your assistance."

"I wasn't attempting to assist her." The pleasant feelings so apparent upon his face when he saw his revived pig were replaced now with something more troubled and difficult.

"It's all the same if one of you turns a carriage over and someone is hurt!" said the wife. This storm was brief and to the point, however, and blew itself out as quickly as the morning's rain.

"Yes," drawled Mr. Fern. He had recalled that it was his aunt and her lover who had sickened Hercules in the first place. But he shook off this dark train of thought and considered what his wife had said. "There's more truth than you know in the charge," he said, and, if his wife's annoyance abated, his embarrassment did not. "I owe Mister Walton and Mr. Moss particular apologies for embroiling them in several adventures last night."

"Certainly not!" said Mister Walton, though there was a pallid hue about the man. "'*All's well that ends well*,' and I would not have missed any of it."

"Mister Walton has had a bad spell while helping to fight the fire," explained Mr. Fern. He was determined to have his guilt fully disclosed.

"I'm fine, I'm fine," said Mister Walton. Sundry looked less certain.

"Please," said Mrs. Fern. "Sit yourselves down."

Mister Walton insisted that he was unharmed by the night's exertions. He had slept at Mrs. Mulligan's. Nonetheless, he still looked tired and Sundry encouraged him into a kitchen chair.

Outside, the pig had sprawled onto his vast side, grunting contentedly— a massive island of white upon the lawn—and the children left him for news of the fire at Iceboro and the chase after Aunt Beatrice and her bridegroom. Hercules rolled onto his back and swung his feet in the air like a dog.

☙❧

It was not typical of Mister Walton to lose interest in his surroundings. His sympathy for nature, human or otherwise, and the general level of his curiosity were, as a rule, quick to lift him from personal travail; action—that is, forward movement of any sort—was almost always enough to generate his famous optimism. Even now, hardly hearing the conversation or tasting breakfast, he was practiced enough at these characteristics so that his hosts would hardly guess that he longed for nothing more than his own home and Phileda McCannon.

Everyone has some aspect of the contrary in their temper, however, and he would have objected had he known that Sundry Moss had already wired Miss McCannon from Iceboro.

Sundry, too, was usually more attuned to his surroundings, and certainly he could do justice to most any meal, but he was as anxious to see Mister Walton home and to have Miss McCannon's opinion on matters. All morning he hardly felt he had his wits about him.

While the Family Fern listened with rapt expressions to the father's tale of pursuit in the night, of fire and hazard in Iceboro, Mister Walton only nodded or said "Yes" when his corroboration seemed needed, and Sundry said less. Mister Walton considered, in the midst of a palatable breakfast, what Mrs. Baffin might be cooking at home, and Sundry—the object of esteem and even awe for his part in curing Hercules and in the adventures of the night— wished his friend and employer (and, by extension, himself) away from all distraction and worry.

But the tale needs be told, and Mr. Fern warmed to his task, describing the precarious chase through the night, the (now) comic exchange between himself and Aunt Beatrice at the ford, and the startling advent of that single bolt of lightning.

"And who should appear at the end of it all," finished Mr. Fern, "but Mister Walton's and Mr. Moss's fellow club members—one arriving in time to rescue a woman from a burning building and the other two assisting a lawman in apprehending burglars!" And this meant, of course, that nothing was finished at all, but that the whole tale—or as much as the farmer and his guests knew of it—must be started at the beginning.

61. The Hospitable Reciprocation
of the Family Spark
(June 1, 1897)

Strolling the lower blocks of Danforth Street in the late-afternoon sun, the members of the club could hardly credit that here was the scene of recent hazard. The street was no more hectic than many another commercial avenue, and the folks along the sidewalk appeared congenial. Ephram, Eagleton, and Thump doffed their newly purchased hats to those they passed and were gratified to be similarly saluted. They had never imagined how divided in character a place might be between sunlit day and fogbound night.

"Is this the Weary Sailor?" they asked themselves. The tavern looked placid, and even homely, as it dozed, and one could almost believe that the exhausted mariner on the sign above the door would find his needed rest in this place. Only the wreck of a piano on the porch gave evidence to what had happened last Thursday night—not a week ago!

And was this . . . well, the house of the "Woman in 12A?" And was that the roof by which they escaped? Again, they were struck by the tranquility, and they paused to number the surrounding buildings, the intervening days, and the events that brought them full circle to this street.

Eagleton stood with his hands behind his back and considered the brown building. "Do you suppose they have moved out?" he wondered. It seemed the only explanation for such a change in the local atmosphere. Then he was conscious of a pretty face smiling out at him from a second-story window. The young lady fluttered delicate fingers at him, and he was quite sure that she winked! Eagleton looked like a soldier standing at attention, which demeanor hardly altered when he walked away. His friends hurried to keep up.

Further up the street, three young fellows were slouched against a storefront wall, and one of these shouted, "Did your ship come in, Thaddeus? I thought you must be the mayor and his friends."

Ephram, Eagleton, and Thump raised their hats as they hastened past. Curiously, the three young men sported toppers that were very much like the Moosepathian's own new hats, which, in turn, were identical to those gone missing on Friday night.

"Several days of seasonable weather expected," announced Eagleton, glancing with great interest at these three well-crowned fellows. "Winds shifting to the southwest, with scattered clouds in the forecast."

"High tide at twelve minutes before eleven," announced Thump, his eyes wide with curiosity.

"It's thirty-five minutes past the hour of five," informed Ephram. He almost tripped while casting a look over his shoulder.

"That's not Thaddeus," said one of the slouchers, and, "Don't you know?" said another. "That's Mr. Thump who saved Calvin Drum and put Fuzz Hadley in his place. They say he's a long-lost cousin to Thaddeus. He made his fortune digging up Captain Kidd's treasure up toward Scotia."

The men on the porch craned their necks to keep the three men in sight, and when, as one, the Moosepathians looked back, the storefront slouchers raised their hats.

The Moosepathians were pleased to reach Brackett Street, however amiable Danforth Street in daylight had proved. Another man and then a woman greeted Thump with the name of Thaddeus and approving, if mystified, smiles.

What halted the members of the club next was the sign of the Faithful Mermaid. On their previous visit, they had entered the tavern by the back door and had not been privy to the prevailing spirit of the place. They had heard of mermaids, of course, and even seen a modest rendition of one or two—in the newspapers or perhaps a book of children's tales—but they had never seen (nor even imagined) anything so conspicuously ladylike that was also so . . . well, so *conspicuously ladylike*.

"That is a very striking emblem," said Eagleton.

"She does seem very . . . *faithful*," said Ephram. It touched him to see the mermaid gaze upon the heart in her hand with such ardent expression.

"Hmmm," said Thump. There was a robust quality about the mermaid that he did admire. Tightly gripping the day's *Portland Courier*, he cleared his throat and said "Hmmm" again.

"It's Mr. Thump!" called Minerva, when the three men entered the tavern. She hurried to the double doors at the back of the tavern room, stuck her head into the kitchen, and repeated her news. "It's Mr. Thump and his friends!"

An interested stir had prefaced this announcement; some were simply surprised to see such obvious gentlemen entering the Faithful Mermaid; others had met the Moosepath League on their last visit; everyone had been informed of them, about the business on Danforth Street and the search for Mrs. Roberto. The kitchen doors burst wide and Thaddeus Q. Spark barreled into the room, startling the members of the club all over again with his resemblance to Thump.

"Mr. Thump! Mr. Thump!" he piped in his high voice. "Mr. Eagleton! Mr.

Ephram! We heard you were back in town!" He greeted them with handshakes that were positively Moosepathian in their honest delight and energy. "'Oh, the rumor mill is never still,' my mother used to say."

The rest of the family, as well as the large and looming Jefford Paisley, the Todd brothers Tom and Patrick (who weren't related), Captains Broad and Huffle, and some of the laundrywomen pressed around the celebrated fellows, and the tavern room grew noisy with exclamation and inquiry.

"We heard you rescued Mrs. Roberto from a band of thieves and a burning building!" said Patrick Todd.

"Oh, dear!" said one of the laundrywomen. "I don't know if my heart can take it!" The laundrywomen were fully enamored of the Moosepath League by now and it was an agony to think of its gallant members in such dangerous straits.

"What were the villains up to?" Captain Huffle wondered aloud.

"They told me," said Tom Todd, "that you went into a camp of hoboes and raised them like an army!" He did not characterize who *they* were.

"There *was* Mr. Pfelt," admitted Eagleton. "And his fellows."

"Not Paulus Pfelt?" said Thaddeus.

"He never told us his Christian appellation," said Eagleton.

"He had a singular *sobriquet*," admitted Ephram

"He had a what?" said one of the Todd brothers.

"He called himself . . ." Ephram hesitated—"Big Eye."

"Gory!" said someone.

"Big Eye Pfelt!" said Jefford. Others echoed his amazement that the Moosepath had fallen in with one of the most notorious road men known to the State of Maine.

Two Indian scouts rushed into the tavern room, looking like they had spotted a whole war party of Hurons. "We heard up the street that Mr. Thump was here!" declared Timothy Spark. His blond hair stuck out like surprise in several places.

"Why, it's the young gentlemen who rescued us the other night," said Ephram without embarrassment. He and his fellows offered their hands again.

"How good it is to see you again," said Eagleton.

"We will not soon forget the service you did us," promised Thump.

"We're keeping them a little closer these days," said Thaddeus.

"They are good boys," said Eagleton.

One of them is, thought Thaddeus, and he almost said this aloud.

Several people in the room might have said something like it. Most people were at a loss to know what to think about Melanie Ring. She was a mystery, and they could not imagine how they had ever imagined that she was a boy. No one had seen very far behind that dirty face, and now that it was washed clean, more or less, her features seemed much too fine for a boy's.

Eyes that had peered from sooty surroundings like starlight in a well looked less hollow and only large and expressive. "Her mother was a pretty woman," said someone. Melanie was still dressed like a boy, and the members of the club were unaware of the change in the child they knew as Mailon (or, rather, the change in people's perception of her).

"Move aside," said Mabel Spark, then, "Right there. Serve them up," as if her daughters didn't know how to wait on guests. The young women piled the table with the best the house could provide—plates laden with onion-smothered beef and gravy, baked vegetables and potato, yeast rolls the size of Thump's fist, and great flagons of spring water purchased in yard-high bottles from Poland Spring. (The abstemious proclivities of the Moosepath League had been made plain to the Sparks.) "And bring coffee," Mabel said as her daughters hurried back to the kitchen for further comestibles. "You are hungry, gentlemen?" she inquired, almost fearfully.

They were famished. They were always famished after an excursion (and quite often before one as well). They were only a little indefinite about the precipitate manner in which they had been served. Things moved at a more stately pace at the Shipswood Restaurant. Violin music was played. The waiter offered a variety of dishes, and perhaps half an hour or forty-five minutes was necessary to decide on the evening's repast. For all its headlong preperation, the meal before them was not only adequate but hearty in the extreme.

Ephram cleared his throat.

"It looks marvelous," said Eagleton; and if his capacity were half as big as his eyes he would do the meal proper justice.

Thump looked up from his dish and said, "I believe that I have brought my appetite with me, Mrs. Spark." It was something Mr. Moss often said.

"Very good, Thump!" said Ephram.

"Ever in the fore!" said Eagleton, truer words than which had never been said, for, even as they spoke, Thump was gallantly addressing his plate with fork and knife.

Mabel Spark looked as pleased as she might to see a baby take its first drink from a cup, the general response around the table was one of sympathetic pleasure, and the members of the club indulged their hunger amid the sort of privacy bears at the zoo can expect at dinnertime. All chairs and tables were oriented in their direction, and all gazes attentively marked the completeness of their appetite, as well as the very decorous manner in which it was satisfied. Jefford Paisley promised how he'd "never seen anyone eat so nice or so well."

✺❧✺

"It is no wonder things turned out well," said Ephram when they were considering the apple pie served up for dessert. "Our chairman was there." Then he added, "Mister Walton."

"Mister Walton," said Thaddeus, as if this name should mean something to him. He was seated with his arms folded over the back of his chair. He had a pipe clenched in his teeth.

"And Sundry Moss," added Eagleton.

"Sundry Moss?" said Thaddeus. *There* was a name he couldn't mistake. "I met those fellows out in front of the Shipswood," he said.

"Yes, they said they met you," said Eagleton, remembering now.

"When were you at the Shipswood?" asked Mabel of her husband.

"You should have brought them along," said Thaddeus, neatly avoiding the question.

"They are in Bowdoinham still," ventured Ephram, "but I should not be surprised to hear that they are home on the morrow."

"You must bring them by," said Thaddeus.

When the Moosepathians were finished eating and coffee made the rounds, they told the story of their recent adventures as accurately as they could recall. The tavern was tense with people eager to know how the Moosepath League had tracked down Mrs. Roberto and her assailants, how they had raised an army of hoboes and arrived in time to help put out the fire at Iceboro, how Ephram and Eagleton aided in the capture of looters, and, most of all, how Thump had rescued the extraordinary ascensionist who had herself been bravely rescuing poor animals from certain death.

Timothy and Melanie sat in a corner trying to be inconspicuous.

"My!" said Melanie when the tale was finished. "That was *some* business!"

Everyone agreed, and the humble way in which the members of the club expressed their involvement only served to raise them in the estimation of their listeners. The laundrywomen, who ordered drinks at an ever increasing rate as the tale unfolded, were near to wailing when it was done.

"And to think it began with a calling card!" said Mabel Spark.

"A calling card?" said someone.

"Oh, yes," said another who was privy to the early details of the adventure. And so the front of the tale must be told, this time by several people, and finally someone asked to see the storied piece of pasteboard.

"Alas," said Thump, "my wallet went missing that night."

"Ah!" said Thaddeus Q. Spark, and he pulled Thump's wallet from his pocket. "You left it in your coat, Mr. Thump. I found it when I came home that night and have been carrying it ever since."

Thump was elated and thanked his host several times over. From the wallet he carefully removed a white piece of paper, which he held reverently over the table. No one offered to touch the card, much less take it from him, but they all crowded about, leaned forward with their hands behind their backs, and considered the flowing script upon it.

"*Mrs. Roberto*," read someone aloud. The summer sun and sunlit meadows and bright summer skies might have been invested in that single piece of pasteboard.

"Well, God bless her," said Mrs. Spark. "And God bless you good men for protecting her." After a moment, she added, "Thaddeus, don't forget to give Mr. Thump his clothes."

62. . . . And What They Didn't Know
(June 2, 1897)

"Ah, well," said Mother Pilican to Ezra Porch, which creature slumbered in her lap. "I wouldn't know what to think if my own name was on the back of a book." She had signed the last page with the name of *Miss Marion Elfaid Plotte.* It was a young woman's book, she thought. Melanie Bright's decision, in the end, to forsake Roger Dald, despite his confession and his assurances against all future misdeed, was perhaps a little bold for Miss Plotte's readers, but Mrs. Rudolpha Limington Harold would never have written it, and Mr. Wilmington Edward Northstrophe would have sent Melanie off to someplace exotic like Turkey or Argentina instead of Paris.

"What's that?" said Dee. She came in from the pantry with a plate in her hands. "You're not going to use your name?"

"I hardly believe I write them, once they're done." Mother Pilican flexed her hand, looking at it as if it were strange. "What would your father have thought?" She had said this before.

"What *would* he have thought?" said Dee.

"Oh, God bless him! He would have laughed."

Dee thought her father would have laughed, but with pleasure. "I don't think I'll go to Portland this summer," she said.

"What?"

"I think I'll see what summer in Dresden is like. It's been too long."

"Oh, Dee! I'm fine. And Fale hasn't changed for ten years."

"I know. But wouldn't it be fun with Teddy and Bill?"

Mrs. Pilican smiled just to think of them. "They would certainly love to have you." She would never tell Dee that every June the whole lot of them walked around in a daze of melancholy for a week after she left.

"I think I'll stay this summer." Dee almost spoke in a whisper.

"I won't say I'll be sorry to have you." The old woman stroked the sleeping cat, without thinking what she was doing and soon Mr. Porch was stretching his yellow sides, showing his claws while he yawned, and blinking back as if he didn't know her. She tickled his chin.

Mr. Porch trilled contentedly and stretched some more. Then he fell off Mother Pilican's lap with a maladroit flop. He looked startled, but was quick to regain his dignity, or the pretense of it. He paid no attention to their laughter and washed one of his forefeet. Dee picked him up, which was just what they both needed. "Did Mr. Siegfried's letter explain about his mysterious telegram?" she asked. They had received the telegram on Sunday; the letter had arrived that morning.

"He explained," said the old woman, "but I don't know if he made it any less mysterious. And who do you suppose those three men turned out to be?"

She was reaching into her dress pocket when they heard someone on the front steps. The door opened and Fale stepped inside. "Company," he said. A shadow fell across the threshold, and, even before he appeared with his hat in hand, Dee knew it was Olin Bell.

"Olin!" said Mother Pilican, and Dee also spoke his name, but silently.

"I just came by to see how you were," he said, taking them all in with a glance but meaning Dee.

"I just put the last sentence to my last book," said the old woman.

Fale laughed.

"I consider it great good luck that you should arrive at just this minute," said Mother Pilican to Olin.

Olin couldn't imagine it. He reddened and Dee thought she should rescue him. "We still see smoke, now and again, over the hill," she said. She walked to the hall with Mr. Porch in her arms and looked out the door.

"It's an awful mess," said Olin. He had been over to Iceboro, the last day or so, helping to clean up after the fire.

"There's Hank," said Dee, catching sight of the tall gray horse tied up on the other side of the fence across the street.

"Yes," said Olin wryly. "He lets me ride him."

"And you want to put a plow behind him," chided Dee playfully.

"It would make him useful to a farmer," said Olin, but he gazed after the horse with obvious pride.

A cloud of late mayflies hovered in the morning air above the fence. Hank tossed his head at them and nickered in a bass tone. The odd call of a cowbird rose from the hill beyond. Dee was briefly lost in the scene. Olin reached up to stroke the cat in her arms and Mr. Porch reacted with a lightning strike. "Whoa!" said Olin, and he pulled his hand back.

"Ezra Porch!" declared Dee, and she dropped the cat. Mr. Porch let out a jealous *rowl* and skittered up the stairs, where he watched balefully from between the balusters. "Olin, I'm sorry!" said Dee, and she took up the man's hand in hers.

Olin laughed. "It's nothing alongside being kicked by a cow."

"But you're bleeding!"

He almost snatched his hand away from her, partly in embarrassment, partly to put the scratch to his mouth, but he stopped as if to see what would happen. Dee realized, then, that she was holding his hand, that it was strong and callous in her soft palm, and that she felt a wave of sudden pleasure. She looked up into his blue eyes, imagined that he was experiencing something similar, and what she felt was suddenly elevated by several degrees of geometric progression. It had something to do with an absolute lack of fear.

It seemed like a very long time when she thought back on it, but it was only a moment. Fale said he had some salve in the kitchen. Olin retrieved his hand and put it to his mouth, insisting that it was nothing, and Dee very naturally went out with him after he said his good-byes to the older folk.

"I forgot to tell Dee about Mr. Siegfried's letter," said the old woman. "It's the strangest thing! What are you up to?"

It was pretty obvious what Fale was up to as he stood at the window with the curtain pulled aside an inch or two, but for an answer he only let out a low sound, like a chuckle.

"Well, what are *they* up to?" asked Mother Pilican. Mr. Porch had come halfway down the stairs and was peering at her through the banister.

⚸⚹⚸

Dee didn't say she was going further than the fence, and Olin didn't ask her; he simply helped her across, lifting her down once she was seated on the upper rail. He led Hank while they sauntered up the hill, feet kicking ever so slightly so that the toes of their boots (or buttoned shoes, in the case of Dee) made brief appearances above the grass with every step.

At the top of the hill, Olin said he was thinking of buying a boat. "I'd like to see those islands again," he said, pointing back over the Pilican home and the field beyond to the Eastern River.

"Would you invite me this time?" asked Dee.

"I guess I know better now," he said.

Hank seemed restless till Dee stroked his muzzle.

Without thinking, Olin put his hand to his mouth again. "So, what do you do, up there in Portland?" he asked.

"What do *I* do?"

"That fellow the other night seemed to recognize you."

Oh, thought Dee. "Oh," she said after a moment.

"Who's Mrs. Roberto?" he asked. "There was quite a lot of talk through the crowd, but I couldn't catch the most of it."

Dee laughed lightly. "Well, if you *must* know."

Olin shrugged, and by his expression offered to go on to other things.

"I didn't want to tell my mother and Uncle Fale that I've been up in a balloon," she said.

"Then you are this . . . Mrs. Roberto."

"I didn't say that."

Olin frowned. Hank tugged at his reins till he had leash enough to pull at some grass. "Now I *do* must know," said Olin.

"A friend of mine in Portland first brought me to see her. This was two or three years ago. Three years, it will be, this summer. Jeannie said I had to come and see the woman perform her parachute drop, but mostly because we were, she insisted, absolute twins. We *might* be sisters, really, but she is a few years older than myself, if I do say so, and standing side by side it isn't so difficult to tell us apart. Her hair is much darker than mine."

Olin's expression was only a little less doubtful.

Dee beamed. "Mrs. Roberto is an ascensionist. A hot-air balloon is tethered out to, oh, a thousand feet, I'm sure, and she jumps from it with a parachute. It's magnificent, really!"

"I'd like to see it."

"When she came down that day, Jeannie hurried up to get us side by side—with me protesting all the way, of course. Mrs. Roberto was very gracious and quite taken by our resemblance, it seems, for she invited me to ride in her balloon. I happily, if a little fearfully, accepted." Dee looked rhapsodic as she recalled the experience. "I was frightened, at first, but once I grew used to the sensation I thought I knew how an eagle felt. You have not seen the Earth till you have seen it look so small and tidy from such a height." Dee was leaning against Hank now, hugging her own shoulders as she grew lost with the memory. "I almost envy her." Then she laughed. "But I could never make that jump, I assure you."

"I'm glad to hear it," said Olin. Just the thought made him dizzy. He pulled a stem of grass from the ground and chewed the sweet end of it.

"I suppose I could tell Mom, but it's been a bit of my secret."

"I'm sorry to pry it from you," said Olin sincerely.

"No, no," she replied. "It's good to share it with someone. You'd like Mrs. Roberto."

"If she looks like you," he agreed.

Dee reached out and touched his sleeve. "No," she said. "There is something else about her that quite . . . *takes* people. I've seen her a few times since, but that was the only time I was ever in a balloon. It was difficult to know how to thank her, but she is a great reader and I gave her a set of Mom's books." Dee thought for a moment and said, "I'll have to send her the latest now. I sort of hope Mom uses her own name on this one."

"Her last book?" said Olin.

"Yes" said Dee. "Her fifth or sixth last book."

"I hope she has a dozen more."

They looked out toward Iceboro and the black ruins where the icehouse had stood only four days ago. Mounds of ice still stood amongst the wreckage.

"It was something, though," she said. "That fellow thinking I was Mrs. Roberto. I told the gentleman with the glasses that I was Dee Pilican, but I didn't press it very much. It was a little fun thinking of those fellows thinking I was her. You're not very disappointed, are you, that I'm not?"

"No, I'm not disappointed."

"I'm not going to Portland this summer," Dee said suddenly.

"No?" Olin looked like a man who doesn't quite trust to good luck.

She shook her head. "Now that you know my deep, dark secret, and what I do in the big town, I'll have to keep an eye on you."

Hank lifted his head and tugged at the reins. Slowly they walked toward the river, or Olin's farm, or perhaps the farm across the way.

"I should have asked sooner," said Olin Bell.

63. Deep and Philosophic

"I'm going over to the Smithy's and say good morning to Mr. Poulter," said Sundry to Mister Walton and Mr. Fern. The train had just pulled into Bowdoinham Station and they had a few minutes to board.

"Oh?" said Mr. Fern. He hardly remembered that the two men had met.

"Be sure to give him my best," said Mister Walton.

Sundry greeted people on the sidewalk and exchanged pleasantries with two idlers outside Jonas Fink's General Store and Post Office. He and Mister Walton had grown famous for gladdening the Ferns' pig, and there were still a lot of questions in the air. "You should write about it for *Country Gentleman*," said one of these fellows.

"Do you think?" said Sundry as he strode past.

"I'd read it."

"Mister Walton is the real genius."

"I know," stated this potential subscriber. "He raised a lot of them."

Sundry smiled, cocked his head, and continued on his way. He heard an insistent clang from the blacksmith's shop and felt the heat of the forge when he reached the open doors. Johnny was in his leather apron, his face and forearms dark with soot and exertion. He frowned at a smoldering piece of iron, which he held before him with a pair of tongs.

"I think you must have about a week," said Sundry.

Johnny was not a man to be startled. He finished his inspection of the hot iron, then looked over his shoulder. "A week?"

"I can't imagine it will be much longer before some fellow rides up and asks her to marry him."

"Madeline?" Johnny looked dumbfounded, then horrified.

"All *I* needed was a steep slope and a fast horse and I might have asked her myself."

"Madeline," said Johnny. Sundry's heart went out to the man. "Who do you think it will be?" asked the blacksmith thoughtfully. "Did she tell you?"

"Not in so many words, but I got the distinct impression there's *some* fellow she is awfully fond of."

"Oh," said Johnny. He looked *all in* of a sudden.

"I'd think you'd want to find out who it is," said Sundry.

"I don't think I want to know," said Johnny, his head hanging.

"No," said Sundry with a curt nod, "I think you do."

Johnny's expression altered as he tried to make something of this last statement. Sundry was walking back to the station.

"You really think so?" Johnny called after him.

"I really do," said Sundry. He took a few steps backward so that he could see Johnny while he spoke to him. "She has a beautiful singing voice."

"I know," said Johnny in a near whisper.

"Good luck!" said Sundry. The *all aboard* was being called when he reached the platform. Sundry and Mister Walton shook hands with Mr. Fern, exchanging assurances that they would see one another again. Mr. Fern thanked them for rescuing Hercules, and they thanked him for his family's splendid hospitality.

"Is there something wrong, Mr. Moss?" asked Mr. Fern when a troubled look passed over Sundry's face.

"No," said Sundry. "It's just I forgot that Madeline asked me to give her best to Mr. Poulter if I saw him."

"Oh?" said Mr. Fern, puzzled. It seemed little enough to worry about.

"Good-bye, Mr. Fern," said Sundry.

The farmer stood at the platform and waved them from the station.

Once aboard the train, Mister Walton looked pleased to be heading home. Sundry would not hear of going to Norridgewock. "Any more adventures and Miss McCannon won't trust us to go for the mail," said Sundry, but Mister Walton knew that concern for him was behind the thought and he was touched. In the end, Mister Walton had not protested too much. The rhythm of the rails was like a balm to him this day, just as long as it was the sound of going home.

Sundry was quiet for the first few miles. He watched the passing landscape with an expression of deep thought. Finally, just before Topsham Station, he said to Mister Walton, "Did you ever raise a lot of pigs?"

Mister Walton laughed. "No, I never did."

Sundry nodded. Mister Walton was cheerful, but his usual rosy glow hadn't completely returned. "I didn't think," said Sundry.

"We'll probably never know how I became such an expert on the subject. I did like Hercules very much, however."

"He's a good pig," said Sundry.

✦❀✦

Johnny Poulter left his work to stand out in front of the smithy, kicking dirt with the toe of his boot. His chest felt heavy, and every breath was hard to come by. The two idlers in front of Fink's store watched him. Johnny appeared to be studying something at his feet. A farmer driving by glanced down at the ground before the young man, as if the blacksmith were Archimedes scratching geometry in the dust. Johnny looked up when someone hailed him. He hailed back and went inside.

A few minutes later he came out again and paced the yard. The two idlers watched him. Looking up at the sound of another carriage coming down from the train station, Johnny saw Mr. Fern pull up before the store. The sight of anyone or anything associated with Madeline made his heart jump, and he raised a hand and called out a greeting to the farmer.

"Good morning, Johnny," said Mr. Fern. He had a list on a piece of paper and he studied this before mounting the steps. Shopping for staples was a long process in those days—part negotiation, part social event. A person considered carefully what he needed and how much he needed it. Mr. Fern was still reading his wife's list when he climbed the porch steps. He was almost inside the store when he stopped and called back to Johnny, "Madeline sends her best, by the way."

"She does?" said Johnny. From the look on his face, Mr. Fern might have told him that Hercules had taken wing.

Mr. Fern paused a little longer at the threshold. "Yes," he said absently, "that's what Mr. Moss tells me." He waved with continued absence of mind and disappeared inside.

Johnny went back to the smithy but came out again almost immediately. He walked a single wide circle in the yard, then called to one of the idlers in front of the store. "Jimmy," he said, "come watch the forge for me." Jimmy nodded lazily and shuffled over with his fellow idler in tow. "Bank up the fire, will you?" said Johnny. "And close it down. I'll buy you a sarsaparilla when I get back."

"Where you going, Johnny?" asked Jimmy.

"I have an errand to run," said the blacksmith. He threw off his leather apron, then washed his head and neck in the trough outside the smithy. He put on a shirt that was hanging on the door. Johnny went around back and called his horse in from the meadow, and in a few minutes he was riding north on the River Road.

The day was bright, almost unreal in its beauty. The horse was pleased to be out and moving at a good clip. Johnny hardly steered the animal and wasn't aware of how fast they were riding till he passed the farmer that had passed him some minutes before. When he came over the hill above Fern Farm, the first thing to greet his eye was the great white pig in the yard. Hercules grunted sociably as he met the young man at the edge of the drive.

"Hey, fellow," said Johnny. He hopped down and tossed the horse's reins over the fence. Then he leaned down to thump Hercules on the side. The pig talked some more, sounding affable. The backdoor opened and Johnny looked up to see Madeline on the stoop.

"Good morning, Johnny," she said.

"Good morning, Madeline."

"I saw you through the kitchen window." Madeline leaned out of the doorway and looked around the yard. The last time Johnny had come by, he had brought Mister Walton and Sundry Moss.

"I saw your father in town," he said.

"Oh?" She wondered what this might have to do with his unexpected visit. "He took Mister Walton and Mr. Moss in to meet the train."

Johnny nodded. They looked at one another a while longer and then he said, "Would you like to go for a walk?"

"Yes," she said, though she did not stir from the stoop. One of the little boys poked his head out past his sister and she scolded him back inside. There was a short colloquy between the young woman and someone in the kitchen—Mrs. Fern, Johnny thought—and Madeline came down the steps closing the door behind her.

They walked in the direction of the back fields without discussion. Hercules grunted his good wishes, but, understanding certain principles regarding company and crowds, he lagged behind and finally sprawled his great white bulk in the shade of a chestnut at the back of the house. The ducks saw him lay down and came by to socialize.

There are dances that mimic, however knowingly, the duel movements of young people at court—the hands clasped behind, the feet kicking ever so slightly so that the toe of the boot (or the kitchen slipper, in the case of Madeline Fern) makes a brief appearance above the grass with every step. The courtship cotillion is not straight but circuitous and wandering, like a country road. It follows, for a while, the path of least resistance, then suddenly makes a decisive climb to some small eminence, only to return to seemingly aimless wandering. It accommodates both silence and soft conversation. It comes as naturally to the children of toil as it does to the heirs of leisure, and no debutante or junior partner, having attended the finest schools, could walk this dance with more grace, and requisite terror, than this farmer's daughter and this young blacksmith.

Even their hands moved in interesting ways. Madeline had slowly realized that she was not as carefully tended as she might want to be. She had been cleaning house all morning and should have pulled her hair back or worn a kerchief. Her dress, she thought, was a little rumpled. Her hands performed involuntary jerks as she touched her hair at several principal points, and she gave a short, hopefully unseen, tug at the waist of her blouse.

Johnny only saw that she was every bit as beautiful as he had ever thought her to be, and perhaps a little more besides. He felt uncomfortably hot, and he hooked a finger in his collar, took off his hat, and shrugged largely in his shirt. He put his hat back on, and rubbed at the side of his face to ascertain if he had shaved this morning.

From the kitchen window, Mrs. Fern watched them disappear over the next rise. She held a dish towel in her hands as if it were something cherished and full of memories. Her smile was wistful. She blinked several times before returning to work.

Madeline and Johnny went over the knoll and reached the fence along the eastern perimeter of the farmyard. "The blackflies haven't been so bad this spring," said Johnny. To anyone born and raised in Maine, this is an issue of spring and one of first importance.

"It's been dry," said Madeline, which was both an agreement with and a theory as to why the previous statement might be true. They may have said and heard these things (or that the blackflies had been quite bad and that it had been wet) several thousand times in their lives. They did not have to think to say these things. They could say them, and several things more, without thinking.

"Even that rain the other day didn't stay long," said Johnny.

"I hope the summer isn't dry," said Madeline. She looked at him anxiously from the corner of her eye.

He understood that she was watching him and looked straight ahead. He almost stumbled against the root of an old elm that had snuck beneath the fence. They came to a small knoll, where the larger acres of Fern Farm could be seen. There was another hill, not far away, and a stream alongside it—only visible, from where they stood, as a dark crease in the land. The wind was shifting. A bird sang in a grove of birch below the hill. The sun was shining. Clouds of fleece glowed in a blue sky. Johnny could not have wanted a better venue for his purpose.

They looked out over the quiet land. A hawk, over toward the Kennebec, skimmed the horizon. The breeze tugged at Madeline's auburn hair. Johnny took off his hat and tapped it at the side of his leg.

"We heard a fox last night," said Madeline, her heart racing.

"I am quite fond of you, Madeline!" said Johnny.

"Oh," she said. She was still looking out over her father's acres.

Johnny hardly dared look at her. "Well . . . I am," he said.

"Oh."

"I'm sorry," he said after a moment.

"Please, don't be," she replied.

"No?"

"No," she said. "Please."

"I thought—" he began. He had almost said "Mr. Moss said—" but instead the words "you might like me a bit" came out.

"But I do," said Madeline.

"You do?"

Madeline felt dizzy.

"Well," he began again, "maybe more than a bit."

"But I do," she said.

"Oh," he said.

For the first time since this lyric conversation began, he looked at her and she looked at him.

"Oh," he said again. He was trying to locate the thumping engine inside of him; it seemed to bounce around so and even to take up his entire chest all at once. "Oh!" he said a little more emphatically than before.

They were still looking at one another, neither very sure what to do or say next. The solution to their quandary might seem simple to those who have not been in similar straits, or to those who have forgotten just how narrow and constricting those straits can be. Traveling by train at ten or twelve miles an hour out in the open fields may seem slow enough, but traveling at similar speeds through a town, with all of life and the buildings looming close will seem reckless. Madeline and Johnny might have been standing out in a field, in the physical sense, but in their minds things were pressing very closely as they sped faster than they had ever gone before.

Madeline offered a simple and direct utterance that seemed to carry great philosophy and depth. It was remarkable how much could be gotten out of three syllables. She felt, at that moment, as if she had spoken first, after all, and would have to think very hard in later years to convince herself that he spoke first and from out of the blue sky. She got flushed and embarrassed on the instant, but it was too late.

Johnny echoed those three syllables back to her, reflecting the same sort of philosophy, and certainly the same amount of depth. In fact, those words seemed so deep and so profound, and they gave him such pleasure—almost religious in its emotion—that he said them again. A third party might have grown a little weary of this rudimentary phrase before these two were done, but to the young man and the young woman the words only grew the more deep and philosophic with repetition.

But at some point Johnny thought that even these words no longer sufficed.

Back by the house, lying in the shade of the spreading chestnut with the ducks gossiping about him, the great white spirit of Fern Farm—like some conductor of local telluric currents—gave out a series of seemingly unmotivated, but contented, grunts and shifted his massive self to lie on his other side.

64. A Letter from Abidjan

The train ride south was pleasant enough, most of all (for Sundry, at least) because Mister Walton appeared to have recovered from whatever had felled him at Iceboro. Sundry breathed a small bit easier.

A carriage waited for them when they came out of Portland's Grand Trunk Depot, and it occurred to Mister Walton that Sundry had wired ahead, perhaps even the day before.

The portly gentleman did not admit to being weary when they pulled up to the house on Spruce Street; he insisted on carrying his valise and only chuckled at Sundry's frown. The day was bright and warm. Noon was only a few minutes away. Mister Walton startled his friend by lagging behind, but he had only paused to look around at the billowing foliage of elm and oak and chestnut, to smell the breeze that reached Spruce Street from the harbor, to listen to the birds and spot a squirrel on the lawn. There were robins hopping on their stiff legs—perhaps the very robins he had seen almost a week before, for there were seven of them. "How did Mr. Eagleton's verse go?" he asked.

Sundry couldn't begin to remember.

"My family's doctor should have had your concern," said Mister Walton. "I stepped on an old nail once and he said it would sturdy me up. Said my posture was lacking." He took another breath of the sea breeze. "If I smell Mrs. Baffin's cooking when we get inside, I'll know you did more than wire for a carriage."

They mounted the steps and Sundry held the door. Mister Walton stepped into the front hall with a strange mix of sensations. He smelled something wonderful from the kitchen, and he looked forward to the kind attentions of the elderly Mrs. and Mr. Baffin, but he was still counting the days till he would see Phileda again. Weariness had reawakened his recent melancholy.

Then she was at the end of the hall, a kitchen towel in her hands and a look of concern on her face. Her brown hair was done up in a practical bun and she wore a dark blue dress and an ivory blouse that Mister Walton had seen before (and thought of since). "Phileda!" he said. He almost dropped the valise.

"Oh, Toby, you do look pale!" she declared as she met him at the door. Sundry ducked past the doorway and hurried upstairs with the bags.

Phileda put her soft cool hands on either side of Mister Walton's face, then pressed his cheek against hers.

"Oh, my!" he was saying. "Oh, my! I am like an empty house without you, Phileda. Everything inside me just rattles around to no end or purpose."

There were tears behind his spectacles, and then there were tears behind hers. She kissed him, and whatever color his face had lacked till that moment returned to him. As he embraced her slim body, he could hear voices in the kitchen; Sundry had gone down the backstairs to greet the Baffins.

"I will speak to that young man," he said with some firmness. "I am somewhat put out with him."

"Are you?" she said, holding him at arm's length.

He did not look put out at all. He smiled and said, "Not really. Not even a little bit."

With a lace handkerchief from her pocket, she dabbed at her eyes. He made similar adjustments, all the while taking large, life-filled breaths.

"It is a shame for you to leave your aunt's," he said. "Whatever Sundry told you, I am fine."

"There wasn't anything left for me to do," she said. "I left the key with the neighbors, and really, Toby, you are not the only empty house when we are apart." This statement did little to dispel the tears in either of them, and soon they were laughing at themselves, they thought they must look so silly standing there in the hall weeping.

"I am hungry!" he said suddenly, trying to look stern. In her state of high sensation—tears and happiness—Phileda laughed, then put her hand over her mouth.

"Good heavens, what is it?" they could hear Mrs. Baffin's call from the kitchen.

"Oh, Toby," said Phileda, as if she had just remembered something. She put a hand to her breast and breathed hard from the roil of emotions. "There's a letter that arrived the other day. It's from your sister."

"Elizabeth?" he said. Phileda thought he paled again.

"It's postmarked from Abidjan," she said

"Elizabeth," he said. His sister was the only other family he had left alive, and he had not heard from her for almost ten years. He was shaking as he walked the hall, Phileda firmly on his arm.

"Why haven't you heard from her till now?" asked Phileda in a whisper.

"I don't know," he said. "My mother didn't approve of her husband." He laughed softly but regretfully. "He was an Episcopalian, you know. But I know Mother would never have said anything. I do think she was upset when Elizabeth told her she was going with him to Africa, though. I was away—in Indiana, I think—when Mother wrote me about it." They paused at the threshold, and Mister Walton realized that Sundry Moss and the Baffins were poised in the kitchen waiting to discover what was happening.

"My, but dinner smells marvelous!" he said with an appreciative sigh.

Mrs. Baffin's sweet face crinkled with pleasure at the sight and sound of him. "You sit right down, young Toby." she said. "I suppose the kitchen is grand enough for corned beef and cabbage. Sundry, you sit down," she dictated. "Miss McCannon."

Mister Walton closed in on the kitchen table, but it was the white envelope on its surface that garnered his full attention. He was still shaking a little when he sat down and opened the letter with a kitchen knife. It was a fat enclosure, and he shook from it a large sheaf of folded, tan-colored paper, the pages of which were filled with a regular, flowing script. He unfurled this missive and proceeded on the instant to read.

Phileda sat beside him and did her best to read his face. Sundry leaned against the counter. He had cut himself a piece of bread, which he folded in half and munched. Mrs. and Mr. Baffin, who had loved Elizabeth (and, in fact, the entire Walton clan) as much as they loved Toby, stood waiting and finally sat, too, at the table, waiting.

"Oh, dear," said Mister Walton, nearly under his breath but loud enough to be heard in that quiet room. He looked up when he realized what anxiety he might be causing and said, "It's only that my recent adventures pale before hers." He returned to the letter, but several times he let out an exclamation of wonder or disbelief. Toward the end of the letter, he grew silent, and he scanned the last page twice and three times over before he laid the missive on the table and took off his spectacles.

"Three months," he said in an absent voice.

"Toby?" sad Phileda. She put a hand on his.

"Elizabeth's husband has died," he said. "She is working at a hospital on the Ivory Coast. And she has a seven-year-old son. Victor." There was more silence. "I'm thirsty," he said, upon which announcement he realized that Sundry had placed a glass of cold water before him ten minutes ago. Mister Walton took a long drink and thought it tasted wonderful. "She has sent her son to England till the doctors there are sure he has recovered from a bout of fever. He's to sail from Bristol, then, to Halifax. He is, in fact, probably on his way."

"Toby!" said Phileda with quite a different inflection. She knew how much it would mean to him to have family by his side again. She pressed his arm and smiled softly.

"In the instance that this letter did not find me, or did not find me alive, there are arrangements for her husband's family to take Victor in. Poor Elizabeth. To have lost her husband so young." Mister Walton came out of the middle distances to regard Phileda with sudden perception. "He might be in Halifax now."

She did not let go his arm.

"Or arriving any day." He looked weary again. "It means my missing the ball, of course."

She nodded. Inside she was as disappointed as any young girl awaiting her first dance, but she showed nothing of her feelings. She thought herself small and selfish.

Sundry bent over a simmering pot as if he might pick something from it.

"And you left what you were doing to come down for me," said Mister Walton to Phileda.

"Elizabeth's son," said Mr. Baffin to himself.

None of them could think what it meant—least of all, what it meant to Mister Walton and Phileda McCannon and any future they might imagine together to have a seven-year-old boy coming to live on Spruce Street.

"I must go to Halifax," said Mister Walton.

"Of course," said Phileda.

"Sundry?" said Mister Walton. One might have guessed he was asking the young man's opinion.

"I'll check the steamer schedules," said Sundry.

"Thank you." Mister Walton couldn't imagine doing it himself, he felt so confused and distracted.

"Elizabeth's son," said Mr. Baffin again.

"Hush," said Mrs. Baffin, but softly.

Phileda looked to Sundry with an expression of concern. She was missing Mister Walton already, but, more than that, she had recently been swept up by her beau's sense of time passing all too swiftly—a sense (or an intuition, perhaps) that was all the more potent for her knowledge of his recent *spell*.

Sundry was no happier with the thought of Mister Walton traveling, and he was also conscious of the anxiety that must accompany such a new charge. He showed nothing of these misgivings, however, and simply nodded to Miss McCannon with an expression of immutable confidence.

65. Another Knot (or Two)

Sundry imagined that the solution was simple enough, though he understood that it might seem otherwise, were he in Mister Walton's place. He knew he'd been more than a little tongue-tied himself in the presence of Miss Morningside. In fact, reflecting upon Mister Walton and Miss McCannon, his thoughts quickly associated themselves with the young woman, and he experienced such a series of complex emotions that he was glad to step outside and into the day again.

The breeze had shifted into the west, and the ocean seemed further away when the fragrance of salt water was less palpable, but he heard the toot of a distant tug and the answering call of a steamer that might even now be standing into the harbor. The sun was just past its height and every blade of grass upon the front lawn was articulated against its own shadow. The trees were so green they almost hurt Sundry's eyes; they had not been leafed out so long that he could take them for granted. There were robins on the lawn and he thought to count them, though he couldn't remember what the number seven was supposed to auger.

He was in search of a newspaper and the departure schedules for ships communicating between Portland and Halifax. He was hankering for some roasted peanuts. Most of all, he thought it meet to get out from underfoot; Mister Walton might view his situation in simpler terms were there fewer people in the house, and particularly if everyone but Miss McCannon cleared out.

On the sidewalk, Sundry paused and considered Spruce Street in all its June glory. A gentleman with a top hat and cane came down the hill, greeting Sundry with quiet dignity as he passed. He put Sundry in mind of certain acquaintances, and it occurred to him that a newspaper was surely to be had on upper Danforth Street at the home of Matthew Ephram. He had never been to Mr. Ephram's apartments but he knew the address, which was not far away.

It was one of the older houses on Danforth Street—a handsome, white clapboard home of the Colonial style, square and upright. A maid answered the door and was very intent on Sundry as he asked for Mr. Matthew Ephram; he might have found his own way up the single flight of stairs, but she accompanied him, chatting pleasantly about the weather and how very kind Mr. Ephram was. She was a few years older than himself, Sundry guessed—a round-faced woman with bright eyes and rather obviously enamored of the second-floor tenant. "He's been very adventurous of late!" she declared. "Are you a member of his club?"

"I have heard of it." Sundry waited patiently for her to realize that they had reached the landing.

"The papers have followed them very closely," she said, wide-eyed. "Oh! Let me knock for you. I'm sure he's home."

Even before the door opened and Mr. Ephram appeared on the other side of it, Sundry was conscious of a gathered medley of ticks and tocks that had discovered sympathy in the very walls around them, so that the plaster and lathes and the woodwork seemed themselves to tick and tock. But this was nothing to the symphony that grew in volume when the door opened, and Sundry thought the experience was not unlike walking into a concert hall when the performance has already begun.

"Mr. Ephram," said the maid. "I beg your pardon, but Mr. Moss is here to see you."

"Mr. Moss?" said Ephram. "Mr. Moss?" he said again when he had located Sundry beside the maid. "Mr. Moss! How very good to see you! And how very kind of you to stop by! Please come in! Thank you, Miss Blythe."

The maid curtsied prettily and hurried down the stairs. Sundry stepped past Ephram's beckoning arm and thought he had visited the home of Father Time himself. All about him were clocks and chronometers, swinging pendulums and shivering indicators. Sundry peered from wall to table, from settee to wall, his hands behind him as if he were walking the corridors of a museum.

"Please, please," Ephram was saying. "Come in, please. How is Mister Walton? Recovered, I hope?" A stricken look then showed on his face as this line of thought coalesced with the possible reason for Sundry's unexpected visit. "Good heavens, Mr. Moss! The chairman is well, isn't he?"

"He's much better, I think," assured Sundry. "He's going to Halifax."

"Oh, my!" said Ephram. He looked so amazed, Sundry might have told him that Mister Walton was swimming to China.

"I was looking for a newspaper," said Sundry. "The departure schedules on the shipping page."

"Certainly, yes," said Ephram. "That would be the place to look." Then he looked amazed all over again and realized that Sundry wanted to peruse his *Eastern Argus*. "Why, yes! Come in, come in!" Ephram led the way, through a room or two, past any number of clocks, till they came to a comfortable den lined with books and populated by three overstuffed chairs. A table stood before the single window, and here there were certain mementos and oddments, along with a short stack of books, a small standing clock, a pair of reading glasses, and a neatly folded newspaper.

Ephram watched while Sundry perused the timetables in the shipping column. "The *Manitoba* is leaving on Saturday morning for Halifax," said Sundry. "She's down at the Atlantic and St. Lawrence Railroad Wharf."

"That's on the other end of Commercial Street," informed Ephram, "just across from Thump's family business."

"Is it?" Sundry carefully folded the newspaper and laid it on the table. "Maybe that's a good sign."

Ephram was delighted when Sundry invited him along for the walk. He gathered his watches and calling cards, a ring with two keys, and a billfold, then matched each of these articles to the proper pockets about his person, found his new hat, checked one of his watches against the clock in the den, and he was ready.

✻✺✻

"Mr. Spark's establishment is not far from here," said Ephram when they were near the corner where they would turn off Danforth Street. "The Faithful Mermaid."

"Is it?" said Sundry. He remembered, now, that the fellow outside the Shipswood Restaurant had spoken of the place. "Nearby, you say?"

A few minutes later they were standing before the tavern, and Sundry considered the lady above the door with great interest. There was something generous about her that made a person feel hopeful. Sundry was further impressed by the level of excitement occasioned by their entrance. Several people, including a coterie of older women in one corner, greeted Ephram familiarly and one or two even raised a glass, as if he might join them in a quaff of ale. (Sundry could smell the tavern's primary item of trade.) The news of their arrival found its way very quickly to the kitchen, and the image of Mr. Thump came striding out to welcome them heartily.

"Yes, Mr. Moss! I do remember you," said Thaddeus Spark in his high piping voice. "Welcome! Welcome! Mr. Ephram, you continue to honor us with your presence!"

Mrs. Spark came out, wiping her hands on her apron, and she was introduced to Sundry. The daughters came out to look and be looked at, as well. Sundry thought the mermaid had hardly lied.

"Will you stay to eat?" said Thaddeus. "Or just a piece of pie and a cup of coffee?"

Sundry begged off. Sounding as gallant as Mister Walton, he said, "I couldn't resist stopping by after hearing such praise about the place."

"Oh, but you must meet Mr. Gunwight before you go," insisted Thaddeus, and he conducted them toward the darkest corner of the room where a peculiar-looking fellow sat with a stack of green-bound copybooks and a steaming cup of something on the table before him. "Ben Gun!" declared Thaddeus. "I've been telling you about the Moosepath League. Well, here's a pair of them just walked in to say hello."

The fellow at the table stood slowly, mild interest lighting his face. He was perhaps fifty years old, with salt-and-pepper hair that grew a little wild. His spectacles were missing a lens, his collar had not recently been laundered, and his chin not shaven for a day or so, but he offered his hand and bowed as if he were at court.

"Mr. Ephram, Mr. Moss," Thaddeus was saying. "Mr. Benjamin Gunwight."

"Benjamin Granite Gunwight," said the fellow, not by way of correction, but simply as amendment to this gracious introduction.

Thaddeus said, "I gathered that you gentlemen are fond of books, and Mr. Gunwight, here, is a writer of some pretty fine ones."

"Are you indeed?" said Ephram, who was instantly fascinated.

Mr. Gunwight let out a high laugh—almost a giggle. "Mr. Spark is very kind," said Ben Gun (as he was familiarly known). "I have written several—no, many—volumes, some of which you may have seen."

"You should read his books!" averred Thaddeus. "He's got old Daniel Boone down to a bright penny! I read them to the boys, you know."

"*Daniel Boone Conquers the Amazon* was my latest," said Mr. Gun.

"I never knew he did," said Sundry.

"And my last, as it happens."

"It's a corker," promised Thaddeus.

"Is it?" said Ephram. He was not familiar with the term.

"Absolutely bust your buttons!"

Ephram was startled by this contention.

"Your last, Mr. Gun?" said Sundry.

"Yes," Thaddeus answered for the man. "They've gone and fired him."

"Good heavens!" said Ephram. It sounded a very discourteous thing.

"Alas, yes," said Ben Gun. "Forty-two volumes of Daniel Boone, seventeen of Davy Crockett, and several tales of Hawk of the Hurons, Paul Bunyan, and Wilma of the Mountains, but I have penned my last tale for the Intrepid Publishing Company of Portland, Maine!" He declaimed this like an actor; Ephram was much impressed, and very sorry, that Mr. Gun should be so cast to the winds.

"I've been telling Ben he needs another subject," said Thaddeus. "He should be writing about yourselves, is what I think. He's thinking of writing *romantics* for old wives and spinsters—women fainting when they discover their husbands' bad investments and Italian doctors running off with heiresses and the like. My own wife reads them like gossip. But it's hardly healthy, in my mind, for a fellow to mix himself up in all those trianglements!"

"Oh, my!" said Ephram. He had just finished a book about a Spanish doctor and a wealthy heiress.

"And why pace about your room trying to think what will happen next," asked Thaddeus, "when the Moosepath League is here to provide you with the whole kit and caboodle?"

"The Moosepath League," said Ben Gun quietly, then he shot a hand in the air and declaimed, "Moving with practiced skill through the verdant forest! Following the ancient pathways of Indian and deer! Or parting the thickets to tread those wards unfamiliar with the boot of civilized humanity!"

Ephram hadn't the slightest idea who the man could be talking about.

"A pretty fair description," admitted Sundry with a thoughtful nod.

Mr. Gunwight focused his eyes somewhere above their heads. "The wilderness!" he said. "The stoic endeavors of the forested brotherhood!"

Ephram looked up at the ceiling.

"Mr. Ephram almost captured Captain Kidd's buried treasure," said Sundry, who was content to further excite the man.

"Good heavens!" said Ephram. It was more than he would have said.

But Ben Gun was inspired. His talk devolved into incomplete sentences, splashed with phrases concerning pirates and pitched battle, skulking figures sneaking through dark forests, and the small but intrepid membership of the Moosepath League.

"What do you say, Chief," said Thaddeus. The two youngsters of the household had appeared from the kitchen and were listening to the writer's meanderings with expressions of awe. Timothy's face was the more impressive for a swollen eye. "Ben Gun is going to write about the Moosepath League," said Thaddeus to his son as he inspected this shiner. "I swear, that eye of yours is blacker than an hour ago."

Timothy shrugged. He was more interested in Mr. Gun's writing career. Melanie, still dressed like a boy, and looking uncertain, said it was "some business!"

Sundry and Ephram made for the door with Thaddeus and the boys and Mr. Gun in tow. They spilled out onto the sidewalk, Mr. Gun with pencil and copybook in hand. He was writing furiously as he asked Ephram questions about things like yardarms and bowsprits. He'd been in the wilderness with Boone and Crockett for years and needed to brush up on things piratical. Ephram referred him to Mr. Joseph Thump of India Street.

"You'll come again, Mr. Moss," Thaddeus was saying. "And bring your friend, Mister Walton, and the lady he was with. She seemed very pleasant."

"Miss McCannon, yes," said Sundry. He was remembering his mission and thought they should be going.

Timothy and Melanie went up the street. A little ways on, Melanie paused and Timothy called after her. "You be careful, Chief," Thaddeus shouted. "And stay on the street here."

Sundry wondered why the one with the black eye should appear the most confident. That black eye troubled him. "They seem like good boys," he said.

"One of them, at any rate," said Thaddeus.

Sundry revealed his interest with a frown.

"The small one?" said Thaddeus. "That's Melanie Ring."

"Melanie?"

"She's a girl." Thaddeus had almost said "He's a girl."

"I wouldn't have guessed," said Sundry.

"*We* never did. Found out the other day." He explained the child's situation. "We thought we'd adopt him, then found out he's a her, or she's a her, and thought we'd adopt her. Her father's near to killing himself with drink and—she or he—Melanie's a good kid, as you say."

"You *thought* you'd adopt her," said Sundry.

"Well, it's tough," said Thaddeus. He had come to respect the Moosepath League and anyone connected with them, and didn't mind hearing this young man's opinion. "It surprises a person when a boy turns out to be a girl, and there are folks who are having a problem with it."

"I wouldn't say it was anybody's business," suggested Sundry.

"I wouldn't either, but there's always someone, or several of them, if you take my meaning. And the kids around about have made things difficult. Timothy took that shiner in her defense just this morning." He regarded Sundry with the look of a man who wants to know what the listener thinks. "I think she's got to go live someplace, wearing a dress where no one has seen her wear anything else. The problem is, *where*. Other people's kids aren't in huge demand, as far as I can tell. Now, where have they gone?" The father took a step or two up the sidewalk and looked for Tim and Melanie. "I told that boy to keep close. I'd better go after them. A pleasure to meet you again, Mr. Moss." Thaddeus waved, rather than pause to shake hands, before hurrying up the street.

"My, he looks like Thump!" said Ephram.

It was remarkable, Sundry agreed. They continued their progress east, Ephram greatly absorbed in Ben Gun's questions, the writer's flights of inspiration pouring forth, and his occasional dissertations on varied subjects. The man exhausted a block and a half describing the eccentric behavior of Wild Bill Hickok's childhood nurse, who saw pookas and talked to plants, and he was so enraptured by his own tale of Henry VIII sitting on his crown (and the wound inflicted thereby) that he halted in the midst of Commercial Street and was almost run over by the trolley.

At the steamship company, Sundry spoke with a man behind a desk about berths on the *Manitoba*. He and Mister Walton would have separate quarters, but he was interested in what the man called "our *double staterooms*."

"He was a very nice gentleman," said Ephram when they came out onto Commercial Street and blinked in the sunlight.

"And yet he assisted in arrangements he could not understand," said Ben Gun, "contracting with men bent upon adventure and expedition!"

"I think those single rooms might be bought up pretty soon," said Sundry. "He didn't seem to have too many left."

Ephram had not been under the same impression. "Perhaps we should reserve two of them."

"They would search the seas themselves for further exploit!" said Ben Gun. He liked this and wrote it down in his copybook

"I'm not very keen on traveling by water," said Sundry.

Ephram thought this strangely unenthusiastic of the young man who had always seemed so ready for anything.

"I am a farmer by birth," explained Sundry. He spotted a peanut vendor.

Ephram felt his legs flagging and he suggested a cab. "We are not far from Thump's place," he said, thinking that Mr. Moss might benefit from that man's dutiful presence.

Ensconced in his apartments and surrounded by books and charts, Thump had been inspecting the tide tables when the knock came at his door. He was immensely pleased with the unexpected company. Straightaway, Mr. Gun informed him of the difference between the armadillo of the American southwest and the African pangolin. "I've never seen them," Thump admitted.

"You could throw them to first base, they make such a perfect ball when they roll up," said Ben Gun.

Thump wondered what he had said to encourage this information.

They were soon back in the hired carriage, and nothing would do but they find Eagleton on Chestnut Street. He was standing at the window, looking toward the ocean, when the visitors were announced; he hadn't noticed the cab pull up to the sidewalk. Eagleton had thought he might take a trip to the Portland Observatory, from the top of which he always felt a little nearer to the weather, but he was overjoyed to be interrupted in this design.

When they were all crammed into the cab, Sundry thought that he had done things a little backward. He had intended to give Mister Walton and Miss McCannon time alone together and now he was returning with a cab full of men. The members of the club were uncertain whether they should be calling on their chairman unannounced, and Sundry knew, then, that Mister Walton could not be imposed upon by his friends, and that he would find Ben Gun of great interest.

Ben Gun was delighted that the Moosepath League was soon to be gathered complete before his eyes. "And you have a woman in your club!" he marveled when they told him about Miss McCannon. It was his authorial opinion that this feminine exception gave their society a distinctly bohemian touch.

Their arrival had something of an event about it; even Sundry felt it when they piled out of the cab on Spruce Street and Ephram paid the driver. They had not gone very far up the front walk when they were hailed by Mister Walton and Miss McCannon themselves. The two were coming around from the east lawn, arm in arm and looking as happy as Sundry had ever seen them.

The sun had sunk behind the green crown of an immense chestnut, its light winking through the leaves as they were stirred by a freshening breeze. A gray squirrel watched the group of humans from a safe distance, his broad tail forming a question mark.

Mister Walton looked like a man who has just been accorded a wondrous honor, and Sundry was struck by an unsubstantiated and unheralded certainty, rather as if he'd been hit in the chest. He'd never seen the bespectacled fellow stand so erect or with his chin raised to such a degree. In any other man, the posture would have looked vain and even arrogant. Miss McCannon appeared misty eyed and particularly beautiful. She held Mister Walton's arm with both her hands, as if a breeze might come and take him away.

"Gentlemen, gentlemen!" Mister Walton was saying. He was clearly ecstatic to see them all. "Sir," he said to Ben Gun, "how are you? Mr. Ephram!"

"Mister Walton," said Ephram. He was almost dizzy with the light from the chairman's beaming face. And Miss McCannon was so striking! "Miss McCannon!" he pronounced.

She only smiled.

"Mr. Eagleton!" said Mister Walton.

"Mister Walton!" said Eagleton. He was shaking a little. "Miss McCannon!" he said.

She only smiled for reply.

"Mr. Thump!" said Mister Walton. There was no sense of preference or hierarchy in the order in which he named them.

"Hmmm!" said Thump. "Mister Walton!" He stood as straight as the chairman, though he occupied less vertical space. He hmmmed several more times, his expression invisible behind his beard. "Miss McCannon!"

Miss McCannon's smile widened and Thump started as if he were hit.

"Sundry," said Mister Walton. His face clouded unexpectedly, and, contrarily, Sundry laughed. "I hope you will not be offended," said the great man, "if I suggest that you take some respite from my company."

"On the contrary," said Sundry, "I would congratulate you." He held his hand out to Mister Walton, with whom he had not shaken hands since he first became the portly fellow's *gentleman's gentleman*. Mister Walton gripped

Sundry's hand and shook it with great feeling. "Congratulations, Miss Mc-Cannon," said Sundry. He didn't know which of them was the most fortunate.

Phileda leaned forward and embraced Sundry—not briefly but with a long, heartfelt squeeze. The members were astonished, and not any less so when she treated them each with the same attention.

And when she had done this, and Mister Walton had vigorously shaken each of their hands, he considered their mystified expressions—himself beaming—and said, "Miss McCannon has honored me by accepting my proposal of marriage! We have spoken with Reverend Seacost by telephone and he will perform the ceremony here on the lawn, weather permitting, on Friday afternoon."

"Fair weather expected for the remainder of the week!" announced an astonished Eagleton.

"It's twenty minutes before the hour of noon," said an awestruck Ephram, referring to one of the three or four watches that he kept about his person.

"There are several *double staterooms* available on the steamer for Halifax," said Sundry.

"High tide at 1:18 P.M." said a wide-eyed Thump.

Ben Gun was writing furiously in his green-bound copybook.

❧ EPILOGUE ❧
THE WOMAN HERSELF

June 3, 1897

S undry was finishing a letter to his mother when he heard laughter outside his room. He stuck his head into the hall to see Mister Walton at the landing with his hands at his side and his round face lifted in merriment. Sundry went so far as to consider the ceiling to understand the source of his friend's humor.

Mister Walton leaned forward, then, and Sundry had a flash of the man falling over at Iceboro. Sundry let out a small shout, but his friend was only slapping his knees. "Oh!" said Mister Walton, his surprise at Sundry's shout merely an extension of his humor. Sundry had to laugh himself. "It comes to me now," said Mister Walton, still laughing under his speech.

"Does it?" said Sundry.

"Do you know what I told those gentlemen at the store in Bowdoinham?"

"Well, I don't."

"I told them that Iowa is a great pig producer," said Mister Walton, expressing this verity with the same contracted words that had confused Mr. Fink.

"You do surprise me," replied Sundry.

"'*Important* pig producer,' I believe is how I put it."

"It's a side of you I never knew."

"No, no," explained Mister Walton, laughing still. "*Iowa . . . is . . . an important producer of pigs.*"

Sundry began to laugh all over again. "You did say that?"

Mister Walton was shaking all over and there were tears in his eyes. "I'm afraid I did."

"Well, God bless the error."

"I must write the Ferns."

"Do you think you should?"

"Oh, it is too good to let go," said Mister Walton. "Otherwise, I would say, let sleeping pigs lie."

"What are you boys up to now?" came Mrs. Baffin's small voice from the foot of the stairs. She beamed from ear to ear to hear such laughter in the old house, though she had been beaming since hearing of the impending wedding.

Preparations were fast under way. Messrs. Ephram, Eagleton, and Thump were shopping for clothes suitable for such an occasion. People had been hastily invited—friends from Hallowell and Portland. A rehearsal would take place on Thursday, and a dinner would celebrate the coming marriage, quite fittingly, on Thursday evening at the Shipswood Restaurant. Miss McCannon's brother Jared, an antiquarian for the Peabody Museum at Harvard, was coming to "give her away," which phrase Phileda declared "scandalous."

Jared McCannon was, in fact, arriving at Portland's Boston and Maine Station at about the same moment that Mister Walton realized the reason for the confusion at Bowdoinham. Phileda was waiting on the platform to meet her brother. On the train, Jared had met a dark-haired, dark-eyed, and extremely handsome woman, who, in her middle years, carried herself with an unaffected air of sophistication and impressed him as something of a sensualist and (contradictorily) an innocent. He was dazzled.

Phileda watched with fascination as her brother helped this enchantress down from the train, bowing over her hand like a courtier. The woman said good-bye with sincere warmth and thanked him for making the miles so short with such interesting conversation, but it was *he*, he was sure, who must thank *her*. A handsome, confident man, Jared realized too late that he had never asked the woman her name.

"I don't know," he said after they had greeted one another and the sister inquired with raised eyebrows who that striking personage had been. "And so, this Mister Walton I met last summer is to be my brother-in-law," he said. "I quite liked him." But Jared cast a glance or two up the platform for another sight of the woman he had met on the train.

Phileda smiled past her brother. She was surprised to see the elegant woman met by an old curmudgeon she had been observing on the platform. The old man carried a cane as if he was unused to it, and he grumbled and waved the stick when someone offered him a seat. His face lost its grumpy expression, however, when the woman from the train greeted him.

"Mrs. Roberto," he said out of Phileda's and Jared's hearing.

"Nicholai," said the woman musically. She put her hand out as a dancer might and he took it, his own hand shaking slightly. "What a pleasure to see you again," she said.

"I'm sorry to make you come sooner than you might," said Nicholai Bergen.

The conductor had personally taken charge of Mrs. Roberto's things and soon a small caravan of chests and trunks followed them to the curb, where a carriage waited. All the men tipped their hats when she approached; the driver almost fell from his seat rushing to open the door for her. Her thanks and greetings were always gracious, and more than enough reward.

In the cab, she asked Nicholai Bergen what had happened in her absence.

"It's a proper muddle, I should tell you, ma'am," he pronounced. "I tossed one fellow out who was skulking in your room, and that was weeks ago, but last Friday I was set upon by a gang of them and would be lying there still, tied up like a Christmas goose—begging your pardon—if not for Thaddeus Spark from the Faithful Mermaid and these fellows from the Moosepath League." He pronounced this last appellation as if he hardly believed it.

"The Moosepath League!" said Mrs. Roberto. She had never heard of such a society but thought the name delightful.

"Yes," said Nicholai. "There's a fellow among them who thought you were in danger. He had me a good deal concerned, I want to tell you."

"Oh!" said Mrs. Roberto, and she patted the old man's hand.

"But he was hard by to rescuing you, whatever the cost," continued Nicholai. "His name was Thump, and he claimed to have a calling card of yours, though I never saw it."

"A calling card? Thump?" said Mrs. Roberto, her eyes flashing as she searched her memory. "Did you have his first name?"

"Thump," said Nicholai. "Just Mr. Thump, they said. A short fellow. Broad as a stump."

"Did he have a beard?"

"Aye."

"A *marvelous* beard?"

"It was a proper sheaf of hay, to be sure."

Mrs. Roberto sat back, and the carriage rattled on for a block or two before she spoke again. "The dear man!"

"They took one of your parachutes, the daft beggars! Not the Moosepath League or this Mr. Thump, but the fellows who conked my head and tied me up!"

She took the old man's hand again and held it. "My poor Nicholai!"

All complaint left him, and he leaned back.

"Mr. Thump," she said, still holding the old man's hand. "The dear man." The carriage pulled up before Mr. Bergen's place on Winter Street.

"Here we are," said the old fellow.

"Thank you, Nicholai. I'm sure I met Mr. Thump last summer. I must thank him for his concern, however mistaken." She stepped out of the carriage onto the wooden sidewalk of Winter Street. "Another summer," she said. It was a narrow avenue, filled with clattering wagons and carriages, and frequented by the laboring classes. A man in the dress of a mariner raised his watchcap to her, saying, "Ma'am." Several young men hurried up with her name on their lips, offering to help her with her things. "They're going to the hotel," she explained, "but thank you."

Nicholai drove the young fellows away and let her gaze about for a moment. She always did this when she first arrived. She always took in the air, and appeared to count the very doors and windows along the street. One would have never guessed she had been born there. Nicholai certainly didn't.

"Thank you," she said when the old man opened the door for her.

"I straightened things up as best I could," he said.

"That's her, that's her," Timothy Spark was saying to Melanie Ring. They were standing on the opposite sidewalk. "Mr. Thump saved her from a burning building!" Timothy shook his head. He wished he could save Mrs. Roberto someday. He was quite in love with her, for all his eight years. "And she was rescuing some poor horses, tied up in that stable, and a dog with her puppies." You just *had* to love a person who would rescue a dog.

Melanie Ring gazed about them. She was apprehensive of the street ever since Timothy had taken a black eye from a bigger kid; he had been trying to stop a couple of boys from tormenting her. She almost wished she were still a boy herself, and wasn't entirely sure why she didn't wish it with all her heart. Only adding to her confusion was the excitement of being invited into the Spark household, as well as the fear that she was abandoning her father. The little girl was taken by the sight of Mrs. Roberto, however, and she allowed herself to be swept up in Timothy's admiration.

"Yes," he said. "They rescued her from a burning building and a gang of kidnappers!"

The door to Bergen's place had closed behind the old man and the beautiful ascensionist. The carriage waited at the curb, but otherwise traffic on Winter Street carried on as usual.

Melanie solemnly shook her head. "That was *some* business!"

Timothy tugged at her elbow. He had seen trouble in the form of a roaming gang of boys coming up the sidewalk. In a moment he and she had skipped over a fence and scaled a shed. Soon they were skimming the roofs toward Danforth Street like Indians on the wild hills of yore, or like their notion of the Moosepath League in search of hazard and heroics.

❧ AUTHOR'S NOTE ❧

No member or satellite of the Moosepath League has ever caused more confusion for the novice historian of that society than did Benjamin Granite Gunwight. Even certain *authoritative* sources have aspired to make something significant out of his presence at the announcement of Mister Walton's and Miss McCannon's engagement, but latterly this has been considered a stretch.

Ben Gun would make his fortune chronicling the adventures of the Moosepath League (later "the Caribou Club"), and, in his own indirect and inadvertent way, contribute to some of them. One critic, Basil Penwall, has characterized Ben Gun's writing as *"harboring a peculiar, purple charm,"* while admitting that the writer was *"not only inaccurate in his portrayal of characters and events but sometimes wildly and willfully eccentric! The only saving grace about these books is that Mr. Gunwight had the discretion to employ fictitious names, even if he did, in the first volume, make actual use of the term 'Moosepath League' like a canopy over his bare-faced liberalities."*

A sample of Mr. Gun's prose will suffice to inform the reader. (The parenthetical marks are mine.)

> *Myriad Canebrake* (meant to stand in for Sundry Moss) *attempted to wrest his friend from his desperate purpose, but the powerful Jeremiah Pound* (Mr. Gun's version of Joseph Thump) *shook off this well-intended restraint and plunged headlong into the raging inferno of the doomed icehouse. With the desperate cries of the beautiful Mrs. Rambineaux* (guess who) *in his ears, and the white-hot flames singeing his broad beard, he was yet blinded to all but his valiant goal . . .*
>
> from Chapter Seventeen: "Flame and Ice!"
> The Caribou Club and the Icehouse Firestorm (1898)

Clearly, several elements in this narrative (in the words of Mr. Penwall again) *"are out of plumb."* But nothing could have startled the reticent Mr. Thump any more than to read that his fictive counterpart *"held the rescued*

Mrs. Rambineaux to his own panting breast and pressed his lips, heated as much by the flames of his passion as by the inferno he so recently braved, upon her full, red mouth, reviving her with the electricity of his emotions." It is no wonder that Sundry Moss and Mister Walton sought out Mr. Gunwight in his new digs on Munjoy Hill to politely request that he desist from, at the very least, using the actual name of the club. Nonetheless, it is telling that the members never missed a single volume, and Sundry Moss relates that Mister Walton could be heard "hooting with laughter" whenever he ensconced himself in the parlor to read Mr. Gunwight's frenzied prose. "It would quite cheer you to hear him," Sundry said more than once, years later.

The Moosepath League became the Caribou Club in subsequent volumes, which explains why some people have believed the society originated in that Aroostook County town. This fictitious name was, in part, responsible for bringing the Moosepath League to Caribou in the 1920s for the still-perplexing "Adventure of the Dancing Deer."

But change the name though he did, the damage (in so many words) was done, and, more than once, people in strange or desperate straits showed up at the door of one or another of the members like clients at the steps of 221B Baker Street. Life followed art as unpredictably as the converse.

Bright Deeds by Miss Marion Elfaid Plotte, was not Deborah Pilican's last book, but it was her next to last. In the winter of 1898–1899 Siegfried and Son of Bangor published *Always By the Way* by Mrs. Rudolpha Limington Harold, and in it later Moosepathians have discovered three oddly familiar personalities—Mr. Eldton, Mr. Everide, and Mr. Thor. This trio of supporting characters move like guardian angels throughout the book's narrative and exhibit (in the words of the heroine) *"a stern resolve to right wrongs and derail misdeeds— that resolve softened by the most gentle of natures and the most charitable of hearts."*

Ephram, Eagleton, and Thump each purchased a copy of *Always By the Way*, but they apparently did not recognize themselves in it. Only Eagleton's journal makes reference to the fictive trio. In his words, he *"greatly admired them."*

᠅

The events of May 1897 described in *this* volume are variously termed, (among Moosepathian members and historians) as the "Adventure of the Pasteboard Card," the "Adventure of the Startled Ascensionist" (a label that must owe something to Ben Gun's version of events), and the "Adventure of the Widow's Brigade." It is not difficult to stumble across other versions of the affair surrounding "the woman in 12A," but I urge the reader to pay no attention to these.

As the present narrative closes, the members of the club have much to anticipate—the wedding of Mister Walton and Miss McCannon, Mrs. Morrell's annual June Ball, and summer in general. Sundry Moss planned, early on, to visit his family in Edgecomb, but there are only small hints as to his concern for the soon-to-be-orphaned Melanie Ring, and few suspicions of that little girl's spunk and determination. Never was Sundry Moss's ingenuity more obvious than in the events that began the evening before the celebrated wedding, though he was soon without recourse to the chairman's presence and wisdom as well as the charter members' willing assistance. The situation in which he and Melanie Ring would soon be involved—instigated by her father, Burne Ring—would come to be known as "the Adventure of Fiddler's Green," and also as "the Adventure of the Midstream Horse." Present-day members of the Moosepath League insist on calling it "the Adventure of the Gentleman's Gentleman." Someday it may be told.

✦❧✦

The story of Maine's ice industry is surprising and dramatic. The waters of the Kennebec River were famous throughout the world for providing a clear, bubbleless ice, and from 1860 to the early years of the twentieth century a thriving business was to be had from the frozen surface of the river. South America, Hawaii, and even China would know Kennebec ice. Roger F. Duncan's exceptional book *Coastal Maine: A Maritime History* gives us some telling statistics. In one mild winter in the late 1860s "*30,000 tons of ice were cut on the Kennebec, requiring 1,000 vessels to carry it.*" But that was nothing to 1894, when 1,050,000 tons were cut "*on or near the Kennebec . . .*" and "*in 1890, 25,000 men and 10,900 horses*" were employed on that river alone. "*When an icehouse burned,*" writes Mr. Duncan, "*it made a spectacular fire and left a huge stack of ice with no house around it.*"

The birch tree is much beloved, not only for its beauty but, for the wintergreen flavor of its sap and of its twigs and bark when boiled. We in the Northeast are blessed with a nonalcoholic refreshment known as birch beer, that is bottled locally. It's almost as delicious as Moxie but doesn't take as much getting used to.

Birch bark, I am to understand, has certain quantities of salicylic acid (the active ingredient in aspirin), so it is no wonder that American Indians considered birch-bark tea a revivifying drink. I do not honestly know or recommend its effect on pigs, but I will admit to having brewed with some friends a more potent concoction from birch tree sap following the directions in Euell Gibbons's *Stalking the Wild Asparagus* and coming up with a sockdolager of a drink that tasted pretty awful (I blame the brewers and not Mr. Gibbons) and, contrarily, produced some pretty acute headaches—this happening in the days of my misspent youth. One can only imagine what Sundry Moss would have said.

The origin of the term *hobo* is lost, it seems, to history, though at least two likelihoods are suggested (from other sources) in the preceding narrative. Hoboes were a breed apart. They formed something of a migratory workforce in the late nineteenth century, and many of them considered themselves "knights of the road," with their own strict code of honor.

For bibliography, I would direct the reader to the author's note in the previous Moosepath adventure, *Daniel Plainway*, and to which list I would add *Maine: Guide "Down East"* by Workers of the Federal Writer's Project of the WPA of the State of Maine; *Village Down East* by John Wallace; *Imagining New England* by Joseph A. Conforti; the second volume of W. H. Bunting's *A Day's Work, a Sampler of Historic Maine Photographs 1860–1920*; *American Musical Life: A History* by Richard Crawford; *A Natural History of Trees of Eastern and Central North America* by Donald Culross Peattie; *The Facts on File Encyclopedia of Word and Phrase Origins* by Robert Hendrickson; and *Listening to America* by Stuart Berg Flexner.

A wonderful and hard-working group of people are, even as we speak, in the process of revivifying the Wiscasset, Waterville, and Farmington Railroad. There is a station and museum in Alna, as well the opportunity to travel, by narrow-guage, on a mile (and counting) of track. More can be learned about this enterprise—both historic and present day—at www.wwfry.org.

✦S✦

For me, one of the great pleasures derived from these books has been hearing from "Friends of the Moosepath League" by way of the mail, the Moosepath League's website (www.moosepath.com), or my e-mail address (vanreid@midcoast.com)—readers who have, to a person, proved kind, generous, and thoughtful. Thanks also to the book clubs and libraries that have kindly given my books room in their events and discussions. It has been a pleasure to communicate with these folks and to answer questions via e-mail.

I am not working at the Maine Coast Book Shop in Damariscotta these days, but I will always think of the people there as friends and colleagues. Thanks to Susan and Barnaby Porter, Penny and Ewing Walker, Joanne Cotton, Pat Boynton, Frank Slack, and everyone else at the Maine Coast Book Shop for their constant support and goodwill, with particular appreciation to Kathleen Creamer, Jane and Mark Bisco, and Trudy Price.

Much gratitude to my agent, Barbara Hogenson; and her assistant, Nicole Verity; as well as to my editor, Carolyn Carlson; and her assistant, Lucia Watson.

Thanks to the bookstores that hosted me this past summer and fall—including *Books Etc.* in Falmouth, *Sherman's* in Boothbay, *Bookland* of Brunswick, *Longfellow Books* in Portland, and *Nonesuch Books* in South Portland, *Books and Things* in Oxford, and the *Owl and the Turtle* in Camden. Thanks also to Jami Reed, the folks at CentralBooking.com, and Rebecca Willow at *Parkplace Books* in Kirkland, Washington, for their support and generous thoughts.

For camaraderie, advice, and the plain fun of talking shop—best wishes and thanks to writers and artists Michael Uhl, Carol Brightman, James L. Nelson, Nicholas Dean, Mary Beth Owens, Cynthia Furlong Reynolds, Jeannie Brett, Monica Woods, Michael Crummey, Tom DeMarco, and Norman G. Gautreau. Continued appreciation to David and Susan Morse, Joan Grant, and everyone at the Lincoln County *Weekly*. Thanks also to Dr. Edward Kitfield for identifying the metatarsal pads for me.

Thanks go to my parents, brothers and sisters, and my terrific in-laws for their continual interest, encouragement, and humor. And, of course, more thanks than can be articulated to my wife, Maggie, for always providing the calm amidst the hectic business of life; and to our children, Hunter and Mary, for providing the music of laughter, questions, and centuries-old revelations found new in their hearts and minds. Every day my family, my friends, my wife and children encourage my faith in the humor and goodwill, the courage and generosity that finds its way into the hearts and minds of Mister Walton, Sundry Moss, and the honorable members of the *Moosepath League!*

Van Reid's thrilling conclusion to the Moosepath League Series is now available from Viking

Fiddler's Green Or a Wedding, a Ball, and the Singular Adventures of Sundry Moss
Escape to Maine in 1897, where Reid's evocative writing delivers a long-awaited wedding, a society ball, a kidnapping, and a mystical rural nether-world where a bitter family feud comes close to causing the death of the preternaturally cool Mr. Sundry Moss. Full of romantic yearning, knock-about comedy, and touching drama, fans and newcomers alike will be pleased to keep company with the honorable "Gentlemen of the Club."
ISBN 0-670-03320-0

Lose yourself in Van Reid's superb storytelling with the Moosepath League and other colorful novels from Penguin

Cordelia Underwood Or the Marvelous Beginnings of the Moosepath League
The young, beautiful redhead Cordelia Underwood is aided in her quest to unearth a family secret by Mister Tobias Walton, who has never heard of an adventure he isn't eager to join. Together with the Moosepath League, they embark on a most entertaining and audacious adventure teeming with Cupid's arrows, opinionated relatives, runaway horses, apparitions, kidnapping, smuggling, and thievery.
ISBN 0-14-028010-3

Mollie Peer Or the Underground Adventure of the Moosepath League
In the second hilarious adventure of the Moosepath League, Mollie Peer, the feisty society columnist for the *Eastern Argus*, follows up on a lead that lands her in danger and is thrown together with the hapless, lovable members of the Moosepath League.
ISBN 0-14-029185-7

Daniel Plainway Or the Holiday Haunting of the Moosepath League
Following the disappearance of a neighboring family, good-hearted country lawyer Daniel Plainway sets off on an odyssey that changes his life as well as the lives of an orphaned child, a big-hearted ballplayer, and an extraordinary woman whom he meets along the way.
ISBN 0-14-100190-9

Mrs. Roberto Or the Widowy Worries of the Moosepath League
Mrs. Roberto finds the portly and jovial Tobias Walton and his aide-de-camp, Sundry Moss, as unexpected guests at the eccentric Fern Farm, unlikely counselors to a downhearted pig, and unintentional puzzlers over a peculiar family secret. Meanwhile, other members of the Moosepath League run afoul of Portland's toughest gangster, the nefarious Fuzz Hadley, and search for the elusive and possibly imperiled beautiful balloonist Mrs. Roberto.

ISBN 0-14-200453-7

Peter Loon: A Novel
Deep in the north woods of Maine, as the Revolutionary War comes to an end, a young man named Peter Loon falls into a series of startling entanglements and adventures. Providentially, he befriends a nomadic parson whose humble intelligence and steady head prove useful, especially when the two find themselves in the middle of a bitter land battle. *ISBN 0-14-200311-5*